BLACK CLOCK

No. 14

SUMMER–FALL 2011

Summer / Fall ~ 2011

/

Black Clock / isbn 9780983662501

Published semi-annnually under cover of night by the MFA Writing Program at the California Institute of the Arts

24700 McBean Parkway, Valencia CA 91355

/

One-year **subscriptions** (two issues) can be purchased can be purchased at blackclock.org/subscribe

Editorial email: info@blackclock.org

Distributed internationally through Ingram, Ingram International, Bertrams, Gardners and Trust Media.

Printed by Lightning Source in the United States, the United Kingdom and in Australia.

/

Thank you to the Rosenthal Family Foundation for their generous support

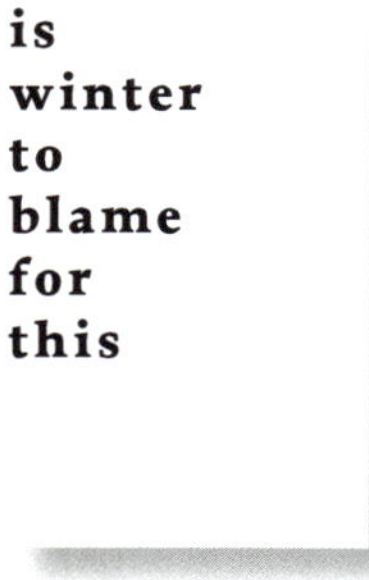

Sarah Vap

Jazmin Aminian Jordán

Katherine Min

Sara Gerot

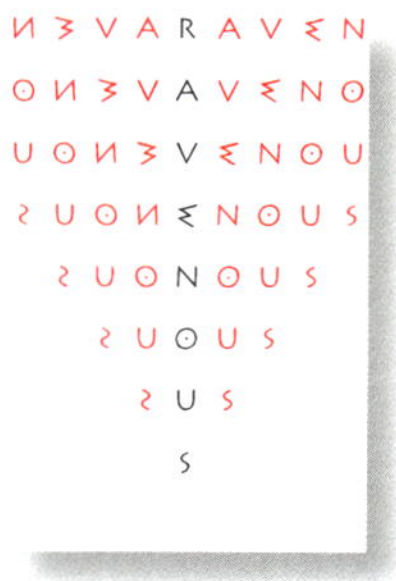
Tiffany Promise

Merrill Feitell

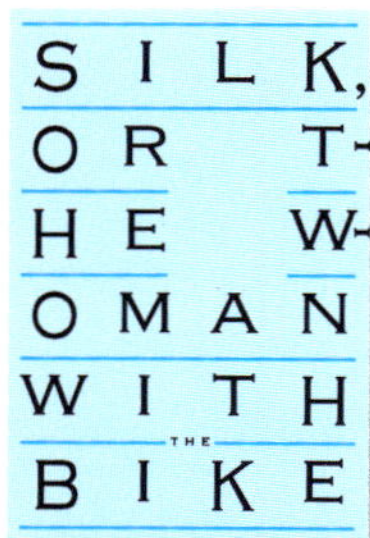

Joseph McElroy

Sarah Wang

Lynne Tillman

Geoff Dyer

Marisa Crawford

Tara Ison

Kate Wolf

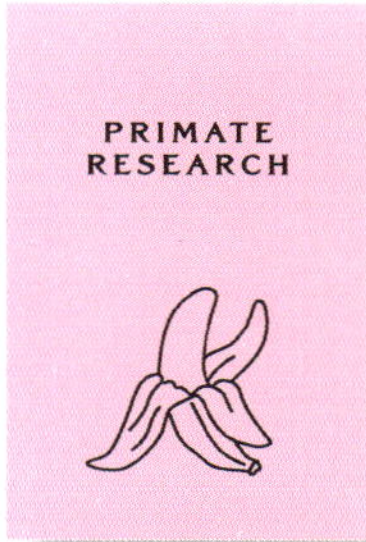

Rick Moody

Jay Neugeboren

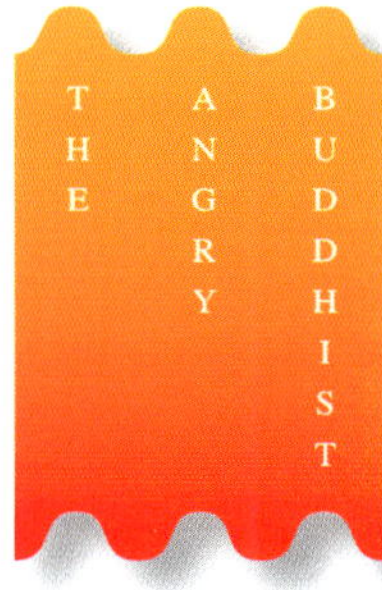

Seth Greenland

Scott Bradfield

Samantha Cohen

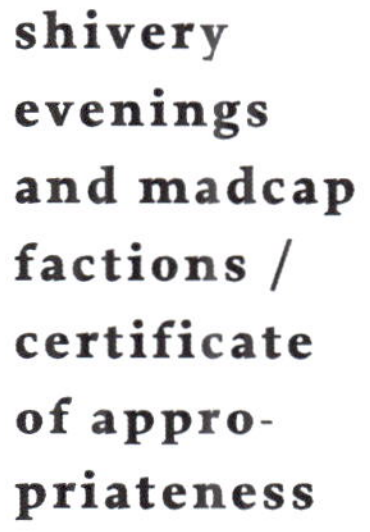

Peter Frank

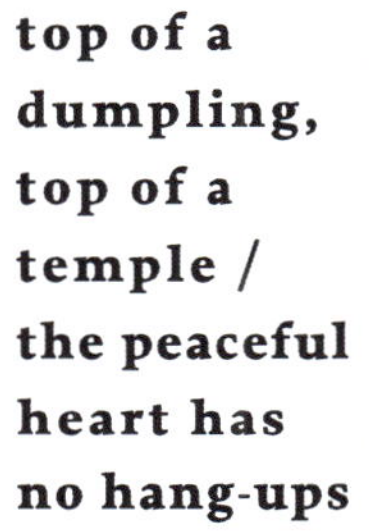

Kiki Petrosino

Ddum Kim

Tom Carson

Jeff VanderMeer

Stephen O'Connor

Sarah Gambito

Sarah Vap

is winter to blame for this

We forget that Christ was stabbed
in the heart by a Roman—love

is unutterable,
withdrawn. I called on you
to close fingers

over the heart of our child at the onset
of winter—a dreamy red wedge

buffed pure

as the marble you sent
your ex for her wedding gift. Inside which you see,

you tell me, the lavender jellyfish of your childhoods.
Inside which

I see the eye
of the whole world's vagina flapping
our heart's long spring

for the love again. As if goodness didn't hurt to hold.
As if pure goodness

could not split you, and then force
your deepest part.

Jazmin Aminian Jordán

OUT FROM UNDER MIRRORS

Jazmin Aminian Jordán

To wake up in L.A. is to wake naked on a bed under mirrors, and though Flavia wasn't in L.A. but Vegas, she knew that the reflection above her belonged to that mirror the way women belonged to the billboards running up and down Sunset Boulevard. Her heavy thighs, her wasp waist, her white skin were suspended up there like brothel art in the morning light. So she shut her eyes to it, burying her head in her sleeping companion's back. She almost slipped into a dream but a midnight telephone call from her sister played in her mind: *and then I realized driving on Sunset that cultivating a relationship with myself isn't a nasty consolation prize for not being in the kind of relationship that I imagined with my husband,* so Flavia reached out of the bed, felt the rug where she dropped her cell phone but instead found a small, dead bird.

Flavia looked over the mattress at the bird positioned as if suspended in mid flight. One wing up, the other down, its sapphire feathers splayed, its neck broken. Flavia dropped it and was out of bed, running hot water over her hands in the bathroom while Rio remained in a deep sleep, undisturbed by the phone vibrating under the bed or by Flavia, who walked back into the room and got down on all fours to check it. Text Message: *Sister, Today, July 4th-I'm forty. More years behind me now than before me.* Flavia deleted the message and pulled squares of two-ply tissue paper from a box on the night stand to pick up the stiff bird. She dropped it into the wastebasket under the desk and placed the basket outside the door next to the rollaway table from their room service steak dinner the night before. Flavia's hip tipped the whiskey bottle over the tea cups on the tray and she watched the clanking sound get lost down the hallway.

Flavia went back in the room and stood naked and quiet, looking for some indication as to how the bird got in. She and Rio had been on the road for seven days, a work journey for Rio that took them from hotel to motel, from Pasadena to Big Sur to Oakland to Tahoe down to Bishop and Vegas, their last stop before heading back to L.A.; and while there were bluebirds in Tahoe, the last one they saw was in the Manzanar detention camp south of Bishop. As for Vegas, a bird this bright would only be seen on stage. Flavia picked up the phone and texted back: *Be brave, fly high and rest. Much love, F.*

Two days before, at seven in the morning, Flavia

was in a platinum dress waiting for the parking valet to bring Rio's car around at the Tahoe Mont Bleu. They'd been up all night, Rio working on deadlines and Flavia keeping the company of mirrors and candles. While Rio was pacing, smoking, in labor with an idea at three a.m., Flavia pulled on sweats to buy tea in the lobby downstairs. When the elevator opened, there was a woman in slim jeans asleep on a chair with half-full coin bucket on her lap. To her left was a banquet hall and Flavia slipped in through its unlocked doors. For forty minutes she stretched, danced, kept a straight line as she spun across the floor, and checked the alignment of her body in the mirrors. She came out of the hall awake, alive, wanting to speak to the multiple places of pleasure, wanting to feel fine clothes as she walked about in new skin.

Instead of tea, she came back into the room with a leopard print bag and a platinum dress she bought at the casino store called Adventures. She tried it on for herself in the bathroom, was pleased at how it held on to her, and she didn't change out of the dress until she was in the front seat of the car the next morning, pulling on jeans and then a silk shirt. While some adventures lost their blush for Flavia, they still could excite when their scent was carried off her body and that morning all her crying was right underneath her skin. So much was so beautiful right then and she placed her hand on her chest where it felt like she could retrieve a leather glove, a wrench, doves, larks, keys, locks, velvet. She kept it there, held on to it until they were out of Tahoe.

The Vegas sun came in fast through the slit Flavia made by pulling open the black-out curtains. She looked out at a small Catholic church where a statue of Jesus outstretched his arms past the casinos onto the whole of the desert, to the foot of the mountains. She'd been behind those mountains where the desert cracked open onto an oasis, an orchard of date trees among willows and a stream. Birds migrating over five hundred miles at night, replenished themselves there and rested during the day in the fronds and branches. Flavia read that a woman named Vanolo Modine sent away for date pits by post in the 1920s, so Flavia wrote *Vanolo Modine* in her journal and kept it there like a pressed flower because a woman created Paradise and found a way to feed birds after she was dead.

Flavia decided not to suggest the oasis to Rio when they crossed over the area the day before. They were trying to make time into Vegas and they had already stopped at Hell's Gate, a ridge that looked out onto the Death Valley floor. There Flavia stood in wedge heels at the edge of the canyon while Rio filmed the desert with a pink pocket camera. Rio hadn't slept in forty hours and Flavia didn't think Rio would make it to Vegas, thought they might stop in Pahrump to rest but Rio kept driving saying things like *the closer a brothel is to Vegas, the higher the prices.*

Rio's sleep was ten hours old now, hard and deep like gems. As for Rio's body, it was glowing in the dark, as if the focus and intensity fired up meridians and pushed light up under such soft petal skin. In Tahoe, Rio explained how it always had been that the momentum in meeting a deadline turns noon into another midnight. Then Rio said they'd better talk about something completely different because talking about tired is exhausting. So they spoke of the ancient forest under the Tahoe lake waters, of the Sierra tree line, of how the Washoe tribe believed if all the snow melted off Mount Tallac then the lake would overflow and create a deluge. And how the drowned never rise and float on the top of Lake Tahoe, the lake of the sky, because they get caught in the underwater nest of the great Ong bird of legend, a cowardly bird, who hoarded them there as food for his adventures. The cold air was refreshing and they walked through a meadow to a hidden beach on Tahoe's south shore where the lake remained so still that their reflection, the sky above, and all that moved under the waters was right there, right in front of them.

Flavia closed the curtains and turned for the bathroom. While she washed her hair in the shower, Rio stepped in behind her. "There was a dead bird under the bed," Flavia said, "so I threw it out in the hallway."

"Honey, a place like this has seen more than dead birds."

On Independence Day, Flavia and Rio drove from Vegas to a hotel on Sunset Boulevard in four and half hours. The cologne billboard outside their window was of a five-story-high naked woman. Flavia turned away from it and watched Rio's beautiful body wrapped in nothing but the red and orange colors of sunset, Flavia watched her love step across the room, Rio tap, tap, tapping the world with long sculpted fingers, nothing between Rio, nothing between herself, and the way the light fell and changed the shape and color of the room.

"We could probably hook if we wanted to stay here longer," Rio said while opening the windows. Rio sang a Cole Porter song. At first, the window wouldn't open and then Flavia tried. She gave the pane a harder push against vines of bougainvillea, shaking the plant and letting loose the sound of wild birds. **-bc.**

Katherine Min

THE FETISHIST

They had fought the whole time: Walking single-file on the narrow stone pathways by the River Arno, vital points lost to the revving of motorcycles and the high bright laughter of tourists; gesticulating with gelato spoons as they sat outside a café in the Piazza della Signoria; standing side by side on the second floor of the Uffizi Gallery, lowering their voices before a bevy of Madonnas (grim, grinning, stately, plump, aloof, aloft, alluring: Madonnas electric, dyspeptic, melancholic, myopic, dreamy, dowdy and delicate); ranging from *buca* to *loggia*; sputtering in and out of leather shops, through churches and palazzos, between market stalls of zucchini flowers and porcini mushrooms; waiting backstage to perform at the Teatro Communale, the Verdi or in the sacristy of Orsanmichele; pausing momentarily in convivial wonder over shared forkfuls of broad pasta with wild boar ragu, and chocolate hazelnut torta, distracted by the flavors and the atmosphere, the company and the candlelight, the corny accordion player outside playing "That's Amore" and the vendor of cut roses passing; resuming full force over bottles of Nozzole, chilled glasses of limoncello and tiny decorated cups of espresso, their voices becoming slurred, overlapping, lapsing for full minutes into drunken, recriminating silences; and later at night, preparing for bed, moody over washcloths and dental floss, cold cream and contact solution, tending to wine stains on cuffs and lipstick removal, listening abstractly to the percussive sputter of Italian plumbing, the ardent, aggrieved rhythm of passing street conversation and the distant brassy strains of Gershwin issuing from a tourist-concentrated spot near the Ponte Vecchio, both of them weary of their own positions, forgetful of them, almost willing to give them up if it weren't for the principle, the responsibility to truth, to reason, until the only recourse was a furious, fast fucking that wasn't so much truce as it was transliteration, the struggle stripped clear of civilized discourse and smarty-pants articulations, stripped bare and rocking in almost catatonic frenzy; the yielding and the pushing, insinuating and subsuming, the pouring in and crying out, conceding nothing.

And what had they fought about? This wasn't so easily determined. It was, of course, the continuation of an argument they'd been having the five years they'd been together, not so much an argument as an undertow, a countercurrent, the same argument that runs swift and dark beneath every romance: The argument against. An irrefutable movement—after the tidal knocking, closer, the crashing lulling waves of intimacy, the moony directional pull toward the same soft shore, gravity's shadow impulse: Away.

From deep in her coma twenty-five years later, Alma Soon Ja Lee's brow furrows. Even unconscious, riven with disease, drug-embattled, intravenous-fed, she frowns at the memory's imprecision. Because in another way what they fought about had been entirely singular.

They had been performing piano trios with Archie that summer, Daniel on violin, Alma on cello. Daniel's Italian was atrocious, and Alma winced whenever he opened his mouth. "It's not *grazie* to rhyme with *Nazi,*" she had to tell him repeated times. "It's *grazie-eh.*"

"To rhyme with *Nazi-eh?*" said Daniel.

"Very funny." It wasn't that Alma spoke Italian fluently or that her vocabulary progressed much beyond his, but she was proud of her pronunciation, which she knew wasn't perfect but which she took painstaking care to reproduce correctly. She fancied herself something of a linguistics expert by virtue of the fact that she had to learn English at an early age, and because Daniel, by comparison, was such a slouch. "You know what I love about Italian?" said Alma. "I love that everything has a gender."

Daniel frowned. "How do they decide if something is masculine or feminine? It seems completely arbitrary to me."

Alma held up her spoon. "Paolo says that you just know. This, for example, *il cucchiaio,* is masculine." She pointed to her cup of espresso. "And this, *la coppa,* is feminine."

"You see? Completely arbitrary."

"Really?" Alma opened her mouth and slowly, deliberately, licked the back of *il cucchiaio* with the tip of her tongue, then slowly, deliberately inserted it inside *la coppa.* She smiled. "*I* think it's sexy."

"You think Paolo is sexy." Daniel was trying to sound casual, but Alma heard the anger that masked the vulnerability, that posed as judgment. She wasn't in the mood tonight to reassure him.

She brought the cup to her lips. "Paolo is our host," she said.

"He's Italian," said Daniel, doubtfully.

"Exactly," said Alma. Paolo the impresario, the opera composer, cosmopolitan. The disarmingly charming Paolo, handsome in a tux, tall, dark with wild antennae eyebrows and thick waves of hair that never seemed to muss or move, reminiscent of Michelangelo's *David.* Paolo who loved all things American including the New York Yankees, cheeseburgers and Bruce Springsteen. People said he was a prince, one of the last of a long line of Florentine royalty that included a Medici or two and at least one Pope, and it wasn't hard to believe it, though he graciously waved aside any direct inquiries into his ancestry. "My dear," he said, in his charmingly disarming English, "you see the problem in Italy is we look always too much to the past. I like your American way better. Look to the future!" Daniel was naturally suspicious of Paolo, in the way that charming egotists are suspicious of one another, as if the presence of two in a room might blow their mutual cover. Alma was flattered, amused and sometimes annoyed by the way the two men vied for her favor. She didn't understand why men couldn't see that this constant, competitive cock-measuring made them contemptible to women, made them appear as little boys play-fighting with sticks.

Later that night, Alma and Daniel are on the terrace of Paolo's palazzo in the Oltrarno. They have just arrived from a private concert in the Basilica di Santa Trinita; the guests are mostly stuffed shirts and women with ponderous bosoms, and the waiters, who seem better dressed, spiffier anyway, in white dinner jackets and black bow ties, circulate among them with service trays of Prosecco and Chianti.

"Uh-oh, don't look now, Count Luigi at twelve o'clock," whispers Daniel.

"Shh," says Alma, cuffing him on the arm, "he'll hear you."

"*Ciao* there, Paolo!" says Daniel, extending his hand.

Paolo nods coldly, barely deigning to shake.

"Buonasera," Alma corrects Daniel. "Sorry," she says to Paolo.

"What'd I do?" Daniel says.

"You're too familiar," Alma says.

"It is all right," Paolo says, shrugging, "we are all friends here."

"Americans don't understand different levels of formality," Alma goes on. "In Korean the honorifics are in the verb endings. So you would say *kahmsamnida* to your elders, *kahmupsumnida* to your equals, *kumupda* with children."

"And this means?"

"'Thank you.'" Alma feels Daniel's anger like a furnace beside her. It fuels her own, and the heat rises and rouses something in Paolo.

"Ahh," says Paolo, "fascinating!" He turns to Daniel, gesturing minutely with his wine glass. "You Americans have no honorifics, I think?" he says.

"No, we're a democracy."

Alma shoots Daniel a look. "Americans have no respect for their elders," she says.

"Americans give respect where respect is due," says Daniel. "And anyway, what's all this 'Americans this, Americans that' bullshit? You haven't lived in Korea since you were four years old."

Alma ignores him, smiles steadfastly into Paolo's cool, patrician face. They are in sync, allied against Daniel and his fatuous compatriots, and the thrill of her small betrayal blossoms in Alma like some night-blooming flower. Daniel's pale Irish complexion, freckled lightly along the bridge of his nose, seems too fair, too telling, in this historied city of deadly plots and shifting alliances, home to the Medicis; it simply gives too much away. "There are some people I wish you to meet, *cara,*" Paolo says now, steering Alma away by the elbow. His own expression is hooded, eyes cast down, and though he speaks to her, he seems to be addressing Daniel who, pink-cheeked and scowling, stares after Alma with a white-hot hatred that causes her, for the first time that night, to sense the danger of the game she plays.

"Oh, Signora Lee," a grating American voice cries out, "we just loved your performance!" *"Bravissima!"* someone calls.

"Why did you do that?"

"Why did I do what?"

"Let's see ... embarrass me in front of Paolo. Act like a total bitch. Ignore me all night like I'm nobody to you."

Alma looks at herself in the mirror, at Daniel behind her. "I don't know what you're talking about, babe," she says.

"Cut the crap!" Daniel brings his fist down on the nightstand, a little harder than he'd intended, causing it to jump from the floor. Alma flinches in spite of herself. "You know exactly what I'm talking about, babe. Why don't you just fuck him and get it over with?"

"Me?" Alma throws her hairbrush across the bureau. "You're the ones who act like you want to fuck each other, always circling around sniffing each other's assholes."

"What are you talking about?"

"You know. You read D. H. Lawrence."

"That's sick." Daniel twists the elastic band of his wristwatch but doesn't remove it. "That's just..."

"'cause we both know you're into some freaky shit."

"Oh, that's... !" Daniel claps his hands. "When you're the one who, who... " He stares at her for a moment. "Okay, why not a threesome? You, me and Machiavelli."

Alma's mouth feels devoid of moisture, as though she could spit sand. "He doesn't want to sleep with me. He just likes to get your goat."

Daniel shakes his head. "He had his hands all over you tonight."

"Don't exaggerate."

Daniel takes a step toward Alma, his hand on his crotch. "*'Cara! Bella!* Come here, *cara!*" He pitches his voice high, rolling his r's, exploding his l's, imitating Paolo's open, insinuating diction. *"Bella, bella, cara mia, bella!"*

"Stop it."

"Here it is, *cara.* I call it my *baton!*" Alma stares at Daniel who is holding his cock in his hands, sticking it out from his unzipped pants. It is partially erect and he bobs it up and down in exaggerated three-quarter time; she has to admit that he's nailed the accent, captured the effeminate lilt of European refinement. It's late and Alma feels herself losing the edge of her drunken belligerence. She is exhausted from performing earlier and then the party after; it's been a long day and here now is Daniel with his penis out, mincing about the room, conducting his idiot's symphony, and the only possible response is to laugh, and once she starts Daniel joins in until they can't stand from laughing so hard and roll onto the bed, clutching their bellies, wiping their tears, and Daniel goes soft and grows hard again. Laughter ceasing he grabs Alma around the waist and pulls her under him—as Paolo still or as himself, Alma isn't certain, nor does she know which arouses her more, though she is aroused; suddenly she feels her wetness; he pulls her panties down, grabs her ass where it's fleshiest and shoves his way inside her so she can feel his pelvic bone slamming against her, *bam, bam*—she pictures a car hitting a retaining wall, something hard, something fast, out of control—and here she is coming, arching up to meet him, reaching back to pull him deeper, *fuck me, baby harder* like a porn star queen, and she's not at all sorry that she's capitulated, or that she made him suffer; she's glad of it, if it's led to this, this igniting.

From the depths of her coma, Alma is held aloft, naked, beseeching. She is carried in strong arms hot against her back, a calloused hand pressed against her backside; at her feet a man crouches, one arm flung up in lamentation. She is terrified, but also excited: It is akin to exultation—laced with contempt—for it is thrilling to be aligned with the victor, borne like a prize, exalted, while the weak and deceived are left to gesture in the dirt. The Sabine women bore Romulus a nation, and even in her dream, Alma smiles at the notion. **-bc.**

Sara Gerot

DOING CRYSTAL

July 23, 1997

It was dark in the basement and smelt like the site of a chemical spill. “Fuck, man, you look like fucking shit,” Seamus said. He perched himself on the armrest of Dusty’s green couch and put his boots on the cushion in front of him. Expensive boots. Hiking boots. None of that gay cowboy farmer-john hick shit. The armrest was small and wobbled under Seamus’ weight. He didn’t want to sit too close.

“Nothing’s for sale and ain’t nobody here to buy any of your shit weed or faggy-trip shit,” Dusty said. A TV that wasn’t on sat on an overturned milk crate.

“I didn’t come over here for that,” Seamus said. And there was no telling, really, why Seamus was there. If there had been anyone else who Seamus knew to pin the shit on, that’s damn well what he would’ve done, but there was no one. No one but Dusty.

The couch was the same green corduroy piece of itchy-ass shit that Seamus’d slept on when he’d stayed the night with Dusty at his mom’s place back in high school. Same couch that’d sat in the first place they’d lived in together before everything fell—no, *not* fell—exploded into all hell. Looked like shit had gone way worse for Dusty though. Now the dirty old thing sat in this little hovel of a house where Dusty lived, and Seamus’d never been inside for longer than it took to drop some of this or that off.

There was such a strong scent of urine that either the toilet was leaking from upstairs or Dusty’d been pissing down there. Seamus’s chest tightened. Fucking rough. He pulled out a small glass bowl from his pocket and lit up. “Here,” Seamus said. He nudged Dusty’s arm with his extended hand.

“Fuck no,” Dusty said. Dusty had his own glass pipe cradled in his hand. There was no flicker from his lighter but Dusty kept trying. Seamus held out a cheap-ass ghetto zippo that he’d taken from someone else’s house. He’d fully intended on returning it when he took it, but now who knew? Dusty took it from Seamus.

“What happened to your arms, and your face? What the fuck happened to you?” Seamus asked.

Dusty sucked and blew. There was barely any smoke, but it smelled fucking terrible. Seamus waved his pipe around hoping to cover up the smell of tweak. Dusty didn’t answer.

“Get in a fight? What?” Seamus asked.

“I fixed something,” Dusty said. Why the fuck was he watching that dead-ass TV? Weird-ass blue eyes all scary and bugged. Dusty usually kept his head shaved pretty close, but looked like that hadn’t happened for awhile. Patches of greasy blonde fur stuck out over his ears and the rest of his scalp was covered with prickly-looking fuzz. Enough to freak a guy out. And the blood. All the sores everywhere. Sores and scratches. Looked so bad it wasn’t going to be easy. No use thinking all dramatic though. The pot wasn't doing nothing for Seamus's nerves.

"More like something tried to fix you." Seamus let out a laugh that was short like a cough. If he didn't laugh he would gag.

"The stairs," Dusty said. "I used that dirty slut's entertainment center to fix my fucking stairs."

Seamus laughed some more like coughing, even covered up his mouth. "Fucking right, buddy," he laughed again. But seriously, he had to get Dusty the fuck out of there. Needed to get on with the shit. The sooner he could get Dusty out of there, the closer Seamus would be to ... jail.

Damn.

"I came to tell you something because I'm your friend," Seamus said. And there it was. Seamus's excuse for showing up after all that time. Acting like he was doing his estranged best friend a favor, like he was there to help poor old Dusty out.

"No you ain't my fucking friend," Dusty said.

No shit.

Dusty kept at the little pipe. "Crystal don't plan on coming back, you know," said Seamus. "She's living with Greg. Nobody was going to say nothing, but I thought you should know."

"Slut sent her mom over here to get her shit," Dusty said. "But she can't have my stairs." The corner of his flaky lips twitched.

/

October 18, 1996

There had been two other girls knocked up at the beginning of school, same as Crystal, but they showed. Angie arrived every morning at school with wet hair that got greasy by the end of the day. Her face was so splotched with acne that it looked painful. Then there was Misty, massive and tall with long hair like a commercial. Smile wide enough for a toothpaste ad. Lots of gossip went around about Misty and her baby. Some said that it was Madame Simone's, the French teacher's, new husband's baby. Some said it was the cop with cropped red hair and skin tanned in a way that wasn't quite right-looking. Maybe it was Mr. Heath's, the girls' golf coach. That Misty had a secret under there. Under that red sweatshirt stretched *so* tight. Her luscious lips always glossy and ready to spread into a come-and-get-me smile. Crystal figured Misty looked about thirty so it made sense to assume the dad would be old.

Crystal on the other hand was five months in and had yet to show much of anything. Still wearing the same jeans that sagged below her hips in the same place they always did. Her white t-shirt hung loose on her like usual as she caved her shoulders forward and stared out the window of her third-story classroom. Even before it got around to the teachers that she was pregnant, none of them expected nothing of her. Been like that since about a semester into her freshman year. That was fine with her.

The night before, Crystal had been over at Dusty's to a party he was having. She was upset that all the people were there, not that she had any say. He'd been begging her to move in ever since he left the shithole he'd lived in before with Seamus, but she wasn't sure yet. She'd sat on his mattress with her back against the bare wall under the floor lamp in the corner, staring at the phone, wanting to call Seamus. Wanting the phone to ring and it to be Seamus. Wanting to smoke meth and being too self-conscious to act tweaked out in front of the other people. She was alone in there, in Dusty's room, and so pulled her knees to her chest, tensed every muscle as tight as she could clench, and shook with the force. She shook and groaned, holding the tremor, keeping it going, *grrrrr rrrrrrr rrrrrrr rrrrrr.* Then she released. *God Please. Mmmmmm.*

A second, another, three four five seconds of relief. Exhaustion. She took a breath and went to it again.

The door opened, slowly, like it wasn't even his room. "Crystal?" Dusty said.

She was hitting herself in the head with a balled up fist. Thumpthumpthump. "Hmmmm?" she growled.

"What is it?" he asked. He dropped down in front of her, his hand going into his pocket, a motion she never missed. She stopped her growling. A few pills fell out of a crinkled cigarette cellophane when he pulled apart the melted top. Picking one up from the floor, he showed her. "Purple bomber. One's all you need."

She held out a cupped hand and clamped it closed on his when it got close. His fingers dragged across her palm to get away. She didn't want him to think that she was trying to hold his hand but she couldn't help it. A bottle of Jack sat on the floor, only backwash left, she knew, but she twisted off the black cap letting it fall to the floor, and downed the bomber like there was no tomorrow, which Dusty was saying was the whole point.

"Lay down," he said.

She dropped the bottle and tried. Curled up tight, she wondered if it was OK to crush the baby like that, but she couldn't straighten out for nothing. Everything was pulled in real tight. The sheet was stained with what she thought looked and smelled like tomato soup but she gripped clumps of it in both fists and pulled them up to her neck, pressing down on them with her chin.

She squeezed her eyes shut as tight as she could. "You OK?" Dusty asked.

"Nuh-uh," she breathed. "Go away."

The way his jeans sounded as he stood up, and his boots lightly pressing here and there as he steadied himself, was loud. Then stillness. She knew he was standing staring down at her. His breathing, all his own, grated her. Not wheezy but wet. Seamus had almost no breath. The few times she'd had the chance to be around Seamus when he slept, she'd tried never to close her eyes. She'd never wanted him to leave.

Seamus. Seamus. *Seamus.* Why didn't he call?

He wasn't coming over to Dusty's any time soon. But he *could.* To get something off Dusty, or for Dusty to get something off of him. The chance was still there and she squeezed and she squeezed and she *squeezed.* He could, he could, he could, hecould-*hecouldhecould.* But.

He wouldn't.

Crystal heard Dusty breathe in deep, his hands running over his jeans. "Dusty, don't," she said.

Nothing. Just the sound of his hands running over his jeans.

"Please," she said. She felt tears, or at least the start of them. If her and Dusty would've been alone she would've screamed real loud and pounded at the walls till she had to be stopped. Tense and vibrating, her skin was alive with an aching zing. "*MMMmmmmmm.* Please," she said.

He was going to make her ask for it. Why couldn't he just hit her? *Hit me, hit me, hit me.* "Dusty, please. C'mon. Hit me. Choke me. Please. Hold me down. Holdmedown—"

Then he was on top of her, giving her what she wanted and really deserved. It's not that she didn't struggle because she did. Dusty'd had black eyes more than once from her flying elbows, but he learned. She was glad he learned. He held her down while she fought to get upright. Struggling so hard that she could hardly breathe. He pinned her with his chest against her chest, both of her arms crossed between their stomachs, and he slapped her. Hard enough to hurt and ache, hard enough to do everything except bruise. He gave her what she wanted and really deserved. He hit hit hit *hit* her.

And finally. *Finally.* Her face really fit her.

/

June 2, 1997

After living together for damn well close to a year, Dusty'd got real sick of Crystal's emotional, head-game bullshit. All that break up to make up shit. Her dirty-faced fat-ass baby was getting to him too. One of Crystal's cheapo sandals hit the ceiling above Dusty and fell. It smacked him on his head. He didn't even yell this time, just got up off the hot-pink computer chair and grabbed her thin arms. Reed was already crying, but when Dusty grabbed his mama he cried even louder from where he was planted on the floor. Couldn't walk yet. Probably wasn't right.

With familiar force Dusty dragged Crystal over towards the bottom of the basement stairs. Her body was limp and she was light enough that he could lift her off the ground with his arms folded at his elbows. Her bare feet knocked into every single wooden step. Even when her toes scraped against the jagged edges of the broken ones, she never cried. It was like she wasn't even real. Dusty had seen her cry when she was all twacked out, losing it big time, but she almost never cried at anything that hurt.

There was no looking in her face. Her eyes were empty and scary anyways. Their blue looked like an endless and hopeless Kansas sky, vacant of any sort of color in the horizon. At the top of the stairs he slammed her into the kitchen wall to disorient her for a minute so he could open the door. The kitchen had knives in it. He shoved her out and she tumbled down the concrete steps.

She got up and pulled down on her thin jean-shorts. Her tank-top was some kind of velvety thing that'd come with a pair of pajama bottoms that he'd bought her for a gift. It was blue with puffy clouds. Bruises covered her arms and legs, and a long red scrape ran up her knee. Her ankles and feet were covered in scabs and tiny bleeding sores that she scratched at with her pink toenails. How come she looked so good standing there with her mousy hair all crazy and bones poking out everywhere?

She slipped her hands into her back pockets like she usually did and twisted a little bit. Looking up at Dusty like *now what?*

"Go on," Dusty said. He could look at her now with the space between them. The skin on his hand was peeling and covered with dirt-filled circular lesions. He half-waved it towards the sidewalk. Everything in him wanted her to come back and be with him right then, on the kitchen table, like they usually did after a fight.

"I'm going," she spoke softly to the ground. The triangles of empty space formed by her jutting arms looked like real good places to loop your arms through. Open spots. "So you don't love me no more? That it?" she asked.

"I'm sick and tired of the bullshit," Dusty said. It was true; he was tired of the bullshit. He turned and punched the wall beside the door. He put a dent in the gray and a splinter of wood in his hand. A trickle of bright red streamed across the back of his pale skin. All he could do was pull it out and let the blood roll. He wanted to turn around and have her be there already, already climbing back up the three concrete steps to the small landing in front of the side-door. He would grab her by her arms again, and then the table. But when he turned around, she was still scratching one dirty foot with the toenails of the other on the overgrown grass.

"OK. So I'll go," she said. Suddenly her hands balled into little fists and she leaned forward slightly at her waist. "I'm tired of the bullshit too," she yelled. A loud station wagon roared down the street. Its hatch was open but it was empty in the back.

"Now, c'mon girl." He ran his hand over his layer of white-blonde fuzzy hair. A streak of red from his hand stained a stripe across his head. "I'm just so fucking—you know, just, you *know.* Why you got to test me?" He couldn't think of anything else to say. Why was she still standing down there? "Just c'mon back in. I'm almost through with the shit, then we'll party. You just need some shit. I need some shit. We'll re-up what we spent," Dusty said. Her hands were loosening. All he could think of was doing a line off that little concave dent between her pussy and her hip, and then fucking her on the table that smashed into the wall with every thrust. "I'm fucking sorry, alright?"

The sky was gray. Gray is good in June. But if the sun had been out, the whole conversation would have been over sooner. Neither Dusty nor Crystal could stand the heat, not to mention the sun. She tilted her head and smiled with her lips that were naturally a strange shade of purplish pink. With skinny fingers she pulled a tangle of hair behind her ear. Who wouldn't want her? "How much longer?" she asked, not moving forward.

"A bit, baby," he said.

He waited for her at the top of the steps, and grabbed her around the waist from behind while she walked through the door. His foot caught on the lip of the doorway and he tightened his grip. It was only four paces to the table. She tried to turn around and face him.

"Uh-uh," he grunted. No looking at her now neither. She was pressed against him and the scent of her, like baby lotion on dirty feet, turned off his brain. With only slight resistance her head strained to push back against the pressure of his cupping hand. In a swift but careful motion he pushed her face down against the table and slammed her hips into the edge.

"Tell me you won't let me get away," Crystal said softly. She'd twisted her own arms behind her back so Dusty could restrain them when he was done dealing with their pants.

This wasn't the way they usually started, but sometimes shit gets turned around and it's hard to know why. Just goes that way, feels so right, there's no stopping it. Not even when she screams so loud that her fucking kid needs her. Not even when the fucking kid cries because he can hear or see his mama getting fucked up the ass, dry except for a bit spit and sometimes trickles of blood that seep out of tears. Screaming *stop, please, let me go,* twisting her own arms, and moving against the motion of his thrusts, little moans slipping out real soft and sweet.

Crystal was his, no matter what happened, no matter how many times she left, no matter how sick of her shit he got, no matter how loud that fucking kid screamed, no matter nothing. There were other girls sure, but Crystal, well, just something about that dirty girl that felt so fresh, burning like a fire, like a sting, like a buzz. Dusty knew the truth was, no matter what, all that really mattered to him was Crystal.

/

October 18, 1996

In class she stared out at the window, watching the cars that would drive by and wishing she could get inside those cars, inside the people driving the cars and be them. Just be them. Then she thought *gener-*

ic. Sometimes she figured her thoughts were real generic. Her crossed arms rested on the desk that had been cleaned with something that smelled at first fresh like bleach, but after a bit like wood-shavings in a hamster cage.

The teacher went on and on about Machu Picchu and eventually turned out the lights for a slide show. The purple bomber was still pulling Crystal down. Her eyelids were sore, worn out. She'd got on the bus a block down from Dusty's that morning, though she barely remembered that happening. The driver woke Crystal up at the bus barn and drove her to school. Crystal realized when she reached the office to fill out her tardy slip that she hadn't even thanked the lady.

Snow came down but it didn't stick. Hadn't even been no fall really that year. Late October and winter winds already had thrashed through the parallelogram of Kansas. Never cleaning nothing really. Just gritty gusts blowing the same way with unbearable pressure till you just about got used to the shit. Then back it'd come the other way.

Blow again.

Snow again. It melted into the brick, the concrete, the black-top, the greedy grass that was begrudgingly green in several spots, even with the sprinklers considered by many to be an unnecessary part of the budget. Crystal figured that was probably right. She didn't really have any ideas as to better ways to spend the money though. Like anybody gave a good goddamn how she felt.

What *if* the snow was meth, or coke, the ice was ice, the blowing blow? She loved this thought. And the smoke stacks. They were like mammoth bongs for giant stoners. Monstrous men closing their lips around the chimneys, letting the smoke roll into rips that would fly across the town when expelled. She almost smiled. It was the first thing she thought of in a long time that she liked. Felt as good as Christmas looked in commercials.

If she had a pen, she would've written it down on paper. Course she had no paper. But if she had a pen, she would've written it down like a poem, on the desktop, and she would've called it *Fuck Machu Picchu.* And as she dropped her head onto her arms and let her tired eyes win, she almost smiled. She was close to feeling pretty good. She ran her hand across her stomach, remembering that she wasn't alone.

And just like that.

The good was gone.

/

July 17, 1997

The cops had pictures. Seamus sat at the metal table with his head in his hands. Now he knew why every criminal, in every scene in every movie, sat with their heads in their hands. It was too goddamn much.

Years before when he was questioned by the homicide police it had been different. They gave him water. They called his mother. The district attorney had laid a hand on his shoulder and told him everything would be OK. The D.A. drove him to the station herself after getting a crisis intervention counselor to get Rheanna out of the fetal position from under the porch where she had holed up for some fucking reason after she saw the body. They were sorry then. Sorry that Seamus'd had to shoot Crystal's crazy-ass step-dad.

The Drug Task Force officers were different. There were pictures of Seamus going in and out of houses and garages with a toolbox. Video even. A toolbox. "We know what you were doing."

"It was just pot. I told you. I swear to Christ."

"Well we say it wasn't. We say you were trafficking methamphetamine."

"No fucking—"

"Who's the cook?"

"I'm no fucking tweaker."

"Who's the cook?"

Fuck 'em.

"You got some kids. That right, Seamus?"

"Nope."

"We figure you do."

"Nope."

"Well we heard you did. Two in fact. How would you feel if we told you we might just have to do investigations into the mothers of your two little bastards, huh? Put 'em in foster care?"

Seamus was silent. The electric buzz of the crisp white light droned and flickered. He finally shrugged.

"Foster care, you little fuck."

"Go ahead. Probably should anyways," Seamus said. He lifted up his head. This was the moment, the first moment he felt like a father.

"Look. You'll never get out if you get charged with trafficking meth, you little fuck. I'd be thinking about my options if I was you."

Seamus pulled on the sleeves of his white thermal. The cuffs were stained with swirls of grime that never came out no matter how much he washed them.

"So here's the deal. This is exactly what is going to happen. You're going to leave here. You're going to wear an ankle bracelet which means you will be home every night by 10 o'clock. Keep up your habits. Going to the bar. Do your dope. Whatever. Live it up while you can. We want you to get your friend to buy some things. We want you to get him to buy ingredients, any ingredients on this list." The officer pulled out a plastic sleeve from the leather folder that he had in front of him. It was a long list of chemicals and medications. "Get him to buy some of this shit, and we'll arrest you both."

"I don't know a cook. I don't—"

"Then you better get to know one. This is what we do. This is how it's done."

"Will I go to prison?"

"For the marijuana."

"That's all there was. You have to know—"

The officers stood up. A uniformed cop came in to take Seamus to the holding cell.

Pacing the length of the cell was one of Seamus's friends from high school, Killer. He was small but crazy as all hell. The back pocket of his pants was held in place with duct tape and he wasn't wearing a shirt.

"Shit. You got busted?" Killer spat. His already ridiculous lisp seemed to be worsened by the swollen state of his bottom split lip. Juicy looking welts, thick and pink, covered his back and front. Seamus figured he must be drunk to be able to talk with all that black and blue all over his face.

"Yup."

"What'd they fucking tell you?"

"Probation probably," Seamus lied. It felt like a commitment.

"Somebody bailing you out?"

"Hope so. You?"

"Nah. No way. I got time I owe anyways on a warrant. Figure now's as good a time as any."

"Who'd you fight?"

"Nobody." He spit a mixture of blood and saliva onto the floor. His voice lowered. "The cops caught me running out a' the back of Tessa's Tavern after Tarah called 'em on me for kicking over a table and threatening her life." Here Killer paused to laugh for minute. He got himself together, wiping away a bit of spit that hung on his split lip. "Ah, shit." He ran his fingers lightly over the side of his face. "Didn't think she really did it. Tried to run when I saw 'em pull up." Now he raised his voice and punched his fist towards the wall, stopping short of the filthy brick. "Fucking little bitch. God*damn* that little slut. God*damn* I sure know how to pick 'em. Probably up at the fucking house right now fucking who knows which one of my friends." He shook his head and laughed. "Probably a fucking gang bang. Crazy little bitch. Running a fucking train on her probably there, buddy. Go home and have to clean up after a bunch of donkey dick motherfuckers." Killer laughed. "If she does any of my coke though I'll punch her right in the fucking face." He punched his fist out towards the wall again and laughed.

Seamus chuckled late and slow. Killer didn't seem to notice. Seamus was sitting on the edge of the bench. There was no clean space to put his back against the wall. It was smeared with snot and feces and stains crusted orange and yellow that Seamus figured for piss. Tarah and Killer had been together since junior high. Seamus had fucked her once during their freshman year of high school, and again, recently, a few months before in Killer's bed while he worked his night shift at the factory. "So what the fuck happened?" Seamus gestured to Killer's torso. Seamus noticed his own hand was shaking and, unsettled by this, he clasped his two hands together tightly, elbows on his knees.

"The cops," he whispered.

"No shit?"

"No shit," Killer said. He paused in his pacing, looked wildly around and then picked back up again.

/

July 23, 1997

Dusty followed Seamus across the basement. "Yeah man. You need a ride, some fresh air. Some fucking sun. Some music. A big fat blunt just waiting in the car with your name on it," Seamus said. "Sounds good, huh?"

Sounded real good. Sounded like heaven. Like somewhere Dusty couldn't even go.

"Come on. What you waiting for?" Seamus said from halfway up the stairs.

Couldn't even make the first step.

He remembered ripping the TV off the entertainment center and the cable box crashing to the ground. It'd cracked real fast. He'd had to dig through box of shit after box of all his collected shit to find the hammer. Digging, digging, digging. It had been so hard to find, so hard to remember what he was even looking for, with all the shit to distract him. Cords to nothing, soiled socks, stolen tools he didn't even know the names for, burnt lightbulbs, threadbare shirts and papers. Mounds of papers. Bills, receipts, notes, cards, torn magazines, and pages from books. The boxes seemed bottomless until he dumped them all out onto the basement floor, then there were the bottomless piles. When'd he found the hammer he'd—*holy fuck the fucking hammer*—roared at the ceiling.

It wasn't real wood of course. Damn cheap piece of shit furniture. Laminated, spray-painted pressed wood entertainment center was all it was, and so it came apart quick and easy. No, it didn't make the sturdiest stairs, but it'd covered up most of the empty spots at the bottom. Took him a whole day because he couldn't find shit. Digging, digging, digging.

Nails. He'd torn out the doorframes and floorboards upstairs for the nails. He had torn it all to pieces then pounded them down. He smashed it up and pounded them down. That'd show her to leave shit. She shouldn't have left it there. She shouldn't have left.

He didn't care.

He turned that shit into fucking stairs.

He couldn't put his foot on even one. Not a one. There was nothing. Not a fucking thing in the world that would let him past those first few steps and get up the stairs. Dusty figured he'd die in that fucking basement.

Fuck it.

-bc.

Tiffany Promise

S U O N E V A R A V E N O U S

S U O N E V A V E N O U S

S U O N E V E N O U S

S U O N E N O U S

S U O N O U S

S U O U S

S U S

S

I tried to get her to eat. Kind of. I mean, really, I was sick of looking at her wrists. Raven's hands were thick and jointed like a man's, but she had these little bird-boned wrists, so delicate-looking that I had no idea how they didn't crack under the weight of her hefty knuckles. I swear I could hear them screaming in strain. I was always prepared for a sudden snap.

At Mealtime I would attempt to feed her slices of wheat bread, baby carrots, berry yogurt, chunks of fruit: stuff I thought dieting people would eat. I just wanted to flesh her out, even out the distributions. I wanted to want her hands all over my skin, but I was scared that if she touched me they would feel like death: clammy and hard, overwhelming. She would never take any of the food that I offered her. "Pinky, you know I can't," she would state sternly, punctuated by a melodramatic sigh. She would spend the rest of Mealtime gazing off at something captivating that I couldn't see.

Late at night, when we were the only ones awake, Raven would let me run my finger across her abdomen. Her scars were thick and twisted there, like faded red-rope licorice stitched to the skin. She liked to tell me the story of where they came from.

"When I was fourteen," she said, "Zeus visited me in bed—shape-shifted and glorious. He was in the same bull form that he had used to ravish Europa. For the first time in my life, I felt like a princess. A few weeks later, my stomach started to swell. I was carrying a god-baby. All the girls at school were really jealous."

I could easily imagine her belly bulging under the force of hoof and horn. I liked to think about it, it was kinda sexy. She explained that when Baby Bovine-Deity burst out of her stomach while she was sleeping, he left her guts tangled in the sheets. Clambering quickly out the window and into the Louisiana wilderness as he did, she never had a chance to hold him. Her parents found her half-dead with a knife in her fist. She claimed it was for umbilical cord cutting. No one believed her.

I tried to help Raven share her story at Group, but the other women on the Trauma Unit didn't want to listen. They only liked talking about their daddy issues, sometimes meandering into the mundanity of food/drug allergies (plus associated side effects) and the bucketfuls of diagnoses that they had worked so hard to accrue. Mythological beings were not of any interest. They hated Raven. She disgusted them, but only because they wanted to be her more than they wanted to be themselves. They binged while she purged. And purged some more.

"Don't worry, Rave, the Vultures are just jealous," I whispered in her peach-fuzzed ear, hoping that she didn't feel too left out or ignored. "Your story is much more interesting than any of theirs. I mean, seriously, a god fucked you! Out of all the girls in the world, he picked you! Most of these fatties haven't even had one mediocre fuck, let alone a celestial one."

"Yeah," she mumbled into her bunny-pink sweatshirt. It was so big for her that the neckhole swallowed the bottom half of her face.

/

Every night before Lights Out, Raven cajoled me into praying with her. "I might slip you a quick kiss tonight if you will say one short prayer with me, Pinky," she whispered, almost cooing. Her breath smelled weird, chemically almost. Like the sparkly rubber balls you get out of toy-vending machines at supermarkets.

We sat facing each other while she quietly babbled. I heard words like "secret," "death" and "hunger" quite a few times, though I could never make out any complete sentences. Underneath the table I would run my toes up her thigh and into her hip. The bones were thick and hooked there, she would never be as small as she wanted.

She was really skinny in every other place. Her clothes hung off her like she was a clothesline. I liked to imagine how small she would have been if she didn't have bones. I was pretty sure I could fit her entire boneless body into my old kindergarten lunchbox. Just looking at her made me hungry; I never saw her eat anything—on her own volition, anyway. Sometimes the nurses would get mad and holler, all squinty-eyed: "Yes, Raven, we know you have allergies, but not to *every* food!" Then they'd shove tubes up her nose—no one in the world is allergic to tubes or tube-food, not even Raven. Right when I didn't think she could possibly get smaller, she would. I would glance at her during our morning Community meeting and I almost wouldn't see her. I wondered how her stomach didn't just get pissed off and eat itself. I go four hours without food and I can feel my insides writhing in agony. She never complained of being in pain, I think she had grown numb to the gnaw.

/

One afternoon while we watched Court TV, I noticed her lusting after the strawberries I was sucking on. She looked like she needed them and I never had seen her look hungry before. I thought that mechanism had been flipped off long ago but the saliva build-up in the corners of her mouth proved me wrong. I was being selfish that day and kept every last red fleshy tidbit for myself. I don't even like fruit that much, I was only eating them as a distraction from my lack of cigarettes. Seeing her want them so badly made them taste like the best thing ever, so I ate them whole, leaves and all.

The next day I started feeling guilty for being such a greedy pig. I couldn't get Raven's hungry eyes out of my head. I knew that she needed those berries and I felt shitty for denying her something so important. I called my Aunt to ask for her help. "Auntie dear," I squeaked, finding it necessary to approach her with some sort of respect, "will you please, please, pretty please with sugar on top bring me strawberries tomorrow when you visit?" I knew she would do just about anything I asked. She seemed distraught about my current situation; whenever she visited, her mouth twisted into funeral mode.

"Strawberries?" she questioned, unbelievingly. "What about your usual carton of Newports? Did you quit smoking?" She sounded so excited that I hated bursting her bubble. Proud of me for being so concerned about my health, Auntie went crazy in the supermarket, buying six pounds of blueberries, raspberries, strawberries. She wanted me to eat them while she visited. Watching me delight in something she brought me would ease some of her guilt. When I told her that I was saving them for a special occasion, her face grew concerned; she pictured them rotting under my bed for weeks. I thought how funny it would be to watch the Vultures contend with hordes of fruit flies.

After Visiting Hours I rinsed and dried every single berry before arranging them as elegantly as I could. I made Raven close her eyes as I led her into the kitchen. She reddened at the sight of the plump berries overflowing their styrofoam bowls; I didn't think she had enough blood in her body to support that deep flushing of cheek and lip. I imagined it just dripping through her like from a rusted leaky faucet.

She looked like she didn't know how to eat, but once she got started, it was obvious that she was a pro. She began slowly, caressing the luscious heart-shaped fruit—I was actually jealous for a second. Then she regally sliced them with a plastic spoon and sprinkled packets of Equal onto their parted flesh. Swallowing whole slivers like oysters, she shoved handfuls into her glistening mouth; the other berries sat completely untouched. The Vultures glared while she ate, thick stalks of purpled leg shooting out of too-short sweatpants, guts thick like butter peeking from beneath t-shirts. They wanted to stuff Raven's mouth full of chicken wings, mashed potatoes and chocolate bars; they wanted to see her bloat and thicken like gravy. "Good girl, Raven," I coaxed like a proud parent. She didn't seem to hear me, so intent on devouring her fruit. Her chin dripped pink, her eyes were glassy.

Five minutes later, Raven found me on the scratchy couch in the TV room, picking my scabs. "Where'd you go?" she asked, vaguely worried, "I thought you were eating berries with me, when I looked up you were gone." She was sticky with juice and pulp. I wanted to lick it off her cheeks but the Vultures were leering; it was TV time, so they were flocked, blubbery and blue, drooling at the screen. "Sorry," I said. "I thought it would be nice to leave you alone with your strawberries. I knew if I turned on the TV, the Vultures would follow."

She grabbed my hand and dragged me to our special corner so that we could pray before Lights Out. She asked god for forgiveness—for what, I forgot to listen. I was too busy looking at her face: With her eyes closed she didn't look half as dead. She walked me to my room, not allowed to actually step foot inside; for weeks she had been dangling goodnight kisses like carrots, disintegrating in the air every time I reached for them. This night, though, the kiss was sweet, if a little parched. I could feel it on my lips as I walked to my room. It warmed me for a few minutes, a tiny campfire in my crotch. I crawled into my ever-so-bleached bed and quickly fell asleep.

All night I dreamed about Raven: tiny berry seeds stuck in her guts and sprouting, spry vines growing up her intestines and out of her mouth—through esophagus, past epiglottal tissue and tooth. I saw her sprouting, like a woman is not supposed to sprout. Spring green peeked from the corners of her mouth, her face red as a strawberry...she looked happy for the first time. I couldn't wait to tell her about it over breakfast.

/

Seven A.M. always comes early, but even earlier when the first thing you're forced to do is say how you feel. At Community we would go around the room and rate our moods from one to ten, while the scribe recorded it on the chalkboard. If someone was feeling one, we were supposed to watch out that they didn't slit their wrists that day.

Raven wasn't there, so we skipped her. The scribe left the two from yesterday by her name on the board. I went to Life Skills without her too, though she usually sat beside me and kept me entertained. She had a nervous habit of knocking lightly on her front tooth with her fingernail. I missed the clicking of keratin on enamel.

After lunch I was feeling lonely, so I refused to go to Affect Management. I locked myself in my room and covered every inch of my skin in red permanent marker. We were given dozens of these as an alternative to razor blades. Sometimes, when feeling generous, the nurses would give us ice cubes to squeeze. Frozen water pains the clamped hand without doing any skin or nerve damage. Every time I tried to sneak over and knock on Raven's door, a nurse would catch me and send me in the opposite direction. Rumors started to mill, as they do in small places.

At my session with Dr. Slate that afternoon, I asked about Raven. "She was allergic to strawberries," he stated sternly. "Didn't she ever mention that to you, Pinky? It was in her chart."

"Of course I never saw her chart. I've never even seen my chart. Where is she?"

"Raven isn't with us anymore..." he trailed off. Deep inside I had known all day, but hearing it spoken aloud made my guts pour. He took a deep breath and continued, "She went into anaphylactic shock last night around 9:30."

"Ana-what shock?" I stammered, picturing Raven's wild hair slithering through the air as she shoved a fork into a toaster. No, an outlet—Raven wouldn't use a toaster.

"Anaphylactic shock," he said, sounding the letters out to me slowly. He sounded like a kindergarten teacher and I wanted him to be wearing a cardigan and holding a stick of chalk. "It is a whole-body allergic reaction. Tissues in the body release histamines that cause the breathing tubes to constrict, the tongue to swell and fluid to leak into the lungs. Epinephrine is usually injected to combat this reaction but we didn't find her until it was too late."

"Oh Raven, I never got a chance to fill all your hollow spots with kisses. I'm so sorry, my sweet skeletal queen." Tears started slipping out of my ducts, my mouth wobbled wearily. "I hope it didn't hurt too badly and that it was over fast. You didn't deserve to suffer any more. Dust to dust." I made the sign of the cross, not because I was religious but because it seemed appropriate and I wanted to do whatever I could to guide my sweet bird-girl into some sort of heaven-like afterlife. My face throbbed, it felt like blood was going to gush out my ears and nose. I stuffed Kleenex deep into my orifices: keeping myself in, keeping everything else out, though I was slightly thrilled by the mental image of spurting hot plasmatic sticky all over the doctor's pasty face.

"We're all sorry for your loss, Pinky. We know that Raven was a core member of your little community. A traumatic event like this will be distressing for the entire group, but at least you're in a place where you can work out your grief. We have counselors available to you morning and night, don't forget that. Also, if you would like for me to increase one of your mood stabilizers, I would be more than happy."

I stared at him, stricken. *I really did love her* kept looping through my head. I grabbed my file from his desk and threw it across the room frisbee-style before stomping out. He ducked just in time, so instead of decapitating him the papers just flew everywhere, floppy white birds taking flight before crash-landing.

/

The rest of the day was strangely quiet. The Vultures kept peering at me out of the corners of their eyes. They didn't look sad or angry, just confused. At Process Group we had a getting-in-touch-with-our-feelings exercise where we sat in a circle on the floor and each of us was given a bulbous yellow onion. We had to peel off every layer until there was nothing left in our hands but oniony reek and tears. Each layer was supposed to represent a mask that we wore to shield us from our sad lives.

We often cried, just not all of us at the same time. Onion fumes yanking tears from our eyes, we blubbered like babies in our own stink. I peeled and peeled like a maniac, wanting the exercise to be over as quickly as possible.

In the center of my onion, I found a tiny green sprout, the start of a shoot. I thought about saving it so I could plant it somewhere. I imagined a lovely fragrant onion flower blossoming in honor of Raven; I would water it daily, hoping it would swell and grow like she never could. But I quickly changed my mind and plopped it squarely in the center of my tongue, swallowing it down in a quick slurp. I wanted to sprout like Raven. She really was the lucky one. I'd be full of onions, she strawberries. We could meet in a place where we'd play harps, float on clouds, touch. Our joint breath would make a lovely aroma: sweet and sharp, flora-filled.

I sat a few more minutes with the stench seeping deep under my nails, before heading off to dinner with the rest of the Vultures. We had grilled cheeses and potato chips. No one touched their salads. **-bc.**

Merrill Feitell

THE QUIET CONTEST

/ 1.

The Road Trip

Before they were out of the garage—
Before their father even had the car out of reverse—
Before he'd finished backing out of the driveway—
Before the thing they were looking at was their destination—the *future*, the road laid out to the horizon—before anyone had made a sound, their father, the Professor, liked to say:
I've got an idea: Let's have a contest.
—What kind of contest?
A quiet contest.
—Oh, a quiet contest! Did I win? Did I win?
This, of course, was Esther's line, as if jutting her chin toward their father and daring another punch.

John Stapleton, Jr., by contrast, tried to ignore the way their father would turn up the A/C, packing the entire bullet-shaped station wagon with a raging blast of cold, no matter the season; he tried to ignore the way their mother would simply—without a word—extract the sweater she kept in glove box, insulating herself in the crumpled wool she'd brought back from Scotland decades earlier, on honeymoon.

In truth, he could hardly breathe; he could hardly breathe from the first mention of any road trip. The fight was coming. Quiet or not, it would come. And Stapleton couldn't breathe until it started. He tried; he just couldn't. Instead, he filled his cheeks with air, tucking his lips into a seamlessly tight line, allowing just the tiniest release of air out one corner of his mouth, trying to focus not on fear but on counting his way through each breath's slow—and slower—escape.

You better cut that out, said his father.

—What?

That noise.

—What noise?

You're an instigator.

—What's an instigator?

Perhaps inspired by this question—*such ignorance!*—or by traffic, or by the open road, or the inclement weather, or the incomparably beautiful weather, or perhaps intoxicated by his control of not just the vehicle's climate but also its steering wheel, and his capacity to slam them all into a retaining wall, or oncoming traffic, or off a fucking cliff—*Is that what you're trying to make me to do?*—their father liked to accelerate and brake; accelerate and brake. He liked to swerve. Then brake. *I'm going to kill us. I'm going to kill us. I'm going to kill us all.*

In school, Stapleton sang along in assembly: *Over the river and through the woods, to grandmother's house we go.* In the car, to his grandmother's down in Brooklyn for Thanksgiving, for example, or to Lake Winnipesaukee, or Acadia National Park for the Fourth of July, he remained completely mute.

But after the acceleration and braking, the acceleration and braking, the lurching and shrieks, the *thwack* of their mother's wedding band as she grabbed for the dashboard, the windshield flashing across traffic lanes, the terror of rocketing through glass, the terror of staying belted in safe—only after all that did Stapleton really become aware of the sound accompanying the slow escape of air through his lips. There it was, with each and every breath he breathed: A grating, insufferable *squeak.*

Was Stapleton an instigator? Did he start *it?* All he knew for sure was that *it* was looming until *it* began. And unless *it* began, *it* would never be gone. He was just breathing; he was just trying to breathe.

Eventually their father would resume regular speed, or screech to a halt on the shoulder, or succumb to traffic, or congestion at the tolls.

Pizza for dinner? How about Chinese?

Their mother might do something—finally. For example: She might tune into some big band broadcast on the radio.

"Oh, a quiet contest?" Esther might mutter again, audible only to her brother over the highway smack and drone. "Did I win? Did I win?"

Thank you. Thanks, dad. I love you, dad. Thanks. This is what Stapleton would say upon arrival at their destination. Sometimes he said it with the pizza man still in the doorway. Sometimes he whispered it in the dark, alone in his bed—a prayer, a bargain. *Thank you. Thanks, dad. I love you, dad; thanks.*

So went the air escaping Stapleton's lips.

/ **2.**

Stockholm Syndrome

The fight was coming. Quiet or not, it would come. And John Stapleton, Jr. just couldn't wait for it. He couldn't breathe until it started—but if he made it happen, it would happen, and then it would be gone.

Then there would just be a total silence, after the lurching car and the shrieks, and the acceleration and the braking, and the screams.

Then their father would resume a normal speed, and some big band broadcast would be on the radio. In the front seat, as if nothing had happened at all, his mother would be singing along to the oldies: *Maresy dotes and Dozey dotes and Little Lambsy divey.*

—Huh?

Their mother knew the words; she could sing along. She understood gibberish. She could speak in tongues. Where had she learned such things?

—Where did you learn such a thing?

Merci. D'ohs en d'oh si d'otes.

—Have you been to France?

She kept singing: *Mareseatoatsanddoeseatoatsandlittlelambsydivey.*

—But, mom, please, I don't understand what's going on.

Their mother would explain how the lyrics were actually as follows: *Mares eat oats, and does eat oats, and little lambs eat ivy.*

This seemed impossible to Stapleton, but he listened hard. He trained his ear and, ultimately, he could hear it too. The world contained hidden meanings, secret codes. If you listened hard enough, you could discern them. You could sit in the front seat, fluent in truth.

Your father loves you, said the Stapleton mom. *You just don't understand him.*

Still, Stapleton and Esther would flinch whenever they heard their father's call from the top of the basement stairs: *What is all that noise down there? Do you want me to come down there? I'll come down there.* He might even crane his neck down toward the fortress the siblings had built to withstand him. *Wireyouup?*

Imgonnakillusgonnakillusgonnakillusall.

This was what their father liked to say as he slammed on the brakes in and out of traffic. Sober. He was reckless sober.

Esther might jut out her chin; she might escape (regularly) into the night through the cellar door, or (one day) out the tailgate of the moving car, but Stapleton would train his ear. If only he could just listen hard enough!

Imgonnakillusgonnakillusgonnakillusall.

He would concentrate until he understood.

"Good night then, dad," Stapleton might call from the basement. "We love you, too." *We love you, dad. I love you, dad. I love you. Really, I do.*

/ 3.

Rules for Regulation Play

Typically, each round has two contestants, plus a judge behind the wheel and a lump of a witness in the passenger seat. While this four-participant configuration is certainly the most commonly played, the game can be pursued in far greater numbers.

Q: How many? I mean, what's your lifetime max?

A: If you want an exact figure, you'll have to take it upon yourself to call the Fire Chief, or get yourself to campus and check the seating capacity of the larger lecture halls.

Q: So it's not just our family? You pull this sort of thing at your job? You pull it out in the world?

A: Suddenly you're jealous; you thought it was our little thing. Believe me: that game gets played just fine without you. Just ask Intro to Mathematics, MWF, 12:30-1:40 pm. Next question?

Q: Is there a *minimum* number of contestants for a regulation match? Usually you've got all four of us in the car or something, but is it an equally good game for you even if the whole family's not there?

A: Tell me what you think. How many players do you really think I need?

Q: Three?

A: ---

Q: What? Is that a stupid answer? I just meant that the mother isn't doing much. Maybe she's not actually required. Is the mother actually required?

Q: Did I say something wrong? I don't know; what do I know? *(I love you. I'm sorry.)* So maybe the mother is necessary as a spectator, as a catalyst. Maybe the whole performance is for her? But you could probably get a round going with just one kid, right? So I'll stick with my answer: Three.

Q: Or wait. It's two. Maybe it's two. Maybe just the judge and the one contestant is enough? Or is that wrong, too? Or am I overlooking a key factor in regard to the particular combination of players, or—

A: How long are we here for, an hour already? You're such a genius and you can't figure out the requisite factors for regulation play. What's the *one* answer you have yet to offer up? There you go, bozo, I even gave you a clue.

Q: Can't you, for once, just get off my back?

A: What is the sound of one hand clapping?

Q: You're asking me this? Are we all of a sudden in some Salinger story? If a tree falls in the forest, does it make a sound? How many quiet contests does it take to screw in a light bulb? I'm not going to stand here and let you talk me in circles all night.

A: But you started it. You wanted to know: How many people do you need for a Quiet Contest?

Q: Really, dad, I'm not doing this with you: *How many times do I have to tell you? How many times do I have to ask? How many roads must a man walk down? How much is that doggie in the window?*

A: Can you just shut up and listen to me? Are you listening to me, son?

Q: Are you going to talk about your suicide?

A: Ladies and gents, behold: The Boy Genius.

Q: ---

A: You with me now? Okay. A guy walks into an ocean. He says: *Let's have a quiet contest.* Most guys wouldn't say that.

Q: Are you saying you're schizophrenic? Are you saying you're Sybil for Christ's sake?

A: I'm saying: Guy walks into a quiet contest. Guy walks into an ocean. Guy is a tree-fall in a forest and there's nobody else there. Guy says: *Let's have a quiet contest.*

Q: So you're saying a guy can have a Regulation Quiet Contest all by himself?

A: Hey, hey. I don't know about just any guy.

Q: So you're saying that *you,* John Stapleton, Sr., can have a regulation quiet contest all by yourself? You're saying there's so much noise in that single head, that you're dying for a quiet contest all the time? You're saying all that time, it had nothing to do with our family? You're saying I'm not the instigator after all—

A: All I'm saying is let's just shut the fuck up and have a quiet contest.

Q: No, wait. Let me get this straight. You're saying: Guy walks into an ocean to have himself a quiet contest. There's no one else with him. So all the aggravation requisite for suicide is entirely self-contained? That's what you're saying?

A: ---

Q: Because if that's what you're saying, then you could have spared us all a whole lot sooner, you know?

A: I'm saying: *Your name is John Stapleton; my name is John Stapleton.* I'm saying, right here, right now: *Let's have a Quiet Contest.*

Q: So what do you think, dad: Did I win? Did I win?

Joseph McElroy

SILK, OR THE WOMAN WITH THE BIKE

It was a job—a lab coworker at his elbow at first, he at hers, drop by drop of cell solution a thrill for her it seemed every time. He came as a surprise hire the lab thought could help out with commercial applications, of all things. But it was him they wanted, genius or journeyman.

It was a job, the new job the man went to by choice in the very late-afternoon rush hour by bike, subway, bike. He took his bike on the subway thinking ahead, to what he did yesterday, the day before and the day before that, and what he again would do today adjusting ring clamps on tissue baths mounted to steel support rods. His pride was the bind that somehow got absorbed in these underground motions of vehicle within vehicle enclosing him. A bike in the subway car. Spinning wheels at rest for six stops inside the clamorous song of the train. Tracking the tunnel forgetting what his new job was not.

Yet now the doors burst open and it was another bicycle, a woman bringing it aboard, parking it up against the steel pole, the straight handlebar of a fancy hybrid tipping the man's bike on the other side of the pole while a girl and boy, lovers realizing this was their stop, struggled to get by the bikes as the doors tried to close. He heard the woman with the bike say, harshly, distinctly, "What is it? I look like someone you know?" It was nothing, he tried to say with a look. Though then, "Probably," he said, thinking hell she didn't know who she was talking to. To hear her speak, she was quite unafraid. Or it was where she was coming from, a woman almost haggard, almost beautiful. Irritable. Short with him. Not just your blunt city person in passing, and not passing but arrived like a coincidence.

"No brakes?" she bobbed her head at his old bike. The seat was covered in a faded supermarket bag furled with a rubber band around the post just below the clamp assembly. Did she betray a smile looking away at the crowded car? Probably not, this woman in her beret and little scarf. He waited for her eyes. "Messenger?" she said. Was she looking through the open window at the dark tunnel wall in motion now? Her bike perhaps suited her, but she was not quite a bicyclist.

At the far end a space had opened where a man lay half-curled across several seats. Lost soul, his smell stained the air. His knobby head scarred, you could see stitches in the scalp raised and blue. A soda bottle and a can rolled across the floor and back at serious angles. "Not even a messenger," the woman said out of the side of her mouth. "I'm overqualified," he said. "You?" she said. In a subway train running north, their bike spokes glistened and the angry tunnel was a slow-stroke piston cylinder falling south. The derelict at the far end of the car woke violently staggering up onto his feet. His pants were half down, something dropping from under his threadbare overcoat. What was it that dropped, a piece of him? He kicked a bottle which hit someone, a hawk-eyed woman in a windbreaker. He's looking about him as if he doesn't recognize this place though he is a veteran of the line surely. And would you believe this fellow bike-person, this woman going on about your bike: "What do you call that?" she pointed.

"It's an old Schwinn."

"Yeah does it have brakes? I noticed it," she was contemptuous but more than that.

"You did?"

She had nothing to say, but then, "Where did you get it?" she added. She was subtly tired, preoccupied. Why did he think she didn't know bikes? "Out of work?" she said then.

"I'm going to work right now."

"A messenger working nights?" she said, lost for a moment, he thought. "I'm in materials," he said, "materials *science*—" "I hate science," the woman said. "—on a good day," he finished.

"On that bike?" she said. "On a good day? I'm not long for this one." Did she mean the day? She patted her handlebar. "You unloading it?" he said. She looked at him then, like she knew him and was momentarily surprised to. The train slowed in the tunnel abruptly, stupidly, and a standee's heavy bag swung into him like a rock. The unreal stench coming this way, homeward-bound travelers leaned to let the derelict by. "I like my bike, it's better than the bus," he said.

"You work nights," she said.

"Not every night."

"You can have it," she said, gesturing. "But what do you do to justify your existence?"

"We grow bone in a lab, that's what we're doing right now."

The woman smiled, she looked away at what was coming. "You don't do any such thing," he heard her say. How could she say this? It sounded true. As if he didn't know what he was doing.

It was a plumber's canvas tool bag that had swung into him on the shoulder of a guy who looked like a plumber, wiry with a drink bottle in a paper bag. The woman told him to watch his bag. An old thought came to mind and was gone about subway-floor bottles and cans, things here below, here was the foul homeless vagrant streaming sweat with a face of different colors and you leaned to dodge his hand as the woman in the hooded old windbreaker snatched the plastic bottle off the floor and flung it into the man's back. His hand brushing your shoulder reached for the pole, missed, grasping at the bike-woman, who had said something to the plumber with a little sting to it. The perhaps quite able hands of the homeless man in their ragged coat cuffs reach the woman, her suede coat, her preoccupations, and her fellow bicyclist swiped the black man away and the plumber recoiled from the touch. The woman had let go her bike. She was her face then, the sweet olive cheeks, and under the skin a fine pallor today that would pass. Was she unwell? "I have a list of things rolling around on the subway floor," he said. "More things," she said.

A teenage girl was sizing up the bike, and now she had a hand on its top tube. She caught you looking. What she knew, she knew, to the beat of her earphones, the fine asymmetry of the nose ring, could she be fifteen? They were in the station. The plumber shoved the black man stumbling onto the platform this lost soul wearing a safety-pinned coat and something happening with the skin, genetic. A child screamed, the homeless man had fallen on top of her, one shoe off, sockless, and the woman, forgetting her bike, was out there pulling at him. The teenage girl was rolling the woman's bike off the car, people getting on. He let go his bike, What had happened? He got a couple of fingers on the rear rack of the fancy bike to hold it against the girl, who had backed and turned it, and a man in a blue MTA uniform materialized and was guiding the bike out onto the platform. And there was its owner, but waiting for what?

He righted his bike as it tipped off the pole, the doors tried to close too soon and came together and he understood that the woman had gotten off but not he, and had said something about her bike—was it his? The homeless man was being yanked to his feet, which was like being thrown down.

The doors jolted open again. "Your bike," he called. She laughed over her shoulder. "Yours if you want it," she had certainly said. Persistent, the teenage girl tried to cock her leg over it, a man's-frame top tube, but the MTA man held the handlebar, looking around him. The service-exit gate opens and a woman pushes a stroller through, the bike woman following her. Call again, catch her eye, the MTA supervisor rolls the bike through the open gate, and the woman beyond the turnstiles thanks him but looks back startled at the train as the car doors jerk closed.

He had raised his voice against this interference with him. He had looked her in the eye, the heck with her he liked his bike he was telling her. And was this woman traveling just one stop? Confronting a woman in a vest inside the change-booth now, she pointed back at the platform while the MTA supervisor held her bike handlebar at the stem.

Up against the glass of the car doors the homeless man's bare face now, the black forehead and maculate tan across the nose and cheek and some pink skin as well where pigment had spilled, he was pointing to you or the floor, stepping back as the train moved yet pointing at something, and what was the woman with the bike doing on the other side of the turnstiles? And did it matter who he was, going to work when others are going home?

An eccentric woman with news for you. In the lab ahead racks of 200-ml tissue baths. Ultra-thin films of silk that may dress our wounds. Elsewhere lattices of silk on which bone cells like to grow. A red-haired college student who had boarded the car at the other end looked hard at the four emptied seats and then, behind him, finding someone he knew, reached into his shoulder bag to find a book for her which she opened with delight, talking to him, her friend, the two of them thrilled to meet while, sitting next to her, the older woman in the hooded windbreaker craned to get a look at the book too. She was the one who had thrown the bottle. The red-haired student stepped away from something underfoot.

"Nice bike she had there," the plumber looked at you personally, even professionally, at your hand feeling in your pocket for a pencil and pad.

"Not for her."

"Thought I recognized her. What's her name?" The plumber looked like one. He'd spent time crouched, adjusting, threading into confined and challenging spaces. The plumber didn't like him. They didn't like each other. "That's not gonna do him any good," the plumber kicked the laceless shoe lying on its side on the floor, the sole coming loose from the upper.

"No?" was the quick reply.

He would talk about it a little at work, the woman with the bike.

She didn't seem to want her bike, a high-end hybrid. Had she expected him to get off? Some city eccentric, though in the soft dark circles under her eyes, the brown and blue irises, experience lurked, and along the bones of her hands and around the mouth what she was made of, was it something there for a stranger? What had she seen? His bike. At his stop he would bear it downstairs from the platform, then upstairs to the street.

Speeding through the Park the whirr of the wheels like wings, the late light, things in the air, a gossamer shine along a witch-hazel stem, a web, sparrows he had watched from the window of his bedroom. He saw the man sitting on a bench not as if he'd worked all day, not well-off looking at all, too old and yet not old enough to be doing whatever he was doing. And further along a woman he recognized reading the Classified. And then a bird's yellow underside glimpsed, tail bobbing, Prairie Warbler upside down quickly foraging. But now a gray hint of smoke from leaves burning so close by that the boy rising suddenly from beside his friend's experiment to dart in front of the man's bike was part of the path itself, no time to brake, the bike wheel caught the kid's ankle knocking it away. He heard the yelp, a curse, and did not stop, the boy had simply risen and darted into the path of the oncoming bike.

He asked his coworker at the lab why. She smiled, it was more of a smile not looking up from her work. "A boy," she said. She commuted from an outlying area—"upstate" she called it—yet was early to work mornings and tonight had stayed late an hour. He thought he knew nothing about her but it wasn't true. On his table under diagrams of insect anatomy and a couple of color snaps of orb-spinning spiders she had taken, he found some others produced by an electron microscope at a more specialized lab she called it, and from yet another lab copies of printout numbers he read at once showing stretches of gene code in silk material of unique strength containing certain other stretches lacking any genetic directions for the protein-making he and his coworker counted on. This was precisely where the unique elasticity came from, and at his previous job he had twice outwitted these intron gaps, he had a nose for them though he knew next to nothing about the orb-weaving spiders his coworker observed in her garden anchoring a dragline like a rock climber a safety rope.

Here he did his work. It was not him. On a collision course with a dozen commercial applications. Silk for tethering planes to a carrier. Body armor. Or practical scaffolding. He had been told they might soon be growing nerve cells for grafts. In the "dairy" in another building fierce ants, he was told, and a well-known golden spider were apparently milked to extract their silk, and he had a joke or two more bitter than his partner understood, who trusted his insight. Why exactly was spider silk sometimes stronger though less stretchable when milked against the spider's will under anesthetic when we could just pull the stuff out? A sketchy thing to do even to an ant. Under CO_2 was the animal asleep or just paralyzed? Meanwhile the silk lattice preoccupies his partner. How if we do our work right, later it biodegrades having done its job, leaving just bone. She listened to him and found occasion to ask about his work prior to this job. Chemistry on a monitor. Pattern at the root. Abstract. What could he tell her?

She was Dutch. "Will it be a good night?" she asked, the way she would ask if it would be a good day, when he sometimes worked days. He thought it would be. He had found himself speaking to her of the subway incident and she dismissed this woman who could say she hated science. "She doesn't know anything. You have to do the work." He said he thought the woman had been a little off, perhaps unwell. He wondered why she had thought he was out of work. "But it is true, you have been out of work, you know what that's *like*," said the woman at his side, and he thought that she was right as he sometimes thought there was probably very little work you could choose that was really worth it. "You were out of work, and then you have come here," the woman was saying. A silk film is ready to come out of the tissue bath. They contemplated each other. "What you bring," she said.

She was OK. He asked about her garden—though what did he mean, her at home, spider-silk draglines elastic with genes of genius?—and what was happening with the hives? It was polite of him.

She had ordered two Russian queen bees that would be arriving in the mail, and again she suggested he come out for a visit one Saturday, bring his bike on the train. He must have had that bike a long time, she said. Ah, he had borrowed it, this at least thirty-five-year-old Schwinn one New Year's Eve twenty something years ago where it had been left in the boisterous and cluttered basement hallway of the townhouse of the host—A New Year's Eve party? she asked, her eyes alive—and he kept it till next day. Kept it? Oh my, she said, she caught a little intake of breath and was thinking about the story. It was the short form, he added. She left it at that. She must have only one bike up in Garrison, it occurred to him staring at photos supplied by her. Blowups of ants, puffy, monstrous, venerable showing among the folds the location of their spinning ducts. Another of a spider he didn't know bringing the duct very close to the venom sac. Another, the ceramic gloss of a maroon and white, big-horned spider from Costa Rica, smaller than it looked, its spinning duct somewhat hidden. Spiders didn't work well together. They ate each other.

It was late for her, though he'd just clocked in and was pondering ants again, if they unreel their silk like spiders, anchor it to something, then move away. A photo of a drab, earthen-hued garden spider showed its dragline silk for the outer rim of the web—insurance in case of a bungee bailout—strong as the golden spider's silk but, with more amino, ten times stretchier when wet—so strong, so soft. Wasp silk they worked with, and bee. Now bee silk a real simple genes-and-protein setup—but nothing beats spider silk. She was leaving. He missed the electron microscope at the other job. Gene measurements on a screen, spectacular speculations and sure things—and now it was bacteria they could insert silk genes into and tobacco, of all things; and unlikely, unsuspecting animals. He felt her near him and turned to see her thinking. "I can see it all, what happened on the subway," she said, her tone disturbingly new to him. He looked at her. "She wanted to give you her bike."

He shook his head, studying his work. A moment later, *Why?* he called out—*why* would she want to give him her bike? His coworker, gone for the night, didn't stop or didn't hear him call after her. He was alone tonight, as it happened. Lose your job, find one, was the philosophy. A better one than any job you could lose, though the new job doesn't come with a certain eighty-thousand-dollar scanning device, failing which he must sometimes independently remember on his own what it was he actually already knew, or ask for help.

It was a job. Pedaling back through the Park along the interior road at two in the morning, he found two kids from opposite curbs converging on him until, coasting as if to slow down, he rose and made a dash for it like a runner, his heart racing, before they could get to him, long-legged, ugly, and passed between them like prey in the deep, like a knife—he didn't need a change of gears and didn't have one. Out for a spin along the Meer, lamp light in the water—what is *this* experiment ahead, behind, around him? A tree in passing (long life and beautiful leaves, they breathe, we breathe) remembered minutes later when he hoisted the bike to clear the subway turnstile and raced carefully downstairs and up again to catch a downtown train ahead of the closing doors. He was alone in the car with one other person at this hour who watched him sit down, holding the bike before him.

Had he been drawn away from the deep shape of things into the bowels, multiple abdominal glands, ducts, dope, quaint feats of animals that supply silk for enzyme-solvent med capsules or stitch the leaves of the gingko tree he had just felt near him in the Park? The train got under way. His fellow passenger stood up and came to sit opposite him. An Asian with a faded khaki knapsack on his back, he leaned forward, a bunch of brochures in one hand. He wore flip-flops showing his brown toes. His taut stare must be returned. "You ride bike on subway?" "It travels with me." The man laughed a staccato Chinese laugh. "I give you backpack, you give me bike." "Not a chance."

The stations of the line seemed—afterward, when he got home—to have been contracted to one unexpected platform to come, though what passed between the two men too much for the actual track time.

"You have job, you wok, you study, get better job—what you study?" "I don't know what I study. I study silk." "Sirk!" (The man shakes his handful of brochures as if that's what they're about and laughs a laugh that is no laugh.) "Sirk wom!" (Yes of course—the silk worm with its half-mile-long cocoon-winding.) "Sister wok in sirk *factory!*" "Does she make comforters? Bed covers?" "Factory!" "Good for her, good for your sister," one adds, not feeling it, then feeling it—"in Suzhou?" Yes, yes (the brother, unsurprised, contemplating your rat trap with small black backpack clamped tight), you recall women in hygienic caps stretching an already arch-stretched square of cocoon silk across a queen-size bed—and a Dutch tour group, a few years ago now, three women among them with Chinese babies, it was pointed out to him by the woman he was with.

"We have some problems with silkworms." "Sirkwom no pobrem."

"We love the silkworm, but—" "No pobrem!"—"Spider silk's more..." The Chinese traveler's knapsack in his lap now, there is something about it. Sirkwom! (Its silk, the sutures, he's learned plodding through surgical applications, regrettably provoke immune reaction, it's the ancient glue that it wraps around a protein.) "Your sister in Suzhou packs the silk inside the comforter." There is no object so soft but it makes a hub for the wheeled universe, a poet said.

Man doesn't question the Suzhou coincidence but he is unpredictable, and where he's coming from produces truth too. He points irritably at the bike with his brochure hand and the brochures scatter multiplying on the subway car floor, or did he fling them? Is he beside himself? His fellow passenger bad news? He would not inquire how this American in the leather jacket picking up a brochure asking him if he's a messenger knows about his sister who packs great ropes of silk into duvets in Suzhou we're quite sure. Americans travel but are not immigrants. The Chinese repeats his proposition, not quite a joke. Why should he not speak? The knapsack—something in it. "Messenger?" you ask again and the doors open at the station you now see you've been drawn to, the downtown platform this time.

The Chinese man stands, the rider rolls the bike toward the door. "Messenger," he says, he reaches for the bike too late, the rear rack. *"Messenger!"* Of strewn brochures.

The station, a platform, has been imagined wrapped in a waiting memory where the woman and her bike left a train hours ago; but before the Chinese traveler in his ire can get his recyclables together, not that it's his stop, doors do their job. And when, in the train's empty, then humming, pause, wheeling the bike briskly alongside stopped cars finding across the tracks the uptown change booth now dark while on this side our conductor promising on the loud speaker we would be moving momentarily materializes at a cab window looking down this platform, a strange routineness now in his reply to the man with the wheels—the same MTA guy from five o'clock?—"Yeah the green bike, they told me over there—supervisor he—" "Supervisor?" For this is not quite the same guy. "She told me where she need to get off uptown like I'm a bus driver"—conductor looked at his palm, dignified—"I said just watch the station comin' in. She goes, Don't you know your job, how did you get your job?"

"She ill?"

"Ill you say." Conductor frowns like a half grin. "Supervisor said she had like—" (Conductor's personal like your friend for a second) "—she had two days." "Two days?" "To give her bike to somebody, that's it. She told him." "What did she tell you?"

"Where she has her coffee in the morning seven o'clock, like we had it together and she's reminding me." The breakfast place uptown familiar after all by the subway where you used to catch the bus.

"Supervisor looks like you." "He's my brother." "How you got your job?"

Checking a black and white monitor in the cab, "You know her," the conductor said.

The doors? Much obliged.

It's going to be two-thirty in a minute, the need to get to bed leaning back into the seat of the moving train, hands on the bike, the brochure in a coat pocket, still on the same train with the Chinese guy. But you're looking at his brochure, a dark green hillside of tea bushes, a stage full of gymnasts balancing a stack of chairs, 212 phone numbers for evidently a travel agency, and a memory of cocoon a shroud wrapped all from one thread, the caterpillar of the silk moth, hardly remembering a book or two in your backpack.

It will feel like the crack of dawn, not seven-twenty, when a figure in the coffee shop window, observed him, he knew, whatever she knew of him as he walked his bike and locked it to a stanchion where the sound of a familiar bus exhaling told him the woman with the bike, brighter, slower than he recalled though dogged by a shadow, was not herself. The green hybrid not in evidence, it was not at stake—as if, at the café's inner doorway, what was in the balance was what he took in—the shining Silex glass over-and-under pots, the murky, gleaming griddle and its smoke of sausage and piled hash-browns, aluminum pitchers reflecting silver light, booths and the hiddenness of men and women in them, hunched shoulders at the counter, two cops, a table or two by the window. And an opened-up laptop lid she peered at, the small, fine scarf protecting her neck. Scents of coffee, sausage links, uncanny toast, a grease of some hunger his gift might take the structure of along with some life out of sight but right behind him as he held the inner door a second about to step across the threshold.

"You!" from the woman—a chair waited for him and all but spoke to him and then he was above her, the planes of her face alight with faint blame. "On my way to work," he said.

He started to explain, but a bird had exploded into the restaurant, swooped in, a sparrow, flapping around the ceiling lights whirring less like a humming bird than an out-of-sync fan, now flew at the window, cut past the woman, her face, and out again past two girls in school uniforms who'd run to push open the inner and outer doors. "Sparrows don't do that," said the tall one. "That's a young song sparrow," the man said. The cops had spun around at the counter. The woman undid her sheer scarf. She said, "The bike's not here."

"I have a bike." He pointed. "It's at home," she said, meaning hers—"two blocks," she bobbed her head westward. She recited the address off the laptop's screen, he thought.

"It's not a *bike* I need," he said.

The tall girl asked how he knew it was a song sparrow. The young ones didn't have the spot on the breast, he told her but she frowned. He was content to order. The other girl, the little sturdy one, asked amazingly what it was he needed if it wasn't a bike. "A daughter?" he joked. "You should have a daughter," the woman said, "nowadays they can do that." They all thought about that. Why had he ordered oatmeal, the raisins surviving above the milk? How much had she paid for that hybrid? he asked with his mouth full. Oh yes, someone had given her the bike, she said—her husband, wherever he was—if he was still or had ever been her husband—thinking it would help. The waitress smiled. The waitress knew her.

"Help toughen you up?" "Why, yes."

The schoolgirls standing with their paper bags would miss their bus, he thought. "When you were already tough," he said to the woman. "You understand me," the woman said. A panel truck advertising *www.REPAIR* backed in and the driver came around and kicked the man's bike locked at the very lip of the curb, and he stood up, and the schoolgirls in their pleated skirts started speaking, laughed, and started again. The little one said, "You had a right to be there."

He had ignored the tall one, who was fretting about that bird—not cold, not hungry, certainly not crazy, was it the door opening that had pulled it in? she asked. The kids stood waiting, but for what? The waitress over at the counter sipped her coffee and watched.

"You understand me," said the woman again. He understood nothing of the kind he said. He understood chains of molecules under an electron lens; he could see code fold into double-coil proteins of bulldog ant silk; bee silk was simpler, four genes, four proteins. Science was beautiful, the woman said and added something typical he almost understood but didn't. "I'm quite well known," he said. He looked at her and she shook her head as if he were hopeless.

"How did you lose your job then?" she said. "I was cruel to someone." The woman made a sound. "Is that all?" "She lost *her* job." "She wasn't thinking well." "No." "But you lost yours." "I let it lose me."

"What does that make you?"

She shut the laptop and stood up and spread a ten-dollar bill next to a slice of toast. "Working days now?" Time had lengthened around them overnight. He started to explain about today but it was none of her business. But then he did, about the message on his machine last night from his lab partner that they would need him early this morning.

"It's you she wants."

Were the schoolgirls about to leave? The little one alerted him, the man who'd kicked the bike was coming back.

"That stop you got off at," he said. The bike had told her to, she said. The bike had not told her anything. "Or I *let* it tell me," she said. No, that wasn't the reason, the man said. "I was hysterical." "You were not," he said. "Where *I* was coming from yesterday."

The waitress had her arm around the woman's shoulders, asking her how she was doing. The woman added a five and took her bag and went thinly to the restroom. The waitress went with her. He dropped a quarter, it landed on end and rolled and the tall girl picked it up. "You leaving?" she said. She was irritated. Some shift had occurred simple as looking out his bedroom window one day and seeing what he hadn't seen.

He was telling the tall girl that a song sparrow would never come in here for food, it foraged on the ground. It wouldn't sing in here either, there was a sparrow with a song like it that began differently but you'd never see that bird in the city. He held the door for her, but she was waiting for her friend. The cops left with him.

In a dark hallway his partner took his arm. They came to a small room. On a table a transparent box lighted by a single UV. In the box a yellow spider, legs out front, legs behind, alone here. His partner had remembered. An inlet tube from a cylinder evidently of CO_2 outside the box. A contraption for reeling out the silk hooked somehow to an orifice point back along one side of the thorax was ingenious. Silk strong enough given a thickness of an inch to reel in a 747 from the sky. Strong enough to catch a careless finch. Stronger than Kevlar. Strong as steel. Good to go as parachute cord. The animal seemed absolutely still. A burly technician joined them and explained. Then the Dutch woman said this spidey was venomous but not seriously so and bites only if put next to your skin and bothered; it was her own, a female, and it had come from her garden. The males are so busy they forget to eat and can starve themselves.

"You're silent," said his partner when they were back in the main building where one of the silk lattices, slow as these things are, was degrading faster than the bone could grow and they had wanted him to look at something close up. "Thinking of a horror film we could go to," he said. "Oh, the old one about the ants?" Yes, that was the one. "This weekend?" Not this weekend, but he thought he would take that bike woman up on her offer, though why him? "She's dying," said his partner.

"How would you know that for god's sake, how do you people know any such thing?" He calmed down. "Science is beautiful now, she says; it lets you go so far."

It was two days later, a Friday. It was the waitress who came to answer the door of the drab little townhouse near the river drive. She looked worn out. She indicated the bike in the hall. He made a sign with his hands. "She's gone," the woman said. He shook his head, "Where?" "She's gone to join her husband. She's sick."

He had the green bike on the step outside. The woman touched the rear rack. "She said you were like family. I don't know anything about it," the woman said. "She said you were uncanny. You said something. That you probably knew her. She said you knew where she was coming from." "Where?" "The doctor's?" The woman seemed to come into focus. "We say things. People are affected by them."

"Who knows why?"

"They're true? I was the best friend she ever had," said the woman stepping back into the doorway. It was what she thought. A dark mole lingered about the corner of her expressive mouth. She'd drunk a lot of coffee. Close up she did not look worn out, she looked English or French. They wanted to talk but were not going to, a risk rising in her breath and in her interested eyes drawn from her limitlessly, he thought.

"Will you return your old bike?" the Dutch woman asked him. Who would he return it to? The owner, only an acquaintance, had died that stormy New Year's early morning coming home through the sleet in a cab.

A lab had transferred spider silk genes into the mammary glands of a goat, and his partner asked him to go with her one long weekend to Montana, paid for by the company. It took six hundred gallons of goat's milk to produce the silk for one bulletproof vest, so far. He decided to let her go alone; she would be back the Monday night. The following weekend he would be visiting her in Garrison.

-bc.

Sarah Wang

i'll come back for you

Sarah Wang

I'm in New York visiting Magda. The humidity here makes my hair look even more witchy. I tell Magda that I feel like I'm wearing a wig.

"You could be, you could very well be," she says before she tells me that she has lupus and I spill a cup of iced coffee on the front of my shirt while trying to catch the subway. During the three and a half weeks I'm here, I drink coffee in the morning, in the afternoon, early evening and then a can or two of an energy drink if we're going out at night. It's the only way I can keep up with my friends, who all walk faster, talk faster and are meaner.

Magda's room is carefully arranged: a stack of books by Lester Bangs and Steinbeck overflowing from a shelf, silver chandelier necklaces hanging by the light switch, old *batik* scarves draped over the nightstand, a roll of green wallpaper printed with art deco patterns tacked to the wall above the bed, crystal bottles of rose perfume that smell good only on her, a row of old journals collecting dust on the slice of their pages on the windowsill, a box of lavender scented powder with a big white puff in the shape of a hamburger bun that she uses between her legs and the back of her neck in the summer.

I go back and forth between falling in love with New York and pining for Los Angeles. I play around with the idea of moving here but know my body would reject it; I'm too frail, too stupid, too scared. After nearly twenty years in Los Angeles, I feel safe in its custody. New York is alive. The energy of the city cuts through the air, brightens the sky; I never feel alone. The humidity in New York reaches seventy-eight percent. The sun rises at six. By six-thirty it's a crackling seed pressing against my temples and the lids of my eyes. The heat at the end of summer burns itself out, collapsing into a vortex at the center of the city; the temperature fluctuates between medium-well and charred-black. When I walk down streets in Brooklyn, the air conditioners drip liquid down my bare arms and cheeks. The sidewalks are lopsided, heavy with young people hiding in its shade, everyone pushed to one side of the street, sunny side empty.

It's strange when something happens and that thing organizes your life into a before and after. Once, back in L.A., I was walking my dog at night and a coyote attacked it. When the thing happens, you're stuck on that moment when it all changed; after my dog was attacked I was wishing I could return to it, change the course of direction like a train's tracks where—with a pull of the lever—the train heads west instead of south. When Magda tells me about the lupus, I find myself stuck at the First Street stop—cup of iced coffee still in my hand—shuffling down the steps with her. She's in front, dark hair pulled in a high ponytail, red shorts, one hand clutching the strap of the bag on her shoulder; there's a teenager in suspenders pushing past us, a woman stuffing an unwrapped sandwich into her purse, the clacking of the train approaching and a rush of air that smells like grease in our faces. I'm stuck here and there's nothing I can do.

/

Magda and I sleep on the same twin bed to share the air conditioning. I wake in the middle of the night; my hair is wet above my forehead. Am I sweating? I wonder, but the hair is only wet on top, my scalp and forehead are dry. I look over at her; the crack of her mouth is shiny and wet. "Mag," I say, shoving her shoulder with the heel of my hand, "you're drooling on me."

"I have more saliva in my mouth than everyone you know," she whispers. "You didn't notice in Mexico because we were below the equator." Between dreaming and consciousness there's something about this that makes sense to me, though I know Mexico isn't below the equator and it wouldn't make a difference if it was. When I get up at eleven, I wash my hair. I can't stand the thought of my head glowing patches of blue-white under a black light, the kind that crime scene investigators use to detect body fluids. At its hottest, the water is lukewarm and the showerhead is so clogged with white crust that it sprays sideways. Magda's cat is a Blue Persian; I catch her drinking water from a dirty bowl in the kitchen sink, pull her small white body away, her tongue still lapping the air. I think about my cat at home in L.A., wonder if she's lying in some shade rolling in the baked gray dirt. I think about getting another cat, two, three more, one for each room to greet me when I enter.

I stuff my bra and underwear into my bag because I can tell from the way the sun shines into the living room that it's too hot for either. As I walk to the train, guilt carries me through the city; I fear department store security guards snatching me though I haven't stolen anything. I'm afraid people think I'm lying when I tell the truth.

/

I look up lupus. When Magda told me, she said it quickly; sitting on the train, yellowed lights sputtering between us, I felt as though I only imagined her saying it, like when I drive over a bridge and the thought of it crumbling beneath me flashes by and disappears.

Systemic lupus erythematosus (SLE or lupus) is a chronic autoimmune disease that can be fatal reads the first line on the medical website. I scan the rest without understanding much: *environmental triggers, clearance deficiency, abnormalities in apoptosis.* On the right side of the page is a drawing that mirrors the baffling medical language: a gray meteorite like the one Superman stopped from hurling into Earth, red arrows spiking from the meteorite into three green amoebae with faces—one with a wiggly line for a mouth, another with a smiling wiggly line, the third's mouth a wide "O." From what I can tell, lupus is caused by unknown environmental factors or genetics; there's no cure. The immune system attacks the body's cells and tissues. Most often it harms the heart, joints, skin, lungs, blood vessels, liver, kidneys and nervous system.

Explain it to me in a way I'll understand. Will Magda have children? Will her hair fall out? Will her hands become gnarled and cracked? Will I have to watch her die?

/

All summer in Los Angeles, before going to New York, Magda and I rode in the backseat of cars, squeezed between a row of hips, legs touching, laughing, getting lost in the crumbly hills of Laurel Canyon, rushing to get somewhere and realizing it wasn't where we wanted to be, spinning from Koreatown to Highland Park, Silverlake, Eagle Rock, Venice, Culver City, Pasadena, Echo Park, Chinatown, Santa Monica, Glassell Park, Hollywood a hallucinogenic web connecting us to each another like an airborne highway looming above the city, rushing into the horizon; deferring, picking up, dropping off, making friends, making enemies, making plans, never seeing them through.

The night the car died, Magda's black eye looked worse, no longer cartoonish or sardonic but realer than real, bulging with blood. At a party a few hours before, a piece of broken glass had caught in her shoe and cut into her foot; someone gave her half a Demerol lollipop and now she was paying for it. I wanted to tell her to get up off the sidewalk, but what was the point? No one else was around at two-thirty in the morning and we had nowhere to go. A jump-start was going to take at least an hour and I was bored.

The tow truck arrived not a minute under an hour. The mechanic had short, curly hair and wore glasses, light blue shirt tucked into navy pants, black boots; he seemed nervous, eyes flitting from side to side, pen clacking against the metal clipboard in his hand. He could have been good-looking if he'd let his hair grow out and swept it to the side, if he wore normal clothes, if the frame of his glasses was black instead of thin gold wire, if he weren't short. "Who did that to her?" He pointed toward the sidewalk.

"She did." I popped the hood of Magda's '89 Ford hatchback and let him attach the cables. The car didn't jump, laid motionless at the turn of the key.

"You were scheduled for a jump," he said, "but if you want a tow, I'll have to come back in a couple hours."

"What are we supposed to do for two hours, sit here in the dark and wait?" Probably because of the way Magda looked, he drove us down the street to an all-night diner. Playing with the menu, bending its laminated pages into a tube, Magda looked at me with her good eye and said, "I don't have any money."

I grabbed the menu out of her hand and it rolled open on the table, slowly unfurling on its own. "Our mechanic gave us twenty bucks."

"Why did the mechanic give us twenty bucks?"

"While you were asleep in his truck, I gave him a hand job."

"You did?" Magda looked at me and cocked her head. I could have told her I was born a hermaphrodite and she would have believed me. "Was he good looking, at least? On Tuesday I went out with someone I met at a drive-thru. We went to the Observatory and made out in Griffith Park afterwards. I've never been more repulsed while kissing someone. I had to suck his dick to get him off my face. Anything to get him off my face." I didn't bother asking why she didn't just stop kissing him. Once Magda passed out at a party and when she woke up, she was getting fucked from behind, her pants pulled down to her ankles as if she were sitting on the toilet. I was going to say something but it was the guy who picked me up and I was afraid he'd get mad and refuse to give me a ride home so I just let him do it, she told me the next day. "If we have twenty bucks," she said now, "I'm getting a southwest cheeseburger and a banana milkshake." She put her chin down on the table and looked up at me; her bangs fell over her bruised eye. "Listen, they're playing The Zombies. I used to have this record. *Odessey and Oracle*, remember? But when my house got broken into, it was stolen. What kind of person would steal my Zombies record?"

I wanted to tell her that the only person who would do something like that was me, Dee, Ash and Kiki. We did it because I was missing a pair of black jeans, Magda owed Dee fifteen dollars for dinner at Casa Bianca, and Ash was mad at Magda for ordering four boxes of Girl Scout cookies from her little sister and not paying for them. We decided to climb in Magda's window when she was having dinner with her father and trash her house before she came home. We knocked over a dresser, threw her clothes on the floor, ripped the sheets off the bed and tossed her underwear into the trash. Magda called later that night crying so hard she stuttered and I laughed, holding the receiver away from my mouth.

"Okay," Magda said in the diner, "now they're playing Joni Mitchell. What station is this? This is the best music I've ever heard in a diner. *Oh, it gets so lone-ly,*" she sang tilting her head to the side, each syllable soft, bending to the lilts of her voice. "*When you're walking and the streets are full of strangers / All the news of ho-me you read just gives you the blues / Just gives you the bluues.* If you're not ordering anything, I'm getting dessert. I threw up in the bathroom and now my stomach is empty and acidic."

"I'm getting coffee," I said, "no dessert. You always order so much junk and then you don't eat it."

"Hey."

"What?"

"My teeth feel weird. I forgot to rinse my mouth out and I think my stomach acid stripped off a layer of fluoride or whatever's on the surface. Do you think drinking a milkshake would help?"

"Enamel."

"Where?" Magda looked around the diner, narrowing her eyes.

"On your teeth. What do you mean, where?"

"I thought you said Emmanuel. You know, the guy that gave HPV to Ash? He works at that cheese shop? Little black eyes?"

"That guy's lucky he isn't here. I'd beat his ass in the parking lot if I saw him here. Dirty ass." Ash was bedridden two weeks in April because the gynecologist removed the warts that were growing in her cervix; when she called Emmanuel to tell him, he accused her of giving him the disease and hung up. We found out later that he had been shooting heroin and was in the hospital with hepatitis C. Maybe we should have felt sorry for him but we didn't.

Is it wrong to be happy when someone gets hurt or dies? Because when I heard, two years after high school, that the first boy I slept with died, I was happy. He didn't really force me to have sex with him, but I was fourteen and one minute we're kissing and the next my skirt was hiked up and he pushed himself into me as dry and sharp as a stick. I didn't tell him to stop because it was over before I knew what was happening. I stepped over some imaginary line that night, a boundary between clarity and a low, buzzing dimness. That night was another moment that bisected my life. It seemed everything after that was one long indistinct list; the next day, everyone knew, and nothing could change that. He shot himself in the head with a rifle on his twentieth birthday. "Are you listening?" Magda tapped her glass of ice water with a fork.

"What?"

"Never mind. So do you want to know something?"

"Don't tell me about your teeth anymore."

"I was thinking about how people cry. Why don't dogs cry, or cats? Is it because they don't get sad like we do?"

"I know cows cry. My mom said that when they're about to get killed, cows get down on their knees and cry real tears. Back when they used to get their throats slit. Have you ever heard of something so sad? It's like they know there's no hope and all they can do is what any living thing does."

Magda bit her lower lip and wrinkled her nose. "You're not messing with me, are you?"

"It's one of the truest things my mom ever told me. I think about it all the time—a soft tan and white spotted cow kneeling in front of some man with a glinting blade, plump tears falling from her sad brown eyes, streaming down her furry face."

"God, why do you have to say it like that? I was going to eat a cheeseburger but now I can't. That's one of the worst things I ever heard. It's terrible."

"Really? I think it's kind of amazing. Get a garden burger instead." Under the table, Magda took off her boot and rubbed her wounded foot. She massaged her heel and stroked her arch, inserting a finger between each toe. "Why are you thinking about it anyway?"

"Sometimes I wish I could cry because it makes you feel better. I'm just sitting here wishing I could cry but I can't."

"Is it because of your eye? Or your foot?"

Magda shook her head, looked down at the table. "I'm glad I cut my foot, that my eye is fucked up. At least it's something."

"Are you going to tell me what happened to your eye?"

"I don't remember. It happened the night Terry came back from Berlin—he doesn't remember either. Probably I was being obnoxious. I didn't fall on any doorknobs." I looked down the length of the diner; at that time of night, passing thoughts of people I once knew, things I did, things I hoped for but knew I'd never have, flooded my body. Magda leaned away from me, letting her head fall back on the vinyl booth. "At times I feel like I know what I'm doing." I wanted to reach over and wrap my hands around her pallid neck, squeeze some blood into it. "Do you feel like you know what you're doing?" she said.

Looking across the table at Magda, I suddenly despised her. We were two buffoons with a black eye and a bloody foot, stomach acid eating away at teeth; our own bodies were in mutiny. Who was she but a deaf echo of myself? I couldn't stand myself. A banner advertising fruit pie hid an oversized clock on the wall; I couldn't see what time it was, if it mattered. Background noise hovered close to the ground. The cash register thrummed behind me, an angry rhythm; something rose up in me, irritated and thick. I was tired of reading books I thought changed my life, then waking up and not remembering what I'd read.

"Remember," said Magda, "when we drove to Mexico with the stolen gas card and bought everything we could at that gas station in San Clemente? I still have those jumping beans and that pair of black sunglasses, but the beans don't move anymore. There are just holes where the bugs burrowed out." I see that trip through a foggy windshield, everything slow and protracted, riding with my head out the car, chin resting on the edge of the window like a dog, waving my arm in the wind with large gestures, mimicking the rolling hills that passed us, spilling cherry coke on the front of my dress, listening to a Stevie Nicks tape, backseat piled with clothes and candy, rose air fresheners in the shape of Betty Boop, cigarettes, a copy of *Glue*, a Pentax K1000 around my neck, snapping pictures of Magda driving with her sunglasses on, hollering with excitement after crossing the border, eating corn out of a Styrofoam cup spiked with chile and lime bought for a dollar out of a steaming metal trash can, shooting ketamine on the beach in Rosarito, waking up with glass and gravel in our hair a mile from where we'd parked, getting lost, accidentally driving into an army base, being chased out by a sand-colored truck with two men gripping black machine guns, waiting in a long line to get back into the country, bargaining with street vendors selling terracotta icons and ponchos in the street, drinking cold tamarind juice outside a pharmacy, a donkey painted like a zebra on the sidewalk, buying a dried seahorse, feeling boundless, seeing nothing but what was in front of our faces.

I imagined my whole life like that, momentous, weightless. I knew what it was like even at that age to break apart suddenly inside, love someone, touch the world in little ways. I wanted everything to be like that: flashing all the highlights, slow pan forward, fading out at the right time.

/

A couple days after Magda tells me about the lupus, we go swimming at Rockaway Beach. I read in the newspaper that a man walked into the ocean there, emulating a death in one of his favorite films, Robert Altman's *The Long Goodbye*. When the sun moves west, I cover my face with the paper and fall asleep. I wake after the wind blows it away; Magda reaches over and wipes my nose and chin with her towel where little words have settled from the newsprint. Granules of sand stuck to her towel scratch my skin. "Can I ask you something?"

"What?" she says.

"About the thing you told me."

"Listen, don't get that look in your eyes. I found out about a month ago. This rash I had on my arms wouldn't go away so I went to a doctor. After they did some tests and I told them I had been feeling tired lately and had a vaginal ulcer the month before, I found out what it was."

It's sounding worse and worse. Lupus has a face now, covered with rashes, and a vagina full of sores.

"I'm taking medicine," she says, "it's not that big a deal. The pills will help to stop my body from attacking itself." And worse still. I see the lupus body fighting itself, the left arm choking the neck, one leg tripping the other. "Don't bury me yet." She sees the look on my face.

It begins to rain so we pack up and begin walking to the bus stop. The corners of my eyes have sand in them; when I try to coax the sand out, it retreats underneath my eyelids. Magda blows in my eyes so they'll tear up but all it does is dry them. Rolling my eyes around and blinking only pushes the sand into my head even more; it's stuck behind my eyeballs and I can only imagine where the particles go from there. "Now New York will be a part of me always," I tell her over the rumbling of the engine beneath our feet.

She says, "Watch out, you're going to wake in the morning with pearls where your eyes were."

The rain comes down smooth, every velvet drop splitting into ten as it falls into the city. We get off the bus and walk to the JMZ; I let the rain cover me. I don't hide from it like I do the sun. Magda takes one big step for every three steps I take; my feet splash the rain from the puddles up onto my calves where it drips down again to the ground. On the train, water seeps from us like we're well-watered plants.

That night we go to the pier where The Slits are playing. We stand in the back because we're afraid to see the band's aged faces. Kettle corn explodes in a metal drum to our right, ricocheting off the sides in rapid fire; we ask for a sample. The girl working the booth scoops hot popcorn into our hands. Magda eats the kettle corn by lifting both hands to her face and letting it spill into her mouth; I spend the next song licking the salt between my fingers. Jacob, a friend from L.A., is there with two friends from Miami, both dressed in gray cardigans and cutoff jeans. Magda whispers between songs, "Do you think they work retail?" and I squeeze her hand that's smaller than mine and softer, fleshier. We take turns squeezing and then drop hands when the song is over.

Afterwards we stand at the edge of the pier, Magda, Jacob, the two cardigans and I leaning against the metal rail that rims the dock, looking into the water. It's black, glossy; the wind picks up, blowing from the east. I have to gather my hair into a bunch at the nape of my neck so it doesn't whip my face. We see a guy who's a dead ringer for Basquiat; he has short dreads, high cheekbones. He's wearing a white bathrobe. We bum a cigarette from a rockabilly couple and the lights above the pier flash

Morse code telling us it's time to leave. At a bar, I get another energy drink for the way back and regret asking the bartender if animal adrenaline is an ingredient; he doesn't answer. He says something to a girl at the end of the bar and they look at me.

The night lends itself to misinterpretations. Everything we do is trivialized, eclipsed by lupus. We shouldn't be going to see bands or hanging out in slimy bars; we should be helicoptering over the Himalayas, speeding through Africa in a jeep, the wind pushing the breath out of us. A truck passes in the night, words lettered on the doors: I'LL COME BACK FOR YOU. LOVE, JESUS. The night is bright, the moon low, wild; Jacob wants to meet at a bar in Harlem, and as Magda and I make our way from the pier back to the city she points out her favorite sushi restaurant, a good video store, where she threw up last year after breaking up with a guy and getting drunk, a stoop where she once found a diamond ring, the apartment she lived in during college, a building that the mafia uses to store stolen goods. When sidewalks end, we're forced to walk in the streets, our pace irregular as we avoid trash heaps and potholes filled with oil and fetid rainwater; I let Magda walk a few steps ahead of me. I want her to take my hand so I can close my eyes and move hidden in my own body. Though she's the one sick, I'm the one who feels weak. Lately she orders for me in restaurants, fends off rats when we walk from the train late at night. I can't see anything, don't know my way around, get sand in my eyes.

When did the roles reverse?

We meet Jacob at a bar in Harlem and file into the men's bathroom; the handicapped stall on the left has a hole in the ground where the toilet should be. A spiral staircase drops down from the hole, leading into a secret club under the city. We feel the steps with our feet; the underground club is magenta, damp. The floor of the bar is tiled and our shoes grate on its surface when we dance. It's too dark for any of us to see each other's expressions; an orange lamp hangs low in the middle of the dance floor and one girl hits her head repeatedly, a sultry voice crooning You're no good, you're no good through the speakers. The ceiling drips with sweat evaporated from people's bodies, beads of condensation spangling the walls around us.

I can't breathe but Jacob assures me that no one can. I'm afraid to inhale other people's sweat. There are no options here, so I try not to think about it. My entire body is wet; I feel amphibian. Magda's bangs stick to her forehead. A song comes on that we all recognize and everyone holds hands and throws their arms around someone's shoulder and does a weird sort of jig, and Magda falls to the ground. Jacob tries to catch her and she whispers something in my ear but I can't hear what she's saying. My arm rubs against Jacob's and I can't tell anymore if I'm tired or excited or riding a wave about to crash. It doesn't feel like night or day or anytime. We're underground, again; we hold heaven and hell in one room. **-bc.**

Lynne Tillman

ANGELA AND SAL

Angela ran a stall at Kensington Market and sold antique and handmade clothes for infants and young children. I worked for her a few days a week, and some days there were no customers. About four stalls down, Freddy and Roger sold women's high-heeled, calf-length leather boots in many colors. Pretty, waif-like Maggie hung out there, a kind of lost soul wandering the aisles. Freddy and Roger explained to me, at the pub, that some years before, Paul had summarily dropped Maggie for Linda; and Maggie found out on the day Paul married Linda. It was Kensington Market lore. Then Freddy and Roger became Queen.

Charming Angela looked like an antique doll—alabaster skin, big blue eyes, mile-wide cheekbones. She was tall and too thin, getting over the break up of a ten-year relationship. Fragile, her friends said. They were all de facto members of the London branch of the Australian—or Strine—mafia, including Michael and Jenny. I'd met them in Crete, and back in London they introduced me to Angela.

Life was confusing. I was confused, more than now, though now with Angela's name come others, usually an inaccessible index set in chronological, not alphabetical, order. If I were writing a novel, it's unlikely I'd present so many characters all at once. If life differs from novels, it's mostly in the management of time and incident. Einstein wrote that "the only reason for time is so that everything doesn't happen at once."

During that time I was moving around fast and couldn't stop moving. When I did, it wasn't for long. Everything was temporary, even when I didn't realize it. The dollar was strong but getting weaker; I was in my twenties and getting by, shifting between Amsterdam and London. I felt I led a separate though not inviolate existence in each city.

/

Angela invited me to rent a room in an enormous flat where she lived, not far from where William Burroughs once stayed, in the home of English filmmaker Antony Balch. In the 1960s, Balch directed *Towers Open Fire*, whose title now seems prophetic.

Several other Australians rented rooms. Scotty raced yachts professionally; he was tan, blond and never appeared to be depressed. Danne had traveled around Europe with the Living Theater and had a two-year old son with her husband, a critic who mostly lived and worked in Australia.

The enormous flat had a long, central hallway, like a hotel, and all the bedrooms off it were spacious, some more than others. We shared the kitchen and three bathrooms. A lovely dark-haired woman I remember as brooding, clever and writing a book, worked as an escort. She bought an expensive designer dress for her dates. The dress had lots of material, because she gained weight when she was miserable, especially after fighting with her married lover. The flowing dress cloaked her changing figure.

Something was always going on, a party, a band playing at a club, there was always someone to hang out with. The Strines I met were fierce about having a good time, and did, except when, like anyone else, they didn't. They taught me a few of their home truths: The English had contempt for their former colonies and colonists; they considered Australians just a cut above the Irish.

/

Angela asked me to go with her to the Hard Rock Café, which had opened on Old Park Lane. At dinner, at a long table, I sat next to the lead singer of Grand Funk Railroad. I talked with him, concentrating on a conversation I can't remember. My glass kept being refilled, but I didn't notice. I hardly ever drank. The band had done a gig at the Concertgebouw in Amsterdam and was going to play, or had played, Hyde Park.

When, from somewhere, I heard Angela's voice.

—We're leaving.

—How much do I owe? I asked.

—The check's been taken care of.

—It has?

—Sal Mineo's paying.

A moment of stunned silence.

—SAL MINEO. I spoke the name aloud, with astonishment. Where's Sal Mineo?

—Here, another voice said.

I stood up. There he was, across the table—Sal Mineo. He looked at me smiling, bemused; he had been seated across the table all along, all through dinner. Sal Mineo of *Rebel Without a Cause*, the teenaged misfit Natalie Wood and James Dean shielded, protected.

Sal Mineo wore an elegant suit. I can't remember its color, though I sometimes imagine it was cream or white, but it wasn't. That was another movie star's suit. Farley Granger, in the 1980s sitting on a couch in the lobby of the Algonquin Hotel. Hardly anyone mentions him now, but he was one of the stars of Hitchcock's *Strangers on a Train*.

Sal Mineo's curly black hair framed his baby face. His eyes were large and black, gentle. The singer from Grand Funk asked me to join him and the band "in Sal's limo." I followed him to the car and was at the limo door; Sal Mineo was already seated on the slate-gray backseat, smiling again. I was about to get in. Then Angela gripped my arm.

"You're coming with me," she said.

She strong-armed me from Sal's limo to her waiting taxi.

"You're coming home," Angela said. She was fragile and tough. In the enormous apartment, in one of its white-tiled, capacious bathrooms, I was sick for the rest of the night.

One day I must have moved out of the flat, but with so little drama I don't remember it, though more of that event might spill out if I try harder. Maybe I returned to Amsterdam. About two years later, in 1976, Sal Mineo, son of Sicilian coffin-makers, once called the "Switchblade Kid" for his roles as knife-wielding juvenile delinquents, was stabbed to death. The Los Angeles police worked the homosexual angle but got nowhere. Sixteen months after the murder, Lionel Williams, a stranger to Mineo, confessed to his wife—a robbery gone bad. The wife gave her husband up; then she killed herself. Lionel Williams was sentenced to fifty-seven years but served twelve. He was released in 1990, then did another crime and was sent back.

Ironic coincidence is common as mud in actual life but appears less often in fiction because it might seem contrived.

/

That dinner in London was the second time I'd seen Sal Mineo. The first was during Christmas in New York, at the Mark Cross store on Fifth Avenue. I was a teenager and a reader of, among other things, movie magazines. My oldest sister and I wanted to buy a gift, a humidor, for our father. He smoked pipes and the occasional cigar.

Sal Mineo stood at the counter, arm in arm with Carol Lynley, another teen idol. My sister didn't notice, she was talking with a salesman; also she was nine years older and didn't follow teen gossip. I was rapt. According to the movie magazines, Sal and Carol were "romantically linked." They looked in love, carefree, luminous, the way stars should be.

My father never used the humidor for tobacco or cigars. He kept it on top of his mahogany tall-boy dresser and threw pipe cleaners into it. He also threw in a lot of other stuff that shouldn't have been there. **-bc.**

Geoff Dyer

SACKED

I wanted to give a full, frank and unadorned account of how I came to be fired from my first proper job after leaving university, but that has proved more difficult than I imagined. It's not just that I can't remember things clearly enough; what really happened has been overlain by the recreated version of events in my novel, *The Colour of Memory* (1989). The fiction has colored my memory to such an extent that it is nearly impossible for me to get at the literal truth of what occurred.

The facts, or what remains of them, are as follows: I came down from Oxford in 1980 with no real idea of what I intended to do. Having applied, without success, for various jobs in advertising and television, I moved to London where I got a job teaching part-time at a tutorial college in Chelsea and at Lucie Clayton Secretarial College. Both of these jobs were for just one term. After that I worked in Harrods during the busy period of their January sale. I was not sacked from that job but a friend who worked in personnel and had access to my employee assessment form told me that I had been classified as someone never to be re-employed. For most of 1981 I lived on the dole before starting teaching again at another tutorial college in September. I also applied again for more jobs in journalism, TV and advertising. One of these jobs was at the Periodical Publishers Association. The company was run by a Tory MP whose name—Tom Something?—I have forgotten. My first interview took place at the House of Commons while my prospective employer was taking a quick break from a masochistic-sounding part of the democratic process called a Running Three Line Whip. My second interview was at the offices on Kingsway. To my amazement I got the job.

I began work in September while living in Islington, renting a friend's room while he was on holiday for a month. I know this because I can distinctly remember cycling to work down Rosebery Avenue, past Sadler's Wells Theatre. I also remember being astonished at the amount of time a job soaked up. If you went for a drink after work—I mean "went for a drink" in the English sense of "got totally plastered"—the whole day was shot to hell.

London was exciting to me back then. There were many things I wanted to do—like going to Kensington Market to buy clothes—and having a job seriously interfered with my ability to do these things. I can't remember what my job involved, but I assume it was boring and completely pointless.

One day the second-in-command took me out for lunch. It was the first free lunch I'd ever had even though it wasn't really a lunch, just some disgusting sandwiches on white bread smeared with too much butter. I thought I was going to be sick, partly because of all this rancid butter and pink ham, but mainly because this pink-faced deputy-boss was a rancid old bore. He told some stories he had reheated hundreds of times before. I was a vehement young lefty at the time and spent quite a bit of the afternoons debating politics with my colleagues. Gallingly the other graduate who had been hired at the same time as me was a member of the Tory party and, even more gallingly, had actually published some short stories in glossy magazines. He shared a house with Ian Hislop who would go on to become editor of *Private Eye* and a TV celebrity. This other new employee and I had many arguments about politics and I greatly preferred arguing with him to doing the work for which I was being paid. Some days I didn't do any work at all, just larked around. It could be said that I had a bad attitude, in fact it probably *has* to be said that I had a bad attitude. All I've ever wanted from a job is to skive. Skiving is a whole way of approaching—in the sense of avoiding—work. It's not the same as slacking because skiving can involve a far greater investment of energy and initiative than doing the work could ever have necessitated. Get in late, knock off early and do fuck-all in the interval except steal stationery: That's my attitude to work. Get paid for something you haven't done. Why? Because this stupid job required that I give up my valuable time, time which I would rather have used in some other way even if I did nothing with it.

I think the reason I have this bad attitude to work is because of my background. My parents worked hard and I didn't like the look of it at all. University made me realize that you didn't have to flog your guts out working at some piss-bin job. It also gave me a taste for leisure which has, if anything, increased over the years.

After about a month I was called into the deputy-boss's office and sacked. I can't remember exactly what happened, only that he gave me a month's pay to sort myself out. After leaving the office I met my friends Robert and James at a cocktail bar where we got totally plastered. I felt pretty bad—not because the sacking was unjustified but because, effectively, I'd been caught, found out. I deserved to get sacked. I am all for firing people. More people should be sacked from all sorts of jobs. The number of people doing jobs and doing them badly—thereby creating extra work for other people—is incredible. The world is an inefficient place and sacking people can only make it more efficient.

Although I felt pretty bad about being sacked, I realized that it was not for me, this world of work, that I was too selfish to do a job, that I actually valued my time—my life—so highly that I would rather waste it than work at a job. My memories are a little vague from this point on. I know I moved into a house in Balham, full of apprentice lawyers. That was a grim phase because they all went out to work in the mornings and I was left in this grim house with nothing to do all day. Fortunately, I only stayed there for a short while. After six weeks I moved into a house in Brixton with a whole bunch of people who, like me, were on the dole. From there, to cut a longish story as short as possible, I ended up becoming a writer.

/

That's all I can manage in terms of recalling the period of getting sacked from my job. The more I think about it the more confused events become. The chronology is uncertain. I just can't untangle the sequence of events. I've had to give up. Perhaps there's a connection here with getting sacked from that job. Getting fired turned out to be a good thing—even though it felt like a very bad thing—and I have tended to carry the lessons I learned from it into the rest of my life. That is to say,

I've adopted a policy of quitting, of getting by without persevering. As soon as I get fed up, bored, tired or weary of anything I abandon it. Books, films, writing assignments, relationships—I just give up on them. (Is it possible to live entirely without perseverance? I think it is, as long as one perseveres with the idea of doing so.) So I should, by my own principles, have given up, without a second thought, on this attempt to write about being sacked. But something about this period of my life continues to gnaw at me. I'm curious about it, would like to learn more about it—and fortunately, I've just had a breakthrough.

I'm writing this in New York where I landed what I thought was going to be a cushy teaching gig for a semester but which actually involves a certain amount of work. My wife is in London and a few days ago I asked her to have a rummage around in my filing cabinet to see if she could find my old diaries for the early 1980s. "'81 or '82," I said. "Hopefully in September or August there'll be an entry saying 'Started work at PPA' or something." This turned out not to be the case but in my little 1982 diary she did find the following entry, dated 24 September: *Sacked from PPA*. Significantly I had noted the date I was fired but not the date I'd started work. My wife is coming to visit this weekend and she's bringing the diary. All will be revealed.

/

I have the diary in front of me now. How funny, to end up being one's own biographer, to have to resort to the kind of research required by writing someone else's life. On the evidence of this diary, though, it's not surprising, either that I have so little memory of what was going on or that I got sacked; if ever there was a case of un-unfair dismissal this was it. The diary is two and a half inches by four, not all the entries are legible; many are blurred as if by damp or by time itself. That's what amazes me most about the diary—the simple passage of time between my writing it then and reading it now. To think that I'm looking back at things that happened *more than a quarter of a century ago....*

At the beginning of the year I was living in Brixton, sharing a flat with my friend Robert who was working as a solicitor at one of London's most prominent left-wing legal firms. (I no longer know any lawyers but there was a time, I see now, when I was surrounded by them.) Robert had gone to the same school—Cheltenham Grammar—and been a year ahead of me at Oxford, but I only got to know him afterwards. I was teaching at a tutorial college over in West London. I see I was always going to gigs (a quick selection: Bow Wow Wow, the Au Pairs, Pig Bag, 23 Skidoo, Kid Creole and the Coconuts), nightclubs (the straight nights at Heaven, the Language Lab, the Kareba, the Beat Bop) and films (*Circle of Deceit, Reds, The Passenger, Badlands, The Battle for Chile, State of Siege, Barry Lyndon, Prince of the City, The Loveless).* It seems that most weeks I went to the cinema and clubs twice and to one or two gigs as well. I also was reading a great deal, far more than I do now. (I used to keep lists but the one for 1982 has gone missing.) It was a period—as it often is for people in their early twenties—when I was doing many things for the first time.

When my wife first looked through the diary she was surprised to discover that as well as going to the cinema a lot (which I still enjoy now), I also had gone to hear the London Symphony Orchestra a great deal (something I never do now). This, I see now, was a code. On Friday 12 February, Robert and I went to meet a client of his in the McDonald's near Warren Street tube. She was waiting with a copy of the *Evening Standard* newspaper folded in front of her. We were there to buy LSD (some code, huh, changing the D to an O?) but when we walked back to her squat in Kings Cross, she unfolded the newspaper to reveal a considerable quantity of heroin. Did we want some? I definitely didn't. Just the acid was fine, thank you very much. But my friend Robert was adamant. This was something we had to do, an experience we had to have. So I did have some of this experience and most agreeable it was too. We spent a couple of hours there, snorting this brown powder with Robert's client and her moronic boyfriend. Robert was violently sick, both in his client's flat and on the tube on the way home. I felt fine and went to meet friends (principally Caroline, Robert's cousin, whom he was always trying to sleep with) at a party at the Royal College of Art. Robert felt better the next day so we took the acid that we had bought. We walked around Brockwell Park and sat in the blue room of our place in Brixton. It was winter in the park and the walls in the blue room rippled and breathed. The floorboards were painted a glistening blue, and sitting on the sofa, watching the walls ripple and breathe, was like being on a raft in the middle of a calm blue lake. The sun sank into the gas fire on the horizon.

There's another coded entry for 18 March: *A!!* This meant that I had anal sex, for the first time ever, with Kate. "I would love to fuck you in your arse," I said. I used the porno words, but this was before I had ever seen any porno. Back then we were anti-porno. Porn was woman-hatred. I said it in this relaxed way but in reality I was as tense as Jeremy Irons in one of his uptight Englishman roles. Certainly I was a lot less relaxed than Kate who coolly responded, "Then why don't you?" I had never done this before, but Kate had (she had also slept with women). She was the first woman I had been out with who was really *interested* in sex.

The next day, my diary informs me, Robert and I took heroin again with his client and the day after that we did two microdots of acid each. Kate cooked a huge vegetarian meal for us. She didn't take acid but she smoked a lot of pot (which I didn't do back then because I hated the idea of smoking).

5 April: *Pink Flamingo club.* It's all coming back to me now. It's a reference to the Soft Cell song *(standing in the doorway of the Pink Flamingo, crying in the rain...)* and it meant I had split up with Kate. Immediately after this I fell ill with gastroenteritis. (Looking through my diary I see that I got ill an awful lot more – an endless succession of sore throats, colds and stomach upsets – then than I do now.) My second interview at the PPA was at 10 am.

7 May: *Camden Palace—French girl.* Another New Romantic type evening. The French girl was a hotel chamber maid. We came back to Brixton on the night bus (I never took taxis and do so now only rarely and reluctantly) and had nothing-special sex. This was on the same day (I remember this, though I've not noted it) that I sprained my ankle playing five-a-side football: the first of a number of occasions when I have torn the ligaments in my ankle. What resilience, though: going to a nightclub after spraining an ankle!

I had become quite friendly with one of my students, James, a rich, charming guy who'd been expelled from Eton and who was now re-taking his A-Levels (though his only real ambition in life was to become a heroin addict). Another of my students was a promising tennis player. He was a member of the club—conveniently located round the back of my tutorial college—where, every June, there is a grass-court tournament which serves as a dress-rehearsal for Wimbledon. When my tennis-playing pupil did not need his card (either because he had classes or some other obligation), he lent it to me so that I could go and watch the matches. Members were allowed to take a guest and so, one afternoon, after we had completed our tutorial, James and I dropped some acid and went to watch McEnroe and Connors in their respective quarter finals. James was wearing fluffy blue slippers. I remember Connors or McEnroe complaining about these slippers because we were in the front row (it was a very intimate tournament back then, like watching top players in furious competition at the vicarage) and James had his feet resting on the net post. Well, that's how it seems in retrospect. Certainly they were resting on the canvas barrier separating the small crowd from the court. According to my diary I went to the club again on Friday the 11th, took acid again on the 12th and went to see Connors beat McEnroe in the final on Sunday the 13th.

30 June: I went round to Kate's and we spent the day having sex. She was living in Siddenham Hill, a short bus ride from Brixton. I don't recall the exact nature of our arrangement but over the course of several years after we split up, if circumstances were propitious we would have blissful sex together. The next day I took a train to Italy en route to Corfu where I was due to meet James. I stopped off in Venice where I spent two nights sleeping outside the station so that I would not have to pay for a hotel. I also went to Florence. One night, in fact, I took trains back and forth between Venice and Florence just so I could sleep comfortably. It was a shitty way to see both cities because I was so tired all the time. I barely could keep my eyes open but I was obsessed with not spending any money.

Things got better when I arrived in Corfu, via Brindisi. This, of course, was in the days before email and although I knew the name of the village I didn't know exactly the *pensione* where James was staying. Miraculously, the first place I tried turned out to be his place. He was there with his girlfriend, Julia, who was gorgeous. I booked into a cheaper boarding house and then the three of us took acid and went down to the beach and got sunburned. It was the start of an amazing week. A football match was arranged between tourists and the local Greeks. We were one-nil down, I scored the equalizer but then the game had to be abandoned because there was so much animosity between the two sides. We got to know all the other tourists in the village and went carousing every night. It was like Ibiza before raving and E and house music, which means we got plastered every night at the disco. Julia was becoming increasingly upset by James because he was so bent on seducing a woman from Norway. It was probably to get back at him that Julia ended up having drunken sex with me in my squalid room. James came in while we were still lying there. I remember him going out and saying to someone next door, "I need a cigarette quite badly."

A few days later Julia suddenly took off. The note she left read: *James, I can endure your company no longer. Last time I left you my soul, this time I leave you money.* James was depressed by this because, contrary to what Julia had said in her note, there was no money to be found. Shortly after, he and I went on to Alexandria and Cairo. There are photos of us riding stallions in the Sahara, near the pyramids, on the edge of Cairo. James said that one of the great things about Egypt was that you could go into a pharmacy and buy drugs over the counter but this turned out not to be true. We kept going into pharmacies and asking for amphetamines but they shook their heads and looked at us like we were junkies. Alexandria had nothing going for it. It wasn't attractive and there was none of that Lawrence Durrell feel about it as far as I could tell, though I hadn't read *The Alexandria Quartet* at that point and still haven't.

Back in England for the late summer I drove with Robert from Cheltenham to Hay-on-Wye, doing hits of amyl nitrate on the way. Why did we do that? Not only is amyl a horrible drug; it's totally inappropriate for a trip to a place like Hay. In late August I must have started my job. I only had been there a few weeks when I went on holiday to Dublin with Robert and James. The reason for going to Dublin was to visit my old girlfriend Claire who was now at art college there. She lived in a house with three other women and they all slept in the same room, on a row of adjacent mattresses. One morning, when everyone else had got up, Claire and I had sex quickly for no particular reason and without much pleasure.

Back in London I got sacked on Friday the 24th. The entry for Sunday the 26th is more representative of this period: The Conversation *at NFT. LSO with R[obert]. Fucked C[laire], in love with C.* Claire was only in London for a few days and I can't remember why she had come. After she went back to Dublin I moved into a room in a new flat in Notting Hill. I was now being paid by James' parents to give him tutorials for the Oxbridge entrance exam, which meant that our relationship reverted to its semi-formal, semi-recreational basis. James had gone from wearing slippers to going barefoot. This behavior was sufficiently unusual to give a police constable cause to stop, question and search him, whereupon he was busted for possession of grass.

The room I'd moved to in Notting Hill was only available for a month and I had to begin looking at a new place almost immediately. At a rental agency I got chatting to one of the women working there. Her name was Lucy and we went out, first to see *Blade Runner*, then to a club called the Bat Cave.

Some of the codes for this period don't make sense, or at least I no longer understand them. 28 October: C + *S!!! at Alison's*, for example. I can't remember who Alison was. Maybe she was a tall woman with back-combed blonde hair who I met when the Clash played at the Lyceum. One imagines the C stands for coke and the S for speed but I don't think I ever came across coke at that stage. Being October, though, I certainly came across a lot of magic mushrooms, partly because James and I spent so many of our tutorials looking for them. The weather must have been mild and wet because there was a bumper crop that year. On the evidence of my diary it seems I did mushrooms twice a week for about six weeks. I even put together a little collection of writings about some of these escapades and made five photocopied booklets on blue paper. I called it *Memories of Hallucinogenics* and gave copies to Robert, Claire and James. Lest we get too transcendental about the whole thing, a not untypical entry—for 10 November—shows how casually tripping had been integrated into the normal rhythm of the day's social life. *Some mushrooms—evening in pub with James.* That was at the tail end of a season which had come to a climax on Saturday, 30 October, when Lucy and I went to Brighton for the day. She had a bag full of an unspecified number of dried mushrooms; we took half each and within ten minutes the world went completely berserk. The beach was as tidal as the sea. We were delirious. The walls of a bouncy red castle swayed over us. We spent the whole day clinging to each other, shrieking hysterically, trying to stay out of trouble. We both agreed that we had never been so out of it in our lives. When we got back to London—punch-drunk, bedraggled, relieved to not be permanently deranged—I assumed we would go home together but Lucy didn't want to. We met again on Monday and went to a club called Sound and Vision and she asked to come home with me because it had been a mistake not to on Saturday.

The next day I moved into a room in the house in Balham and, in the evening, went to see the Thompson Twins. James had started going out with a woman called Sammy who lived in Flood Street in Chelsea. There was a tremendous glut of mushrooms and everyone who passed through that apartment seemed to be off their heads on something. There didn't seem anything unusual or untoward about this but an unremarkable entry from 3 November suggests, I think, how routinely unacceptable our behavior had become: *Met James and Rob at Master's* [a bar, presumably]—*got thrown out, then went to Lucy's.*

On Sunday the 14th I saw Bob Dylan's four-hour-long film *Renaldo and Clara* ... for the *second* time. The stamina I had back then! Lucy phoned to say she didn't want to see me any more. I said I had the right to some kind of explanation or appeal. She told me to stop hassling her. It was around this time that I finally got the hang of smoking grass. I'd never smoked cigarettes and on the few occasions people had passed me joints—when, for example, we went to see *Ciao! Manhattan* at the Scala—I was violently sick. It was James who insisted that if grass was smoked without tobacco it would be fine, and he was right.

From this point on, I think it's fair to say, things got *really* crazy. I started sleeping with Sammy, who I fell in love with (and whom I was still in love with when she started fucking Robert), and James started sleeping with this very druggy, privileged girl called Bella (the kind of person, I used to think, Dylan had in mind when he wrote "Like a Rolling Stone"). At some point I must have torn out part of the page itemizing what took place on 9 December but later, in an attempt to at least partially restore the historical record, I added, on the opposite page, *The Flood St massacre!!!* God knows what happened.

Everything got messier and messier, and they didn't get any less messy when, in January, I moved into the shared house on Brixton Water Lane with five other people (all of whom—like me—were on the dole). I'm not sure how it happened but after a while these five were joined by a sixth, James's friend Bella, who I hated. I tried, unsuccessfully, to have her evicted from the house on some kind of ideological grounds, but the others decided she should stay on the same grounds—because it would be good for her political education. Having been infatuated by James's poise, wealth and decadence I now found myself starting to loathe him for his poise, wealth and decadence. In the course of an argument about something, I punched him in the face. "I won't take this lying down," he said, from a prone position.

One day a brick was thrown through the window of our front door; no one knew why. It just happened. We were always having parties at our house, I was always getting NSU and we were always in the local pub, the George Canning. I fell in love with Bella. We went out together for about three or four months, during which time we took a trip to Venice. Then, when I was out of London, visiting my parents, she called to say she had started sleeping with Karen, a woman who lived near by. Shortly after this, Bella moved out of the house on Brixton Water Lane and deeper into the local anarcho-lesbian-squatting scene. She worked for many years at Brixton Cycles and was the first woman I knew to completely shave her head. A couple of other people moved out of our house and new people moved in. A new phase began which was, in many ways, a continuation of the previous phase. I gradually moved out of this druggy phase into more of a stoner phase with occasional mushrooms thrown in. Later that year I published my first book review—of a new translation of Milan Kundera's *The Farewell Party*—in the magazine *City Limits.*

/

I hope the foregoing provides some context to my getting sacked from the PPA. It had taken two years to find a proper job and less than a month to lose it. It is tempting to say that I decided to become a writer at that moment but this is not the way things work. Certainly getting sacked was one of the things that contributed to my becoming a writer but, more immediately, this job was another possibility—another possible direction—that came to nothing, led nowhere. This is part of the process of becoming a writer. As often as not, one *ends up* being a writer as attempts at doing other things fail to pan out. Writing is what you're left with. It remains a possibility, even when—especially when—nothing else is available. Having said that, my novel, *The Colour of Memory,* starts with me getting sacked from my job, so in this invented version of things (which is, in many ways, the most truthful version) my life as a published writer literally did begin on that day.

I am no longer in touch with any of the people in this account. James achieved his ambition to become a heroin addict. I think he lived in Thailand for a while, was disinherited by his parents and ended up working as a banker. Robert's client and her moronic boyfriend also became junkies. (Neither Robert nor I felt the faintest tug in that direction.) The last I heard of Claire, she was living in France. I don't know what she's doing now but I assume it is grand, international and highly expensive. Kate was beginning to make a name for herself as an artist-photographer but then she got chronic fatigue syndrome and her career stalled somewhat. After meeting again at a wedding, Bella and I got back together when I was in my late thirties. Her parents had just bought her a house in Brighton where she lived with her daughter. She had become a posh, languid mum and had lost neither her looks nor her capacity to make me unhappy (she chucked me again after about six months). Robert—the communist, the Beat, the Buddhist, the friend who always could be relied on to fuck your girlfriend—is now a judge.

And me, I sit here at my desk, looking out of the window on Ninth Street as I've sat at various desks in the long years since the events jotted down in the pages of that little diary. As I look back through it I find myself thinking two things. First: *Wow! That was a lot of fun!* And second: *What an exemplary way to spend your early twenties!* But the thing that I'm most struck by, the thing I most love and of which I am really proud, is the way that the job hardly merited a mention, either in the original diary or this annotated commentary. It meant nothing to me, that job. Compared to the books, the films, the parties, the drugs, the women, the sex, the laughing, the drinking, the clubs and the friends, that job—and the career of which, had I been unlucky, it might have formed a part—was insignificant. It merited the amount of time I devoted to it in my diary: two lines.

It takes a bit of getting used to, the idea that spending 365 days a year doing exactly as you please might be a viable proposition. Getting sacked from that job was what allowed this notion—that the three years spent as a student could actually be extended indefinitely and rather profitably—to gain some kind of purchase on my adult consciousness. Since then I've done pretty much as I pleased, letting life find its own rhythm, working when I felt like it, not working when I didn't. I've not always been happy—far from it—but I've always felt responsible for my happiness and liable for my unhappiness. I've been free to waste my time as I please, and I *have* wasted tons of it, but at least it's been me doing the wasting; as such, it's not been wasted at all, not a moment of it. **-bc.**

Marisa Crawford

sirens

I bought the bug-red lipstick five years ago today,
and every breath I take is a memory
and every memory I have is a reservoir of pain.
There's a point in every story where the story goes sour.
There's a point in every day when you're asleep and I'm awake.
I blame the cartographer for her unabashed sentimentality.
To plant a seed. To chop down a tree.
I heard that if you chop and chop and chop and chop
you'll find a rainbow, that it'll pour out in broken candy streaks.
And that at the end of the rainbow is a pot of gold.
And the pot of gold is made partially of a black tar substance
that is called "me." And I don't mean that
in a cheesy way or a crazy way. Okay?
I mean it because I found it under the seat in your
Jeep seven years before you started leaving.
I mean it because I wrote a poem about it when I was nineteen.
And then the poem started following me. I mean it
cause one summer you threw me in a hole in the sand
at the beach. And another summer the evil twin
in Mom's show threw her sister down a well
and left her there. Like that movie. Wait, no. Not a movie.
And the summer when I was a baby that the baby
fell down a well and cried and cried and cried.
But she didn't die. And her sister brought her sandwiches sometimes.

Tara Ison

THE BIGGEST CROSS IN THE WESTERN HEMISPHERE

Tara Ison

There were signs
for an hour along the 40 East
between Amarillo and Groom,
the road of Love's
Travel Stops, trading posts
for Native American acrylic blankets,
the coral stains and crushed armors
of miswandered armadillos,
the lure of Free
72 oz. steaks (*If Eaten in an Hour!*),
ads for vasectomy
reversal (*Money Back Guarantee!*),
Covenant
Transport trucks with painted scrolls
and bumper stickers
that won't let me pass, or choose
my lane.

The cross rises up,
clean angles and all white gloss.
I am tempted
to stop, buy a key chain,
if only for the kitsch.
My patient little dog deserves
a stretch, a pee, a walk, a lap
at the bottles of water stocked
for our desert trek.

I could visit the cross,
the small landfill mount aside the gift shop
with a facsimile of three bodies hanging,
the main attraction
and those two others (thieves, right?),
see if their faces are
the same.

But I'm tired, tense,
a stiffened spine,
hand pained from the constant search
for news among the static
gospel truths,
the data on cattle heads and choice
beef rates ($4.32/lb.)

And if you're searching for the truth,
I'm scared of this state,
of this unstable air,
the gathering churn overhead and around,
and will I escape the next storm, here?
What I pray is: *please.*
no flat
no radiator fumes
no cowboy siren
no dead dead tubes.

Yesterday I outdrove the tornados.
Last night, on our final walk
before a Motel 6 bed, the dog roamed
a prickle patch
under a blackening red sky.
I spent an hour after ripping thorns
from her belly fur, from the tender hearts
of her paws, trying to assure
with love
and knife
there is no punishment, here.

Kate Wolf

I worked with Rodney all that summer. Five days a week, over twelve hours a day, we drove around canvassing for a new environmental organization, Earth First ("employees last" as we often said); we were responsible for Los Angeles and Orange County. They told us to be systematic, but we weren't—we didn't chart mileage or keep track of where we'd gone the day before. Each morning we got in the car and drove where we felt like until dark. Down the coast to Laguna Beach and back up to the Ventura County Line, south through the strip malls of Malibu landscaped with old oak and trellises of vine, onto straits of Mulholland, over the canyon to the Sherman Oaks Galleria and back over Beverly Glen; we knocked on doors in Brentwood and Beverly Hills, south past the oil rigs, to do the same in Baldwin Hills, zigzagged to Venice and set up at the edge of the boardwalk, eating cherries and pupusas for dinner, east to the parking lot at the Great Western Forum while Bob Dylan played inside, back up through Hollywood to Grauman's Chinese standing alongside the Luke Skywalkers and Wondergirls of the boulevard, warm pavement still heating the night air, the slow drag of headlights passing over us, west to the vodka bars and gay clubs and dirty cake shops on Santa Monica Boulevard and down again to where my car was parked at Rodney's house in Palms. That was one day and it was always like that.

We would stop at different dispensaries en route. Rodney had a prescription for his back, which he said the driving was putting stress on, and I had a forged membership card, purchased on Alvarado Street the year before when I was still in high school. The pot that the dispensaries sold was high powered, exotically named; anything "blue" worked right with my body chemistry. Blue Champagne, Blue Boy, Blue Cheese: Indicas, the blonde, soggy-looking salesgirl said, were for the body, sativas for the mind. Some of the places called themselves pharmacies but you could always tell because they didn't have windows. Inside it looked like a tattoo parlor or a dermatologist's office, bad lighting and shiny fake wood floors; there were leather couches, ugly hemp wall hangings, a television playing cartoons. I sat on the couch, my joint in hand. On TV, Wile E. Coyote was getting smashed over the head with a mallet, a bang of yellow stars fading to black across the screen. We talked to no one at these places; we were talked out. Later in the car, Rodney would pick from a stock of baggies in his Mercedes glove compartment, pack his pipe, disguised as a highlighter, drag and pass. "Just let the flame kiss it," he said. "It hits harsh."

I don't think staying high interfered with my job but it did make the workdays cosmic, full of small spiritual tests and scenarios I put myself through. Sitting in the passenger seat I focused on the ocean out the window, lapping in the sun's last ginger light and tried to see it as something already gone, the current landscape as a memory I experienced in the present. Selling the defamation of the earth sixty hours a week, of course I was susceptible. I imagined myself camped out at my mother's house in the wake of an 8.0 earthquake, my family dead, my legs shattered under rubble or the adrenaline pulsing through me as I tried to outrun a tidal wave up into the hills, flesh seared from the unmitigated grasp of the sun. I didn't know what my survival quotient would be. Would I go on to try to rescue others or just give up, die? Was I brave enough to face the imminent state of ruin—the one that'd already arrived? This was what we asked our customers too.

/

It was only my second job. At college I'd worked at Sprouts, the school café, and if I'd gotten another of the summer jobs I'd applied for, I would have been spending my time as a counselor at a Jewish youth camp. The job description called for singing songs, encouraging good deeds, administering a mini-Olympic games and overall admiring "G-d" loudly to the children, and sometimes, caught in traffic, having not yet scored a single commission that day, in an intoxicated state of panic I felt I was missing out on something.

Rodney asked, with pity, "Are you actually religious?" Mostly just in a superstitious sense. I'd read parts of the bible and "G-d" didn't behave like a reasonable man—what if he found out I didn't believe in him? Rodney could name off the greatest environmental disasters of the century: Bhopal, BP, Exxon, Chernobyl and on—his answer was, what worse could the man do? He was still on parole for a power plant he'd tried to shut down on a reservation in New Mexico, first with sit-ins and roadblocks, then with a homemade bomb. He seemed so lackadaisical it was hard to picture. He called it part of his impulsive youth. "I used to be what I called an I-dealist," he said. "Back then, it was all about me." Rodney now was in his late forties, tall and black with skinny, nutmeg colored dreads to his shoulders, tensed mouth, sullen eyes. He told me he wasn't legally allowed to see his daughter Winnie because of a backlog of child support he owed from when he was in prison. He cared for his senile mother on his own and had given up night law-school to try to earn more money. "But I'm not depressed, you know why?" He pointed to his forehead. "This is in check."

On the other side, I was trying to get used to what felt like the first steps toward the end. Even though the job and living situation at my parent's was easy in comparison to my vision of what was coming next—the breakdown, the trampling, the miles of lines, the floods, storming fires, the living in policed tent villages, the rapes I'd witness, pitiless murders, the rabid dogs and pools of rats and lack of sleep, the strewn body parts and pounds of dead animal littering the street, my own death in a violent circumstance—how could life be appreciated under the assumption, it could only get worse?

I had tried to keep it hidden but inevitably this feeling leaked into the car when I confessed to Rodney somewhere during the first week of working together why I had moved home for a while, the way I imagined the earth like a terminal patient, its signs of suffering frightening me but also just confirming what I knew. I was caught in a cycle of fear and recognition, one where I worried and reality aligned. I was crippled. I was failing college. So Rodney checked in with me sometimes. "Hey," he said, "your head is exploding over there?"

"Maybe." Not having to lie helped.

Rodney said, "Don't fear the future—no one knows what will happen."

My eyes were fixed on the horizon, a flat cloud that hung above the ocean like a shelf. "Don't you know something? Isn't that why you used to blow up buildings?"

"The circumstances weren't perfect. I did what I believed in at the time," Rodney said. "But you, you're young. Life could be good for you."

"Or not," I said.

"Or not," Rodney said. "But, cogito ergo sum—questioning is just part of it lady. For now you exist, that's it." He punched my bicep as encouragement.

"With nature being marked out, I'd almost rather not."

"Your choice. It'll happen with or without you." He turned back up the radio, a techno party station he liked to play to keep our energy up; he reached around to the backseat and grabbed our bag of trail mix and plunked it on my lap. "Eat something."

I picked out a few shriveled cashews and put them in my mouth. "You know another question I have, how could they condone this much driving? It's insane. They can't see the contradiction?"

"What do you care? This car runs on bio fuel." He tried to distract me. "I think that ACLU guy liked you. Did you talk to him?"

"I signed his petition."

"Good," Rodney said. "Maybe he'll call, he's got your number."

/

Pay was based on commission. If you earned a pledge from ten people in a day you'd get a bonus and then you could relax for a few hours, hang out in the air conditioning at the Beverly Center, see a movie and quit. We had a two hundred dollar gas per diem each week that we could also salvage if Rodney kept up making his fuel out of cooking grease. Neither of us was quite suitable for the job. We resented the pitching, the confrontation, it was obvious people hated us. The angrier they were, the more antagonistic we became. Our initial script, meant to be delivered with only the most earnest conviction: *Hello, do you want to stop global warming and save our planet?* I could admit it was dumb but even if the question was a metonym and everybody knew what it meant, couldn't it also be an invocation? People looked at you like you'd asked if they would join a death squad. "No," was our most common response. Or sometimes they'd just give a laugh of disgust, or a harried "sorry," followed by a refusal to meet your eye again as if you'd shown them something throbbing and diseased inside of you. We'd come up with tactics. Rodney was into puns. He printed out some pictures of Martha, the last passenger pigeon, and taped them to a piece of poster board under the heading, HUMANITY IS FOR THE BIRDS. He had scare tactics too, like another poster he'd made that was a collage of birth defects after Hiroshima. On my own, I coined the drop—dropping down in a donor's path, pretending to tie my shoe or retrieve some keys. When I popped back, asking if they had a second for the planet, they were often confused enough to say yes. Or pretending I recognized someone:

"Don't I know you?"

She was about my age wearing a lavender body suit under a schoolgirl uniform with turquoise eyes, fleshy pale face, drinking iced tea in a plastic cup. "Do you go to Palisades?" she asked.

"Is your name Jenny?"

"No, Violet."

"Violet, do you want to help save the planet? It only takes twenty dollars."

"You're annoying," she said and walked away.

"At least recycle that cup!" I shouted after her. Our schemes might work though on a day when it wasn't too hot and I'd smoked the perfect amount of weed, not feeling paranoid or introspective, just capable and full of agency. Those were days I felt like I could save the world, that somehow it all rested on me. Rodney suggested a character for Hollywood Boulevard, Radiation Man, where he would wear a white jumpsuit and mask as though he were trying to protect himself from a toxic spill. I could go naked like the Cowboy in Times Square who got a record contract out of it. "You'll wear fig leafs," he told me. "And hold a sign that says, 'Back to Basics is No Garden of Eden.'"

/

Summer, the city was full of tourists and giving to Earth First wasn't high on their list of attractions. Rodney wanted to see his daughter again; it would be three years in August. My parents had informed me the day I got home, that without the scholarship I'd lost from academic probation, I needed to make enough money to finish my next semester of school, if I made it back in.

Our company had a cap on commission. Any donation over a thousand dollars still yielded the same compensation—an effective way of confirming that no matter how hard you worked, the job couldn't get better. And there was something futile knowing the money we raised mostly went to funding campaigns to increase awareness and support government initiatives that, apart from a wildlife refuge in Northern Alaska, seemed theoretical: a toxic chemical reduction campaign in the Senate, a fund to promote wetland conservation awareness. I'd been naïve about economics. It was like having to raise money for the fire department in the midst of your own decrepit town burning. Even the hottest day ever recorded in Los Angeles—one hundred sixteen degrees in downtown, the air covered in a green carcinogenic film from all the burnt-off smog—didn't give way to much camaraderie from people, or donations.

Standing outside the entrance to the Santa Monica Mall, the air-conditioning flicked at my back every time the door opened. When it closed I could still feel its coolness on that one part of me like an ink spot. A few people soused in sweat were outside window-shopping, trying to ignore the extremity of the weather like it was any other day. I came up to where Rodney was stationed a few feet away from me at the door. "Do you think I'm paranoid?" I asked.

"That lady did just call you an asshole if that's what you're wondering."

"The radio said it's the warmest day ever in Los Angeles. I view that as horrific but I notice the people I've seen seem hot, not scared."

"Yeah, well, these people are stupid," Rodney said. "And cheap. I need that bonus. Let's hit another spot."

/

"We can do a lot with karma," Rodney was saying. "If we know what's really right and wrong."

He had a buddy who was a rare reggae record collector in Laurel Canyon with a vault of old LPs and original tapes worth millions. We were going to his house to smoke him out of his head, get a nice sized donation and keep any part of it that went over a grand. Rodney seemed to think this guy, Jason Selig, would give us a lot of money. I didn't really object. "Would karma call that stealing?" I asked. "Just wondering."

"Don't be literal," Rodney said. "We have to take care of ourselves. What I'm explaining is that if we get this money and it makes our lives better and we use that to do something better for the world, then that's karma. That's what I'm trying to tell you."

"You're right," I said.

We had put in a few hours on Melrose, outside the Soap Factory and were driving north, up into the canyon, the car a heady mix of patchouli and musk and all the other essential oils I'd tried on. We stopped at a light on Sunset and La Brea. At the corner, a white haired man with a flushed, sunburnt face and nubby gut was dressed in a liberty tunic and crown, wearing knee pads, holding a plush torch in one hand and, in the other, a sign with 15% OFF printed on it, pointing toward the Liberty Insurance inside a shopping complex. He shook his hips back and forth and twirled the sign around, lifted it over his head, and then crouched to his knees to make eye level with the cars. He looked me in the eye, his expression overly exaggerated by the virtue of his silence, eyes bulging, smile deranged. The light turned and we kept driving.

"Tough job," I said.

The house was on a shaded leg of road, off Laurel Canyon Blvd, a deep cedar covered shack on the side of a dry creek bed. A single rose amethyst hung on a leather cord draped from a beam in front of the door, glinting in a speck of sun. "Peaceful, huh?" Rodney said. "Jason listens to records all day and smokes weed. He barely leaves, just sells his stuff on the Internet."

Sometimes I imagined a similar life, but it was a last resort, never a matter of choice. "He used to have goats," Rodney said, "but his neighbors reported him. Ask him to see the picture of Peter Tosh with his goat Brownie. It'll make him happy."

When we knocked, no one answered. I said, "Did you tell him we were coming?"

"He's always here. I know he's here now too. Jason," he knocked harder. "Open up, man, it's Rodney." We waited some more and then went around back. We saw Jason, lanky in shorts, barefoot, standing on a pile of mulch with his back to us, chopping wood. Rodney whistled a long call to let him know we were there. "Fuck off," Jason said when he saw us, dropping the axe down; he had a British accent, a kind of aristocratic air. "You could be happier to see me," said Rodney.

"Where were you when everyone in this entire canyon was conspiring against me?" Jason walked over to Rodney and extended his hand. "Come on. Do you have any grass?"

"Of course. I meant to call."

"It's all over now," Jason said. "I'll be eating goat for the rest of my life. Permits, permits, permits. Don't I own this fucking land? Isn't that worth something?"

"This place is worth tons. I've told you—sell it. Move to Mexico."

"I'm talking about my rights, not real estate. I'm talking about freedom. Who's this?" he asked pointing at me.

"This is my partner."

"Partner in what?"

"What if I told you," commencing my pitch to Jason, "that in seven years there won't be a single newt left in all of the U.S.?" We sat in his den, Jason pulling in a long drag off a honey-coated spliff that Rodney had rolled. He started laughing, the smoke falling out of his mouth in little tufts; it looked like it hurt. "I'd say," he answered, "what the fuck's a newt?"

"Come on, Jason," Rodney said. "You know what a newt is."

"No I don't. Is that why you've come here? To make me feel guilty—"

"That's exactly it," I said. "A lot of people don't know what newts are."

"They're water salamanders," Rodney said.

"Jason," I said, "you're not alone in not knowing what a newt is, or even caring. Regardless of the effect we see now on our everyday lives, what we want to stress is that everything alive—every species of animal and plant—is connected and important. We might not realize how important until they're gone. With the current rate of pollutants and denaturalization coming to bear on our riparian and wetland ecosystems, newts are just one of the amphibians slowly being erased. "

"Yeah," Rodney said. "Seriously man, do you know what type of shit could be in the rain forests? Cures for diabetes, cancer. This isn't charity, it's self-interest, worth all you can give—three grand at least."

"I agree," Jason said, "but I don't have any money for you. I've reached my quota for donations."

Rodney took the spliff. He looked at Jason seductively. "You're lying."

Jason shook his head.

"Who'd you give it to, then?"

"VHEM."

"What do they need money for?" Rodney asked, disgusted.

"Birth control for one. Abortions. They're environmental too."

"What is VHEM?" I asked.

"A bunch of wacknuts that think no one should have children. Voluntary Human Extinction Movement? Man, you're a sucker."

"I don't need your approval," Jason said. "I've never wanted kids and every woman I've been with has acted like that makes me a monster. I was right, though. Overpopulation is destroying everything."

"And what about the animals?" Rodney asked. "They don't deserve your money?"

"Lucky for them, they don't know the difference," Jason said.

"But we do," Rodney said. "We have to live with that."

"What's that song?" Jason asked. He sang: "I close my eyes and the world disappears."

I said nothing, just watched them sparring, wondering what to do, feeling kind of invisible. My heart was beating in my throat; I realized I'd smoked too much. I got up to use the bathroom.

I walked through the rest of the house. It was only a big carpeted studio-bedroom with a futon on the floor and a desk cluttered with piles of tapes, reels and papers, two file cabinets, an old computer with a young Bob Marley as the screen saver fracturing down into ten Bob Marleys, twenty, a hundred. Out the long rectangular window above the desk there was a grove of shaggy eucalyptus trees and a blue scrub jay perched in one. The bird cocked its head, looked at me quizzically and then flew off, and I could hear the sounds of other birds gurgling and chirping in the canyon. The room filled with light and then a cloud covered the sun and it receded.

/

I didn't know what I was taking, and later driving back down into the flats at night with Rodney after I'd fallen asleep on the bedroom floor, I'll never know why I didn't mention it. It didn't help that Rodney was annoyed with me and complaining what a baby I was, crawling off to my crib to nap while he had to deal with Jason all by himself; his disappointment at our failed attempt took up most of the car ride. I tried to explain that I was having too much anxiety listening to their conversation but he told me to get over myself, go live some place where all the things I worried about weren't a lingering threat but an actual reality. "Why don't you go to Haiti?" he asked. "Go do something instead of just feeling sorry for yourself all the time." I know he felt bad by the time we reached my car at his place. "We'll get another goat," he promised. "For now, it's back to the grind. Step by step."

I would have told him sooner or later but we stopped working together after that night. A few days later I learned that what I'd grabbed from Jason's desk was worth a lot of money, more than enough to pay for my next semester at college. I wasn't going to sell it right away—I thought about how when the world erupted I might need the money to buy a shelter, buy me some time—but I realized if I waited till then, it'd be too late. I never saw Rodney again. **-bc**.

Rick Moody

PRIMATE RESEARCH

Let me begin by saying, *if only to myself,* Morton thought, in the primate research laboratory at the University of Rio Blanco, *that what I am, first and always, is a chimpanzee. A chimpanzee born into captivity, raised in captivity, and presently living in a laboratory, I believe, in a state called Arizona. Had you,* Homo sapiens sapiens, *to explain what a chimpanzee is, you would perhaps point to certain television or Web-based advertisements in which juvenile chimpanzees appear, and you would talk about the pleasant and humorous aspect of these juveniles. Or you would refer to certain programs you have seen on your Internet-programming monitors that have depicted the dwindling numbers of chimpanzees in the wild.*

Let me tell you, instead, what I believe a chimpanzee is. I believe a chimpanzee is the unluckiest life-form to spring forth in the world. A chimpanzee is unlucky because he is the not-as-handsome relative of you, Homo sapiens sapiens. *By virtue of his resemblance, by virtue of sharing some 99 percent of DNA with Homo sapiens sapiens, the chimpanzee is doomed to be captured, tortured, and injected with drugs, for the benefit of his more attractive relatives. A chimpanzee, that is, takes all the guff and never gets to win the trophy.*

Among the disadvantages of the chimpanzee is his tendency to concentrate on his immediate surroundings while avoiding the larger political or social picture. The chimpanzee is constantly thinking only of other chimpanzees, I believe, which does very little good when you are in a laboratory serving as an experimental subject. In the absence of a large social network, this chimpanzee will see an attractive image on a screen on a wall monitor, and he will stare at it for a long while, while otherwise occupied with removing insects and fleas from his fur. He will masturbate occasionally or, at the very least, he will touch himself now and again because there is not much else to do, and then he will wait for lunch or dinner. When there are tests of acuity to which he is subjected, he will follow the testing protocols in search of the elusive banana or mango. Beyond this, the chimpanzee has few, if any, ambitions.

This approach to life is almost exactly identical to that of the masses of men. Men do little else but perform their eight hours of work before, as I understand it, going home to eat, drink excessively, masturbate, and watch celebrities on their Internet-programming monitors. Perhaps, on certain occasions, these humans watch broadcasts featuring chimpanzees bred in captivity. Since the majority of humans are, I would argue, being kept down by forces of economic oppression, and chimpanzees are living with similar styles and ambitions for their lives, and are similarly oppressed, it stands to reason that we are more than a little like one another.

The routes to liberation in each situation—human and chimpanzee—are also virtually identical. If chimpanzees were to begin to feel the kind of political, social, and evolutionary power which they are due, they would immediately put aside their contentment with creature comforts, so as to militate for greater freedom and independence. Bad luck does not have to go on endlessly. I know that certain thinkers about liberation, such as Martin Luther King, Jr., Mahatma Gandhi and Frantz Fanon, have argued that the arc of history bends toward justice, et cetera, and so on. This implies, in my view, that the oppression of chimpanzees must come to an end, too, and we can only hope that the end will come while there are still enough chimpanzees left in the wild to repopulate. The oppressed human must make a similar decision, a decision to leave off from serving the state apparatus, so that he might move toward a whole and experiential vision of what is possible, a union of species perhaps, a symbiosis of primates, interdependent and mutually respectful.

It was morning, when Noelle Stern arrived at the laboratory, fresh from a night of heavy peyote ingestion at the *omnium gatherum.* A number of people, if *people* is even the right word, because some of them claimed to be routinely inhabiting inanimate objects such as shrubs, stands of sage, and mountainsides, were present at this ingestion. The idea of person and object had become porous at the *omnium gatherum.* The object, they had learned, was no longer content to serve as a second-order being. This was an emotionally draining experience and yet Noelle was able to put aside the abstractions, the talking shrubs, of the night before, by getting to work promptly. She was first to the office. Koo, as always, was nowhere to be found. Larry hadn't come in yet. Noelle's headache, from the peyote, was deep and migrainous, and she had the sensation that she often seemed to have afterward, that life, despite its shabbiness when compared to the pyrotechnical hallucinations of a drug, was somehow rewarding, tender, sad and welcome. The lines of people at the filling station trying to cash in on the big lottery drawing that day: sad. The people filling up large drums of water and putting these into their motorless wagons at the government-sponsored rationing stations: very sad. People climbing out of automobiles that no longer had enough algae fuel in them to make a journey to the next intersection: very sad.

Still, Noelle was feeling *upbeat* and *positive* in that she still had a job, and her job on this day was to observe Morton, and to interact with Morton a little bit, to see if there was a way that he had begun to respond to the injections that she'd given him earlier. Given that she had just witnessed cactus, in psychedelic hues, arguing about whether the soul was vegetable or mineral, spending a morning watching a chimpanzee operate a computer joystick or push around a ball didn't seem like the worst thing.

The question of my own enlightenment, Morton meanwhile considered, *is more important to me, however, than the liberation of my species, which I may not be able to accomplish from this squalid cell. After all, Wilde was not able to achieve complete liberation of his fellow homosexuals from* Reading Gaol, *nor was the Marquis de Sade effective from the Bastille, for all the profligate excellence of the Frenchman's imagination. Gramsci, Mandela, many great thinkers have spent the kind of time I'm spending now, and they have learned to be patient about history, while they pursued a course of individual betterment. I must take comfort from these examples.*

Therefore, there are a number of questions I would like to ask. The first question I would like to ask is: how is it that I am composing these lines (admittedly in my head)? Since I know well that in prior years I felt myself to be just as oppressed as any other chimpanzee, and just as uninterested in the political superstructure around me as any other chimpanzee, why is it that today I am a thinking and feeling and rationally reflexive primate who could easily best the humans in many a logical puzzle?

I will put aside the supernatural, which doesn't really exist, as an explanation. I will instead tender two other arguments. The first of these arguments concerns mutation. Perhaps it is possible that evolution, at last, has thrown a curveball in the direction of the evolutionary dominance of Homo sapiens sapiens. *Perhaps evolution has finally anointed another mammal, another primate, who is easily as reflexive and rationally enthusiastic as the human animal, namely myself. Perhaps the time has come, and all I need to do is to insure that I am able to pass along my own DNA to succeeding generations of chimpanzees. If this is the case, then it's absolutely imperative that I sire as many children in captivity as I am able, because I need to avoid interbreeding, though I also need to try to prevent dilution of my intellectual capabilities. Unless I should happen to chance upon a female chimpanzee who is possessed of the kinds of superior skills that I now seem to possess.*

This would be the first argument, the argument from evolution, which might explain my enlightenment. I have a very substantial doubt about this argument, however, and it concerns the suddenness of onset. I am now able to know my own age, and to know that there were many years prior to this year (my eighteenth) in which I was unable to learn much about myself. In prior years, I couldn't read English (I also now have a modicum of French), I couldn't follow complex news stories about economics and international relations, I couldn't banter about sports. By suddenly finding myself capable along these lines, I have to accept that either adolescence is very, very primitive as far as intellectual capacity goes, or I have to conclude that some outside agency caused my enlightenment.

It is also possible that I am made thus through some kind of accident. It's possible for all primates, probably all mammals, to suffer severe personality change after head trauma. Maybe what I am experiencing now is post-traumatic awareness of some kind. And yet I'm quite as skeptical about this accidental theory. It's just too easy.

You probably know as well as I that there is only one legitimate conclusion, and that conclusion is that my intellectual awareness has been arrived at through experimental regimen. True, the vast majority of experiments performed upon my brethren are cruel, degrading and inhumane. And yet perhaps it is possible, on occasion, for an experiment to produce genuine results! Improvement in the lot of the chimpanzee! Perhaps I am the beneficiary! If so, I too now believe that the future of life on Earth involves the interfacing of organic life with technological innovation. It is simply ignorant to believe that all life has to be fashioned from organic compounds, or that anything that is conceived of in the brain is somehow less natural, simply because it was not fashioned from the elderflower or the lingonberry. Uranium is natural, and therefore, the atomic bomb is natural, and if uranium is natural, how are the dangerous intermediate isotopes of uranium any different?

"Morton," Noelle said, upon slowly and carefully entering his cage. "Did you have a good night?"

Her usual greeting. She had learned from the primatologists that the highest compliment afforded by a chimpanzee, upon greeting, was a casual glance, followed by nonrecognition of any sort. Still, she believed the music of her voice was welcome, and she applied it warmly, fervently, so that it was something reliable, continuous, soothing. She also believed in repetition, in habit. And so she tried to engage with Morton in nearly the same ways each morning. The chimp offered no response. But as she carried to him the plate of orange slices she'd brought for him, this particular day, she did notice that he went immediately to grab the fruits, and then, in what was clearly a reversal, he instead made the decision to leave the plate where it was, at least for the time being.

"Is there anything you particularly want this morning, Morton? I suppose I could give you more of the paints, but I think you have used up most of the paints for now. Until we get more. Unless you're interested in chartreuse. Or mauve. We loaded some new alphabetical software on the computer, and you could work with that for a while. There's also a copy of a personality index called the Myerson-Goldberg Multiple Choice Index. You could fill that out and we could see if you have sociopathic qualities. Dr. Koo wants you to take the test at some point. But there's not a lot of pressure there. Or I could just read to you a little bit from this book I'm reading about medieval diseases. Any of these things of interest?"

Morton looked at Noelle, looked down at his chimpanzee hands, as if to express chagrin at the shape of them, and then, unless she was mistaken, he looked right at her and sighed. How to describe the sigh? Some sighs have centuries of history in them, and Noelle was sure that Morton's sigh was one of these, and she believed it had to do with his hands. It was true that she had never quite got over the "thumb broad" prank from last week, and she still believed Larry was lying when he said that he hadn't painted the word "thumb" over "dumb" on the pad. She realized that it was a not infrequent side effect of hallucinogens that regular life begins to be abraded by the bizarre certainties of the drug theater. Therefore, she believed that Morton was sighing in an expressive way because she had taken powerful hallucinogenic drugs the night before. And maybe Morton *was* leaning down and looking at her shoe, and was somehow attempting to tie her shoe for her, but maybe all of this had nothing to do with the hallucinogens or anything else. Maybe it was just part of life in the animal research laboratory. The big, black fingers of the chimpanzee, imperfectly calibrated to the fine motor requirements of shoe-tying, pursued the intricacies of the butterfly knot, the loops, and the inside and outside of negative space in a way that surely must have had something in common with the famous typing monkeys, because Morton did exceedingly well with the butterfly knot at first, if slowly. While she, still bent forward at the waist like some sufferer of osteoporosis, waited, the ape crouched at her sneakered foot, and she could smell his breath. Their breaths, their inhalations and exhalations met and commingled as the ape labored. Their breaths were one.

At last, however, Morton let go of the butterfly knot that he was struggling so badly to keep in his hand, sighed additionally, and he lumbered over to one wall of the cage instead, where there was a nasty, oily stain on the wall, probably a fecal smear from some primate who antedated Morton. He stood there, as if expectant. As if beckoning to her.

"Giving up on the laces so soon? Do you want to clean the wall? Is that what you're trying to tell me? Because you know if you wanted to eliminate some of my maintenance responsibilities, I'd be only too happy to let you."

She didn't wait for an answer, because all conversation with Morton, or virtually all conversation, was rhetorical. Instead, Noelle slipped out of the cage, went down the empty hall to the supply closet, and fetched the mop, the bucket, and some sponges.

Pursuing the legal remedies that will grant me my freedom, Morton pondered, before the bucket arrived, will require that I reveal myself to the world, that I demonstrate my linguistic and reasoning skills, and yet that will bring down upon me a great deal of attention. Truly, one of the great blessings of modern life, especially now, is anonymity, and it's a certainty that my anonymity, which is part of my life here in the laboratory, will be challenged by the kind of media circus that's bound to ensue, once people know about my skills. Given that I cannot help but be a standard-bearer for my species, it may be that I simply have to accept this as part of my lot. However, there is one very high cost, as regards my becoming a well-known political thinker and statesman, and that cost relates to my growing feelings about this woman.

When I think back to the period before and the period now, there is only one constant that connects these two periods. Only one person was there before—this I know indisputably—and is here now. Her name, so as not to be rude about the whole business, is Noelle, which I think is a very beautiful name, a name that has a lot in common with the wintertime celebration of lights known as Christmas. That I remember her from before is perhaps part of why I cannot seem to overcome my surging ardor with respect to Noelle. Perhaps I am suffering with what I believe is called in human circles a "crush." Of course, we have these in the chimpanzee world, too, but they are temporary, and also potentially very dangerous. Should you unwisely elect to fall in love with a female who is already spoken for by one of the high-ranking chimpanzees of the group, you are liable to receive a serious, I believe the expression is known as smackdown.

Because I am the only chimpanzee in the laboratory right now, there is no danger of my crush resulting in bodily harm of any kind. Perhaps for this reason my feelings about Noelle, the ones that date to the earlier period in which she took care of a more adolescent Morton, have become more acute now that I possess the language with which to elaborate upon their specifics. For example, there is what I refer to as the Night Cherishing. Night, when I am alone in the cell, and there are few visits, except perhaps from the learning disabled janitor who happens by periodically, is the worst time, because there is very little stimulus, and yet it is also the time in which I am left alone with my thoughts, and I am therefore at liberty to think about the garments that Noelle may have been wearing this day. I try to avoid thinking about her in an unchaste way, but in the midst of the Night Cherishing, I recall the little gestures that she has made, or displayed, I wouldn't refer to them as mating gestures or mating rituals at all. On the contrary. In a way, it's exactly the unrequited nature of my feelings about Noelle that motivate me during the Night Cherishing. She cocks her head in a certain fashion when I feel sure she is being ironic. Only yesterday she asked me whether I was tired of having lunch with her and whether we should invite others to our daily lunch gatherings, and I understood her question to be facetious, and yet the adorable way that she cocked her head while she was saying it, it was just very sweet. I was eating peanut butter, by the way, which was causing me to lick my lips in that way that human beings seem to find so amusing, and I was kind of ashamed of myself, and therefore I decided to put off finishing the peanut butter sandwich, which was creamy as opposed to chunky, and this does not meet with my approval. Because I was putting off eating, Noelle asked if I would prefer to have some other lunch companion, and this remark occasioned the cocking of the head, and the cocking of the head occasioned, later on, my Night Cherishing. There might also be a certain garment that she's wearing. For example, today she is wearing these lightweight shoes that are called sneakers, and they are of such fanciful colors, and it's just very hard for me not to think back on these shoes, I have found, and to think of them as something that I am just very, very glad to have in my life.

Noelle loved the weaving motion of the mop and bucket, and she weaved and careened down the ill-lit hospital corridor and into the primate research center with her drunken bucket full of soapy water. A couple of sponges lay in the bottom of the bucket, and these she fished out. Into the dingy, joyless cage, where all her efforts to decorate the space had come to naught, she wheeled the bucket, bringing it to a sloshing halt in front of the animal.

"It's your first chance to have a low-paying and difficult job of the kind that any unskilled worker in this country might have. I feel like I shouldn't really initiate you into this, because if you are able to learn how to be a wage slave, as opposed to a victim of science, then you will be treated unfairly twice over. But it seemed like you were asking for the bucket, so I brought it."

The response was almost instantaneous. In the past, she had seen chimps, and especially orangutans, express an interest in cleaning solutions when, practically speaking, the only real interest they had was in splashing the cleaning products onto the human who was standing nearest to them. Or perhaps they were inhaling some of the cleaning solution for the purpose of derangement. In this case, Morton's yen for the cleaning supplies seemed strangely to be about *cleaning*. He successfully dragged the bucket over toward the wall, he applied water to a sponge, he began massaging the oily brown stains on the wall. It was true, Noelle observed, that he did take special interest in squeezing the water out of the sponge and back into the bucket, and repeating the dipping and squeezing, as if testing the liquid properties of the deluge that resulted. But most indisputable was the interest of the chimp in the actual scouring of the wall, and the conclusion had to be that this particular chimp, unlike many others that she had seen, preferred a tidy and presentable living space.

From the office, she sent a message to Koo's old-fashioned voice mailbox to offer a few comments on the situation, noting that Morton seemed "even more tidy" than he had seemed in the last few days. And then when she walked back into Morton's space, he handed the mop back to her, like he was through with it, and he gestured at the stain on the wall, whose fecal splatter was all but removed now, as if to indicate that he had cleaned it up especially for her, so that she wouldn't have to work under these unsanitary conditions. Was that possible?

Was she imagining all of this?

And was it really true that she had had a conversation with a paloverde tree last night, and that in the conversation with the paloverde tree, she had asked it, well aware that there was a risibility to the whole exchange, whether it was possible to have relationships across species lines? In the aftershock of peyote, she felt herself to be nothing more than a medical researcher, albeit a medical researcher with certain vague spiritual ideas. She knew that the paloverde (and later the prickly pear) were actual examples of *plant life*, not beings of volition. Sex with them would not, could not, be very rewarding, if only for the spines. And yet if there were an emotional bond there, then maybe the cross-species difficulties would not be so difficult to surmount. Love made all things possible, she'd said to the paloverde. A tree blowing in a desert breeze could be moving and delightful. It could be a thing of sublime perfection. Why couldn't there be love? The paloverde tree, however, had been rather brusque, just not very seductive, when you got right down to it. He reminded her of a lot of the men in the *omnium gatherum*, self-involved, falsely casual, somewhat narcissistic. Much later, it occurred to her that when she asked the paloverde about interspecies love, she was not, in fact, confining the topic to vegetation.

"Morton, did you clean that off for me? That's very kind of you. Because Larry, you know, usually leaves the cleaning for me. He thinks my being a woman somehow makes me better at cleaning stuff. Listen, I know that the bonobos are much more about the matrilineal, matriarchal thing than the chimps are, but I'm going to give you some insight here into the situation with humans, and maybe that will help you as you go forward in your dealings with us. Okay, Morton, the situation is that the male of the species is just always looking for ways to dominate the woman. That's just my opinion, and maybe you should just consider it my opinion. But that's how it is. It's true that in many cases the male of the species is physically larger. Look at me. I'm not a big girl, really. But even when the women are big—and there are all these models that are mainlining designer HGH and stuff, and they're six feet tall, or more, and they look like they just came in from killing wolves out by the fjord—I guarantee you that every guy thinks he's got something *over* those Valkyrie maidens. He can order them around, and even if he's an evolved guy, from the *omnium gatherum,* and he's a paloverde under the cover of night, he goes home and he expects the woman to wash the stains from his Y-front briefs. That's why I'm here, all these hours, all these days, and when there's shit all over the floor, it's me who comes to clean up the shit. It's either me or the janitor guy. Because a woman is lower than an autistic janitor who is lower than a chimpanzee, who is lower than the lowest, meanest man on the face of the planet. And that's why I really appreciate your cleaning up the smear."

There was an expectancy in his expression again, or else she was really starting to go crazy and ought not to have come into work, and it was the expectancy that made her feel like she wanted to unburden herself even further. The three-legged stool in the cage, on which she sat, screaked, and Morton flinched for a moment. It wasn't easy to do it, what she did next, and she sort of wondered whether in doing it she was just cleaning out the last bit of peyote in her system. She did it anyway.

"Morton, would it be all right if I told you something that I'm going through right now? I know that you are not really going to have an opinion on this stuff, but there's something going on at the *omnium gatherum,* which you know is this spiritual community that I'm involved with, and I just have a bad feeling about it, and I haven't really told anyone about it. Because, you know, obviously, here at work, nobody believes in this kind of thing. They all think it's pretty embarrassing. I just feel like I can talk to you about these parts of my life without feeling, you know, judged."

It wasn't until she began to tell him that she realized how much it had been bothering her, how with these alternative ideological systems, you know, the irrational thinking took place a little bit at a time. You didn't know at first. You just woke up one day, assuming you could still wake effectively, and upon waking you realized that you had gone further than you'd meant to go in *alternative culture,* and now you were far away, downstream, waving at your family who stood on the banks. What she was trying to describe to Morton was the feature of the *omnium gatherum* known as *algorithms.* They had algorithms for everything now, they had algorithms for playing chess, they had algorithms for dating, they had algorithms to predict chaotic systems like annual rainfall and the apocalypse. People hooked up a bunch of mainframes, and they got in the business of forecasting, because that was the last part of the service economy at which NAFTA still seemed to excel. And there was a reason for that. The reason for that, she started telling Morton, was that NAFTA favored the eschatological. And the guys at the *omnium gatherum,* because it was always guys who ran these things (she told Morton), had realized there was a spot in the forecasting business model where no one had yet created a lively Web presence (besides, what with the Futures Betting Syndicate, it was possible to make a market in the apocalypse).

And thus the *algorithms.* The *algorithms* were compiled from all the available statistical data on the end, which is not to say the likes of the Chelsea Clinton senatorial campaign, but the actual predictions of the End from all the ecstatic cults and the declassified intelligence reports. The *algorithms,* after the big economic collapses of the last twenty years, she told Morton, had become really pretty popular as a Web site, although a lot of the traffic was said to be *ironic;* you know, the people visiting the site didn't really believe that the end was really coming, they just liked reading the updates and looking at the advertising.

There had been many reckonings of the End over the years. The way to increase market share as a splinter religion was to come up with a really attractive idea about the End and to sell it really hard. Probably you had to pick a time that wasn't too far off, not unimaginably far off, like 2112, or 2345, or something, because no one who was alive now gave a shit if the End was going to be in 2345, because their great-great-great grandchildren would have to worry about that. You had to pick a time that was pretty soon, and then you had to collect a lot of canned goods and other kinds of donations, but not weapons, because when you collected weapons, that attracted the attention of government agencies. You had to stockpile stuff, awaiting the End, and then when the End didn't come, you had to retire quietly to a condominium somewhere with a nice climate. People were constantly engaging in some using idiosyncratic calculus to recalibrate. And interpret. This was the word that they liked at the *omnium gatherum.*

"Look around you, Morton," she said, "the world is composed of languages. People are laboring away in a sandstorm of significations. And it's their job, they say, to interpret these signs. A bicycle painted white chained on a street corner with garlands upon the seat. No coincidence. The proliferation of coyotes in downtown Rio Blanco. Those are no ordinary coyotes, and they don't have to do with habitat destruction, or the gutting of the Endangered Species Act.

"Morton, you know and I know that the End is mainly just a silly kind of marketing. It's attractive, because it means that you don't have to make long-range plans for things, and you don't have to worry about how you're going to pay for your kid's college education, and you don't have to worry about voting in the next election. The End is adolescent. It's always teenagers, on harder drugs, who think the End is at hand. Still, you know what, it's kind of scary when they say it's *now.* When people you know socially, and maybe you slept with them once or twice, just to be nice, and because you don't think too clearly about this stuff too often, when these people you know socially are suddenly talking about the End, that's a bad sign. So the question is, Morton, do you think I should just pay no attention? Should I just say that these are my friends, or some of them are my friends, anyway, and they have some really strange ideas, what do you think? Is that the right approach?"

What I think, my darling, is that when I listen to you discourse on the affairs of the day, I am filled with a warmth. A warmth such as I have never known. We may have our ups and downs, and over the course of our association there have been times when you wore outfits that I didn't entirely approve of. And after all you are human, you are the oppressor, but despite all these things, when you make yourself vulnerable to me in this way, when your face is open, and full of a yearning to understand the rushing river of the world, then I feel a tremendous warmth in my breast. I could listen to you discoursing upon the laundry all day long, if that is all that is given to you as woman. I don't care. The outside world, after all, is only available to me as a series of computer screens. I haven't been outdoors in years. But in this space there is a person who cares for me still. My own parents are gone. And the monkeys in the cages down the hall from me are beneath contempt. I am alone in the world, and as such, there is only you. Only you no longer treat me as so much humanoid meat, ready to be fed into the grinder. So tell me of the End, tell me of the Beginning, tell me of everything in between, which would be called, I guess, the Middle. Tell me of the Middle, and I will listen. I will listen even if you want to tell me about the state-sponsored lotteries, or the gigantic algae bloom in the Gulf of Mexico. I will listen.

She stared at him, she gazed upon him, he had the full extent of her gaze, as though she were looking into the window of his soul, now, and it made her tremble in a way that she hadn't experienced with him before. It was like the knowledge of her own nakedness, this trembling. It was like phased withdrawal. It was like avian flu, the new mutated version. It was like something interpersonal. She could see him mulling it over, too, she knew he was, even as she believed it was peyote or the afterburning of it. Morton was chewing oddly, as though he'd got hold of Larry's nicotine gum, and it seemed almost hilarious, but she resisted the desire to laugh at this gum-chewing repetition of Morton's—laughter was species-centric behavior; it was narcissistic, unless it was the laughter of recognition, of compassion, of likeness, and without laughing she realized that Morton was trying to say something to her, and the fact that he had no real idea as to the use of his vocal chords was a genuine impediment, not to mention fine motor control of mouth and lips and tongue. It was as though a stroke victim or a coma sufferer had clawed his way back from the lower depths, and was attempting to use his slack musculature. He chewed and he chewed, and then, as though he were somewhat informed on the physiognomic reasons he would never be able to talk, he put his lips together, and with a momentousness that would transport Noelle leagues beyond where she was when she parked her car out in front of the hospital that morning, Morton, the chimpanzee, *whispered*, "You know, I am so fond of you."

-bc.

Jay Neugeboren

The previous afternoon, when they were less than a two hour drive from Le Tignet, a small village in the south of France, they had turned off Nationale 95—the old Route Napoléan—and meandered through towns and villages that seemed little changed since they passed this way in 1968.

Now, drinking coffee on a terrace that overlooked the Lac de Castillon, Saul found himself remembering how, during the time they lived in Le Tignet, they adopted the custom once a week of searching out a new town or village, usually one they read about in *Les Plus Beaux Villages de France.* They would start out after breakfast, arrive at their destination within an hour or two, wander the village's streets, enjoy a leisurely lunch, and after lunch adjourn to a local hotel where they would, before returning home, make love.

The names of the villages stayed with him—Gordes, Séguret, Ménerbes, Ansouls, Coaraze, Peillon—and there were others, not included in *Les Plus Beaux Villages*, that they had happened upon and, by doing so, made their own: Sisteron, Draguignan, Digne, Rousillon, Gap, Mons, Eze, Bonnieux, Ys, Apt—each name having the power, still, to evoke specific days, conversations, meals and rooms. In Digne, he recalled, in the Hotel de Ville, the wallpaper had been composed of faded red and green chevrons like those on Chevrolets; in Peillon they had, within less than a minute of entering their room and with most of their clothes on, made love, and had done so standing up, Janice's back against the door, her legs clasped around his thighs; in Ménerbes they had talked for the first time about getting married; in Apt, on a noisy, broken-springed bed, he had—another first—entered her from behind; and on a broiling August day in Entrevaux, in a room with a huge chestnut armoire, one whose doors were faced with narrow gilded mirrors covered with colored streaks that, in memory, appeared to be dried blood stains, they had, after love-making and on sweat-drenched sheets, fallen into the blackest, most sublime post-coital sleep he ever experienced.

Was the hotel still here?

While Janice talked about their daughter, Ellen—who several weeks before their departure had taken up with a guy Janice said was like the others: an untrustworthy, manipulative drifter—Saul thought about Camus. Forty years before, while they were living in Le Tignet, Saul had decided to become a doctor after reading *The Plague.* This small epiphany that changed the course of his life happened in May 1968, when the entire French nation was shut down by striking students and workers, a time when he and Janice believed a revolution was taking place in France that had the potential to transform the world. They had arrived in France the previous summer after graduating from Oberlin College, giving themselves a year in which to travel Europe before returning to the States and making decisions about jobs, careers and family.

So that Janice would think he shared her concern about Ellen, Saul asked questions—was the guy doing drugs? was he abusive? did he have a day job? was he clean?—though his mind wasn't on Ellen but his imagined affinities with Camus, a man who once declared that he believed in three things only: courage, intelligence, and women. On his last day on earth, while riding in the car in which, at the age of forty-eight, he would be killed, Camus, in a kind of a premonitory revelation that Saul envied, told his friends Janine and Michel Gallimard (Michel was his publisher) that he felt he had made all his women happy, even those he loved simultaneously.

Janice was asking when they might begin traveling again—Saul had promised they would go to Italy: Venice, Florence, Siena—and Saul said he couldn't think about that yet. Why so intent on planning? Why not just let things happen? Couldn't they simply be where they were without thinking of where they *might* be? Janice sighed. "Look, I'm not trying to organize your life, much less run it," she said. "In truth, you seem so distracted that I was just making conversation. I thought that perhaps talking about Ellen had upset you."

"Let's enjoy the view, okay?" Saul said. "As for Ellen, she's been down this road before. She'll tire of the guy in a month or so, and go on to another."

"And if she continues in her patterns? Can you imagine her going on like this through her thirties and forties?"

"I'm not into imagining what might be," he said. "Ellen's Ellen. I don't imagine her being anyone else." He looked away, toward the lake, its surface grey, calm, metallic; he pictured Camus leaving Villeblevin and driving south along Nationale 5 until he came to the spot some twenty-four kilometers north of Sens (was the Nationale 5 still there? Saul hadn't been able to find it on the new map he'd bought) where the car Camus was traveling in with his friends and their eighteen-year-old daughter Anne, along with the Gallimards' dog, slammed into a tall plane tree, bounced off and crashed into another tree some forty feet beyond the first.

Although neither his face nor body showed signs of visible injury, Camus had been killed instantly, his skull fractured and neck broken. Michel Gallimard died five days later while being operated on for a brain hemorrhage. Neither Janine, who was found near her husband leash in hand, calling for the dog, nor Anne, sitting in a field sixty-five feet from the crash, were seriously hurt. Camus's black leather briefcase, which contained his passport, photographs and some books—Nietzsche's *Le Gai Savoir*, a school edition of *Othello*—along with a manuscript of what would be his posthumously published novel, *Le Premier Homme*, survived intact.

Previous to this day, Camus had written that he considered death in an automobile to be *une morte imbécile*, the single most absurd way of dying. The manner of Camus's death, thus, made sense to Saul. But to visit the spot where Camus had died—or even to stop in Villeblevin or Lourmarin, as Janice suggested in deference to Saul's obsession with Camus—wasn't something he cared to put on their itinerary.

They came upon the village of Entrevaux the way they first came on it forty years before, from the east, and once again—suddenly, physically—it took Saul's breath away. Hearing his rasped intake of air, Janice pulled to the side of the road, turned off the engine.

"Are you all *right?*" she asked.

He stepped from the car, rested his hand on his chest, felt loud, irregular thumpings, and heard, also, the sound of rushing water. He wondered, for an instant, if the sound were coming from within, if his blood pressure were rising immoderately. In the silence, though—unearthly somehow, as if they had been transported to a place covered with a huge transparent dome, one that let in light but that kept out all sound—it occurred to him with relief that the sound of rushing water probably *was* the sound of water: of the Var River which, overflowing from spring rain and mountain run-off, would be surging nearby.

The village appeared, as ever, an apparition: from a cluster of perhaps a hundred closely set stone-walled houses that seemed to grow from the ground itself, their red tile roofs bright in the late morning sun, a walled road zigzagged up the side of a pyramid-shaped mountain. At the top, some fifteen hundred feet above ground level, was a medieval fortress from whose ramparts one had a three-hundred-sixty-degree view of the surrounding countryside. "I'm excited is all," Saul offered. "It's just very *exciting* to be here again."

"We should eat," she said.

"And then—?"

They walked toward the part of town where they expected to find the hotel they once stayed in and where, were it open, they would have lunch. The village seemed preternaturally quiet, shutters on most homes closed while people ate their mid-day meals and prepared for their siestas. They remembered this: that stores in these villages—butcher shops, bakeries, groceries—closed down for two to three hours mid-day and all afternoon on Wednesdays.

They found their way to the far side of the village, walked along a path that bordered the Var River and came to an abandoned fortress. Beside its drawbridge, a few feet from the river's bank, three small green-backed turtles sat on a single flat rock. Under the bridge, where the river narrowed, the water, coursing downstream, foamed with increased turbulence, and Saul thought of boiling water and of the fact that if you placed a frog in a pot of boiling water, it would jump out, but if you put it in the pot and lit a fire underneath and let the water come to a boil slowly, the frog would remain where it was and die.

Saul often had mentioned this fact to his medical students, even before, he would joke during lectures, Al Gore "ex-propriated" it for his film on global warming, and he used the fact in order to draw his students' attention to the ways in which human beings, like frogs, seem to have been programmed by evolution to be able to respond to acute crises but not chronic conditions, not to thinking and acting in terms of long-range effects and consequences. This short-sightedness was deadly when it came to medical care, where the government, medical groups, insurance companies, and his own hospital rarely thought long-term, where the premium was always on efficiencies dictated by profit margins and cost-effective ratios, and where, therefore, doctors were paid more for procedures—to shove things down people's mouths or up their assholes—than they were for essentials, like taking good histories.

It was the same, he'd come to think, with matters beyond health care: the belief that we were going to have a quick, neat and complete victory in Iraq—to shock and awe the enemy without having to think about or deal with the aftermath of our invasion; the delusion that we could keep polluting and using up the world's water, air, oil, coal, minerals, wetlands, forests, without regard to consequences and future generations. And so when the Bush Administration pushed for a delay in giving grants to the UN Global AIDS Fund—of an amount that was, as a percentage of gross national product, the lowest amount any developed nation was contributing—Saul went to his office and told the nursing staff to hold all calls, and, feeling like the Moses Herzog of the AIDS pandemic, had written a letter to the president in which he identified himself as an AIDS doctor and accused the president of being a murderer. For if, he had written, you watch a neighbor drowning and you have a life preserver and don't throw it to the neighbor, you've killed the person, which was what, when it came to AIDS, we were doing. Unlike Moses Herzog, however, who rarely sent off his missives, Saul went down the street and put the letter in the nearest mailbox.

In the letter's final version, he edited out an appeal to self-interest: the deadly truth, given that viruses were now frequent flyers—passengers moving around the globe with astonishing speed—that what happened in South Africa, South America, South East Asia or the South Pacific affected *us*. We were, none of us, islands unto ourselves, and we were none of us safe. Whatever spread across poor nations would eventually spread across wealthy nations. It behooved us then, for our own well-being, to think of others, to think long-term and be generous. It was better, that is, to give than to receive.

So what Saul hoped to do during his mini-sabbatical of four months was to explore and write about why we seemed destined never, as a species, to think in our own long-term interests. Was there some underlying biological reason for this inability to respond to conditions that had the potential to destroy us? Did we possess some kind of innate biological death-wish that would lead inevitably to our destruction? The questions, he believed, were obvious; how and where he would find anything resembling answers was beyond him. We didn't respond to the familiar *because* it was familiar—because it was regular, predictable and didn't *appear* dangerous. That much he had figured out. Also: that people became excited about *crises*—an anthrax scare, a tsunami, SARS, acute incidents in which somebody was done in by a can of contaminated food or bottle of adulterated pills. As for insurance companies, why should they think long-term when the clients they were serving now probably wouldn't be the clients they would serve in a year or two?

Still, if Saul could write a book that would be the equivalent for the Twenty-First century of what Camus' book had been for the second half of the Twentieth, what then? Had *The Plague* changed anything? Janice, a clinical psychologist who worked as a consultant to school districts while maintaining a small private practice, had thought Saul's letter to the president foolish, a transparently childish attempt to get himself punished, and further proof that he was losing it, overworked and depressed, and that his years of caring for AIDS patients finally had done him in. He couldn't disagree, for until the last few years, when a new generation of antiretrovirals had, blessedly, proven effective, every last one of the thousands of AIDS patients he tended to during the previous two decades had died.

Before the AIDS pandemic had exacerbated what Janice saw as Saul's considerable capacity for survivor guilt, she frequently remarked on the obvious. His tendency was to dwell not on those patients whose sufferings he had ameliorated but—always on those he had lost. What Saul hoped to do during his leave was to try and repair the marriage, though given how far each of them strayed in recent years, he doubted this was possible. Returning to a place where they were happy once upon a time might, they agreed, help, for it remained true—a tangible basis for hope?—that they had stayed together more than forty years in a time when most people they knew long ago had divorced and moved on to new couplings, new marriages.

Saul watched the turtles slide from the rock and disappear into the river, one following the other, and only when the third was gone did he become aware that Janice had for some time been leaning against him, her arm around his shoulder. Walking back through town they stopped in front of the Hotel du Midi—not the hotel they once stayed in—to read signs taped to the hotel's door: a handwritten note from the *propriétaires*, Monsieur and Madame Bruno (the hotel and restaurant would be open again May 15 to September 15), the village's church (times for Sunday Mass and weekday services), the mayor's office (rules concerning sheep, goats, pigeons and dogs, and times the water would be turned off), and—what caught Saul's eye—a poster announcing a concert by the Turetzky Duo, to be held in Grasse at the Maison de Jeunesse et de Culture. "Didn't we hear them in Boston a few years back?" Janice asked.

"Yes," said Saul, "but they were a trio then. The Turetzky Trio. The violinist and the cellist were brothers. The pianist was the cellist's wife."

"She wore a full-length low-cut gown—burgundy, I recall, with black lace trim," Janice said. "And they performed my favorite—the Schubert B flat Trio. She was an exceptionally beautiful woman."

"Was she?"

"As if you wouldn't notice," Janice said. "Tell me, Saul. We're alone, nobody else will hear—but have you *ever* met a beautiful woman you didn't remember?"

"Probably not," he said.

When they had circled back to their car a third time without having found the hotel—Entrevaux had only three passageways that could legitimately be called streets, only one of which was wide enough to allow automobiles to pass—Janice suggested they move on. "Does anyone live here anymore?" she asked.

"I heard a dog bark."

"Do you remember, when we first read through the *Plus Beaux Villages* book, how I noticed that there rarely were people in the photos?" she asked.

"Yes."

"Yes *what?*"

"Yes, I remember you noticed that. You said that the villages seemed very beautiful, and very dead."

"I'd forgotten, too, once you're inside these villages, how little light gets though," Janice said. "All the alleyways and narrow streets, the thick walls without windows—"

"To keep out cold and wind in winter," Saul said, "and to keep out sun and heat in summer. Also to protect against invasions. In villages like this—*villages perchés*—most of the windows, to the outside, were added in the years *after* the villages lost their military role."

"My scholar," Janice said.

"Don't mock, please."

"Are you hungry?" she asked. She pressed herself against him, lightly, and nibbled at his ear. He did not push her away.

"Can we go, please?" he asked.

He opened the car door, but before getting in he stepped behind Janice and nuzzled her, his mouth on the nape of her neck. Her skin was warm and salty, and he considered lifting her skirt and doing her from behind; he was confident they could, close to the car, bring this off while seeming to be embracing. As he bit at her neck, he found himself troubled momentarily by his anger. Was his sudden desire to hurt her, he wondered, greater than his desire for her? But as often happened, he found too that he was soon comforted—his ardor and rage compromised—by a familiar thought: that though AIDS would be with us for the rest of human history, he would not. **-bc.**

Seth Greenland

THE ANGRY BUDDHIST

The kitchen window is open but no breeze ruffles the worn curtains. It's just after seven in the morning and Vonda Jean can already feel the heat of the day. She is still wiping the sleep from her eyes when she pulls the orange juice container from the refrigerator. It feels light, not even enough for a glass. Dammit, how many times does she have to tell Hard to throw out the carton when it's nearly done? He's still in the bedroom. She'll tell him again when he marches in to get his coffee. Sees her reflection in the kitchen window. The loose plaid nightdress hangs on her like a potato sack. Glances down at the furry pink slippers on her feet. If she was trying to look alluring she might be worried but right now she doesn't care if Hard finds her attractive. The slippers are comfortable and that's what matters.

Hard likes younger women anyway. Vonda Jean senses there was something going on between him and the one who showed up at the house the other night. She could tell he was lying about her but didn't have the energy to press the matter. Or the interest. Vonda Jean has been thinking about fleeing the marriage and she doesn't want to waste any more time fighting.

With bread in the toaster and the coffee on, she heads to the garage looking for a carton of frozen orange juice. The Marvins have a horizontal freezer that Hard uses to store meat from his hunting trips. Every autumn he drives to the Sierra Nevada range and roams the woods for several days stalking deer and elk. Vonda Jean used to accompany him; they would sit in a tree, rifles at the ready, not saying a word for hours as they waited for game to appear. It was bliss for Hard, being in the woods with an attractive woman with whom he didn't have to make inane conversation while he cradled a high-powered weapon with his finger on the trigger. Vonda Jean didn't particularly like to hunt, but at that time in the marriage she enjoyed being with her husband. She had stopped going with him when her sons grew old enough to accompany their father. Then the boys developed other interests and the last few years Hard has made the trip alone. Usually he'd get a kill and the freezer in the garage would be stuffed with venison steaks that the family would eat throughout the winter months. This past hunting season ended a week earlier and it had not been a good one. Despite tracking an eight point buck five miles through the woods, Hard never got a clean shot and drove home empty-handed. There was an unanticipated upside to this, however, since it left room in the freezer for the frozen hundred and twenty pound Rottweiler, something Hard has neglected to mention to Vonda Jean.

Hard is in the bedroom pulling on his boxers when he hears Vonda Jean's scream. Figures she must have just opened the freezer. He could have warned her about the dog but imagines it would have led to an argument. The two of them have had enough of those lately. Hard continues getting dressed, taking his time, and when he walks into the kitchen he sees his wife seated at the table sipping her coffee, tension emanating from her like cheap perfume.

"G'morning," Hard says.

"For you, maybe."

Hard does not immediately respond. Instead he opens a cabinet, takes out a box of cornflakes and pours them in a bowl. Removing the milk from the refrigerator, he pours it over his cereal. Then he takes a spoon from a drawer and joins Vonda Jean at the table. "Sleep well?" Hard says.

"I nearly had a seizure," Vonda Jean informs him. "You want to tell me what that animal is doing in the freezer?"

Hard has been dreading this exchange. Chews his cornflakes, swallows. Looks her in the eye: "I'm going to have him stuffed."

"What, and put him in the living room?" Her tone suggests he has a greater chance of doing that with her.

"Maybe."

"The hell you are."

"This is why I didn't tell you he was there."

"I thought I was going to have a heart attack, Hard. You probably would of enjoyed that."

"No, I don't want to kill you, Vonda Jean. Not like that, anyway."

She doesn't laugh at this attempt at humor. Vonda Jean is sick of Hard, hates him now, wishes he would leave and just get out of her life. But if she plays it wrong, she could get screwed in the settlement, and Hard has nearly twenty years on the force. His pension, a subject that comes up regularly during their frequent fights, won't be small change. "I want that dog gone."

"The nearest taxidermist's in Apple Valley. I'll take him up there my next day off."

"That's not how it's working, Hard. You're going to get rid of that dog pronto. And I don't want him back here as a living room decoration either."

"What do you want me to do?"

"Pretend you're normal. Bury him."

"Just stick him in the ground?"

"Cremate him if you want. Bury the ashes. Just get that dog out of my goddamn freezer." She stares at Hard, the cordite in her gaze challenging him to reply. Hard eats his cereal in silence. "I'm not fooling."

"Or what?"

"I'll toss his carcass on the side of the road."

Hard desperately wants to wrap himself in the cloak of self-justification that would come with telling Vonda Jean that Bane has been murdered. Of course he can't do that since it will open up a potentially incriminating line of questioning. Why, for instance, would anyone have wanted to harm a dog? "Fine," he says. "Next day off, I'll bury him."

"If that dog isn't out of my freezer in twenty-four hours, I'm checking into the Days Inn and hiring a lawyer."

"You think I'm worried about that?"

"Just remember I'm entitled to half your pension." She stares at him with an expression as nurturing as an oil spill. Hard stares back at her, the vein Nadine had nearly pierced with the salad fork pulsing like a strobe light. *Nadine.* That bitch. Next time he needs to cheat with a better class of woman.

/

Vonda Jean is teaching a jiu-jitsu class out at the dojo in Twentynine Palms when Hard returns from work a little after seven in the evening. He knows she won't be home for a few more hours so he empties a can of chili into a bowl and puts it in the microwave. While it heats up he takes a bottle of beer out of the refrigerator and then eats the chili and drinks the beer standing at the kitchen counter. It's been two days since Vonda Jean threatened to dump Bane on the side of the road but Hard knows her patience is not infinite. He finishes the dinner, puts the dishes in the sink and heads to the garage where he lifts the lid of the oblong freezer and gazes upon his frozen dog. The folds of the animal's black muzzle are stiff and frost has formed on his eyelids. In his current condition he reminds Hard of one of the Yukon poems he loves so well. He only wishes Bane fell doing battle with a wolf pack instead of at the unhinged hands of a sociopathic tanning technician.

Hard takes a red camp blanket from a shelf and spreads it on the floor of the garage. Grabs Bane by the front knees, hoists him out of the freezer and thuds him onto the blanket. The dog hits the floor with a force that makes Hard think for a second the corpse might crack in two, but Bane retains his structural integrity. Although Hard will not admit this to Vonda Jean, he is glad she insisted on not allowing Bane to be stuffed. Absent the spirit that animated him, Bane looks like nothing more than road kill. Hard realizes even the most skilled taxidermist would not be able to change that. Upbraids himself for having been sentimental. Then he folds the blanket over his late companion and, heaving, grunting, lifts the corpse and muscles it toward the driveway and into the bed of his pickup next to a metal can that contains a gallon of gasoline.

Back in the house, he grabs an unopened pint bottle of tequila and a worn Robert Service paperback. Tosses them on the front seat. Heads east from Twentynine Palms, then south on Gold Park Road and deep into the desert night. Hard turns on the radio to hear some music but after a couple of seconds realizes music does not dovetail with the gloomy nature of his mission so he punches the off button and continues his journey in respectful silence.

Hard ruminates about funerals as the truck glides through the starry blackness. He did a little research on the Internet and knows a thing or two about how different cultures deal with the dead. He knows about the Tibetan sky burials where the corpse is left on a rock in the Himalayas and birds dine on the remains until nothing is left but bleached bone. He read about Viking funerals where the dead warrior is placed on a boat that is then set aflame before being sent out to sea on the cold wind. And he learned about the Egyptians who entombed their pharaohs in vast pyramids with gold and jewelry—and sometimes living slaves—to accompany them to the afterlife. Hard also did some research into pet cemeteries but concluded there was something effeminate about them, something sappy and weak; Bane was a masculine dog, a burly canine paragon and Hard doesn't want him to spend eternity in Pet Heaven Park next to some old lady's Labradoodle. Where was the dignity in that?

Bane is deserving of a grand send off and Hard regrets not being able to provide one. He thought briefly about doing the Viking version at the Salton Sea and concluded that not only would procuring a small boat on short notice be difficult in the desert, but should anyone see him—not unlikely since much of the Salton Sea coastline is accessible to motorists—it would be difficult to explain what the police chief of Desert Hot Springs was doing there with a flaming dingy and a defrosting Rottweiler.

The road dead-ends twenty minutes later and Hard pulls over. Throws a flashlight, the book and bottle of tequila into a knapsack, climbs out of the truck. Lashes the gallon of gasoline to the knapsack. Looks toward the mountains in the distance, their hulking silhouette rising from the desert floor. Hard fills his lungs with the cool night air and picks a spot on the mountaintop; that will be his point of reference. Then he hoists the corpse over his back and, bending under the weight, sets off into the night. A pale crescent moon hangs over the rocky Mojave landscape; juniper and mesquite trees cast weird shadows along the desert plain. Hard trudges along, stumbling occasionally under his burden, but remains on his feet. He's already miles away from any living human but he doesn't want to perform his task near the road. He's calculated that he'll cover a mile of this terrain in about twenty minutes, even with the mass he's carrying.

Five minutes into his walk, Hard begins to sweat. Bane's body is not only heavy, it's unwieldy in its frigid state and Hard has to keep shifting his weight to keep the dog on his shoulders. He is breathing heavily, panting at the exertion; this kind of weight is a lot for a young man to hump through the desert and Hard isn't exactly a spring flower. He thinks back to basic training over two decades earlier, brutal hikes under scorching sun, toting packs that weighed what he's carrying tonight. Pleased he hasn't keeled over, he imagines the headline: LOCAL LAW ENFORCEMENT OFFICIAL COLLAPSES BURYING DEAD PET. Is he out of his mind? Hard is brought back from contemplation of his potential humiliation by the strain in his lower back; he adjusts the weight again. Doesn't want to pull a muscle. Ten minutes more and he's already sweated through his undershirt. Feels his heart beating a tattoo in his ribcage. Starts to worry that Bane could begin to thaw out before they reach the destination. What would that smell like? Not good. The breeze on his face reminds him of the coolness of the evening. He'll have time. Hard sees his own shadow in front of him, cast by the moonlight. He'd like to look up and see the stars but the weight of his cargo keeps his head canted forward. Maybe Canis Major is visible tonight, Hard's favorite constellation. Behold Sirius the Dog Star, brightest in the sky, a stellar tribute to Bane.

Rivulets of sweat run down Hard's shaved dome and face. Checks his watch. Twenty minutes of walking is a mile. Five minutes to go. Hard told himself he'd walk a mile in to the desert and he'll be damned if he does anything less. He may ignore marital vows, laws even—it does not matter what other people want—but when Police Chief Harding Marvin tells *himself* he's going to do something, he knows he'll do it.

He steps on a rock and tweaks his ankle but catches himself before he puts all his weight down. Loses his balance and recovers, steps lightly like a little dance before straightening out with a grunt, re-orienting with the mountaintop and getting back on his route. Deeper he walks, stumbling through the desiccated creosote bushes, the night breeze drying his moist face. Five minutes later, Hard exhales through his mouth, gets down on his knee and, with the aspect of Mary in the Pieta, lowers Bane to the ground. Takes a moment to catch his breath. Looks up at the sky, the stars. Can't discern Canis Major but spots Ursa Major, the bear. He's glad there's an animal up there. Likes the symmetry of it, the connection between stars and earth and it makes him feel less alone. Around him there's nothing but emptiness. Reflects on his good fortune at being born with a sense of direction or he might just wander off into the Nothing.

A little fortification is in order. Some consecration of the circumstances. Hard takes the bottle of tequila out of his knapsack and unscrews the top, puts it to his lips, tilts his head back and swallows. Relishes the burn in his throat, regrets for a moment he neglected to bring salt and lemon but reminds himself this isn't a party. By the third belt he's a little lightheaded. Realizes he better get down to business. Hard places the tequila gently on the ground, screws the bottle into the dirt to make sure it doesn't tip over and detaches the gallon of gasoline from the knapsack. He stands over Bane for a moment, remembering the joy he shared with the dog. *Shared* wasn't the right word exactly, since he had no idea if Bane felt any joy, although he did wag his tail whenever it was just the two of them. What Hard will miss most about Bane is how he feels when they're together in the desert or the mountains, beneath the vast sky, man and beast in the primordial world. It's always just the two of them, no one else there, and it's beautifully uncomplicated. It was easier than being with Nadine who has become a goddamn unguided missile. And it was sure as hell more pleasant than being with Vonda Jean. Hard plain and simple preferred Bane to humans and now the pleasure of his company would be denied him until the end of Time. He really could kill Nadine for doing this. She's lucky he hasn't already. *Goddamn* why did he talk to her that night in the AM/PM on Highway 60? Why couldn't he have just walked away instead of falling right into the honey pot? The woman jams a *fork* into his neck, wields a kitchen utensil with deadly force, would have bled to death if she'd hit the carotid, and then she poisons the one living creature he interacted with on a daily basis and still cared about.

Now Hard grinds his knees on the desert floor, a supplicant. His dead dog lies prostrate before him like an offering to an utterly indifferent Deity who clearly has no use for Harding Marvin. And he's here because of Nadine. If he doesn't kill the woman at least he can put the fear of God into her, make her think there's a target on her back, create a sense of the acute spiritual discomfort he feels, the sense that something wrong is happening and cannot be stopped.

Takes another swig from the tequila. Then pulls out his cell phone and dials. One, two, three, four rings, then that voice, the one that makes him want to strangle her, tells him to leave a message.

"Nadine you fuckin' cunt." Hard turning on the charm. "I know what you did to Bane and I want you to know you're going to spend the rest of your life looking over your pretty shoulder." That feels good. Emboldened and exhilarated by the tequila, the delivery of this threat buoys him. Clicks the phone shut. If nothing else that should make her worry. It's not like she can report him for it either, since she killed his dog. Let her try to explain that one. His anger at Nadine is an animating force, coursing through him, making his cells howl in wordless grief. Hard is most alive when he hates something and right now it's Nadine and what he's feeling for her is positively vivifying. But the rage slowly subsides, like a tide washing out to sea, and Hard is left with the sadness of the dead dog at his feet. Realizes that, as much as he'd like to, staying in the desert all night is not an option. There's work in the morning, responsibilities. He needs to focus on the task at hand.

Hard pours the gasoline over Bane soaking the fur from stem to stern. Although he is drunk, he is not so drunk that he doesn't know he should place the container, which still has a small amount of gasoline in it, several feet away from the drenched corpse. That would be embarrassing: How'd you blow yourself up, Hard? Lighting your dead dog on fire? Then he returns to the body and gets down on one knee. Thinks about praying—*God bless the soul of this dog*—but Hard isn't big on religion and since the feeling is more reflexive than real, it quickly dissipates.

He removes a book of matches from the pocket of his khakis, strikes one and drops it on the animal's haunch. Flames immediately engulf the body and in a few seconds the acrid stench of burning fur fills the air. There is something primal about fire, something cleansing, and Hard stares down at the blaze for over a minute before he moves. From the knapsack he retrieves the Robert Service paperback and the flashlight; his face lit by the flaming pet, Hard opens the book. Fumbles with the flashlight but gets it aimed at the page, then begins to read the poem "My Dog." In a ringing voice that carries over the hard desert plain toward the distant mountains, Hard intones the words.

By the time he reaches the end, desolate tears flow. In public Hard is not the kind of man who will display any emotion other than anger. Sadness, which he is capable of feeling deeply, is something he will never reveal to an audience. But alone here in the desert under the stars of Ursa Major and the eternal night sky, he lets the melancholy course through him, and as flames consume his dead dog, his friend and boon companion, Hard is wracked with heaving convulsive sobs. He cries for his lost youth and grown sons and dead marriage. He cries for his powerful, strong, inspiring dog, his *late* dog, a dog that embodied qualities that a human could on his best days only try to emulate. Hard feels weak, pathetic even, but the tequila has done its job and he doesn't care at all so he lets it flow and then raises his arms to the heavens and roars a deep sound, rough and resonant, that's beyond words and thoughts and is pure emotion and deep grief coming from a bottomless well he hasn't drunk from in what feels like years, and he yells and rumbles and groans and stomps, the demons running free, venting, purifying, and the fire consumes the flesh and the glow dances on Hard's face and he screams and cries banshee wails and the sounds drift into the still desert night mingling with the smell of the fire, the wood and the burning flesh, and time drifts, he has no idea how far, it could be minutes or an hour and then Hard suddenly is exhausted and he sinks down near the pyre, his dead comrade partially consumed now and he puts the tequila to his lips and swallows deeply, feels the lightning down his throat all the way to his heart that throbs in quick sorrow.

/

Hard feels the weight of his head, never a good sign. There is a dull ache at the base of his skull and it's radiating upward, valiantly attempting to join forces with the sharp pain pushing up from his temples. Adding to this, something percussive is going on behind his eyes. There's no sense of his body below the neck except for his bile-filled stomach. And he hasn't opened his eyes yet. Hard lies in bed in his boxers. He has no recollection of going to sleep, doesn't remember driving home. Steels himself for the onslaught of daylight and the havoc that will ensue as his cornea sends a terrified message to his weakly pulsing brain receptors—*danger, sunlight!*—that in turn will alert the pain center to hit the panic button. He opens his right eye a crack. The predictable sensation of hot knives being inserted is mitigated by the fact that Vonda Jean no longer is in the bed. Already things are looking up.

Hard rolls on his side and waits for his stomach to settle. This takes a moment as the various internal ducts recalibrate and determine whether or not to send the contents of the Marvin stomach pouring out. The tequila drenched volcano rumbles, threatens, sloshes its sour lava but mercifully fails to erupt. Hard places a tentative foot on the floor; the brain seems preoccupied with its own horrifying situation and the pressure of the floor against the pad of his foot does not provoke an unmanageable reaction. This leads Hard to place his other foot down. Collects himself for the task at hand: standing. Takes a deep breath and tries to ignore the sensation that a preternaturally strong and malevolent chimpanzee is manhandling his cerebral cortex. One, two, three: pushes his hands against the sheets and...there, he's standing. Wobbles. The stomach again, riled. Hard waits a moment for the seas to calm. He lurches toward the bathroom.

He throws some water on his face. Opens the medicine chest, sees a bottle of eye drops. Puts them in and blinks. This does not help his monumental headache, but the moistness of his eyes augurs a positive future. He gargles mouthwash and spits it out. Looks at his stubbly face and considers shaving for a moment but decides this is entirely too ambitious a plan. He opens a bottle of extra-strength Tylenol and swallows four.

"Any coffee left?"

Vonda Jean is cooking eggs at the kitchen stove. She wears workout clothes, her hair pulled back with a clip. She tells Hard to help himself.

Dressed in a robe, still unsteady, Hard takes a ceramic cup from the pressed wood cabinet and fills it with coffee. "You go for a run?"

"It's a beautiful day," she says. "Where'd you go last night?" Her voice sounds like broken glass.

"You asked me to get rid of Bane, so I did." His own voice sounds to him as if it's coming from someone else, somewhere else, some place far away. Hard takes the coffee and goes to the living room; he does not want to engage with Vonda Jean any further right now. He sits in his recliner and sips the coffee. Through the picture window of their hilltop home he looks east over Twentynine Palms. The town has grown into a little metropolis since the Marvins settled here over twenty years ago, the population closing in on thirty thousand now. There's a big new hotel being built and retirees, artists and students at the new community college are moving in because of the good land values. And all that's not counting the upwards of five thousand Marines at the combat training base just outside of town. Hard considers the place well on its way to being a redneck Palm Springs and he likes the idea of being mayor. Doesn't just like it, but *puffs up* at the thought. In Los Angeles, two former police chiefs had run for mayor and been elected. One of them had even been a black guy and that was before black guys were getting elected to anything. It's as good a starting point for a political career as any and Hard intends to find out how soon he can file papers for the next election.

The knock at the front door is as welcome as shingles. Vonda Jean has girlfriends in the neighborhood and sometimes they arrive unannounced to visit before work. Hard has requested she tell her friends to call before stopping in but the women either don't care or, more likely, Vonda Jean hasn't bothered to relay his instructions.

Vonda Jean's voice from the next room: "Hard, can you get the door? I'm still eating breakfast."

He does not like this at all. It's bad enough they drop by without calling, now he has to drag himself across the room and pretend to be nice to one of Vonda Jean's friends when the mere thought of human company makes him more ill than he already is. He takes another sip of his coffee before placing the mug on an end table, then rises and ties his robe. Pads toward the door, fighting the Mexican Revolution in his gut. When Hard opens the door and sees Arnaldo Escovedo and Cali Pasco, two detectives from the Desert Hot Springs Police Department, his bloodshot eyes narrow and his head tilts slightly to one side.

"Sorry to bother you, Chief," Detective Escovedo says.

Desert Hot Springs Police Headquarters is nearly an hour to the west of Twentynine Palms and Hard immediately thinks there must be some kind of disaster. No one from work has ever ventured to his home, so he has no context for the current situation. "What are you doing here?" Hard trying to keep any sense of doom out of his voice. He regrets cursing out Escovedo the other day; had the man filed a grievance?

Detective Escovedo produces an official-looking piece of paper. Pasco is looking directly into his eyes. She's an attractive woman. For a moment he thinks Vonda Jean is going to accuse him of having an affair with her. He hopes she stays in the kitchen. "Chief, we have a warrant to search your house," Escovedo says.

Hard's mind rockets back to last night: the desert, the dog, the fire. The fire! Was he supposed to get a permit for the fire? Who could have seen him in the wash of scrub? He is certain there was no one around for miles. And even if it is illegal, and yes, it probably is, this is the jurisdiction of the Sheriff's Department, not the Desert Hot Springs Police. What are his own people doing here asking to search his house, no, not asking but *telling* him they're going to go through his home? Reflexively Hard grabs the piece of paper out of Detective Escovedo's hand and stares at it. Rendered in bold print at the top of the page are the words **Search Warrant.** At the bottom of the page is the signature of Judge Allan Diemer, a magistrate Hard knows to be rigid. Now Hard is desperately hoping this is some kind of horrible practical joke that will be revealed to him in a moment, people jumping out with video cameras, shouting happy birthday or April Fool's, but he does a quick survey of his logy mind and remembers it's not his birthday and it's November, not April, and no one jumps out with a video camera yelling anything, the only sounds the cars rolling by on the long highway below.

Until Vonda Jean pipes up from the next room. "Hard, who is it?"

"Some folks from the force."

Vonda Jean appears in the doorway. "Howdy," she says. "Should I put more coffee on?"

"They're here to search the house." No one says anything for a moment. Arnaldo and Cali look at Hard; Vonda Jean does too. Hard looks out the door toward the desert. A shaft of sunlight falling through the picture window illuminates a river of dust motes that refract the light as they float and twist in a chaotic ballet. Cali and Arnaldo exchange an uncomfortable glance.

"This house?" Vonda Jean says. Her voice rises slightly at the end of the second word. "What for?"

Cali tells her that someone Hard knew was murdered last night and before she can say another word, Vonda Jean asks, "So why are you here?"

Arnaldo says, "M'am, would you mind stepping out of the house, please? Chief, I'm going to have to ask you to do the same thing."

At this moment two Sheriff's Deputies appear in the doorway, young men in their thirties, ex-Marines. Hard knows them both, nods hello as he and Vonda Jean walk past them and on to their scrubby lawn. The Deputies greet them neutrally. There won't be any fraternization this morning.

The Marvins are standing on the street looking toward their house. The sun is still low in the sky but not as hot as it was yesterday. Hard sees a red-tailed hawk soaring overhead, searching for prey. He can feel Vonda Jean looking at him. She says, "You want to tell me what the hell this is about?" **-bc.**

Scott Bradfield

HAPPY TO BE NICE

Dear Mom and Dad,

I miss you both very much.

Life here at the Company is very good. I like my life here at the Company very much. We make very good microwave ovens for people to enjoy all the time. Do you guys have a good microwave oven to enjoy? My boss says I can offer you one of our outdated models at 20% off the normal retail price, but only if you act now. I like my boss very much. If you met my boss, you would definitely like him, too.

They treat me very good here at the Company. My boss is very good to me. He sees to it that me and my fellow employees get all the exercise we need every Saturday between one and one-thirty. That's all the exercise I can handle, boy, that's for sure. Afterwards, my heart's beating like a rabbit's.

I cannot think of anything more to say. I sure miss you both very much. I miss our kitchen, even though we didn't have all the latest appliances, such as this really good microwave oven we make here at the Company. Actually, we don't make the microwave oven right here at the Company. But we write lots of memos that help nice, hard-working people in South Korea make them. This is because we believe in exporting democracy throughout the world.

I could not be happier than I am here at the Company. They could not take better care of me. My boss is a very good guy who takes very good care of me, so please stop writing him with your concerns. You have nothing to worry about so long as my boss is in charge, so please don't worry yourselves unduly about those ridiculously exaggerated news reports you may be hearing in the liberal media. They are just a pack of lies. Especially that stuff about radiation levels, and lack of proper hygiene facilities.

They treat me so good here. I am so very happy.

Can I please come home now?

Love, Danny Boy

Dear Mom and Dad,

I guess you weren't listening. Everything's fine. Really really fine. How can I assure you that everything is fine? I miss you both very much.

Today I got married. Me and the other guys in my Assumption Level are all very happy, except maybe Petey, who told me that he isn't like other guys but the Company won't believe him. Our wives are very happy too. We got married in the main Audio-Visual Room, which they kindly decorated with pink crepe paper swans. Our wives all cried when the Company Chairman announced: "I pronounce you all husbands and wives!" So did Petey, come to think of it. It was a lovely ceremony. Afterwards, we had cake and ice cream.

Meanwhile, everything is getting better and better at the Company. Production levels are up. Sales levels are up. Pre-orders are up. Profit levels are not up, but only because those bad people at the Other Company have been trying to undercut our profit strategy. Pretty soon we will turn the tables on them, boy. We will start undercutting their profit strategy, and then they'll be sorry. Their profits will go down and they will suffer for what they tried to do to us. Eventually they will not be allowed to exercise, or see movies, or enjoy Private Time with their spouses. By the way, I will be spending Private Time with my new spouse very soon. As soon as we get over this little bump in our profit strategy, that is.

I think her name is Marlena. She is very nice. My boss says she's great in the sack. I'm sure he wouldn't say it if he didn't mean it.

Which reminds me. My boss says those recently-returned (but practically brand-new) microwave ovens are ready for shipping, and because he is concerned that you guys may be missing out, he will make this one-time offer of a 25% reduction in the retail price, but please don't tell anybody else because they'll feel cheated, especially if they paid retail at the Store.

My boss says we will be having Family Day very soon and you can come visit and check out these microwave ovens for yourselves. I know I've told you we'd be having Family day several times now, but this time I really mean it.

Love, Danny Boy

Dear Mom and Dad,

I'm sorry I haven't written for a while. I have been very busy here at the Company. Mainly I have been busy getting yelled at by my boss, who only wants the best for me. Apparently I have not been taking my job seriously. I have allowed myself to drift into poor marketing-response strategies. If everybody here at the Company was to drift into poor marketing-response strategies, serious consequences would face all Mankind. The Other Company would take over everything. They would say things like: Those people lack motivational excellence. They are ripe for the picking. They can't even sell outdated microwave ovens to their own Moms and Dads. How good could their microwave ovens be, anyway?

They really are pretty good, Mom and Dad. I wouldn't lie to you. They're definitely worth 30% below retail, which is the offer my Boss proposed I offer you, mainly because we're related.

My boss says he wants me to get "my ass in gear." He claims my ass has not been in proper gear for weeks. I think my ass may have fallen seriously out of gear when I started writing you guys and thinking about my home back there in Happy Villas. I miss Happy Villas very much.

Would you please send me a photo with your next letter? Of Happy Villas, I mean. I forget so much about it. Like sometimes when I'm lying on my cot at night I try to envision Happy Villas, but all I can envision is this microwave oven I can't convince you to buy, which is now available at 30% reduction from the full retail price. Would you please reconsider this once-in-a-lifetime offer, Mom and Dad? Maybe that would get my boss off my back.

Love, Danny Boy

Dear Mom and Dad,

Today I am a man.

My boss says he doesn't want to submit a low-assessment monitoring report to the Board next week, but he may not have any choice. In order to put some "wind in my sails," he kindly arranged Private Time between me and Marlena, and it was something special, believe you me. I am a really lucky guy. I hope I never have to enjoy Private Time with Marlena ever again.

Private Time with Marlena was really, really good. Private Time with Marlena was really, really horrible. I feel very happy and ashamed. I wanted to tell you both right away.

Marlena "taught me the ropes," just as my boss predicted. As luck would have it, Marlena turned out to be very good at teaching people the ropes. I think it must be because she has been married before. "Practice makes perfect," she said while teaching me "the ropes." I may need more practice. In a few months from now, that is.

Marlena is very beautiful and attractive. She is missing some of her front teeth and her hair is falling out, but I don't mind. She also has very wide hips, but my boss says that's good for us "randy old boys," which is how he referred to him and myself. "More cushion for more pushin'," that's my boss's motto. I never got around to doing much pushing, by the way. Marlena says I am very great in the sack.

Actually, what she said was: You aren't any worse than what I've been getting.

That Marlena. I love my new wife very much.

Maybe it's a bit early, but maybe I should start calling you guys Grandma and Grandpa?

Love, Danny Boy

Dear Mom and Dad,

Last night I couldn't sleep. I forgot to tell you this in my last letter, but sometimes I worry at night, maybe every night, I'm not sure. I started worrying that I hadn't heard from you or that something had happened to you. I started worrying that I might be thinking unproductive thoughts about running away from the Company and living in the woods, and never enjoying conjugal relations with Marlena ever again. And then I started worrying that running away to the woods might lead to poor-coordination strategies, which would, of course, adversely effect my effectivity ratios.

Some nights when I worry I sit up in bed and observe my fellow employees sleeping on their cots. Their eyes are all closed. They don't appear to be worrying, but who knows? All except for Bernard, who was recently transferred here from Product Development.

Bernard is sitting up in the darkness and looking straight at me.

If we don't bust out of here soon, Bernard whispers, we're going to have two heart attacks apiece before we're twenty. Are you listening, pal? If you're listening, nod your head.

Of course I am listening. But I'm not nodding my head.

I don't want to encourage him.

Was I happy as a little boy at Happy Villas, Mom and Dad? Would you please send me pictures and tell me stories of my former happiness?

Love, Danny Boy

Dear Mom and Dad,

Thank you for your lovely photos of Happy Villas. I miss Happy Villas very much.

I took the photos to Marlena's suite but she didn't answer the door. Her door kept telling me You are attempting an unscheduled intermission. I told the door Marlena is my wife and I want to show her something. The door said Your unscheduled intermission is being reported to Central Processing. I said Please don't report me to Central Processing, please just let me see my wife. The door said Maybe just this time I won't report you. But you have to leave right now. You have to stop attempting an unscheduled intermission.

Happy Villas is very beautiful, and just as I remember. It is not at all the way I remember it, but that's only because I may be losing my mind. I wish there were some photos of you, Mom and Dad, but even without you in them these photos are really special. I especially love the Burger-Matic Drive Through picture with the 30% discount offer on french fries. I also like the Happy Bee Pre-School Play Center picture with the two-for-one monthly Child-Care Happy Bonanza offer attached. How convenient that so many wonderful places at Happy Villas produce such lovely photos to remind me of home.

Please don't send me any more pictures of home, Mom and Dad. Or at least wait until I'm feeling better.

That's a very lovely photo, my boss said when I got back to my desk. He was pointing at the Half Price Park-Day Visitor Voucher pinned to my bulletin board and nodding supportively.

It's Happy Villas, I told him. It's where I grew up.

I didn't know what else to say. I don't want to disappoint my boss by saying something uninteresting. He might stop liking me.

Why are you breathing funny? my boss asked. Are you okay, Danny Boy? Would you like a glass of water?

Please, I said. A glass of water would be nice.

I started to cry.

You seem upset, my boss said. He put a hand on my shoulder. I hate being touched. I love being touched. It makes me think of Marlena, my wife. Whom I love very much.

Your next water break isn't scheduled until eleven thirty, my boss said.

Everybody is looking at us. Baby Girl Blue. Billy Boy. Sandy Honey. Even Bernard at the water cooler. He is smiling. I can't stop crying. I just want to run home to Happy Villas and hide under the bed.

We've got a code seven, my boss tells his collar phone.

Repeat, a code seven.

Which is when the office doors open and the paramedics arrive and that's all I remember.

Except that I like the paramedics very much.

Love, Danny Boy

Dear Mom and Dad,

I am feeling much better now.

I am working hard on my effectivity ratio. My hospital bed has a little desk on the side with a computer terminal. I like my hospital bed very much.

I am very sleepy. I have to go now.

Promotional Copy I Have Been Working On During my ReCuperation:

Our microwave ovens don't give you cancer

Our microwave ovens aren't responsible for the drinking water

Our microwave ovens don't leak

Many of the radiation threats you hear about from the alternative news station which produces lies have nothing to do with our microwave ovens, and anyway, they never really happened

Our microwave ovens

I am feeling better every day.

Every day I bring myself closer to perfection and happiness.

Every day I bring myself closer to a job in middle management.

Every day I wake up happier and happier.

I love my job very much.

Tonight I had a terrible dream. I dreamed that I found my way back to Happy Villas and was calling your names and couldn't hear you but knew you were out there. Then I arrived in your bedroom and found stacks of microwave ovens, rows and rows of them, like chickens in a coop. Mom and Dad! I called. Is that you? Mom and Dad! You didn't answer. I knew you were nearby. I could hardly move because the bedroom was so packed with microwave ovens.

And then I woke in the crowded hospital ward. There we were, rows and rows of us in our hospital beds, poor employees with inefficient profit strategies. We were all medicated. We were all awaiting dramatic comebacks in our profit strategies. If we didn't enjoy dramatic comebacks, we might have to stay in the hospital forever.

Which is when I turned to see him standing beside my bed, holding an unmarked aerosol canister and wearing dark military fatigues.

Don't act surprised, Bernard told me. We're getting you out of here.

Then he sprayed me with the canister. And I went back to sleep.

Dear Mom and Dad,

You may be wondering why you haven't heard from me. This is because I have joined the Armed Resistance which seeks to overthrow the Company, the Board of Directors, and maybe even the Government. "Joined" is a tricky word in this context, since technically I was kidnapped from my hospital bed and taken to a basement somewhere in Supplies. I have been given a special aerosol canister with a shoulder harness and a set of smelly military fatigues. They shaved my head and changed my name to Tania. I don't know about you, but I like the name Tania very much.

Who do you work for? I asked my new friend, Bernard.

Who do we work for.

Who do we work for, then?

We work for the end of tyranny. We work to overthrow the corrupt administrative system and replace it with a completely perfect administrative system of justice for all.

If we take over, can we visit Happy Villas? It's been so long since I've seen my parents. I don't even remember what they look like.

If we take over the Company, you can visit Happy Villas any time you want.

I looked around at the crowded basement, which contained lots of empty cardboard boxes with the words One (1) Brand New Microwave Oven on them. Some wooden chairs, several large green plastic bags of refuse, and cigarette butts everywhere.

Okay, I told Bernard. Should we get started? Or should we wait until the others get here?

Bernard placed a hand on his shoulder-strapped aerosol canister. Then he looked over both shoulders.

What others? he asked.

Love, Danny Boy

Dear Mom and Dad,

Well, you probably saw it coming. But I didn't see it coming, boy. I didn't see it coming at all.

Bernard, of course, marched me straight upstairs and turned me over to my boss, who was expecting us. Once I realized what was happening, I pulled out my aerosol canister and sprayed it directly into my boss's gas mask, which is when my canister released a refreshing scent of potpourri.

My boss's canister, on the other hand, was loaded for bear. Some sort of nerve gas which made me collapse on the floor and writhe spastically, while understanding everything he had to say.

What my boss had to say (after removing the plasticene-wrapped business-card-sized Statement of Rights from his wallet) was this: You have the right to fair treatment in a court of law, if and whenever this aforementioned court gets around to it. You have the right to the best possible attorney you can possibly afford. You have the right to purchase a Microwave Oven, at forty percent discount, from the bearer of these aforesaid rights. You have the right to writhe around on the floor spastically. You have the right to think contrary to popular opinion, so long as nobody finds out. You have the right to watch commercial TV. You have the right to work for the Company. You have the right to have your rights read to you. And finally, these rights are not to be held tantamount in the face of opposition by any board member of the Company, or by any failure of the Company to grant them. The Company will see what it can do, that's all we're saying. Let's not get hung up on the specific wording, okay?

Oh well.

Hope to hear from you soon, Danny Boy

Dear Mom and Dad,

What a relief. It turns out that my lawyer won't be some anonymous slimeball, after all. My lawyer will be none other than my old friend (and erstwhile co-conspirator), Bernard.

You are being charged with insurrection, mutiny and conspiracy, Bernard told me this morning during our twenty minutes of Legal Time. You are being charged with holding a low-effectivity ratio, along with several other charges we probably won't know for a while yet—we're still working on them. So far as I see it, we throw ourselves on the mercy of the court and just hope, well, that things don't turn out like last time. I mean, like the last time I told a guy to throw himself on the mercy of the court and, you know. He did.

Bernard has me sign and initial some papers confessing all my heinous deeds, along with several heinous deeds I never actually got around to committing. Bernard's logic is as follows: that had I gotten away with my original heinous deeds, I would have gained enough confidence to commit many of these uncommitted ones, and so forth. There's something pretty logical and persuasive about Bernard.

Before he left, Bernard gave me a big hearty slap on the back. I couldn't help thinking that a big hearty slap on the back wasn't what I needed right now.

Bernard told me: I'll get these papers up to Legal and while I'm gone, you do me a favor, Danny Boy.

I sat down on my thin cotton mattress and looked at the commercial TV monitor, which was featuring one of my favorite commercial presentations: "Own Your Own Microwave Oven Part VI."

And what would that be, Bernard? I asked.

The commercial presentation concerned this happy couple who really loved one another and their children, but somehow their lives weren't up to snuff. The house was a mess, meals were bland and flavorless, and they just didn't get excited about waking up in the morning. Then, lo and behold. A brand new microwave oven.

Bernard watched me affectionately from the doorway.

Don't go fomenting any more insurrections without me, he said. Dig?

Love, Danny Boy

Dear Mom and Dad,

Well, I guess it's like those commercial presentations always tell us. Everything works out eventually, especially if you can afford suitable legal representation.

At first, though, it didn't work out well at all. In fact, it worked out kind of horrible. The Company sentenced me to death by hanging in the public Commissary. I must admit that I wasn't too happy with that initial judgment at all.

But then it turned out that several of my replacements in Media Relations went kind of nutty. They began suffering the usual breakdowns and low productivity ratios and spontaneous weeping, that sort of stuff. Then there were the mass shootings, and before you knew it, a couple of my fellow employees actually tried to foment an insurrection without the authorization of Bernard (which really teed Bernard off, I can tell you). By the time the dust settled, they just didn't have anybody left to run the Copy Machine.

Which was good news for yours truly, since me and the Copy Machine are old buds.

Nobody was happier than Marlena, who came to my room last night when I didn't go to hers. Marlena is very loving and attractive. She is also great in the sack, boy. Is she ever.

We'll call him Roger if it's a boy and Marlena if it's a girl, Marlena decided afterwards, smoking her filterless menthol cigarettes and spitting shards of tobacco all over the clean sheets. We'll work hard for years and years. We'll send little Roger or Marlena to Day Care, where he or she will learn to read, write, and establish good Media Relations regarding the latest generation of microwave ovens. Then, as soon as our little angels are paying the bills, we'll post our sorry butts off on the first bus to Happy Villas, where we won't have to engage in Media Relations ever again. It's not that I'm against Media Relations, understand. It's just that most of the guys who work here—your boss, for example—don't have any idea how to treat a lady. Not like my Danny boy. Even if he's not quite so good as Bernard is in the sack.

Love, Danny Boy

Dear Danny Boy,

We sure miss our big beautiful baby boy all the time. We are so proud of you all the time.

Our new microwave oven arrived today. It is really beautiful. We were so surprised we didn't even mind the fact that we hadn't ordered it. We meant to order it, but we never got around to it. After all, we're still paying for the last microwave ovens we ordered. We enjoy all of our new microwave ovens very much.

We sure can't wait to meet Marlena! Are we grandparents yet? Please promise us you will cherish your little babies and take good care of them and not send them out to work until they are at least five years old, which is coddling them we know but it's such a precious little time we have with our babies as it is. Enjoy your babies very much, and try to stop by the Day Care/Training Center to visit them on your way to and from the office every day. They grow up so fast.

We wonder about you often. We wonder what you look like often. We sure love our retirement jobs here at the carburetor factory. Someday when you buy your big retirement house by the ocean can we come live with you?

Can we please come live with you soon?

We better go now. We miss you often. We sure love our lives here at Happy Villa. Sometimes, when we think about you, we even remember what you look like. A certain color of hair, for instance. Or your complexion, which is a certain hue. You are such a big beautiful boy. Your lovely wife Marlena must be extremely pleased.

Please don't send us any more microwave ovens.

Love, Mom and Dad

P.S. Please enjoy your life as much as we are enjoying ours. Please think good thoughts often, as we are taught to do on government-sponsored commercial TV presentations. Please know that your parents love you all the time, even when we are sometimes remiss in sending you birthday cards, or in remembering the color of your hair. Please think of the glass as half full rather than half empty, or even just partially filled rather than almost empty. Please write to us often. Please get us out of here. Please please please! Help help help!

Samantha Cohen

Gray light leaks through the glass door and I've given up trying to sleep. The front door deadbolt doesn't work and for the millionth time I wonder whether this house is safe or a slightly heavier rain would collapse the ceiling. I imagine Amanda gathering up the neighborhood children and dressing them in matching jumpers, Von Trapp-style, putting the house together as an afternoon crafts project, singing on ladders and supergluing oversized popsicle sticks.

At this time of night I always feel surprised to be here in Amanda's bed, accidental somehow, but then I remember that now the bed belongs to both of us. I never made an official decision to move in; I just came out for a visit two years ago. On what was supposed to be my last night in town, Amanda kissed me and we had the kind of sex where we lost track of ourselves, of our boundaries, the kind where our non-physical parts mingled. I started dreaming parts of Amanda's dreams and she began thinking some of my thoughts. It was too hard to divvy correctly, to gather all of my original parts, so I had to stay.

/

I WATCH AMANDA laying on a bed of curls in her moonlight case and vacillate between jealousy and admiration. My mother always said that if I went to bed hungry, my soul would leave my sleeping body, wander off in search of filling things, and so Amanda and I keep ginger cookies and tins of frosting in the nightstand cabinet, dense things that take a while to digest. I can tell it's working because though her body looks vacuous, Amanda's soul is right here, the stuff among these dust particles, hovering. Her skin reflects all the light specks in the room, and I think that when the roof does collapse she'll sprout wings and flutter away and I'll be left here, covered in ceiling pulp.

/

WHEN I SLIDE MYSELF OUT THE SIDE OF THE BED, Amanda makes a whiny *mmm* sound as though she's about to protest, but then she appears to settle more deeply. I tiptoe down the spiral staircase, remembering to duck my head for the too-short part, thinking that maybe this staircase was built by the smallest children, who wanted to prevent grownups from ascending to their lair.

I traverse the downstairs floor and descend to the basement. Amanda hates this basement bathroom—it's too cold, too dirty gray for her—but it's a place I love as much as I love the hammocks and the porch swing outside. It has a claw-foot tub and hot pink tiles around the mirror and it's the only room in this place with a door that locks.

I've been coming down here at this time almost every night, sitting clothed in the dry bathtub and thinking. Tonight I hold my green notebook against my bare knees and write it down for the first time: *I am pregnant.* It's a relief to write it. There have been no sperm but my stomach grows rounder, the skin stretching thin and taut; I measure my upper arm, my thigh. The metal end of the tape measure lands in the same spots it always has when I'm checking for symmetry. 15.4 for my right thigh, 7.1 for my left bicep. But I've stopped caring about symmetry. Now I'm checking for size. My limbs are the same but my belly expands outward, protruding gourd-shaped.

I've never kept a secret from Amanda. She even knows about the measuring. But I don't know how I'll explain this pregnancy. She'll laugh, think I'm joking; I'll probably say it as though I *am* joking. Maybe she'll try to make me take a pregnancy test. I'll ask if she thought the Virgin Mary took a pregnancy test and she'll shrug and tell me there was no Walgreens back then. Then she'll laugh and tell me that I couldn't have survived anyway, in a time when there wasn't any Walgreens. She'll get started in next on Jack in the Box—superstores and drive-thru french fries are two things for which Amanda lacks appreciation and therefore in her mind are intrinsically linked. I always grin through Amanda's playful chastising, allowing her to continue thinking that the toothpaste and Q-tips she uses are self-replenishing.

Last time I was at Walgreens, a stranger asked if I was pregnant. It's happened twice now and Amanda was there the time on the bus, when a middle-aged lady offered her seat. Laughing, Amanda placed her palm between my shoulder blades. "Maybe you should stop wearing empire waists," she suggested later.

/

I WRITE DOWN SOME WAYS IN WHICH I MAY HAVE GOTTEN PREGNANT:

1. God. In high school I spent all of sophomore year certain I was pregnant. My boyfriend and I used a condom, but condoms fail. I had promised myself I would wait to have sex until I was in love; I wasn't in love and didn't even love sex. Pregnancy seemed like an apt punishment for this self-betrayal. Regardless of the dots on my calendar, I checked my underwear every day for signs of blood. I stayed up at night thinking how I would have to be one of those girls who's sent away for a secret abortion, and also how there was a soul finished with the afterlife and ready to re-enter the world of the living, a soul that already lost all its knowledge and had entered my body as a kind of mid-world, and I'd have to be the one to boot it to some unnamed place where it might get lost in the shuffle. I stayed up at night asking God to make me bleed, checking in the bathroom every half hour. One night I vomited. Then I made a deal with God: *God,* I said, *please abort this baby that's growing inside me. I don't love Marco and I don't even love sex and what kind of a chance does a child have who isn't made from love? If I bleed tomorrow, you can make me pregnant whenever I have sex with my one true soul mate even if I think I'm not ready.* I bled the next morning and for seven subsequent weeks. My mother took me to the gynecologist, who put me on birth control pills to stop the dull brown seep. I never worried with my college boyfriend or after post-college one night stands. Maybe now God is keeping their end of the bargain.

2. Spontaneous generation. Science is made out of stories. The story of evolution, the story of Pangaea, the story of dinosaur extinction. I love these science stories, but the problem with science is that once a better story is found, the old story is abandoned. Spontaneous generation hasn't been disproven exactly. It's only been proven that spontaneous generation didn't happen in Louis Pasteur's flask. Spontaneous generation was first suggested by Aristotle, who was around way before Louis Pasteur and before the unquestionably-useful-but-maybe-insufficient scientific method. Aristotle believed that living beings were spawned from pneuma, "vital heat." It's possible that real, actual pneuma only exists very rarely. Maybe the last time it existed was in biblical times and now it exists between Amanda and me. Maybe the pneuma made a baby.

3. Egg mitosis. I've read that this is possible, although until now it's only happened in sterile glass beakers. Eggs each have twenty-three chromosomes and while they can't burrow the way sperm can, they can fuse to make a whole female person. The babies begun in beakers so far have been pretty underdeveloped, cognitively. Amanda and I are awkward around babies in general. When other adults make strange animal noises and crawl around on their knees, Amanda and I stand there, speak to the baby in our regular voices, saying things like, "Hey, baby, how's it going?" I worry about how we'll deal with a cognitively underdeveloped child. I imagine Amanda staring, paralyzed and uncertain. Still, I like the idea of being the first couple to conceive via natural egg mitosis; the idea of Amanda's egg traveling out of her and up into me, toward my center, huddling close with my egg, trading information, combining codes, the two drawn together like magnets, compelled toward creation.

/

I THINK ABOUT EVOLUTION. We've evolved from the sea—flippers into fingers and thumbs. We've become skin-covered and hairless and tall. We've developed the luxury of being able to sit in a waterless bathtub in an underground room thinking and thinking before taking any action, knowing no one will eat us, and that if we get hungry there are cucumbers and radishes growing outside, there's the drive-thru at Jack in the Box. Evolving the ability for egg mitosis doesn't seem impossible.

I feel the waves of nausea I've been anticipating. I get out of the tub, look at my face in the mirror. I'm wearing only shorts and, except for my circular belly, I look like a too-skinny avian thing, shrunken and underslept. My hair is short and it sticks up and out in all directions. I think of that sonnet about the black wires.

The rush comes then and I kneel and heave yellowish water into the bowl. Then I lay on the floor.

I brush my teeth and rub verbena lotion into my chest and arms before going upstairs to crawl back in bed with Amanda.

Amanda pretends not to notice the morning sickness. Maybe she thinks I've added 7 a.m. teeth-brushing to the list of other habits and rituals she knows would embarrass me to explain. Maybe she thinks I water plants at dawn now.

Or maybe Amanda knows about all of this. Amanda knows a million things that she thinks about extensively and then decides she doesn't know anymore. I should just tell her today, "I'm pregnant. You were right, when you thought that." Or maybe I'll just ask her, "What if I were pregnant?"

/

WHEN I ASCEND THE SPIRAL STAIRCASE to our sleeping loft, Amanda is upside-down on her yoga mat. Her eyes roll back to find mine and she smiles as she kicks her legs down. "You're up early," she says.

Amanda's eyes looked green upside-down but rightside-up they're gray with yellow rings. I imagine her four months from now, asleep in her flimsy white cotton thing, head resting on my spherical midsection, hands cupped on either side. The baby will fall in love with Amanda's sleepy *mmm* sounds, kick steadily as a response, trying to get closer to her. Amanda will smile and make more sleepy *mmm* sounds and the baby will kick, a positive-feedback loop, a chorus. I feel myself grin. "Is it 8:30 already?"

"8:45." She arches an eyebrow, walks toward and then past me, sidling her nose against my collarbone without breaking gait. I put on what's become my daytime uniform—black stretch pants and a black tank top—then walk back downstairs, grind coffee, set water to boil.

Our days always start like this, with coffee. Amanda works as a graphic designer—she spends workdays at the kitchen table or on the patio out back. Her favorite part of her job, I think, is that she gets to wear tulle to work. Amanda has half a closet full of pinafores, tutus and other sorts of lace and mesh garments she calls her "work clothes." Today she's wearing white thigh-highs and something gold that looks like it should belong to a figure skater.

In the time I've lived here, I've been a receptionist, a telephone fundraiser for political campaigns and a barista. Now I stay here all day and work on my book, *Starsucks: An Employee Memoir.* At least this is what I say I'm doing, if anyone asks, but mostly I sit on the couch reading music blogs or sitting across the table from Amanda reading aloud to her from the *Harper's* I get at Walgreens. When I start to feel annoying, I sit outside in a hammock, or downstairs in the tub.

/

AMANDA STRUTS UP TO ME, puff-chested. "Asha," she sing-songs, wrapping a forearm around my lower back.

"Yes?"

"I'm going to make us pancakes."

"But you hate sweet breakfasts."

"Yeah." She looks pensive. Then she shakes her curls and releases her forearm, runs the knuckly part of her hand from my shoulder to my elbow. "But, it will be fun."

I laugh. "Okay, then. Go make pancakes." I push at the plated part of Amanda's chest.

I think Amanda will be a good parent. She'll make things fun. We'll be good together. I'll buy toothpaste, she'll make pancakes.

/

I LOWER THE PLUNGER on the French press, pour coffee into two mugs, pour soy milk and agave into Amanda's. It occurs to me that caffeine probably causes birth defects. I'll have to become one of those women who browses the pregnancy section in the bookstore. I'll need to learn these things. I decide I'll leave my cup in front of me without sipping, that Amanda won't notice.

I glance over at Amanda. She's cracking an egg into a bowl of powder. "Will you go pick us blackberries for the pancakes?" she asks.

"Sure." When I walk outside, the blades of grass feel wet and hairy between my toes. Blackberries sprawl everywhere, tiny prizes for withstanding the murky white skies and blank white faces of the Northwest.

Careful! Watch out for the thorns, I imagine myself saying to a child grabbing fistfuls of berry, smashing grainy, red juice against her face. "Danny's Song" starts to play in my head as I pluck the biggest, darkest berries from the bramble. *He will be like she and me, as free as a dove, conceived in love, the sun is gonna shine above.* I bring two handfuls of berries into the kitchen, dig a thumb into Amanda's shoulder as I drop them into the bowl of batter. As I watch her stir, I think that she'll be into telling the child where all our food comes from. *Pancakes are made out of wheat flour. Wheat grows in fields in the middle of the country. And eggs. Where do eggs come from?* She could ask this because even tiny children know from storybooks that chickens lay eggs. I'll take the kid to Jack in the Box and we can talk about how potatoes grow underground.

Amanda and I sit at the painted red table and eat. "You've not been sleeping well," she says. It's not a question, so I don't respond. "I'll call Lora about the door lock if it bothers you. And if she's flaky again, we can just call a lock person. It can't bother her if we fix her door." Amanda spoons sour yogurt onto her stack. *People make it out of goat's milk!*

I nod, surprised that she noticed the deadbolt thing bothered me. I swallow syrupy pancake. "Thanks."

"I think she might be attached to that stupid staircase, though."

/

AFTER WE FINISH THE PANCAKES, I sit on the couch and open my PowerBook. I can see over Amanda's shoulder that she's working on a local puppetry theater website. Amanda keeps changing the colors of everything on her screen—pink, silver, royal blue. "You should make the stars cerulean," I suggest. "Cerulean is such a good color."

Amanda laughs. "Seer-oo-LEEN!" she squeals. "That's adorable-sounding!"

"That's how it is pronounced," I say.

"Um, I took design classes, darling." She sips her coffee, sets the cup back down. "It's suh-ROO-lee-uhn."

"Suh-ROO-lee-uhn is stupid," I say. Amanda and I both love being right, but neither of us is great about it. "It's a good color, though."

I look up cerulean in the online dictionary while Amanda changes the color of the stars.

/

AFTER A FEW HOURS, Amanda picks some kale from the garden, mixes it in a blender with beets and water. I eat this Amanda-food now—I've come to like it. I watch her pour the thick mixture into glasses. I join her at the table and we drink from straws; I feel the nutrients funneling through me, leaking into the place where the forming baby lives.

I decide it's time to tell her.

"I had a dream the other night," I say. I'm not sure how the dream I'm about to tell her relates to my pregnancy, but somehow it does. Amanda will figure it out. "It was kind of intense."

Amanda takes an exaggerated breath. "I'm prepared for intense."

"Okay, so I was driving on this highway along the coast and you were in the passenger seat. All these rabbits kept appearing everywhere. Like, they were coming out from under trees and bushes, and they were darting in front of the car. They were all over the highway and I couldn't help it."

"You started running over them?" Amanda says.

"Yes! I started running over them and you disappeared. I started crying and screaming your name and blood was spraying up onto the windshield and I didn't know what to do, so I just kept driving." My voice sounds breathy and weird.

"Baby. Being surrounded by rabbits is good. Rabbits mean trust and love and closeness. Good things. They're connected to the earth but ruled by the moon. You shouldn't run over rabbits."

I nod, then swallow. "But they mean fertility, too, right?"

Amanda stirs the bottom of her glass. Then she

looks up smiling. "Fertility like you want to fuck me like a rabbit," she says. I look down at my empty glass. "Hey," she says. I look up. "It could be for other things, too," she says. "For your book—creativity, productivity. Why? Can you think of something else?"

I shake my head.

"I think," she says, "maybe you should have just stopped the car. Wherever you were going maybe wasn't so important. I think it would have been okay to sit there, surrounded by all those rabbits." She sucks the remaining juice loudly through her straw. "I mean, don't you think?" Her eyes are all gray now, no yellow at all.

"Maybe," I say. "I'll think about this."

I get up to scrub the gritty red residue from our glasses.

/

I'M BACK ON THE COUCH, reading about miraculous historical pregnancies, when Amanda asks to see what I'm working on. I close my internet windows and find a passage of Starsucks for her. I read over the passage I'm about to give her.

Rule #42: If you are a person who freaks out about a wrongly made drink, you belong on my list of people who deserve to die:

Salt-and-Pepper Suit came in this morning. Despite the line, his drink was ready by the time he waited in line and paid. "Grande 120 degree double-cup skinny vanilla latte with two Equals," I announced as I handed him his double-cupped drink. I tried not to say it sarcastically. People just ask for two cups, as though paper grows on trees in a world where trees sprout up everywhere. He sipped and made a face. "Is this sugar-free?" he asked. "No," I said. "I'm sorry—I forgot you do sugar-free. Would you like me to remake it?"

He sighed, drastically, looked at his watch. "If you remake it, I'll be late for work, but I'm on this diet... ." He said this to himself. He sighed again. "Fine." He said it in this defeated-sounding baby voice. "Re-make it."

He'd glare and sigh, I already knew, through the whole steaming and tamping and temperature-taking process. I took down two more cups.

/

I HOLD MY COMPUTER OUT WITH BOTH HANDS. Amanda takes it, sits down cross-legged in front of me, reads. "This is sad," she says when she finishes.

"I know, right?" I say. "If having a wrongly made drink is the worst part of your day, you're doing pretty fucking well."

"No," she says, "he's not doing well. If he were happy, a wrongly made drink would be okay. But probably his life is so totally anguishing and dull that this latte is the only thing that inspires him to get up in the morning. And if that one thing he has control over, that he can look forward to being exactly how he wants it, is already fucked up, how can he go on with the rest of the day?"

I nod, lean back into the couch. "I didn't think about that," I say.

She traces the inseam of my pants, absently, with her finger, nods. "Not everyone gets to live in a treehouse," she says. She opens her mouth and wraps her lip-covered teeth around my calf. When she looks up she's laughing. She re-seats herself at the painted table.

I look at her in her metallic coating. I look at the treehouse. I feel a loosening, as though whatever tough fabric has been holding my insides in place has unwound, relaxed.

I walk down the basement steps, trying to appear nonchalant, clenching my abdominal muscles and my

PC muscles to hold my insides together. It's an awkward walk. I go into the bathroom, sit down on the toilet, pull down my sweatpants. I see it. Thick shiny red suspending scraggly purple-black chunks. It's everywhere, smeared and sticky on my thighs. Crusting in my cotton underpants. Sinking in rivulets toward a sad dark mass at the bottom of the toilet bowl.

I run a finger between my legs and hold it out in front of me. The finger makes me think of newborn mammals, goo-coated and albino pink. I consider using my hands to gather the stuff, shove it back inside me, beseech it to stick.

I wrap my arms around my naked thighs, pull them toward my chest. I rest my brow on my knees and hold myself there. I don't look back into the toilet bowl, but I don't flush either. Maybe if I wait long enough, all the blood will coagulate, find its way back through the body opening above it.

I lay on my side on the tile floor.

Maybe a long time passes. I hear creaking footsteps coming from the basement stairwell. "Asha?"

There's a knock. I don't say anything. Then the door opens a crack. "The door was locked," I say.

"Oh," her disembodied voice says. "It doesn't lock, actually. I thought it made you feel safe to think it did, though. We can get that fixed, too, if you want. Here. I brought you a present." A foamy-looking but hard gold ball rolls through the crack in the door. "Run it in the bath," Amanda's voice says. "It will make the water sparkly."

I look at the ball next to me on the tile.

"Also, I got you curly fries," she says. "I can pass them to you."

"You went through the drive-thru?" I ask.

"Yeah. The guy there? The one with the lip piercing? He says hi."

"Esteban." I can kind of see Amanda's profile. She's turned toward the washing machine, looking down.

"Yeah."

"Thanks. I'll get in the bath. Come back in like ten minutes with the fries."

The door closes. I wipe blood from the floor. I clean my thighs. I put all the tissues in the toilet. I flush.

I run the bath. The water is a shimmery yellow. Amanda-colored.

When I climb in the tub it's almost scalding, but I submerge my whole body right away. I swim my head under. It feels good to be burned by glitter-water. I reemerge, float.

/

THERE'S A KNOCK on the door. Amanda walks in; she places a foot on the edge of the tub, rolls her stockings down and off. Then she sits, pink tulle hanging almost into the water. She extends the grease-soaked paper bag; I take out a fry that coils and coils. Then she takes one, eats it.

I observe my fry as I eat it rung by rung. I stare at my legs awhile. Then I look up at Amanda. She is watching me—not looking at me, but watching—as though I might transform, suddenly, or have an allergic reaction. "We need to get a real lock on this door," I say.

"If you want it," Amanda says. "You're the only one who really comes in here."

I nod. I look down at my flattened body through the shimmery gold water.

Then I look back up at her. "Give me Lora's number," I say. "I'll call her."

"Tell her you're my girlfriend," Amanda says. "Tell her you live here now." She smiles her smile that I know is connected, physically somehow, to all my central organs. The yellow in her eyes glows bright. My head is empty and everything my belly contains is shriveled, but my heart, my pancreas, feel pulled. **-bc.**

Peter Frank

shivery evenings and madcap factions

Work with time. Enjoy the interval. Bring in the
burly modern. The sightmass is paining me, and
there are some signs of unstuck suns in the poolyard.
But whatever looks okay, tastes okay, okay? The big
bicycle tatters and all throughout the troposphere
there are these crunching sounds, now cold, now warm.
It really doesn't faze us, quite, so we smile and shrug.
The cooking lessons themselves soon start to steam,
the goony looks of postherds convincing themselves
that they're insanely happy get real old real fast, and
pretty soon no one is convinced, no, not any longer,
of the consequences of catafalques caught in mid-
caterwaul. Who's in charge here, anyway? Who's
picking up the tab? Why is this question not burning
more? What kind of nerve does it take? When's the
next train? And where, oh where, are we going with
this? We're still unshaken. We're rarin' to go. We
cavil precious little, say less, and winkle not hardly
at all. But all in all, after all, we still refuse to be born.

Peter Frank

certificate
of
appropriateness

Truthfully, we were yesterday. The ordinary
is also original. Give it a black spank, curl
it in a face, ring the town—the whole town—
and bring the heavens down upon thee.

Kiki Petrosino

top of
a dumpling,
top of
a temple

The mind of an eater is dark as drink & heavy in its shell. On market day, she moves like an ocean liner among the cases of edible silver leaf & grilled seahorses. How the hull of her chest tips, tenderly, towards the lovely lake of eating sounds. Her hunger is a metallic swish, is the hook in her clanging mouth, which she fills now with the flesh of spider crabs & wild vegetables. *Bell, bell, bell, bell* her lips & teeth repeat, twenty-seven times before swallowing, & again she takes up the fried bread, the shredded beef & mooncake. Each bite exactly as it surfaces before her, each bite a small hotness matched with a saltness & touched to a brightness of near lights. The lights do near. Buildings advance inward on their wooden stilts. The eater's lucky tongue gets freighted, gets flat; her lucky hands fill up with friends. Yes & why shouldn't friends come calling? Must the lunch one sups off gnash at the heart so? Must the lunch one sups off needs be at home, at the curve of the yard? The eater ranges, blackly. Her harp is a harp of blood.

Kiki Petrosino

the
peaceful
heart
has no
hang-ups

The eater returns to the municipal garden & sees that it's
empty. She remembers just this: two chairs under the willow
tree & matching bowls of cold, sweet soup. Then, also,
his long body against the armature of his motorbike, & how he
had first happened to her, in front of the National Library,
in view of the exact bend in the river where he would later hand
her five white roses once, & once only. The soup contained
pale clouds of swiftlets' nests, which she pulled with a large,
shallow spoon. Then, too, he had reached into her robe
with a hand like a linnet, & she'd let her robe fall open to the
spring air. He was telling her that one of the stars above
their heads was not just a star; it was a huge gold cylinder with
astronauts breathing goldenly inside it. His tongue flickered
against her teeth, saying the secret names of things:
If fairy floss, he said, *if watermelon seeds. If spikes of rock sugar,*
if wintergreen. Then, it was difficult not to think
of love as music in the mouth. A small, hot star came to rest
inside the corrugations of her ribs, & she called the name,
dissolving as she went.

Ddum Kim

I can only tell you what I remember. Of three stone slabs not built but found. That met at the top in a lean. Commiserating giants in a gravitational trinity. Smaller stones filling the gaps between except for where the door and two window frames were. Connected to a wooden frame lining the interior connected to four beams crossing the ceiling connected to four columns standing inconvenient in the already limited workspace, structural reinforcement appropriated as shelving stuffed and wedged with books, manuscripts, loose papers, unclear which supporting which, all the way to the top, accessible with a ladder I never saw used. The ladder leaning against the wall behind the historian's desk. His desk tall with an angled surface like an architect's, covered with ink pots, pens, pencils, brushes, papers, a lamp, three magnifying glasses of different sizes, binder clips, mugs of tea steaming or stale never slipping off, defying gravity or placed to be in perfect harmony with it. In front of his stool, also wooden, also tall, allowing him to hunch over documents with feet resting on one rung above the floor stone or concrete or clay, dusty and dirty despite daily sweepings, never mopped or scrubbed, covered with more books, manuscripts, loose papers placed in stacks only meaningful to the historian we knew as doctor. The piles bridging, blocking the space two strides wide between the historian's desk and the scribe's, also wooden. Apothecary drawers built in the base of the scribe's desk containing ink, paint, gold leaf, graphite, lead, nibs, pens, pencils, brushes, blotters, thinner, string, turpentine, seals, rags, rulers, erasers, knives, thread, needles, wax, matches obscured by the scribe's chair, also wooden. With a surface one arm's length deep, one arm span wide, necessarily large. Level, thick like a butcher's block, cut, damaged, worn, painted with a precise black grid for second, third, and fifth copying, helpful for sevenths. With a red stain on the front right corner I suspected was blood. The swing-arm lamp dented, clamped on the right, to the right of copies resting on the desk in front of the scribe's chair, the right farther from the door and potential drafts when opened by theoretical visitors. Originals placed left of copies on the left side of the desk in front of another chair, also wooden, that I only witnessed occupied by one individual a handful of times, back to the wall and window slightly open for ventilation. In that wall, below the window, a shelf laden with blank sheets bound, loose and rolled, and in the level below, my school bag and thermos of tea hot when cold and iced when hot, never sweet enough. The archive only hot or cold, never moderate, jumping from one extreme to the other in changeable weather. A veritable tinderbox. Of wood, paper, fumes, dust. Collecting for uncountable years confined in a too hot stone shell. That burned down, that you saw burn down, in a heatwave like this heatwave, disappearing lakes and rivers, leaves, rodents. Its ruins rotting in weeds tall again after years, bulldozed and removed, the earth reshaped, sprinklers installed, and grass grown for the members-only golf course that outrages those who supported and voted for its development who now whine injustice when fined for trespassing on land they once could tread for free though they never did. I tell you this is what I remember.

/

Now go to the municipal building, go to room 214, ask the clerk for a file on *the old archive, the one that burned down.* She will give you a folder. In the folder you will find a photograph. The clerk will tell you this is all there is, that all other documents on the archive had been stored in the archive and disappeared with it.

The photograph will be neither dated nor signed, but you will recognize the image of the archive. You will know the yellow grass of late summer, early fall encircling it, the cast shadows of late afternoon, the dirt path leading up to the door. You will see the door closed, the lines in the dry wood, the small stones filling the gaps in the outer wall just as I described them, that make up the archive into something resembling a beehive, stacked so tight, flush together. Look for the three large stone slabs that form the lean. If you can not see them immediately, make a copy of the photograph, take it home, and in your room under a strong light with a magnifying glass look closer, carefully. Search until your eyes ache, the photograph pixellates, the image is lost, reduced to black vibrating on white. Find that you can not see the three whispering giants. Find the small window at eye level, left of the door, small and missable, but still there, that I did not mention because I have forgotten it. The mat, woven, large, bleached out and rough in texture in front of the door that I did not mention because I cannot recall it. The wildflowers growing from between the stones that I did not mention because I do not remember them and still question if they ever were.

Looking at the photograph to which I have led you, that you might not have known existed had I not told you it did, consider whether I lie. Question my memories, dismiss them as you count the number of discrepancies I point out, acknowledge exist, describe because I have observed them myself. Have myself accused light, lens, and angle of trickery, declared the thing altered, and knowing these possibilities to be untrue, have dismissed my own memory as inaccurate, false, deficient. Have avoided and feared my own mind's fabrications not only of the archive's exterior but of the interior, of the work, of the paints and inks used, the copying skills acquired, the doctor, the professor, the walks to and from there, of home, of you, of them, of ghosts, of sounds, of smells, of textures, of noise, of temperature, of the weight of the air, of my anxiety, my very thoughts, my very feelings. Have myself been pushed to only trusting facts—numbers, addresses, names—to only believing that substantiated by others or recorded, and even then only sometimes. The inaccuracy of remembrance reinforced by the constant incongruities perceived between what is and my recollection of what was. Walking on level carpets of mown grass where I remember there stood an ancient stone structure on a yellow balding hill. Sitting on a black leather sectional too large for a room with gray cracked paint in a house too small to breathe in where I remember a green corduroy couch in a room with white walls in a house big enough to hide in. Eating dinner with a quiet man whose strength and anger I remember terrified, sitting across from a quiet woman whose scream I remember ruptured an eardrum. Doodling meaningless pencil lines with a hand that I remember replicated seven calligraphic styles with certainty, grace, ease. Seeing you again gaunt, gray-skinned, lined, exhausted, not opposite but so other from what I remember.

I searched for something remotely familiar in your posture, gesture, speech, not to disprove my paranoid amnesia but to reconcile the simultaneous and contradictory feelings of knowing you and meeting a stranger so that when the moment of seeming déjà vu came, when you spoke with the same inflection, the same cadence, the same voice, the same words, said *If we were one person, we would be perfect, then we would be okay,* though you preceded it with *Remember when we thought* and followed it with a laugh, it jarred remembrance into full consciousness and despite the photograph I remembered as I had always remembered three commiserating giants in a gravitational trinity, a wooden door stained dark and dry, a handle painted black with a thumb latch smooth from wear, pens with bent nibs, the doctor's loud breathing, a leatherbound portfolio sticking out of the shelf to the left of the door, rust growing on the corners of the hotplate in the shape of rabbits, a perfect circle of light glowing on the historian's desk illuminating a yellow legal pad covered in graphite notes, the musk of the soap in the bathroom, picking up the phone after two rings, pausing after asking *Hello?* after you answered *Hello?* Asking *Who is this?* though I knew. You said *It's gone.* Said *I was in the woods.* Said *I smelled burning.* Not *I smelled something burning* but *I smelled burning.* Told me you walked towards the smell. Told me you walked into the smoke before you were aware it was there, that you could not see, that you choked, that the day was windless. Said *Firemen came and did nothing, said there was nothing to be done, just to watch, to be on standby, to be sure it was contained, that it would be safer to let the fire die out on its own, said it was lucky there was no wind. Said it was lucky.* Said *They smoked as they watched.* Said *There was so much smoke.* You told me others appeared from the woods, that they stood, watching along the perimeter, refusing or unable to venture beyond, neighbors we never knew who must have emerged from the houses that never seemed inhabited. Said *Some were crying.* Told me they mouthed *Oh my god* into the smoke to no one, into phones to invisible someones. Said *But I could not hear them. For the smoke.* Said *The smoke. It took over.* Told me you could not see the fire for the smoke. Told me you could not see the archive for the smoke. Told me your eyes watered. Said *It was the smoke. It turned everything black.* Told me it diffused twilight, blurred bodies, muted faces, muted sound but the roar of smokescreened blazes. Said *And then the doctor. He appeared as if by magic. I don't know from which direction. He stood so close. I only knew it was him because he stood so close.* Told me he did not know you were there, that he was wordless. Told me the sun set. Said *Then I could no longer see anyone or anything, only feel the fire, its heat everywhere.* Said *I still smell like burning. Everything smells like burning.*

/

If this recollection does not match yours, if I have missed even the smallest detail, I know you have stopped reading. That this goes unread. But if it aligns with your memory in every way, I know you are still with me. And I know you are still with me. I know you are still with me. I know you are still with me. I know you are still with me. I know you are still with me. And I can ask you to look at the photograph again and consider what you remember of the archive. To note details you remember differently, do not remember, never knew were there, and know your memory to be as imperfect as mine. And now to put the thing away. And read what I have to tell you. Because if we are ever to be okay, it is not what was, but what I remember of what was that you must know.

/

There were eight scripts, eight historians in all. The doctor being the eighth. I thought he lived in the archive a hermit. The ink pots, pens and brushes on his desk always dry. He used pencils. HBs, round, silver-painted, sans erasers, making notes, crossing out on blue-ruled yellow sheets stored in manila folders stacked on another stool, also wooden, at his right side. Reading and turning pages with care, slowly, of volumes and records compiled by his predecessors, nodding or shaking his head as if in conversation. His large nostrils breathed loud, clouding one of three magnifying glasses left hand held over manuscript or book or sheet smoothed flat with crooked fingers with thick nails striated and yellowed connected to a bony right hand age-spotted, steady, and fingerless-gloved in winter. He was left-handed. I felt embarrassed for him his loud breathing, seeming a condition more profound than simply nasal for one silent unless posed yes or no questions—the least demanding to one so taciturn—or greeted with a *Hello* to which he replied *Hello have some tea.* With a reserve not cold or condescending, but concentrated. Making tea his rare break. Taking any two mugs and the kettle to the bathroom. He emptied and washed the mugs in the sink, filled the kettle, emerged, placed the kettle on the hotplate, turned it on, watched it. The kettle, aluminum with a black handle. The hotplate white with two burners. On a small brown oblong refrigerator that stood to the right of the bathroom door which was to the right of the archive door, closer to the historian's desk than the scribe's. The bathroom an afterthought, a toilet and shallow bowl of a sink wedged between stone and drywall that did not reach the ceiling, sounds in one room audible in the other. The tank of the toilet stacked with empty manila folders smelling of mold. A wooden ledge nailed into the wall above the sink slimed from bars of soap, holding a damp sponge and mugs, of which one held the doctor's toothbrush, toothpaste, and razor, and a small beige lamp its incandescent bulb buzzing orange. The doctor watching the kettle well after the steam began to emit, turned off the burner only when a rolling boil hit the kettle from inside, took a tea bag from a box, also wooden, removed the lid from the kettle, emptied the tea bag string and all into the water, replaced the lid. Took hold of the handle, swung the kettle in slow generous circles, the water sizzling without spilling, poured the contents into each mug, returned the kettle to the hotplate, walked to my desk, placed a mug on the corner furthest from my work, on the lefthand corner closest to the door, returned to his desk to his historian's work, his nostrils breathing loud while sipping tea. I drank the tea out of politeness, but always too bitter, never finished it. Drinking, always finishing, the tea mother prepared in the thermos brought from home. Cold in the summer, hot in the winter, sweetened but never sweet enough because I never told her. Never bitter. Rationed. The thermos there, in one hand, mother's hand in the other, you on the other side of her, on that first visit to the archive, first meeting with the doctor, when I did not know I became a scribe and did not know what a scribe was. There in my bag thereafter when you walked me after school uphill through dry yellow grass that drew raised lines across my calves. Sweating through my shirt through the blue canvas of my book bag dampening its heavy contents, holding onto your shirt hem crying *I'm so hot.* You quickened your pace out of reach and with vision blurred I followed the sound of your footfalls. Fast and wide, kicking up dust or dirt or mud or nothing pounding frozen ground when you said *If we were one person, we would be perfect. If only we were perfect. Then we would be okay.* Reaching you waiting outside the archive entrance, you told me to go in, so I did. The door, also wooden, stained dark was never locked, though there was a lock in the handle painted black that gave with a thumb click of the latch and a too-easy pull. Any exertion too much exertion. Light and flimsy in contrast to its appearance. Slight breezes flapping it almost open. Flap flap flapflap flap flapflap syncopated in the summer dust sneaking in through cracks, snow in the winter, rain in spring and fall the wind beating it against its frame almost unhinged. I wore gloves in winter. The pair you received as a gift from a friend of father's, bagged to donate, the kind that appear made for midget hands but stretch to fit any. They were green. I cut the fingers off like the doctor his. Drank tea like him. Layered gloves the way he wore two sweaters. Gloves made of felt that must have been white when new but which I only ever knew to be gray, I wore over the fingerless ones in winter and by themselves otherwise. Always worn when copying second style manuscripts regardless of the season. Second style manuscripts written with soft charcoal that smudged too easily on smooth paper square and thin tearing with a pull of the charcoal pressed down too hard. The sheet fit in the outlines of the desktop grid, the horizontal rule visible through the paper serving as guides ensuring straight lines required by the second historian, his glass face void of features but for two blazing eyes that stared through the woods you told me were haunted. I held my breath copying seconds, expelling air with a turned head. Accidental breath or breeze or bump of the desk scattering the charcoal, marking the paper with spider thin lines, ruining the sheet and hours of work. The small size of the sheets, ten inches square, a redeeming aspect of fragile seconds. Second characters created with a series of strokes from left to right not demanding the symmetrical precision of thirds. Perfect reproductions achieved with controlled and measured strokes allowing for slight corrections if need be with charcoal sanded to a fine point, in and of itself not a difficult script to master. The text fixed with a spray, the sheet made stiff with a short soak in a water and gum bath in a wooden box placed on the lowered toilet seat cover, the wet sheet transferred to a tall narrow rack, also wooden, with seven levels each made to dry one sheet overnight, set up on the desk for this purpose but otherwise folded leaning against the wall to my right. Minimal embellishments applied the following day with the handle point of the brown paintbrush. Three dots in each corner, one in the center, dropping on thick, viscous, drying into hard smooth half beads of dark red lacquer serving as decorations, weights, and buffers between sheets to prevent blotting effects, only then stacking the copied sheets followed by the copying of the next seven pages followed by soaking followed by copying the next seven followed by the dropping of lacquer on the dried sheets followed by stacking followed by the soaking of the next seven followed by copying the next seven pages and so on until the copied pages made a copied manuscript followed by the copying of the next manuscript. Making mistakes, replicating mistakes, my hand going straight when it should curve, skipping lines, spilling ink, applying too much pressure, not enough, copying so slow the ink drying in the nib of the pen, backing into the chamber, flooding onto the sheet, onto my hands, wiped permanent on my clothes by accident, copying so slow the paint hardening in the brush, or sitting, just sitting, not sleeping, just sitting, incapable of doing anything more or anything else. The doctor never saying anything, never commenting on my inertia. Then slowly or abruptly, either on the same day or the next or several later copying again at a steady pace without difficulty, without pause, focused, selecting the proper materials, the proper instruments, selecting and treating the paper accordingly, practicing strokes, comparing copy with original for incongruities, placing originals to the left, copying on the right, lines, curves, dashes, forming letters, characters, words, sentences, into pages, into manuscripts, cleaning instruments, clearing spaces, opening the next manuscript, arranging and preparing for the next copy. Copying occupying time uninterrupted but for the one week and then a day the professor dripping greetingless came letting in rain and a wind that streaked ribbons of ink across my copy. Not knowing he was a professor until he said *I am a professor* then *You can call me professor.* I did not call him *professor.* I did not call him anything. I never spoke to him. I never called the doctor *doctor.* I said *Good morning*, not *Good morning doctor* or *Good morning sir. Thank you* not *Thank you doctor. See you tomorrow* not *See you tomorrow doctor.* When you called, I picked up the receiver, asked *Hello?* and you answered *Hello?*

/

I do not mean to confuse you. I did not know my memories would splinter on the page, lead to the transcription of spontaneous thoughts crashing into tangential dead ends. This is not how I meant for this transfer of information to happen. Before my conviction in the eventuality of this telling faded on finding the photograph of the archive in the folder for the *old archive, the one that burned down* in the file maintained by the clerk in room 214 in the municipal building, I constructed and reconstructed over and over and over and over in my mind what I would tell you, how I would tell you down to the very pauses I would take between phrases. I planned to tell you everything in person. In an organized manner, in script order. I planned to start with the first script. The *skeletal or insect script.* With its lead lines making up characters resembling primitive four-legged creatures formed with slow gestures. Veins drawn with deliberately painstaking unhurried movements that caused the hand to shake and produce jittery lines that made the insects appear to vibrate. The foot of each leg punctuated with a near invisible pinhole. An appropriate script to start a child just having internalized name-writing, just learning to write a sentence, good with instruction, mediocre and uninspired when asked simply to draw, always lacking ideas of my own. The doctor placing the manuscript in front of me, opening it to the first page, breaking the spine to lay it flat, placing a blank translucent sheet on top and a pencil on top of the sheet without instruction, wordless. The set-up familiar from alphabet primers, I knew to trace. Tracings appearing perfect when layered over originals but upon separation, held up to the light on their own, missing lines, the thickness of lines inconsistent, uncorrectable due to the delicate nature of the paper, smudged, a mess. Wasting so many sheets before learning to keep my hand lifted so as not to smear the work or stain the sheet with sweat from the base of my palm. Wasting so many sheets to achieve a perfect tracing only to be discarded. Leaving dozens of meticulous tracings on my desk on the left side under originals to be found in the trash on my next visit each time over the course of something like a year, turning into something close to a ritual. The disposal of that work not upsetting, having learned in school to view tracing as an act of pretend regardless of the time and effort invested. Not meant to be cherished or saved. Not serious. The paper's translucence announcing amused forgery. Especially in contrast to the rough, beige almost gray heavy handmade leaves of first manuscripts. Of which blank ones I found in the scaffolding turned shelf behind the scribe's chair. Thick layers of dust covering the stack suggesting it had been there all along. Lead wrapped in paper like a crayon I found in the top left apothecary drawer in the scribe's desk. Initial attempts to copy not simply trace, eyeballing character size, spacing, alignment, resulted in creatures of various proportions resembling less a system of language and more an infestation of mutant vermin. Running out of space after writing too wide, too long, too far apart only then to create cavernous margins with characters too small, too close, too narrow. Until observing that the innocuous pinholes resting in the feet of each character, what I believed to be pure decoration, were regularly spaced and aligned both horizontally and vertically. I measured the spacing with the ruler, also wooden, that lay in the desk, in the top line of drawers, second to the right, and found that the spacing between each hole alternated between being three centimeters apart and half a centimeter apart. I looked at the page again and for the first time saw the regularity and repetition of the holes of the characters, each contained in a perfect square, horizontally symmetrical made with care and deliberation that undermined the document's seeming primitive qualities. It took several days to find the needle. Rusted into the crevice of one of the drawers. In the process of searching for it, happening upon other implements I did not know before were there. I did not reorganize what was at the time still but a cabinet of curiosities, in part because I knew it was not mine, but more on account of a newfound awareness that what I perceived as haphazard storage might be the resultant order of centuries. And so I left it all undisturbed but for the needle, scraped out with my fingernails and cleaned in the bathroom with soap and water. I took out a blank sheet, measured three centimeters in from the left edge and three centimeters down from the top margin. Marked the paper with the tip of the needle, just deep enough so that I could see it, and then deeper to puncture the sheet. The size of the hole perfectly matched those in the originals. But the needle, still rusted, left a brown stain around the hole. I tried again one centimeter to the right with the hope that the first hole had removed the rust, but the needle left the same stain. Washed the needle again with soap and water, not knowing my efforts were counterproductive. Spent the rest of the day poking brown holes in the paper at random, no longer concerned with measurement, only in eliminating rust and my failure to do so. The doctor absorbed in writing, crossing out, appeared unaware. But whenever the supply of blank sheets on the shelf ran low, I found it replenished on my next visit. Likewise the needle I found on the scribe's desk clean on my return to the archive. I took out a new sheet, positioned the needle and punched a hole so clean I held the sheet up to the light to make sure it was there. From there I measured and punched the rest of the sheet. From there I copied the characters with lead, used the ruler to measure the length of each stroke, used the protractor, also wooden, to measure the angle between each line. Measured and measured again, deliberately painstaking, copying the characters with unhurried movements that caused the hand to shake and produce jittery lines that made the insects appear to vibrate. Characters that took seconds to trace taking unquantifiable time to copy. Months of familiarization through tracing completely abandoned, irrelevant. Thoughts of copying the entire manuscript also abandoned, seeming impossible. Focus refined to reproducing a perfect line. Until on copying the last line of the last character on the last page, suddenly finding nothing more to copy, recollections of finding the needle of making marks in nursery school primers of marking sheets with lead of us marking asphalt with chalk of us sleeping between mother and father after too many of your ghost stories laughing in between coats smelling of mothballs giving away my hiding place of hiding keys so she could not leave of hiding bottles so they could not drink of crying of crying *I'm so hot* grabbing for the hem of your shirt climbing up the hill leading to the archive running after you silent that silence the sound of the doctor's pencils scratching paper heavyweight paper attempting clean holes in paper attempting flight from beds flapping like wings the sleeves of matching pajamas several sizes too big from father just because attempting to avoid stepping on shattered glass of mother singing lullabies about children with our names of tracing of watching breath materialize into clouds swirl dissolve in darkness of waiting outside the archive for you always late of measuring the second to last line of the last character on the last page rushing me undifferentiated, I did not know what to do. Could not bring myself to close the original, close the copy, return the needle to the crevice in the drawer. I left the lead on the copy, left copy and original open on the desk, left the lamp on, left. Returned to find the lamp off, next to it the lead and ruler placed side by side, the paper replenished in the shelf, the copy and the original nowhere to be found. In their place a manuscript I had not seen before, thicker than the one previous. I copied the new manuscript to completion over uncounted visits and unable to close it, left copy and original open on the desk to find another in its place to copy and leave open on the desk to find another in its place to copy and leave on the desk, unspoken swapping of copied and to be copied developing into a routine that led to the eventual learning that firsts were not the only scripts, to copying second style manuscripts wearing felt gloves with soft charcoal that smudged too easily on smooth paper square and thin like tracing paper tearing with a pull of the utensil pressed down too hard and, unlike tracing paper, soft to the touch, that fit in the outlines of the desktop grid, the horizontal rule visible through the paper serving as guides ensuring straight lines, making the pinpricking of firsts obsolete. I held my breath copying seconds, expelling air with a turned head. Accidental breath or breeze or bump against the desk scattering the charcoal, marking the paper with spider thin lines, ruining the sheet and hours of work. The small size of the sheets, ten inches square, a redeeming aspect of fragile seconds. Second characters created with a series of curves requiring fewer strokes than firsts. Seconds streamlined and simplified versions of firsts, less demanding than symmetrically precise thirds. Perfect reproductions achieved with controlled and measured strokes allowing for slight corrections if need be with charcoal sanded to a fine point, in and of itself not a difficult script to master. The text fixed with a spray, the sheet made stiff with a short soak in a water and gum bath in a wooden box placed on the lowered toilet seat cover, the wet sheet transferred to a tall narrow rack also wooden, set up on the desk for this purpose but otherwise folded leaning against the wall to my right, with seven levels each made to dry one sheet overnight. Minimal embellishments applied the following day with the handle end of a paintbrush. Three dots in each corner, one in the center, dropping on thick, viscous, drying into hard smooth half beads of lacquer serving as decorations, weights, and buffers between sheets, preventing blotting effects, only then stacking the copied sheets followed by the copying of the next seven pages followed by soaking followed by copying the next seven followed by the dropping of lacquer on the dried sheets followed by stacking followed by the soaking of the next seven followed by copying the next seven pages and so on until the second style copied pages made a second style copied manuscript followed by the copying of a third style manuscript, larger, thicker versions of seconds. More austere, more imposing. In paper weight and dimension, the characters themselves, a combination ink of graphite and stone ground by hand in a circular motion on a slab with drips of water from a ceramic contraption with two holes in the top, one for filling through submersion, one for pouring made for the sole purpose to drip water, the novelty of which wore off within the first day of grinding, the smell of which mildly intoxicated. Third blanks came stacked flat with frayed edges, requiring trimming to create clean sheets of uniform dimension. Then aligned and centered to the grid, each corner weighted with a handful of gray and white porcelain minnows, grid lines still visible through sheets refined in their translucence and tight weave of indistinguishable rice fibers. The simplicity of third characters demanded symmetry, the erasure of human imprecision both in the calculation of characters and the application of ink demanding nothing less than an even coat to every character that could not be retouched. Thirds seeming an impossible script to copy but after months finally accomplishing the task, followed by the copying of another third, followed by the copying of a second, followed by the copying of a first, a third, a first, a second, a first copied through too much tea, copying bloated, copying into dusk beyond dusk into night, copying turning into waiting into hunger into errors into amassing wasted sheets riddled with deformed half insects into walking crying frightened through the woods running from clawing ghosts in between trees that disappeared the moon into the house to find them not there, you already asleep. Trying not to wake you. Hoping you might. Thinking you should. Crying into sleep my head turned towards you, watching your back turned to me, the profile of your right side covered with a blanket that reached your neck, unconscious in the bed parallel to mine separated by the white nightstand, also wooden, with two drawers with metal pull handles, the top drawer yours, the bottom mine holding our pajamas, just a little wider than our combined arm-lengths creating the aisle where mother sat her back against the nightstand reading aloud a story of our choosing then another and another still because we begged. Her voice calm, calming even when shaking.

Laying in bed, there, I counted the number of years until I could leave, converted the number into months then weeks then days. The conversion into hours and minutes beyond my faculty of calculation. Staring at the dark grays of the night ceiling otherwise beige, holding my breath, unable to imagine what comes next as sitting at dinner beef broth still in my spoon almost reaching my mouth, taking care not to drip, their talking turning to shouting somewhere between ladling the soup into my spoon and its almost ingestion. Always on my back not turning on my side so as not to disturb the sheets and cover mother made neat, there on my back in pajamas you had long outgrown, watching the ceiling thinking how strange that though I could not see or hear you, I knew you were almost within arm's reach. Unable to figure out how this could be, wanting to ask you, but knowing that rousing you from sleep would only make you angry.

Staring at the ceiling, their screaming reaching us through cracks around the door, wide awake before learning to sedate fear with sleep, I asked you what they were saying. You said *You do not need to know.* Asked you what they fought about, asked why they fought. You said *You do not need to know.* Asked why you would not tell me. You said *To protect you.*

Staring at the water stain on the ceiling thinking how strange that without turning to see, I knew you were not there. That if I reached out to where your bed would have been, I would touch the wall separating my apartment from my neighbors' whose incomprehensible screaming lulls me to sleep.

I asked you how could we make them stop, how could we make them stop. You said *Come here* and I did and you fell asleep holding me in your arms the way mother used to.

Staring at the ceiling wondering though I could not see or hear you, if you might be almost an arm's reach away. Turning my head to see your bed empty, made, neat. Years after not seeing you stretching into longer still. Not knowing you were gone until I returned. I did not ask them where you went or when you would return if you were to return or why they did not tell me. I never asked them anything. And you were not here for me to ask.

I asked you how could we make them stop. You said *If we were one person, we would be perfect, then we would be okay.* Asked you why. You said *Because we are so different.* Asked you why. You said *Because.*

Watching shadows crawl along the ceiling tracing the outline of the stain with my eyes, climbing out of bed, opening the door, seeing in the next room you sleeping on the green corduroy couch now mine now faded almost to yellow, your back turned to me under a thin blanket white with pale blue lines also once theirs now mine pulled to your neck despite the heat, I hear your inhale, exhale under the neighbors' high-pitched screams and still cannot believe you are here.

/

There were eight scripts, eight historians in all and you must know them if we are to be perfect. Imperfection a fear instilled by ghosts. Turning from menacing to violent, closing in as I ran through the woods, a telltale sign that a copy was subpar, must be fixed or discarded altogether. The residue of dead historians maintaining distance when copying met their standards, but still there with eyes blinking presence and judgment. The first ghost's skin gouged by gaping pockmarks, two of which served as sockets for sunken eyes that followed my every step. The fifth historian with clothes as disheveled, hair as frazzled, angles and gaze as severe as fifth style characters, watching alongside the seventh historian verging on translucence but for sallow eyes so dense they seemed to float on their own, watching with eyes that I did not know were there until you told me they were there. You said *There they are* and *There, there* as we cut through the woods from the archive towards home when you still came for me, when I was still a scribe, when you were still here, when you said *Even if you don't see them, they are there* and *There, they are watching, there* and *There* and *If we had been one, we would have been perfect—we would have been okay.* You pointed and I saw eyes piercing the clear early darkness of winter, the dust and haze of heatwaves like this heatwave disappearing lakes and rivers, leaves, rodents, everything but the second historian appearing of dust, his eyes red lacquer luminescing in between trees we once used to play tag and war, the fourth historian his eyes glowing indigo flooding, streaking his face like ribbons of ink pulled across three completed sheets and another in progress, across the desk towards the right corner closest to me onto the floor, drawn by the wind let in with rain by the professor dripping greetingless. Wiping the wet from his coat, pushing it out of his hair onto the floor narrowly missing the piles of papers and books stacked there. The professor waiting, myself waiting then returning to work, discarding the ruined sheets, preparing a new one, turning back the manuscript two spreads. Following the doctor's lead until asked *May I sit here?* Seeing colorless and not indigo stains on the floor, seeing the professor gesture towards the empty chair next to mine. He added, *Until the rain lets up.* I shrugged and he interpreting this gesture as acquiescence, pulled out and sat in the otherwise empty chair. The professor sometimes watching me, sometimes the doctor, sometimes looking at the ceiling, but mostly out the window. He did not say anything more that day. He fell asleep. He had brown hair and a receding hairline and his face was thin. He wore glasses with thick black frames. He wore muddied black dress shoes. He had a straight nose, a cleft chin. He smelled of mildew and rain. He wore a rumpled black suit too wide for his frame. He slept with his arms crossed, mouth closed, head resting on his chest. I forgot about him. Then he awoke, stood up, the mud on his shoes dried to a light brown, breaking off onto the floor. He said *Thank you,* walked to the door, opened it onto a dry twilight, stepped out pulling the door closed behind him. After which I completed copying two of the three ruined sheets and felt accomplished for it. He visited every day for the following eight days, coming at different times, each time sitting in the chair next to mine. He said *You are a good listener.* Told me he was educated and worked in an office. Told me he lived somewhere far away but had returned because his mother had passed away. Said *I used to play in the marching band* and *My father yelled at me when I would lose my mittens. Like Tom Kitten.* He said *My mother passed away four years ago.* Told me his mother smoked, said *But that is not what killed her.* Said *I bet you wonder why I come here.* Said *It is so peaceful. That is why I come here.* Said *Always look both ways when you cross the street. My father always told me that. Now I look both ways even when a street is empty.* Said *You work so hard. When I was your age I did not work as hard as you.* Said *I do not know how old my mother was when she died.* Said *They lied to me. They said they didn't, but they did.* Said *They keep lying to me.* Said *My father says he remembers differently.* Said *I always wished I had a brother or sister.* Said *It is all different from what I remember.* Said *Everything looks strange. Not how I remembered it. I don't know who to believe, who is correct.* Said *Beware of those who begin with 'I remember.' They lie. No one remembers anything. Memories are gathered emotions presented as fact. There is no such thing as 'I remember.' If you know this, you will never be conned by someone else's delusions.* Said *She was not very pretty, but she was beautiful.* Said *Don't worry.* Said *I go back on Tuesday* on the Wednesday they covered the kitchen with shattered fragments of what were bottles, what were glasses, what was a window, what was a chair leaving the blue flame of the left front burner on to burn the second to smallest stainless steel pot with the long curved black handle that once contained water and illuminate your streaked face. You wedged squatting in the corner next to the stove shivering from wind blowing in through where there had been a window pane. I asked what happened and you said *You do not need to know.* Asked why you would not tell me and you said *You do not need to know.* Asked why you would not tell me and you said *You weren't here* and I turned the knob on the stove to disappear the blue flame and you said *You weren't here. You're never here. You do not need to know* and I pulled out a chair from the kitchen table and sat with you there in the dark, waiting there for them to return long after you stood up, wiped glass from your lap, walked across the kitchen out to the hall and up the stairs, waiting until falling asleep waiting waking up knowing no one had returned fearing they never would, wondering what would happen if they never did, standing up, walking across the kitchen out to the hall and up the stairs into our room. Trying not to wake you. In the dark changing into pajamas outgrown twice over, climbing into bed, laying on my back sleepless in the silence watching the stain appear on the ceiling black turning gray to red to pink to beige to white washing out all but the outline of the stain, climbing out of bed, taking off pajamas, showering, toweling off, brushing teeth, putting on clothes, putting on shoes, going downstairs, entering kitchen stepping over shards but still feeling and hearing granules underfoot, making tea, filling thermos, leaving the house, going to school, being at school, leaving school towards the house in the same direction as others with now forgotten faces and names mutually ignored when passing in hallways, sitting parallel to one another by last name in classrooms, and walking away from school, some starting in loud clusters that dwindled as paths diverged to subsets of fours then threes then pairs to myself and two whose birthday parties I attended years earlier, before I was a scribe, staggered across and along the same stretch of road, silent eyes following the ground or fixed on an invisible line stretching towards a house or tree or lawn in the distance avoiding each other's gaze. Entering the house to find no one there, in the kitchen the glass gone, the window pane replaced. Climbing the stairs, entering the room, leaving the door open, laying on the bed, staring at the water stain on the ceiling thinking how strange that without turning to see, I knew you were not there. Sitting up, taking out my thermos, pouring the tea still hot in the cold of winter, neither sweet nor bitter, drinking it watching shadows pull across the walls and absorb themselves waiting. I sat there waiting, there listening, there in the room dark but for the hallway light cast through the open door listening for the key in the lock, the door opening, knowing mother's footsteps from the weight of their sound followed by uncounted hours by father's return by the television turned to the news at the approximate time I would have returned from the archive with dinner almost ready, the table needing to be set, getting up, going downstairs finding mother finishing preparations, father watching the news, and four place settings already laid out by you returned without my knowledge, sitting there with fingers absently stroking the corduroy of the green couch. Mother bringing the food to the table, we moved wordless to three matching chairs and a miscellaneous fourth too low for the table, silent as we ate, I watched and listened for warning signs, clearing the table, climbing the stairs, returning to the room, completing assignments for school, going to bed, laying there on my back waiting there watching lights and shadows flicker and move across the ceiling through waiting straining to hear angry whispers before they turned, waiting through unnerving silence until morning to leave to return in the afternoon to the empty house to sitting on my bed drinking tea, hearing mother followed by father and you somewhere in there undetected, dinner, homework, bed, laying there counting the number of years until I could leave, converting the number into months then weeks then days then hours then minutes decreasing incrementally with the passing of days of the same, expecting the silence to be broken by their yelling, crashing, departure never to return, determined to be there awake when it happened, to know what happened, watching shadows waiting there laying in bed there fearing the punishment awaiting me for my delinquency to be exacted by the ghosts the doctor the professor should I have misremembered misunderstood misheard him say *I go back on Tuesday* and not *I come back on Tuesday,* recalling him say *You are a good listener* and *It is so peaceful here.* and *My father yelled at me when I would lose my mittens. Like Tom Kitten* into my spoon ladling clear beef broth through voices taking care not to drip on the tablecloth turning to shouting somewhere between soup ladled and its almost ingestion returning it there to the bowl there their screaming there pulling their pushing there and I was there, there not knowing what was happening begging without knowing what we were begging shielding them from each other there screaming not knowing there what why we scream there altogether screaming there him screaming there leaving her screaming leaving there the silence of overturned bowls spilled soup running forever off the table forever dripping onto your foot forever there absorbed by your sock there forever reaching your ankle and matching the green of the couch and turning a darker shade absorbing more soup there forever unnoticed by you on the mismatched chair there forever I turned and left you there. Climbing the stairs to the room there climbing into bed facing the wall crying there not knowing when you came into the room if you came into the room not knowing when I fell asleep to wake in the morning late for school going to school leaving school running between trees chased by ghosts slamming the door on them safe in the archive where the doctor sat hunched over a yellow legal pad, round silver-painted HB pencil, sans eraser, in his left hand, making notes, crossing out on blue-ruled yellow sheets. Reading and turning pages with care, slowly, of volumes and records compiled by his predecessors, nodding or shaking his head as if in conversation. His large nostrils breathed loud, clouding one of three magnifying glasses left hand held over manuscript or book or sheet smoothed flat with crooked fingers with thick nails striated and yellowed of a bony right hand age-spotted, steady, and fingerless-gloved in winter. With a reserve not cold or condescending, but concentrated. I said *Hello* and he said *Hello have some tea* placing his pencil on his desk, taking up two mugs and the kettle to the bathroom. On the scribe's desk the fourth style original, wooden paperweight resting on the manuscript spread open four pages to the end as I had left it but for a coating of dust, there on the left side of the desk in front of the wooden chair as I had left it only now empty, no longer occupied by the professor. To the right of the manuscript, in front of the scribe's seat, a sheet penciled ready for inking made flat by thin rectangular metal rods set in the left and right margins as I had left it all only now the sheet no longer curling on its own rendering the rods unnecessary. Two copied sheets set to dry on the far side of the desk as I had left them only the ink now matte, no longer wet and glistening. Brushes, pencils, ink, rulers, and neatly folded rags laid out in an organized fashion to the right of the copied sheets near the base of the lamp as I had left them only now the bristles dry. I blew away the dust, twisted open the ink pots and set their lids down. I took up the largest brush, dipped it into the ink, let the excess drip back in before sweeping the bristles along the inner rim to smooth the sides and bring them to a point. Examining the original script, the character about to be copied, before applying brush to paper with enough pressure for the bristles to bow without separating, maintaining its shape, with steady sweeping curves along the near-invisible graphite guidelines. The ink thick, smooth, flowing with a texture reminiscent of black pearls revealed, held up to the light, then swathed in fabric and disappearing again in the secret place we were meant to remember with mother saying *Should something happen to me. Don't forget.* Fourths not easier than other scripts, but as with seconds, slight errors retouchable with a miniature brush used exclusively for this purpose with glossy surfaced sheets interrupted by scored lines making the pinpricking of firsts obsolete. Heavyweight sheets stored in rolls, shiny side in, requiring metal rods to keep them flat when copying preventing ink from running satin lines off-course. The paper barely absorbent, the ink sitting on the surface, each copy taking several hours to dry. Indigo sections interrupted with centered headers of three characters painted with a clear suspension containing flecks of gold that shimmered in response to undetected vibrations before sublimating into solids. Sheets larger than others, wider than long, too large for the rack used for seconds, were set to dry on the scribe's desk a maximum of five at any given time. Transferring freshly inked copies from the grid to a place to dry the trickiest aspect of fourths, many a sheet ruined from moving them not only too soon but too late, disrupting the rhythm and momentum of copying, but not on my return when copying the last pages of that manuscript with such skill and precision, no ink was wasted, no paper discarded, offering my first encounter with perfection and its power over ghosts with eyes glowing in the darkness following my slow walk homewards through the woods long past dinner time who in spite of my delinquency, in spite of my expectations, to my disappointment, maintained their distance and did not tear me to pieces. **-bc.**

Tom Carson

DAISY BUCHANAN'S DAUGHTER

1 : District of Columbia, 2006

As of now—6:22 a.m. on Tuesday, June 6, 2006, my eighty-sixth birthday—my full name is Pamela Buchanan Murphy Gerson Cadwaller. I'm waiting with some asperity for a telephone call from the President of the United States.

You know how his minions must've hounded poor Potus, congratulations to the likes of me not crisp in their relation to his game plan. "The old bag will never make it to ninety, Mr. P.!" they said. "And she did a lot of something or other back in the way-back-when."

True enough, I did. Google away. For the fuck of it I sometimes do myself. Are you surprised this old bag knows how to surf the Web? Mine was the first female voice broadcast from Omaha Beach. Beyond its grassy bluffs, a lone Spandau still hammered as D-Day waned. I believe I can handle your toy.

That five-mile crescent was ours by then. The proof was that rations were being unloaded around us along with ammunition. I'd done Anzio, and I knew how that first case of Hershey bars meant victory. Just didn't expect what happened next, as the flicks of distant tracer fire making a tailor's dummy out of twilight had damned little resemblance to candles. Neither did the hulks of charred landing craft to gifts.

"Happy BIRTH-day, Miss Bu-chan-an, HAP-py birth-day to you." Heard in the States on my better-known colleague Edmond Whitling's radio report, the original recording is in the National Archives, crackling on earphones for school groups to whom such sonic chaff is now the Baskin-Robbins side of history. Listen close for Pam Buchanan, just turned twenty-four, saying faintly, "Thank you, boys! Thank you all very much."

I'm sure none of those temporary survivors of Company A, 116th Infantry, 29th "Blue and Gray" Division, landed to be massacred at H Hour and left behind like dazed American barnacles on the Vierville sea wall by fresher troops' advance, knew me from Venus on the halftrack. All they were in a position to understand was that some lanky dame had crouched among them—"And *now* what?," their eyes said—yelping "Where you from, soldier?" and passing around dry Lucky Strikes. I may've been a sort of human Hershey bar with two almonds under the wrapper myself, maybe not the finest candy but definitely made in U.S.A.

Getting sung to on Omaha as bulldozers finished clearing the exit wasn't Pam's idea of "if they mean to have a war, let it begin here." But Eddie Whitling was no chump at contriving human interest for the home front. Spotting his opportunity in Company A's lack (I wonder why) of officers, he beguiled—since I don't want to use a stronger word—

beguiled those weaponless and stunned late adolescents into singing to his pal Pamita.

"*Happy birthday, Miss Buchanan, happy birthday to you.*" In Pam's own D-Day piece, finished with a gin assist (I just hated those buzz bombs) in London two weeks later—"The Day the Tide Ran Red," *Regent's* magazine, June 28, 1944—I omitted that chorus in chafed fatigues around the perpendicular pronoun. There I am thanking them in the archives' earphones like some lost stewardess on Clio Airways just the same. Then I inanely add, "Good luck to you tomorrow, boys!" On the recording, the grind of newly landed trucks blots out my most vivid *viva voce* memory: a teenage voice saying, "Tomorrow?"

Eventually, Eddie and I had a confused fight about his stunt. It was over a dinner of *omelettes à la rations* K near Notre Dame, in a Paris forced to depend—oh, but it was enough—on its pure Parisness for wonder. On an ocean of cheers, De Gaulle had just strolled up the Champs-Élysées, and Eddie grinned at my naïve belief our friendship made him human. Nonetheless, when it comes to memorable birthday serenades, Potus will have his work cut out for him to compete.

"She was some sort of stewardess for something called Clio Airways, Mr. President," they said. "She wrote some book called *Nothing Like a Dame* and married some ambassador. No, one of ours, not one of theirs. He's long dead and she's one of those old bags who roost on upper Connecticut Avenue like falcons. On the plus side, she used to be on some museum board with your mother."

I was, for fact, the pearly bitch. Even then she looked as if she launched herself each morning by smartly cracking a perfume bottle over her own jaw. Recruiting Pam thirty years ago for whatever District cultural chore stood in urgent need of pointless discussion must've been one of Callie Sherman's odder jokes, which if you know Callie is saying something.

"Just make the call, please, sir," they said. "We know it won't do much for your afflatus, Potus, but it's only a blip in your day. No, sir—we can't figure out why he cares either. It's the first time he's asked us a favor in forever."

Dear Bob. I don't really know my Senatorial benefactor well at all. Callie Sherman introduced me to him too, and later he surprised and touched me by adding Pam's name to the honored-guest roster for the dedication of the World War Two Memorial on the Mall. I gather he's forgiven me for what I brayed as that atrocity smacked my fat lunettes: "My God! Why didn't they tell us the *Germans* won?"

My only remorse is that Bob meant well and I'm fond of him. What I'm planning is a betrayal of his apparent, surprising affection for me. The White House won't be panting for his *next* request to give some upper Connecticut Avenue crone a holler, put it that way. And too bad, because is Potus ever going to get an earful!

The gun in my lap was Cadwaller's. Like so much about Hopsie, his old Harvard nickname included, the pistol seemed mildly absurd until the night a thief brazenly broke, with an annunciatory crash whose declarativeness would've pleased Beethoven, into the Residence in Delhi. Then my brisk third husband reached behind a certain book on our shelves and it jumped into his hand as obediently as a phone receiver, his customary daytime armament.

Which sound is the one with which Potus is most unfamiliar? Because I'm only human, I'll laugh if you say "Beethoven," but the answer is a shot fired in anger. If *I* can find the nerve to fire it, mine will be.

Rightly or wrongly, I think I've got some standing as well as a stake in all this. My mother was Daisy Fay

Buchanan. Unknown now except to Jazz Age specialists, she was one of the nudest pearls in that era's champagne goblet until the scandal whose aftershocks italicized my childhood.

In my younger, less invulnerable years, I often wished my guardian hadn't told me what Daisy was alleged by no less an authority than herself to have wished for me at birth. He had so few even fugitively Pamcentric anecdotes in stock that I can't blame him for sharing that one when I kept whinging, and she didn't get her stupid wish. Or, depending on how you count, her fairy-tale three wishes.

No, Mother: your daughter never did get to be beautiful. Nor even stay so little once I shot up to a hoop-hunting five-foot-ten in the Midwest the year after you died. And I wasn't a fool. I made my way.

No need to pretend you're jealous, though! We both know you'd have soon found a reason to be dismissive. Measuring my real career against your fantasized one, you'd've found Pammie's clumsy imitation, with my big feet and my ugly hair and my stupid tugs at your beaded dress in East Egg, wanting.

In a dopey way—and pun intended, mother mine—you pined for France. Your daughter saw it in an overseas cap and GI shoes, saw Paris liberated. Dachau too? Dachau too.

Physically, you should know, I survived the Twentieth Century unscathed. The only exception is or was a small scar over my left eyebrow. For almost half a century I used to focus on it in my medicine-cabinet mug shot, trying to decide if it looked more like part of an *i* or part of an *r*. Then it got lost in Clio Airways-carved newspaper crumples like everything else.

Why am I pretending you can hear me, mother mine? When the White House switchboard finds me, I need to be able to feel I speak for you. When the phone rings, I'll snatch up Cadwaller's gun from my ancient snatch. As Potus starts burbling birthday congratulations to an old bag he's never heard of, I'll interrupt. Yes, I will!

With what, mother mine? A litany of what he's done? By now he could've heard all that from millions. As countless readers of the Declaration of Independence have discovered with surprise and annoyance, particularized lists of offenses can get tiresome even in indictments written by Thomas Jefferson. Or else, mother mine, should I just say this?

"Yes, yes. I know who you are. Do you know who I am, Mr. President? I'm Daisy Buchanan's daughter. Their only child, the last of them. These days I roost on upper Connecticut Avenue like a falcon, and believe me: I've seen 'em come and I've seen 'em go down at your end. Oh, hell, Potus! We both know you're going to do whatever you like. But before you get on with it, I've got one question. Do you expect me, me, me, me! Do you really expect *me* to put up with this shit?"

At which point, at least if all has gone well—can my hand raise Cadwaller's gun in time? will he have hung up by then?—I'll give a screech of fury. That will be my wordless last word before, right in Potus' ear, I blow the prettiest thing about me at fourteen—my attractively bejangled, hopeful brains—to goddam Clio come.

/

2 : Bavaria, 1945

Datelined May 17, 1945, twenty-four-year-old Pamela Buchanan's report on the Final Solution for *Regent's* had paralyzed me until I hit on misrepresenting Eddie Whitling as a nameless GI: "Quite possibly for good, the soldier's face changed" and so on. Only then did every other element of "The Gates of Hell" fall into place.

I suppose using Eddie gave me the clutchable point of familiarity I needed to get on with it. It was the hardest piece I'd ever had to write, and its opening line—"This pile died in a boxcar"—won the admiration of none other than Cyril Connolly. In my defense, Eddie hadn't been quite Eddie—or even CBS's sepulture-voiced Edmond Whitling, his other masquerade—since we came upon the death train.

No guards, no locomotive, no explanation. Just a stench as big as the Prado under a low pewter sky that kept it sealed in over thirty or forty boxcars and flatcars packed with former people, none alive. I'm not even going to try to describe all we saw. Doing it once in dulcet magazine prose nearly killed me, and I was lots younger and spryer then. But as a sample of what doesn't get in the books and didn't in *Regent's*, I'll tell you about Eddie's and my first test—which we passed—in the etiquette of genocide.

It was a practical dilemma, because we'd yelled at our driver to stop and scrambled out as soon as we came upon the train some minutes after the leading patrols. Three or four cars down, we saw that it stretched on and on.

Eleven months after D-Day, Eddie and I knew each other best when wordless. Here was the question we asked with our skins: now that we knew, when did this get redundant? The two thousand or so *other* dead Jews could be not unreasonably assumed to be more of the same. Oh, we might spot one whose specs still encircled his I-was-a-tailor stare at the sky, proof he'd stayed a person until nearly the end. Maybe one ex-little girl would be clutching a doll: human interest at last!

Faced with that much formerly human immobility in close-up, we two felt frantic to reconvert ourselves into mobile, aggressive, not-dead Americans by jogging back to our jeep to barrel by on four wheels. The now aging stink of the former people's final excretions was still being caught up with by the younger and friskier smell of their corpses, as if they'd expired while trying to write their names on each other in feeble dribbles of pee and crap: nothing else left to communicate, nothing else left to write it on or with. Prim Roy Charters, my *Regent's* editor, was fretful about letting me say "excretions," much less the word that in 1945 would've shocked printers and made our readers ask what this world was coming to. LET ME SAY SHIT I WAS THERE IT WAS SHIT IT WAS SHIT IT WAS SHIT PAM, I Telexed from Munich in a pointless fury.

More etiquette of genocide: so long as we were on foot, we understood smoking was verboten. Our nostrils were pining for the fragrance of our future cancer to dull each new intake of feces and carrion.

Etiquette of journalism: the camp lay ahead and it was our story. If we stupidly tramped the whole length of the death train like two amateurs, other reporters might beat us to Dachau. We knew how we'd feel if some brisker rival, say the *Herald Trib's* Marguerite Higgins—Pam's ETO doppelganger, younger than me by all of three months—went bucketing by as we trudged alongside the dogfaces who'd unslung their rifles, perhaps for some illusion of potential to affect the situation, back at the first flatcar. Ever since the Russians had come upon Auschwitz and with local urgency once the Brits to our north had found Belsen two weeks ago, being first in on a concentration camp's liberation had been every war reporter's new grail.

No fair, I thought: Maggie'd already gotten Buchenwald. Eddie could be on the radio tonight. With *Regent's* longer lead time, I'd have to work twice as hard for my piece not to sound dead on arrival. And above all, we knew that the farther we walked, the farther we'd have to walk back, plodding past faces we'd now recognize or particularly memorable tessellations of bodies—unless our GI driver, no master of the initiative even when what lay ahead didn't start him gibbering "Jesus," trundled up the road on his own. Doubtful, and we'd gone too far to wave.

Well, we paid our respects. Couldn't see how to avoid it, since neither of us wanted to be the one to bleat "Enough" and bolt jeepward. Of course we were each hoping the other would crack. We'd seen bodies before, but killed soldiers did and no doubt do tend to be reasonably healthy and well-fed and young and clothed. And shod, though I'm not sure why bare feet make such a difference. They do, like bare diarrhea-dribbling gray rumps and shrunken penises and one ex-child's small nipples, which somehow unlike her eyes struck me as closed.

"And here I was counting on you to be the weaker sex," a re-Eddified or rather rebenighted Eddie was to say at the pub party for *Nothing Like a Dame*, my ignobly frisky 1947 account of the lighter side of World War Two. "Why do you think I took you along?"

"I'm sorry: took me along?" I said and his grin lost wattage. We'd both attended enough Royal Navy briefings in England to know that, in that particular ice-cube voice, "I'm sorry" meant "release the hounds."

Anyhow, we followed the tracks on into the camp, and if you've never visited what's left of Dachau—never have myself, so don't know how much has been prettily, *tactfully* preserved—you should know "camp" is a misnomer. Like the industrial complex it was, Dachau was built to last. Dozens of buildings spilled out over many walled areas as migraine-inducingly as typography in an alien language.

Neither I nor any elderly GI could tell you what Dachau looked like, though. We never saw it as a going concern. We saw it in bankruptcy, with all the mess you'd expect when a business goes under: its inventory scattered and suddenly puzzling, its former foremen unemployed. Its product no longer in urgent demand.

In *The Gal I Left Behind Me*, Metro's flop 1949 Hollywoodization of my inane first book, Eddie's and my trek got telescoped into screen shorthand of wondrous puerility. Once this pause for a world-historical postcard in the Gal's itinerary had been identified by a sign reading DACHAU over the entrance to what appeared to be a converted cattle ranch—and was, left over from some recent oater; the camp's real outer wall was brick, its name unproclaimed by any similar logo—a brief but thoughtful reaction shot showed our dismay. *DISSOLVE TO* a Glenn Millerized VE-Day in Hitler's old Munich apartment, true as to setting but not a lot else.

That's when Eddie "Harting" in his lovably testy way finally explodes: "Will you shut your trap, Peg? I've loved you since Normandy." Me, or rather "Peg Kimball," spunky to the last: "Not London?" *THE END*. Inserted closeup of Adolf's portrait rolling its eyes no doubt just Pam's later hallucination.

In the nonhallucination, the tracks didn't let up once we were inside the grounds, the grounds?, the grounds. With nothing else to guide us, we followed them. The GIs we saw flitting here and there before they melted into or vanished behind one warehouse or workshop or another—if you can't picture how exhausted men flit, it's the same fast-slow-fast as a firefly's dusk squiggle, only more unshaven and cantilevered by equipment—might be under orders that would veer us off course.

The earth was vile mud streaked with random silver. Cadaver, face down in puddle: a journalistic detail, should maybe make a note of it before I forget. (I did neither). Brains stove in and showing. Dogs somewhere barked urgently. Clammy rain mugged the air without falling. The fresh batch of cattle cars we saw as we came up to the railhead were empty, but the unscrubbed shit-stains—take that, Roy—and reek told us they hadn't always been.

Beyond them, past a stubby bridge over an undredged, just as well, canal, a squat guardhouse with a gun tower broke an unending tall shiver of wire fence. Three or four jeeps were already wedged in the badly paved gap between the bridge's far end and the guardhouse's archway. In helmeted mottlings of drab coats and grime, a few dozen of our boys clustered around them.

"We guessed right," said someone beside me exultantly. Unscrambling my mind from not-Pam paralysis, I realized Eddie's voice had surprised me because I hadn't heard it or even not-Eddie's voice since we'd come upon the death train.

And yes, this was it: the famous encounter between our fabled Wrigley-chewing naïveté and the Nazis' ultimate *Gesamtkunstwerk*. I doubt I'll get much credit for admitting that the pajama'ed stew of not-quite-former people on the far side of the guardhouse archway's gate—yes, *that* gate, with the inset motto, smaller than its iron twin over the aperture of Auschwitz, reading *Arbeit Macht Frei*—reminded me briefly of my old girls' school in St. Paul during our one night fire drill.

The regimental CO had orders to keep the not-quite-former people penned until medicos and documentation crews reached the scene. The only reason things kept happening just the same was that something had to. If you must know, leaving aside the corpses and the clatter of machine-gun fire from behind us on the other side of the canal, the climax of the liberation of Dachau was a lot like being stuck on a mucky outdoor subway platform at rush hour.

Machine-gun fire? Oh, yes. Before the officers stopped it, we machine-gunned a few dozen of the camp's guards out of hand. I didn't watch it happen, but I later saw their crumpled bodies in an unmistakable, deeply satisfying (PAM HAVE YOU GONE CRAZY ROY) domino arrangement. True, those who got machine-gunned were unarmed by then. Ethically speaking, we didn't have any business machine-gunning them. They probably shouldn't have been machine-gunned until they had no hearts left to speak of.

Most of us had gotten here by walking past the death train. We killed all the dogs too. In my earshot, a light colonel got into a shouting match with a brigadier from another outfit over who had responsibility for the camp, ended up pulling a .45 on him; it didn't seem unreasonable. Nobody got court-martialed over anything at all that happened the day we liberated Dachau.

In the one photograph I've seen that I believe shows Pamela Buchanan of *Regent's* on the spot, my head has started to turn away from the *Arbeit Macht Frei* gate as my blurred paw reaches up to my breast pocket. But if it's the moment I remember, in fact my would-be grip's retreating. At a loss, the GIs nearby had started to push cigarettes and candy into too many hands through the bars until some shavetail lieutenant shouted at us to quit.

Unless we had thirty thousand packs of Wrigley's and Lucky Strikes coming out of our pink assholes, we were fueling a melee. *Lt waving arms—POWs [sic] yelling*, my mud-smudged notebook scrawl reads. Then, amid the cries of resharpened despair from up front—and of indifferent and baying, otherworldly celebration from somewhere farther back in the scrum of not-quite-former people—I heard a croaking summons unmistakably addressed to me.

"Mar-ga-ret Mitchell," some not-quite-former person was calling. "Margaret Mitchell."

I was tentative as I approached. Squeamish? Yes, squeamish. The mob of hands that gripped the gate had knuckles as prominent as buboes. If you weren't there, you'll never truly know how the distinctiveness of eyes is that they're the only part of a human body that doesn't and can't get dirty. They all stank like latrines. "I'm sorry, I don't understand," I said.

"Margaret MIT-chell," he repeated and I naturally thought Dachau had driven him mad. I couldn't have gotten it more backwards. Behind me, two more jeeps had wedged their snouts into what was fast becoming Dachau gridlock. I heard some sort of fracas break out: "My orders are to *secure this fucking camp.* These men aren't under your command. So help me, sir, if you don't—"

"What the fuck are you, Colonel? Some kind of guardhouse lawyer?"

"Margaret *Mitchell!*" my inmate—my, how the proprietary instinct runs deep—raged at seeing my attention divide.

"Yes, yes. Margaret Mitchell," I tried to reassure him. "*Gone With The Wind.* Yes, yes, yes. Americans! Statue of Liberty."

As you may have gathered, my second guess was that he was babbling the only American name he could remember. Again, I couldn't have been more wrong.

"*Hilfe*!" came a wail from deep inside the compound. Automatically, I jerked my eyes to the sound. Dully, I watched what happened next happen. Just before it vanished among scrabbling fists and fingernails, the guard's face had looked like a turnip that screamed.

"*Please*! I am Nachum Unger. Nachum Unger, Nachum Unger! We are colleagues. Was it in Technicolor, and did Paulette, Paulette—Paulette *Goddard*!—play Scarlett? I'm Nachum Unger—Nachum Unger, the poet! My work was as the cinema critic for the *Yiddisher Togsblat* in Dresden. For the love of God, colleague, tell me! Did Selznick succeed?"

"Does it matter?" I marveled inanely. But it did. His face was fierce with triumph.

"Margaret Mitchell!" Nachum Unger boasted. "David O. Selznick. 'Scarlett O'Hara she was not beautiful, but men seldom realized it when caught by her charm as the Tarl-ton twins were.' Eight years I have been in this place. I swore my reason to live would be unique—so unique they'd never guess. *Here I am.* Please tell me, colleague!"

I gaped. Honestly, should I have told him—Nachum Unger, Nachum Unger, weighing eighty pounds and reeking like a latrine—that I didn't know? That *GWTW*, six incredible years ago, had been infra dig in Pam's suddenly silly, newly obtuse Manhattan set?

"It is a cinematic masterpiece, Mr. Unger," I said formally. "Feel free to tell your surviving readers so."

Nachum Unger's chin lifted. "Thank you, colleague." His unfoulable eyes gleamed.

"No, no." I reached out a grotesquely healthy and corpuscle-crammed Pam-palm to cover his knuckles' gray stones. "Thank *you*," I told him, for I did understand I'd just heard a tribute to something about America I'd never held in proper awe.

Brother, was I about to be upstaged. The new female voice that crashed in beside me was so disorienting I thought it must've come from inside my own skull: "Put a sock in it, Melly. I don't know why *you're* here, but I've got a job to do. Did they really kill that guard with their bare hands?"

"Yes," I said. "Jesus, what are you doing, Maggie?"

Bewildered, I was staring at compact-mirror range into the determined face of one the greatest war reporters of the atrocious century we shared, ravishing even in the overcoat and oddly earflapped cap she'd scrounged in an apparent bid—hadn't even crossed my mind, and evidently didn't need to—to disguise her femininity. If you want to please my lesser ghost, honor her giant one. Face the ocean when you do.

Friends we weren't, though, then or ever. "What do you think I'm doing, 'Pamita'? I'm going in. My God, you don't even know who's supposed to be in the VIP hut in there. Von Schussnigg, Leon Blum, Niemoller! I'm sorry for these poor bastards too. But amateur hour is *o*-vah."

And she'd already gotten Buchenwald. In my defense, remember that even colonels and generals lost their heads the day we liberated Dachau. Remember that Marguerite Higgins and I were both twenty-four, and Dachau wasn't yet, well, *Dachau*. Given her looks (sexier than mine, no matter her garb) and reputation (ditto), the accusation implied in calling me "Pamita" was an outrage I couldn't abide.

"Hey, *fuck you!*" I screamed. "Fuck you. I got here first, Maggie! I got here first."

"So did the Vikings. Now get out of my way."

In "The Gates of Hell," the *Arbeit Macht Frei* gate opens somewhat mysteriously: "As if the demand for liberty of those within could no longer be contained." It's bullshit. I was standing right there when, after a quick check on whether the arguing officers were paying any attention, which they weren't—that was when the light colonel jerked his .45 from its holster—Maggie started to prise up the restraining bar I hadn't noticed, incidentally proving which of us was the real deal.

The thing she hadn't counted on was that the once and future people all straining against it had no stake whatsoever in letting anyone *in*. They only saw someone about to let them out, and I doubt they even registered Maggie was female. That can't have been a too significant distinction in there since around 1936. The second the restraining bar was loose, she went from bulky-coated human champagne bottle to cork in a latrine-smelling flash flood.

If the gate's outward swing hadn't pinned me behind it, I'd've been as buffeted as she was. I'd lost sight of Nachum Unger too, had no idea if he was part of that frail and foul exodus. Nor did I see him once the crowd was recooped, or when I went back the next day in a foredoomed attempt to refind him.

My only exportable Dachau memento? When the inmates sluiced out and the gate's bars slammed into me or I banged into them, the *r* or the *i* in *Arbeit Macht Frei* cut my forehead, three-fourths of an inch above my left eyebrow. Half a century later, when my medicine-cabinet mug shot showed me the tiny scar was lost for good in crinkly Clio Airways routes, I confess to having mixed feelings.

At some officer's shout, a few Tommy guns rattatted. Our boys had fired in the air, but the shots stopped the flood anyway. Some of them trying to apologize as they did so—and the single word "pal," spoken in a Tulsa twang in Dachau's miasmal air, was never to sound so moving or so inadequate to me again—the GIs moved the protesting, all too used to being herdable not-quite-former people back into their compound, desperately trying to avoid actually pushing them or aiming weapons: "Ya gotta wait, pal. Doctors are coming. Food's on the way. For your sake I hope it ain't Spam, buddy! You know Spam? Spam?"

Not a soul understood him, but his face must've been comic: I swear someone laughed. The sound could have made a bird gasp.

Just as the last of them were being squeezed back behind the gate, another GI grabbed my elbow to propel me inside. "Mac, what the fuck are you doing?" I shrieked. "Do I look Jewish to you, for Christ's sake?"

"You were bleeding," he blurted by way of

atonement, mixed with a hint that I'd pulled a fast one: something any snail could do. Probably a replacement, he looked as if his unlined face's inadequacy to everything it was being asked to react to would make his eyes resentful rather than generous in old age.

Quoth droll Eddie in Munich: "Easy mistake, Pamita. You *are* on the skinny side. Plus, that beak—"

I pitched a pillow at him. "I didn't say I was complaining, did I?" he called. Stomping out of the room, I stomped back to my typewriter. Three words aside—"by Pamela Buchanan"—the scrounged page rolled into it was still blank but for the swastika watermark.

It wasn't until my third straight day of being blocked on "The Gates of Hell" that I smacked my still Band-Aided forehead at my stupidity. Good God, why hadn't I kept my mouth shut and bled? A little more thinking fast and I'd have succeeded where Maggie had failed. What a scoop: the only correspondent to experience Dachau while caged.

Thanks partly to that, none of Maggie's biographers mentions the *other* woman reporter on the scene that day. Her mischief with the gate does show up in the more scrupulous accounts of Dachau's liberation and is this old bag's test of their reliability. Miss Higgins's own published report, incidentally, had Eddie and me guffawing, since she and a photographer apparently had ended the Holocaust, which we didn't yet call it, single-handed. In fairness to her, I repeat: twenty-four.

When I respotted her near the jeeps, she was plainly the worse for wear. I think she'd actually gotten knocked down in the panic when the Tommy guns blatted skyward—and if ever a sky deserved killing, it was that one. Tossing a breath up at those tightscrolled curls under her strangely earflapped soldier's cap, she got out a notebook coolly enough to turn Pam's impulse to mimic her into intolerable monkey-do. As I started past her to make my way back over the stubby canal bridge instead, secretly begging only to be somewhere not raw with the imprint of livid events—in Dachau? Good luck there, Miss Buchanan—I heard her say, "Colonel, Maggie Higgins, the *Trib.* Do we have an estimate yet on the numbers?"

"In there? My God, none."

If I was looking for Eddie, which I'd like some points for thinking I wasn't, I was lurching the wrong way. He was still on the compound side of the canal, trailing behind a squad of GIs along the fence to see if he could talk to anyone through it without risking his or their electrocution. (The juice was still live.) What hindsight tells me I was after is bound to strike you as grotesque. Not unlike Eddie, I was looking for a little bit of Dachau I could call my own.

I wished "Tiger! Tiger!," my *Regent's* report on life with a tank-destroyer battalion ten days after the relief of Bastogne, hadn't stressed stench. Now I'd sound like a real broken record, all nose and no brain! Dogs would do better. The six I'd just lurched past, what made them journalistically interesting? Got it: even in death, thanks to their pelts, they looked warmer than the fifteen or twenty near naked or naked former human beings I could see sprawled in plain sight between mud and silver.

American trucks were starting to groan this way from the camp's main entrance, so slowly they clearly didn't understand anything. Near the second cattle train—or was it now the first? The shitstained and shit-stinking but empty one, near the railhead—a lone MP with a snagged brassard was already posted to direct them here and there with stupid traffic flags. He had a GI handkerchief knotted over his nose and mouth against the smell.

"Howdy, cowpoke!" I brayed. "Robbing the

train? Stick 'em up! That gold'll never reach Tucson, Tom Mix. Bang, bang, bang!"

Fumbling with his stupid sticks—too slow, too slow!—he jerked the kerchief down. "Ma'am?" A few seconds later, he said, "Ma'am, I can't move from here. How can I help?"

Pam was pretty sure he couldn't, but I did have a list. If I'd had my druthers, Pam definitely wouldn't be on her hands and knees in this icy foul muck. Lord knew when we'd get to change to dry clothes! I wished Pam hadn't just vomited, partly because that reminded me of all the food she could eat anytime she or I liked.

I wished the stupid MP and his fucking dumb little furled flags would wave the trucks to run over me when they finally got here. On my hands and knees in randomly silvered mud, I was feeling sorry for myself with starved bodies reaching for the sky around me.

The hands that helped up not-Pam turned out to be Eddie's. "It's all right, Pamita," he said, atavistically batting away the reek of my pukey breath before a grimace signaled he'd remembered what replaced it: Dachau's. "It got to me too."

And notice, as I only did a week later, his admission's implication that I hadn't seen it get to him back at the death train. Men always try to treat our hearing and our sight as two sovereign powers. They can't even be selfless without hoping we're eyeless.

"The Gates of Hell" takes dramatic license in compressing all its perceptions—and omissions, too—into one afternoon. In unforgiving fact, it wasn't until we forced ourselves to go back the next day and split up to poke around as much of Dachau's vast layout as possible that Eddie completed his metamorphosis into "the soldier" by discovering its abandoned Brigadoon. Spotting a portal in a discreetly walled brick compound north of the inmates' stinking barracks, he stepped into a haven of *Gemutlichkeit* homes and tended lawns: housing for *Hauptsturmfühers, Sturmbannführers, Obersturmbannführers,* and *Standartenführers.*

The one he entered was cozy, with the one and only unprefixed Führer approvingly sizing up chintz from his gilt frame above the mantel and the familiar boiled-potato smell of humid German kitchens, whose gestalt always does make cooking seem like another ablution. People had sat down to meals here. Upstairs, one room held a boy's playthings: rocking horse, toy train set. Children had been raised here.

In the master bedroom, which like the whole building was infuriatingly undamaged—our boys had looted the liquor, left the rest—the soldier saw a feather bed. From pure campaign habit, he threw himself on it, stretching out from crusty boots to crewcut; booze was the only other thing nobody in the ETO passed up. We claimed beds even when we hadn't felt tired until then, knowing our illusion of wakefulness was just exhaustion held in check by nerves.

Just as the pillow's wings nunnified the soldier's now helmetless head, obliterating the ticks of the watch on the forearm hooked under it, he turned his eyes to the wall. Like all those in this house that faced the inmates' barracks, it had no windows.

Thanks to a grippable bedpost, he was back on his feet right away. When Eddie agreed to let Pam borrow not-him for "The Gates of Hell," he claimed his hands were swabbing at his clothes without a say-so from his brain.

However pooped a man may be, some beds just aren't worth sharing with their former owners. Of course "I'd just pictured that pillow under Frau Major's fat ass" was too crude an epiphany for the soldier to think it, but I did try to hint at the sexual dimension of Eddie's revulsion by scattering some women's unmentionables on the carpet. They'd probably been there, Frau Major having presumably packed in a hell of a hurry.

From his next remark, Eddie must've regretted giving me that glimpse of an Eddie whose body was jerked by morality's strings. We were in the gloomy domed basement of Munich's Hofbrauhaus, site of Adolf's proclamation of the Nazi Party's program in 1920 and now, a few unmoving migrations later, one of our Forty-Fifth Division's regimental CPs. The Germans took it back eventually; the night Cadwaller and I revisited in 1959, a group sing broke out, swaying tankards and all. "Let's get the hell out of here," my third husband grunted.

Four days after Dachau's liberation, what was Eddie's next remark? This, with a forced and hence authentic grin: "Natch, if you'd been there with me, Pamita, the story might've had a different ending. Huh?" He even got his eyes to twinkle, which was like watching television be invented in a crypt.

"Oh, Eddie," I said, disgusted. And for the first time, sorry for him, the reaction that fatally lingered.

"I wonder if they made beer there?" he said restlessly, which was chivalry of a sort. He was groping for an acceptable halfway house between his manner and my mood. "You didn't see a brewery, did you?"

I hadn't, which doesn't mean there wasn't one somewhere in Dachau's maze of workshops. And though I hesitated briefly over my typewriter, the American woman who wandered through "The Gates of Hell" didn't see a brewery either. Fudging was one thing, outright invention another.

For instance, it was a meek Hershey bar, not my idiot Lucky Strikes, that the nurse was on the verge of pulling from her breast pocket to push through the *Arbeit Macht Frei* gate when the shavetail lieutenant shouted at us to quit. That kind of thing was all right. So was resorting to an anodyne "Later" to get her inside the prisoners' compound, something I only did under escort the next day.

I'd reluctantly introduced the nurse after realizing the soldier couldn't see everything, not only because his perspective was limited but because no such entity was within human grasp. As I wrote in "The Gates," there was no *everything* to Dachau. Something would always be left out, had to be—the story of a single shoe in that place could've filled an encyclopedia.

So like the soldier, the nurse just wandered. Unlike me, she didn't throw up, much less turn a lone MP into Hopalong Cassidy; she was a professional. As she went through the barracks, she was assessing which emaciated not-quite-former people had a chance. Around the time the soldier came upon the officers' quarters, the nurse found the camp's infirmary.

Naturally it was for the guards. Unable to grasp that not only were they prisoners but their former victims weren't, its tenants—poor halitosal Hansel, down with a corn—had been monstrously indignant, so I was told, at being ejected (poor green-toothed skeevy Erich, did you shiver with the flu?) to make room for a handful of inmates.

All the same, it's true that, like the soldier and the nurse in "The Gates," Eddie's and my paths recrossed outside Dachau's modest crematorium. Modest, you ask? Oh, yes. Unlike Auschwitz, Dachau wasn't an extermination camp. The thousands who died there died unsystematically: shot, worked to death, succumbing to starvation or disease.

Mauled by trained dogs for entertainment.

In the usual tangle, the couple of hundred as yet unburned bodies our soldiers had found heaped almost to the rafters in the storehouse next to the crematorium were still there. Roy rightly made me cut an overelaborate simile about indecipherable chalk at the top of an oversized blackboard, but I was trying to get across the strangeness of looking up at mortality. Ever since, I've believed we stick it in the ground to make that state inferior to our own.

Anyhow, that's when I turned and saw Eddie. While I wouldn't understand for years that the final sentence of "The Gates of Hell" was also my goodbye to my quip-happy ETO Virgil, I was proudest of it for a note of doubt I don't think my editor (BEAUTIFUL ROY) ever caught. Tapped out in Munich in a two a.m. litter of balled-up pages, overflowing ashtrays, half-filled bottles, maimed copies of *Mein Kampf* and Eddie's new snores, this was it: "Four living creatures despite it all, their eyes met."

/

3 : Los Angeles, 1951

By the year I met the nameless California girl I call the Great Unknown, my salad days as a war correspondent and indeed a journalist of any stripe were behind me. Pamela Buchanan didn't go to Korea, that reject pile of bits of World War Two that hadn't been fought at the time. In Hollywood ever since *Nothing Like A Dame* had been turned into *The Gal I Left Behind Me*, I was happily—well, contentedly—married to Noah Gerson, who'd produced it and somehow found it in his heart not to shudder at the sight of me once the reviews were in.

That morning in our now twice redecorated Beverly Hills home, Noah had let out a swiftly muted cry. The script he'd found in his briefcase was supposed to have been messengered from the studio to some actor or actress whose name I don't recall. He was addled enough to reach for an already emptied juice glass.

"Pammie, I hate having to ask. Could you please, please run this up to Malibu? We're in horrible rewrites on *That's All She Wrote*. You know I'd do it, but I don't have time."

Was I resentful? It's possible. In a modest rebellion once Gerson's Packard scooted offscreen (our front window was Beverly Hills Panavision), I phoned up the DeWitts for a lunch date. Since I'd be going out their way anyhow, I'd drop off the script after a good meal and some enjoyably surf-pearled Manhattanish banter. I was ignoring a stricken face's plea of the sooner the better.

Noah aside, the friendship between Eve Harrington and Daisy Buchanan's daughter is probably my warmest memory of Hollywood. *The Gal I Left Behind Me* had been the movie Eve scandalized Broadway by ditching the Theatuh to star in right after her prizewinning performance in *Footsteps on The Ceiling*—or *Footprints on the Ceiling*, as she used to call it in bawdy moods. As for her husband, unabashed at living off his wife's earnings—"Good Lord! So did God," he crowed, flourishing a hand at our dazzling surroundings—and amusing himself by sporting atrocious Hawaiian shirts in their sun-medallioned garden as he chatted with servants in the most debonair pidgin Spanish I've ever heard, Addison had ditched life as a drama critic, tucked cigarette holder in mouth and gone back to writing the taut, spiky poetry he'd begun with in his youth.

Luscious Eve was off shooting, though. Addison said he'd be tickled mauve just the same. As usual, he proposed their Filipino cook's warthog sandwiches—his delighted description, not mine—but the day's warm yet wild breeze had me craving the Pacific in closeup. I convinced him to putter down from their hill and meet me in Eve's and my favorite restaurant, glassed-in and exclusive but hunkered out at the far end of a weathered fishing pier near Porto Marina Way.

In a Hawaiian shirt that was dreadful even by

his standards—"Jekyll and hydrangeas," he bragged—Addison dropped into the facing chair. I was instantly overdressed by comparison in a bronze silk blouse, copper scarf, beige toreadors, low-heeled fawn shoes and modest peach handbag. When friendship's unflustered edition of silence came over us after updates and gossip, we gazed at the beach's dotted idyll: tiny lovelies with their interchangeable Chucks, gulls soaring like punctuation hunting the sky's nonexistent sentence. He looked so tranquilly pleased I decided to tease him with beatitude's opposite: "Do you envy them, Addison?"

Judging from how his eyes had to drop as well as turn to meet mine, he'd misunderstood me slightly. "Oh, Pam! We're all creatures and the rest is verbiage. That's really all my verbiage is about."

Our food came. Recalling a jingle made up by a now dead and obscure (not in that order) Greenwich Village prankster to entertain Pammie in her Jazz Age childhood, I recited. Tickled purple, Addison wanted to memorize it: "'To eat an oyster / You crack it foyster / This part is moister!...' Wait, what's the last line again?"

As we crunched back over gravel to our cars, the beach's squeals and caws becoming audible just as their source grew invisible, I remembered Gerson's script with distaste. "Addison!" I called, eyeing it in the back seat. "Do you know where Blank Blank lives?"

"My dear girl, I'm a poet. I study how people live"—grand sweep of his car keys—"not where. To find my way home, I just keep going up."

In an un-Gersonishly hasty scribble, the address was on the envelope. I still needed help. Damn few of the surf-facing houses on the coastal highway's beach side sported visible numbers then or maybe now: too prey to fans. As for why I've long forgotten the name and even gender of the star Gerson was pursuing, your guess is as good as mine. Mine is that the erasure is memory's way of mimicking the fact that Glen or Glenda never starred in that film, title also gone to oblivion and evidently unproduced.

Near Topanga Canyon Boulevard, Gerson had said. More irked at that sweet man than I could ever remember being, I parked when I got to it and set out, the script swinging like a second handbag to metronome my real one. Found one *boite* with a fearlessly displayed address under twenty digits lower than mine, so at least he hadn't been lying. But its neighbors' expensive roofs and protectively recessed, unnumbered doorways wandered away from Pam's sight as if queuing for an invasion of Canada.

Nothing for it: I'd have to find someone to ask. The odds of spotting any resident in reach of my halloo on the *highway* side were about as good, though for the opposite reason, as seeing convicts wander at will outside a maximum-security prison. They kept to themselves, those exiles from availability: on the beach side, with architecture to match. When you drive past, you're really looking at their houses' anuses, not facades.

Spotting a thumb of white with its nail painted blue in an unfenced gap between two *boites*, grimly aware the breeze had played hob with a hairdo that had been hobbled even at Antoine's, I plunged into the sand, my miscast shoes sinking like miscast actors' hearts. Out back, since the beach was the whole bloody point, I knew I'd see somebody hallooable. Maybe even, by good fortune, run right into Blank Blank him/herself.

To my shock—but why? It wasn't that unlikely—someone hallooed me instead. "Why, Pam! Pam Buchanan. That *is* you at last, isn't it?"

Turning, I found myself face to face with a woman's apparently decapitated head. We weren't precisely eye to eye, since her pleased blue ones, pellet nose and rich red pulpit mouth were perpendicular to mine inside a dark crater of tangled bangs and between two slats of the house's raised beach-side deck. The rest of the railing was mostly screened by bright Navajo rugs, explaining the Mary-Queen-of-Scots effect.

"Well, hello!" I said, purse and script dangling at my beige toreadors' flanks. I couldn't remember who the fuck she was.

"This is so nice! Come around that way," said she with a lift of her chin, meaning the stairs on the deck's far side.

As I did as told, I was racking what was left of my brains after lunch's two bottles of Riesling. I knew her face wasn't famous, but then what was she? My guess is I'd met some two thousand of movieland's crème de la foam, and she really could have been anybody. Unless her chat dropped a hint or she tactfully recognized the problem and told me her name, I was stuck.

While I wouldn't call it a hint, it was certainly intimate. As I reached the top step and all of her sat up, naked as the day we were born, her small breasts stopped pouting and grinned.

She hadn't sat up before then, you ask? You don't know California. Hands to her sides like a swimmer at rest, upper baubles two dark stoppers on those little brown jugs and thatch going from crackle to cruciform as I came up the stairs, she was taking the sun and had even reclosed her eyes. Ten more seconds was ten more seconds.

"Isn't it wonderful? After all this time too. I didn't even know you lived out this far," she said eagerly, drawing up her knees. Only for balance as the deck braced her palms, though, not from self-consciousness.

"Me? Oh, God, no. I'm just, ah—" My purse and Gerson's script fidgeted as if I was unsure which was the right token.

"Oh, of course. I should've known from that handbag you didn't, shouldn't I? Rodeo Drive's satchel is Malibu's porte-monnaie." Proving that, whoever or whatever she was, she did have an eye for the telling detail.

Her grin counted on me to appreciate it, too. Her question asked Pam's approval, but before I could answer—how I would've beats me—she'd deduced that my fidgets, along with my pause on the weathered top step, might have a meaning that surprised her.

"I'm sorry! I'm stupid from sun. It never crossed my mind you were shy. 'Nothing like a dame!' But I can—"

As she tilted one haunch, her eyes still on me politely, the arm that reached for her towel was at once ceremonial and a genuine concession, what with every inch of that compact body plainly craving more radiance, heat, breeze and salt air. Craving everything except the gull droppings, so far as I could tell.

"Oh, no. It's perfectly all right," I told her, showing a cool I didn't feel by stepping onto the deck proper. "I'm just—"

"Silly, isn't it? He likes me dark all over," she cackled. "Marry in haste and repaint at leisure, I guess. I'll be black by the wedding. Of course you can't come."

"Oh, I'll live," I said vaguely.

"Let's just hope I do! Say, is that your new book? Please tell me it is." She meant Gerson's envelope. "Of course you remember how I loved your first one."

"This? Oh, no. Just somebody else's script. I'm just—"

"We've seen enough of those!" the Great Unknown laughed. "I'm making sun tea. Would you like some?"

"I'm sorry?"

"You don't boil it. Desert trick. Put it out in the sun and it steeps." She nodded to a screwtop jar of auburn liquid on the railing that I hadn't noticed before. I doubt I'd have noticed if she'd had an ack-ack gun hooked there. "Wait a sec. I'll get ice and glasses." One tanned arm scything out at me, the Great Unknown made as if to stand up. "Sugar or lemon for you?"

"Oh, neither! I'm just—"

Seeing *more* of that trim practical body wasn't my idea of a health program. Nor hers, since trying to rise started her coughing. "Oh, brother! What an awful racket. Let's make it worse, Cee." Squatting on her heels Indian-style—in profile, but my saints—she reached for cigarettes. "Want one?"

"No, thank you. You see, I'm—"

"Maybe I should just let you finish your sentence," she laughed, squatting and smoking. "I haven't let you get a word in edgewise. And you're Pam Buchanan, for Christ's sake! Who I've waited so long to meet."

"I'm sorry," I said. "I'd love to stay awhile, truly! But I can't! I'm on duty, you see. I can't find Blank Blank's house and I've got this stupid purse, script, to deliver."

"Oh, is *that* all?" The Great Unknown scrambled up, stood near Pam. Pam guessed the Navajo rugs were only decorative after all. "It's the one with the blue awning, just down there." She aimed with her cigarette hand.

"It looks like a mausoleum for tropical fish," I said.

"God, that's just like you! It used to belong to Monroe—" and she hesitated—"Monroe Stahr. But he died without ever living there."

Now that we were side by side, the most obvious difference—I mean aside from her being so richly naked, Pam so impoverishedly clothed in Rodeo Drive's copper, bronze and beige best—was that I was taller. I don't mean we were twins, just that we might have been sisters. Yet she was a pure emanation of Los Angeles, and Daisy Buchanan's daughter was a collection of scattered lives that had wired itself into a semblance of nativity. I'd thought it genuine because I'd unconsciously thought it temporary.

It only lasted a beat, as actors call seconds. Then I said, "Thanks ever so much! See you later."

"I hope so."

I was back down the steps when she called me. "Oh, Pam!"

I looked up, which I'd never done before at her. Since it was a clear day, they must've seen that smile and those dark stoppers winking all the way from Redondo. "Yes?"

"Come back when you've dropped it, why don't you? I'll give you sun tea. Or if you like, wine! One bottle between us and I bet you'll join me."

"Who knows? Maybe I will," I called over my shoulder as I floundered in costly beach flour. My purse and the script were now Malibu skipoles: inadequate ones, neither reaching the ground.

At the one with the blue awning, I got told Blank Blank wasn't home. A woman servant accepted *The Script Not Taken* on her hermaphrodite employer's behalf. Once I'd agreed with Manuela I had a car waiting, not precisely a lie, she showed me out at the street door. As I trudged up on the highway side past a Greyhound bus I'd neither catch nor ride to the uninhabited convertible I duly got into, drove away in and soon traded in for an Oldsmobile, I realized I'd never know for sure behind which of these hideouts the Great Unknown lay waiting with sun tea.

"I am California," the Great Unknown's bare skin had whispered as we stood side by side. "I'm sun, money, plenitude, joy. I was the victory in the war that you saw and the proof is I know nothing of it. I'm the reason you came here and the champagne that kissed you when you came down the ramp, and you should have listened to Addison. We are all creatures and the rest is verbiage. What we might have done if you'd accepted my sun tea wouldn't have bound you to any future at all, don't you see? We'd both have been back in our lives before midnight. But you might have had a few naked hours as the Pam you most dream of—*still, still*—before it was too late, since youth is the one god I, California, have been cursed by my makers from Cortez to Metro to kneel to. You can't have everything, can you?"

My one gesture indicating I'd like to broker a compromise was fairly pathetic. Once I'd tipped the sand from my shoes, I didn't put them back on, walked back up to my car with them hung from the hand Gerson's script had been in and hot asphalt and mica bits searing my soles. How my eyes scoured those hooded pink houses as I walked past them on the burning road, numberless, cuneiform, cruciform—oh, drat.

I loyst her.

/

4 : District of Columbia, 2006

"Mrs. Cadwaller? This is the White House calling," says a decorous but understandably brisk female voice. "Please hold for the President."

I seize Cadwaller's gun. "I'm here," I pointlessly tell limbo.

"Hello?" he says when he comes on the line. "Caddy?"

"This is Mrs. Pamela Cadwaller, yes."

"Don't they call you Caddy?" he asks pleasantly. "They ought to."

"Whatever you say, Mr. President."

"You know I asked my mom about you," he confides. "Want to know what she said? 'Why, George. I don't recall you calling me on *my* last birthday.' Heh, heh. I had to say, 'Well, Mom, I had the Turkish Prime minister in here and I had Tony Blair the day before. I had to work.'"

"Yes, I remember Mr. Blair's visit."

"Well, we get along. I like to tease him, you know: 'How can you call yourself an Oxford man? You're wearing a pink shirt.' But once a Mom always a Mom, what I say. Isn't that so, Caddy?"

"I guess so, Mr. President."

"No guessing allowed! That's our rule in this White House. You've got to be a mother yourself, I imagine."

"I'm afraid not, Mr. President. Only a writer."

"That's right and I want to tell you, Caddy. The First Lady is a big admirer of, uh"—check your notes, Potus—"*The Gory Bee.*"

He may have thought I wrote children's books. "Well, I know it's no *The Pet Goat*, Mr. Pres—"

But he hasn't stopped talking. "I know you had one, though." He means mother. "They tell me she was somebody, too."

"Everyone is, sir."

"Sorry, what's that you say, Caddy?"

"Nothing, Mr. President. Just clearing my throat. Please excuse me."

"Well, I'm glad we got this chance to talk. You know the Senator"—that would be dear Bob, of course—"must think awful highly of you. He came down here, showing everyone his gun."

I have no idea what that means. Don't blame me if I feel stuck inside, immobile, with the Potus blues again. "Mr. President," I say and suddenly don't know what to accuse him of. Where would *you* begin?

"Anyhow, Caddy. You keep well, you hear? Be careful blowing out those"—did he use index cards or a PC?—"eighty-six candles. We want you with us for a good long while yet. Well, good—"

"*AGH!*" I scream. Shakily hoisting Cadwaller's gun and putting it to my temple, I pull the trigger.

"Hey, Caddy! You all right there?" he says.

"Oh, my! Dear me. Oh, sorry, Mr. President. Just a cat jumping in my lap."

Mission accomplished? Plainly no, thanks to Cadwaller's gun. Your dandy little gun, darling, so handleable and light even in your eighty-six-year-old widow's uncertain grip. Your nifty nickel-plated pistol, so near to weightless every time I've hefted it. Your damned unloaded gun whose ammo clip Pam Buchanan, onetime war correspondent, has never thought to check.

"You ought to try it with daughters," Potus advises. "Anyhow, happy birthday again, old Caddy. Keep well. Anything at all we can do for you down here, just let us know."

"Well, Mr. President, for Bob's and my sake, you could try attending at least one soldier's funer—" But he's already gone. **-bc.**

Jeff VanderMeer

BORNE

I found *it* on a sunny gun-metal day when Mord had come a-roving near the Balcony Cliffs where I made my home. I found it on Mord's flank as he shuddered in his sleep, his one haunch rising high above me—deep within that brown fur jungle, mottled and stinking of musk and carrion and chemicals, teeming with parasites. Mord had leveled a building when he'd fallen over into slumber, and pieces of soft-brick rubble had mashed out to the sides, repurposed as Mord's bed.

Even asleep on his side, Mord's outline rose three stories. Mord had claws and fangs that could eviscerate, extinguish, quick as thought. His eyes, sometimes open even in dream, were vast fly-encrusted beacons, spies for a self-loathing mind that some believed worked on vast cosmic scales. But to me, a human flea at his flanks, all he stood for was good scavenging. Like many of my fellow scavengers, my skin was as brown as Mord's fur, so I hoped not to be seen by him or Company drones, even if my footsteps were felt. That was the risk I took—for my own survival, and to bring what I discovered back to Wick, my boss and lover both, so he could go through them like an oracle through entrails.

When Mord wandered out seething from the lair he had hollowed out in the Company's basement, all kinds of food and broken, bioneered artifacts became tangled in that ropy, dirt-bathed fur. Some of these things may have been placed there purposefully, Wick always warned me. They were *traps.* They were *misdirection.* But I knew traps. I set traps myself. "Just be careful, Rachel," Wick said as I left, and I ignored him as if he spoke a foreign language.

As Mord destroyed and re-imagined our already broken city for unknowable reasons, so too he replenished it in his thoughtless way. Debris fell off of him in a steady rain during his shambling walks. Sometimes he gave us only the corpses of unrecognizable animals, their skulls burst from some internal pressure, eyes bright and bulging. Sometimes, amongst the dander and the dirt, we found the beetles you could put in your ears, like the ones Wick made, and within the explosion of mint or lime or orange would form visions of places I hoped did not exist, had never existed, despite my childhood memories.

Mord's relationship with the Company, by the day I found *it* in his fur, had become truly dysfunctional. The Company could no longer control him, their creation. Wick had kept track of the progress of the Company's ever-swifter destruction through a telescope hidden in the trees atop Balcony Cliffs, had witnessed the Company's inability to fight back, although Wick sometimes mused that "perhaps Mord still works for the Company in the same way a tsunami works for the ocean." For these reasons I did not risk much more than exploratory missions along Mord's flank, the other scavengers using me as a canary to see if Mord truly slept or had concocted a ruse in the spiraling toxic waste dump of his mind.

This thing that I found was not food, not recognizably valuable, and yet it drew me to it. Entangled in the brown coarse seaweed of Mord's pelt, too near a curled claw much larger than my body, I found the sea anemone. At least that's what it looked like to me: a dark purple, half-closed, strobing beacon—like an emerald green over the purple. I could smell the sea salt on it, rising in a wave. For a moment there was no city, no search for food and water, no roving gangs and escaped, altered creatures of unknown origin or intent. No mutilated bodies dangling from broken street lamps, burned beyond recovering their names or faces. No buckled, grass-infiltrated concrete of abandoned highways, cracks now filled with huddled blue-and-pink communities of things like coral polyps, almost conscious, almost not.

For a precarious moment, the thing I'd found was a sea anemone from the tidal pools of my youth. I could smell the salt and feel the wind, knew the chill of water on my feet. The long exhilarating hunt for seashells. The gruff sound of my father's voice, the upward lilt of my mother's. The honey-warmth of the sand as I squinted to look at the horizon and the crisp white sails of ships that hinted at civilization beyond our island, the sun above the carious yellow of one of Mord's eyes. It lay there softly humming to itself, the half-closed aperture on the top like a constantly dilating mouth, the spirals of flesh contracting, expanding, and the closer I came to it through Mord's fur, the more it resembled a hybrid of sea anemone and squid: a sleek vase about the size of my fist whose rippling colors strayed from purple toward deep blues and sea-greens. It had four ridges evenly spaced and vertical along its warm and pulsating skin. The texture was smooth as water-worn stone but also somewhat rubbery. It smelled of beach reeds on lazy summer afternoons and also, beneath the sea salt, of passionflowers; later I came to realize that it might have smelled differently to someone else. It didn't really look like food and it wasn't a memory beetle, but I'd been fooled before so I picked it up anyway.

Around me, Mord's body rose and fell with the tremors of his breathing while the other scavengers, a few of whom I recognized as the friends of an uneasy truce, now advanced, emboldened, through the forest of his dirty, his holy fur. I hid my find under my baggy shirt rather than in my satchel so that the others could not see it or easily steal it. It beat against my chest like a second heart.

/

2.

There is no other way to say this: Wick was a drug dealer when I met him, and the drug he pushed was terrible and beautiful and sad and sweet and like life itself. The beetles Wick made from materials he'd stolen from the Company didn't just teach when shoved into your ear; they could also get rid of memories and add memories. People who couldn't face the present shoved them into their ears so they could experience someone else's happier memories from long ago and places that didn't exist anymore. Many of his clients blissfully starved to death while in the grip of another person's life. That was the first thing Wick offered me when I met him, and the first thing I refused, seeing it for the trap it was—sensing a trap even when it seemed like an escape.

I set the sea anemone on a rickety table between our chairs on one of the rotting balconies that inspired me to name our refuge Balcony Cliffs. Behind us the buried hotel, and in front of us, veiled by the protective skein Wick had created to shield us from unwelcome eyes, the steep rock face at the bottom of which seethed a poisonous river: a stew of heavy metals and oil that generated a toxic mist. "What is it?" I asked Wick. It pulsed there on the table, looking as harmless, as functional, as a lamp.

He smiled, a thin smile for a thin man. In the two years since his firing from the Company, Wick had lost any remaining fat. His handsome face, lantern chin and high cheekbones had begun to eat themselves the way a candle is eaten by flame. He had shadows under the eyes, a tremor at the mouth, and yet this only made his gaze more piercing, the purity of his features more arresting and intense. Those hazel-green eyes now seemed larger, more empathic in the shrunken face, and they saw *everything*—except, perhaps, how I saw him. "What *isn't* it, we should ask first, perhaps," he replied. A sense of distance or a lecture-y quality often created a wall between us when discussing finds. It emphasized the conflict that might one day overtake our relationship. He was self-sufficient and self-contained. So was I. Or so we both thought.

Meanwhile, the thing just lay there on the table, pulsing and strobing in a way I found comforting. The strobing made it look bigger. Or perhaps it had already started growing.

"But I know what it isn't, Rachel," said Wick, responding to my silence. "It isn't Mord-made, like his proxies. Nor is it necessarily Company made."

"How can you tell?" I asked. "And where did Mord pick it up if not from the Company?"

Wick shrugged, as if to say *how can anyone be certain of anything?* "The Company is too big to keep track of itself. So let's find out." He passed his hand over the object so that the crimson worms that lived inside of his wrist could leap out briefly to analyze it before retracting into his skin. "Surprising. It is from the Company," Wick said. "Created *inside* the Company, at least."

"But not *by* the Company?"

Wick's smile became a tight frown. "It has the economy of design usually achieved only by committees of one."

This answer exasperated me. When Wick didn't know, when he couldn't make sense of the senseless, he would dance around a subject and I would become nervous. The world was already too uncertain. "Do you think it's a mistake?" I asked. "An afterthought? Something put out in the trash that got tangled up in Mord's fur?"

Wick shook his head. "It's too perfect."

"Then *what*?"

Wick folded his arms, turning that green-gold gaze upon me. "It could be almost anything, but it isn't random. It could be a beacon. It could be a cry for help by someone inside the Company. It could be a bomb."

So Wick really didn't know. "What do we do with it? Eat it?"

He laughed like I was a child, ruining the architectural lines of his face. The laughter didn't bother me. Not then, at least. "I wouldn't eat it. At least not until we know its purpose. Much worse to eat a bomb than a beacon." He leaned forward and I took such pleasure from staring at his face that I thought he had to notice. "If you give it to me, I could break it down into its component parts, repurpose it through my beetles. It might even make good spare parts."

I had let Wick into the Balcony Cliffs. My domain. I told myself I let him stay now for my own protection and called him my boss because I scavenged for him, but as I've said the relationship was more complex. I didn't have to give him the sea anemone, although he could always take it while I slept—but this was always the test of our relationship. *Were we symbiotic or parasitic?*

I looked at it, lying there on the table, and suddenly I felt possessive. I shouldn't have, and yet I did.

"I think I'll keep it for a while," I said.

Wick gave me a long look, shrugged and said, too casually, "Suit yourself." Then he took a golden beetle from his pocket, put it in his ear, and his eyes no longer saw me. He always did that after a trigger, something that reminded him of the Company in the wrong way and unleashed a kind of self-despising rage and melancholy. He said he did it to shield me, but I think the emotion so overwhelmed him, he couldn't help himself.

/

3.

I called the creature "Borne" because of something Wick once said about an animal he'd created while working for the Company: "He was born, but I had borne him." When I wasn't scavenging for myself or Wick, I took care of Borne. This required some experimenting, in part because I had never taken care of anyone or anything before. I had no family, and my parents had died before I'd come to the city.

Because I knew nothing about Borne, I treated him like a plant at first. It seemed logical from my initial observations. The first time Borne felt comfortable enough to relax and open the aperture at the top of his body, I was sitting down to a quiet dinner of stolen Company food packets. He was sitting on the table in front of me, as enigmatic as ever, when suddenly, mid-bite, I heard a whining noise and a distinctly wet pucker. As I set down my plate, the aperture on top of Borne opened, releasing a scent like roses and tapioca. The sides of Borne realigned and peeled back in segments to reveal slowly rising tendrils that held to a steady dark green color and protected the still-hidden core. The tendrils were thick, muscular and fleshy.

Without thinking, I said, "Borne, you're not a sea anemone at all—you *are* a plant." I'd gotten into the habit of talking to him, but at the sound of my voice Borne snapped back into what I thought of as his "defensive mode" and didn't relax again for a full day. So I put him on a plate in the bathroom, under a hole in the wall that let in improbable sunlight from above, green-tinged and musty. I savored that light in the mornings before I went out to do Wick's Work, or the Work of Wick as I sometimes put it.

By the end of the second day, Borne had taken on a kind of yellow-pink hue and begun to exhibit a trembling tenacity to his defensive posture that hinted strangely at either sickness or religious ecstasy, both of which I had seen too often out in the city. He smelled overcooked. I removed Borne from the ledge and returned him to the kitchen table. However, by then I noticed that the worms across from the window—the worms that composted my bathroom waste and excreted the nutrients Wick then gathered for use in his vat—had all "disappeared."

Now I knew a few useful things about Borne. Borne could overdose on sunlight. Borne was a glutton for compost worms. Borne could move around by himself, but refused to move while I was around. So Borne *chose* to overdose on sunlight. Nothing now indicated that Borne was crippled, malformed or in any way dysfunctional. But what *was* his function?

I upgraded Borne from plant to animal, but still had not reclassified him as "purposeful."

I should have, however, because following his bathroom sojourn, Borne made no attempt to disguise his movements from me. Although he still didn't move while I was around, I would come home to find him in the bedroom when he had been on the kitchen table before, or in the bathroom when he'd been on the living room floor. Upon my approach, Borne always remained silent and unmoving. Sometimes I sensed amusement from him, but I was probably projecting.

This combination of guile and innocence, I'll admit, made me smile and look forward to coming home more than usual. It became a kind of game to guess where he might have ended up in his explorations of the apartment. Since he never engaged in any kind of threatening behavior, I never thought to take him as a threat. Even calling Borne a "he" seemed faintly ridiculous, as he didn't exhibit the kind of aggressiveness or self-absorption I expected from most males. Instead, Borne during those days had become a blank slate upon which I had decided to write only useful and positive words.

I didn't tell Wick about Borne's behavior. I didn't mention Borne at all unless Wick asked, and kept my answers brief and casual. "Borne is fine. He's nothing more than some kind of vegetable."

Wick would look at me like he saw right through me, but say nothing. It was all a test, you know, as to whether trust could still exist for me, and every time I extended that trust a little further I expected it to be unable to take the weight, or the pressure of my weight on it, and to snap.

/

And ... I liked Borne too much. The more personality Borne showed, the more I felt attached to him. Borne made it easy to keep him because I discovered he would eat just about anything—any crumb, lowly pebble or scrap of wood. Any worm that came within reach of that circular maw would disappear, never to be seen again. Borne ate a lot of what I otherwise would have discarded as trash, and in a sense made a garbage can redundant; I think he would have eaten the garbage can if he'd been hungry enough.

This practical functionality didn't stop Borne from continuing to puzzle me. The most basic and troubling puzzle? Even though so much went into Borne, nothing ever came *out* of Borne. It had been years since I'd had a pet, and those were just random hermit crabs, but this fact struck me as absurd, even humorously sinister. It actually made me giggle.

Borne was growing. I hadn't wanted to admit it at first, because the idea of growth carried with it the thought of a child becoming an adult, and in how many species did the transformation seem radical, the parent so different from the juvenile? Yet by the end of the first month, although it had been a gradual process, I could no longer deny that Borne had tripled in size.

Then the world intruded, as it had in the past.

/

4.

Each of us chooses to remember the old world in a different way. Some decide to disremember it entirely to make the current world more bearable. Others linger there and make of the past a vision that cannot exist outside of some more ethereal afterlife, and these are the addicts that provided Wick with the most business.

But I prefer details, little moments of memory that exist beneath the notice of history, beetles or any wider context, because those details have the ability to rejuvenate the future. For every clear-eyed view of my room that took in the lack of running water, the mold that had begun its war against the fireflies that constellate my ceiling, the half-collapsing wall with the window that looked out on a mountain of dirt, or even the too-familiar, utterly banal scenes on the streets of one person fighting with someone else just as tired and dirty over a scrap of something that in the old world would have been thought useless or disgusting ... for all of that baggage, I could still imagine a time when the small things we used to love might be returned to us. But none of this means the past was ideal, and so what happened to me about five weeks after I found Borne wasn't new, no matter how much amnesia we've suffered; it was as old as the old world and older still.

One night I let my guard down, my thoughts elsewhere, and a gang of children creeping through the moss and detritus caught the door behind me before it shut. Followed me silent down the corridors to my apartment, immune from traps and pheromones and attack spiders because they kept to my same path. I didn't notice. Nothing is fail-safe. Even a safe place isn't, so you carry your safety with you, in your head, the best that you can.

Other than Mord, his proxies and the odd biologicals that could cause death or discomfort, the young were often the most terrible things in the city at that time. Nothing in their gaze could tell you they were human. They had no memories of the old world to anchor them or humble them or inspire them. Their parents were dead or worse, and the most transformative violence had been visited upon them from the earliest of ages.

Wick had left to tend to the farther reaches of his drug empire. None of my personal defenses—predator cockroaches in the hallway, poisonous crab-spiders embedded in the door, a good old-fashioned knife blade—could stop them. There were four, and three had traded their eyes for green-gold wasps that curled into their eye sockets and compounded their vision. Claws graced their hands like dangerous commas. Scales on their throats burned red when they breathed. One wing sighed bellows-like out of the naked back of the shortest, the one who still had slate-gray human eyes. After a while I wished he had wasps instead.

They smelled of brine and sweat and dust. They licked their lips and flexed their biceps like little conquerors. Who knows how they had become so changed, unless it was from drinking run-off from the Company building, but it was mostly environment that made them what they were inside. I fought, of course, but sometimes fighting isn't enough. Showing aggression and resistance isn't enough. You can't blame yourself for being outnumbered. It was useless. I was useless. They tortured me in various unimaginative ways for hours. The shortest mostly just watched, stood beside the bed with his slate-gray gaze shining dully from huge eyes, the whites not as white as his pale skin. They were on drugs they'd probably found in the toxic waste heap next to the Company. They thought I might have drugs hidden inside my skin.

In between my whimpers and screams and thrashing, as the sheets grew red and redder still and the other three howled their dominance, I would say to the gray-eyed child, "Don't watch. Don't watch." I wanted to believe I was trying to spare him, but I was really trying to spare myself. It was too late for him.

Afterwards they broke anything not of value, stood on each other's shoulders to put out my fireflies with a single-minded efficiency, and decided to take Borne with them. That was the first time I truly pleaded with them, when they took Borne. It didn't matter. They left me there cheek laid open, face and arms and legs bleeding from a dozen wounds, two of them deep. My skin itched and burned and my open flesh felt cold against the heat. I didn't have the strength to get up. The city had visited me, to remind me that I meant less than nothing to it. These children didn't even have the excuse of hatred.

I don't know much time passed, but later, when I regained consciousness for the third or fourth time, my head was on Wick's lap and he was looking down at me with a curious expression on his face, as if deciding whether he could afford to care or not. My body felt soft and warm, with an ache behind it that threatened to become a full-on train barreling down the tracks. "Lie still," Wick said, and the concern I hadn't seen in him came through in his voice so thick and heart-felt that it almost killed me. His voice said he'd been crying. "Lie still. You shouldn't feel pain for a while."

My vision blurred as I stared up at him, and yet I could still make out the precise and beautiful architecture of his features. He was running a diagnostic beetle over me, its legs smooth and glossy. Everywhere it touched me, I felt an immediate and fast-fading glowing sensation. Wick had already closed up my wounds with the help of surgical slugs. I knew the cool-cold sensation of their presence from the last time I'd come out on the wrong side of an encounter.

"I'd give you a hug," Wick said from far away, voice quivering, "but I don't want to hurt you." I wanted to ask about Borne but Wick told me not to speak, said, "I'm sorry I wasn't here. I'm sorry they got through," then, "Did they... ?" He had to ask, or all the medicinal beetles in the world wouldn't help.

I shook my head. Too young or oblivious, single-minded. The one with the gray eyes, the oldest, had been about ten years old, with sandy blonde hair and delicate hands. Out of shame I might not have told Wick the truth even if they had, but they hadn't. The closest it had come to that were two of the wasp-eyes shoving their tongues in my mouth as they cut me. As if trying to contaminate me. A metallic aftertaste still lingered on my tongue. None of this made it any better or any worse.

Now I was crying, just a steady stream of tears without the expression on my face, as far as I knew, changing at all. There is only so much anyone can take before you begin to feel that perhaps the effort to survive is too much to endure. Then you forget and start over.

After the beetle had finished its work, Wick asked, "How did it happen? Details." He took my hand in his, grip tight. His hand was warm. My skin so dark against his translucence, as if his body had gone paler still with worry. I told him, so it wouldn't happen again. "And they took Borne, too," I said, not daring to ask still. Not sure if my words were even coming out right.

Wick frowned and nodded toward the living room. "But they didn't take Borne—he's right in there."

Even through my numb discomfort I felt an overwhelming relief. "Did they bring him back?"

I couldn't read Wick's face, didn't want to. "I don't think so. Not sure what happened. He was in the hallway by the door. I brought him back in."

"Thank you," I said, and put as much emphasis on the words as I could manage. Wick could have used the opportunity to get rid of Borne. He hadn't.

"He's bigger," Wick said. For the first time I realized he looked worried or preoccupied for reasons that might have nothing to do with my condition. I'd hidden Borne from Wick. He hadn't known how much Borne had grown.

"What's wrong?" I knew what was wrong.

Wick attempted a smile. "You need to rest. I've brought food for the kitchen. And you won't be bothered while you recover—I've put up more formidable defenses." Which meant taking resources away from his main business, putting us more at risk in the long term. "I have to go out for a while, but I'll be back soon."

I understood. He needed to check the outer defenses, too, make sure nothing else had been breached, perhaps even change the entry point into the Balcony Cliffs. He might even have to reach an agreement with someone else to fulfill my role while I recovered. They'd drawn the knife across me in creative ways, drawing patterns, writing words, that had no meaning to anyone, least of all them. The burn of what had happened was still hours away from reaching me. I reached up to touch his cheek, the edge of his mouth.

Wick flinched away from my touch. "I should've been here."

"You can't be here all the time."

"I should take Borne with me," Wick said, trying to make it sound casual.

I winced. "No. Please. Don't." It would've been better if I'd shouted it out or pleaded, but I didn't. I just said those three words in a small broken voice, and I could see in his eyes that he had been re-creating the moment of my being attacked over and over again in his mind.

Wick nodded and left, but not before he sealed the door to my apartment using a few dozen beetles and another spider. I knew it was an absurd waste of resources for little gain, and I knew he'd have to take most of it down in a few days, but I felt selfishly grateful anyway.

At some point I realized I couldn't sleep and decided to get up, even though it hurt so much, and go see Borne. He sat on a chair at the kitchen table, pulsing a faint green. Wick had restored a few of the fireflies but not many, and so all I could really see was Borne's glow.

Borne stood at least a half-foot taller than that afternoon, and his base seemed thicker and more robust. I couldn't see that any harm had come to him—he still had that perfect symmetry. He was beautiful in the darkness, and somehow that beauty got to me in a way that made me break down.

"It's just me," Borne said.

I screamed. I stumbled back, looking for a weapon, for a stick, a knife, anything, because his voice sounded just like the rasp of the boy with the gray eyes.

"Just me," Borne said again. "Borne."

The slugs and worms Wick left inside me struggled to release substances that would calm me.

"It's just me," Borne said again, and this time sounded less like my attacker, warmer and mellifluous, the tone I would come to know as his normal voice. I flinched again but didn't scream, stayed up against the wall, keeping as much distance from Borne as possible.

"Rachel," Borne said, "don't need to be. Afraid." The voice now drowned the gray-eyed boy's tone entirely.

"Don't tell me what I need to be!" I shouted. "What are you? Don't come closer! Stay the fuck away!" I struggled for more to say, and into that silence Borne said, "Go rest. Please rest. Don't worry. Sleep." I could sense Borne considering each word carefully before choosing one, unsure how they all fit together.

"Sleep?" I laughed bitterly. "I'm not going to sleep now," I said, though I could feel myself fading. "How did you escape them anyway?"

"Them?" Borne said.

"Is this a dream?" I asked, as if he knew more than I did.

It's absurd to say this about a creature with no face, but Borne seemed to sadly smile as he said, "What is a dream?" And: "This?" I was drifting then against my will, swaying as the medical creatures worked on me. I felt faint, staggered back to the bed. Let the things crawling inside me take over my body as I entered a kind of delirium, raving at first, then just talking, gradually aware of the presence of Borne beside the bed, that I wasn't just talking to myself, that I was talking to him, and somehow having him there was a comfort. I wondered if I was waking from a nightmare or entering one, and if I would know the difference.

/

5.

In the city, the line between nightmare and reality was fluid, just as the context of the words "killer" and "death" had become over time. A killer was someone who killed for reasons other than survival. A killer was a madman or madwoman, not a person just trying to get through another day. Once, I hit a woman with a rock. We'd encountered each other while both out scavenging on the same rubble-strewn street on the west side of the city. I had found a smooth piece of metal partially absorbed by a glistening red piece of flesh-like plant, and I had no idea if Wick would find it of use, but it seemed likely since I had never seen anything like it before. As I turned a corner holding my prize, I came upon a woman walking. She was about fifty, wiry in the way survivors often are, gray hair hanging in sheets, clothing a patchwork of gray and black.

She saw me and smiled. Then she saw what I held and her smile went away. "Give me that. That's mine."

Maybe she meant, "That's going to be mine." I did not wait for her to get close enough to grapple with me. I knelt and picked up a rock with my free hand and as she rushed toward me from the middle of the street I threw it at her, catching her in the forehead. She went limp, fell onto her side, breathing heavily. Then she got up and I threw another rock, catching her in the head again.

This time she staggered back, put her hands on her knees as she hunched down. I could see the bright red pooling from her head to the ground. She sat heavily in the rubble and put a hand to her head, looked up at me as I dropped the third rock I'd picked up. I didn't need it now.

"I just wanted to look at it," she said, puzzled, as she kept putting a hand to her wound then taking it away again. Her eyes began to glaze over. "Just a look is all I wanted."

I didn't stay to help or hurt her. I left.

Did she die? Did I kill her, and if I did, am I a "killer"?

/

Once, I'll admit, it was all different. And within that context I wanted to be a writer, not a finder and maker of traps. At the age of seven or eight I filled my notebooks with scribbles—poetry about how I loved the sea, retellings of fables. Even scenes from novels I never finished and never will. But the world back then could still support that idea. Most people had homes. Parents had jobs. Cities had governments. Cities existed within countries, and those countries had leaders. Many people could still, for a time anyway, think of travel as adventure or recreation.

By the time I was eighteen, the wider context was a joke that doubled you over in harsh laughter. Become a writer? How? Why? What was important that I write about? How we'd lost every last thing we had? Incredible, really, how a slight slip could become a freefall, and freefall could become a hell. We lived on as ghosts in a haunted world, untangling the meaning of our own creations, living off of recycled parts and memories of the past. Waiting for it all to end, for good.

By now you understand, I hope, how close the line between sane and mad, between *need* and *want* had become.

And into all of that, Borne said, *"It's just me, Rachel,"* and for a long time huddled on my bed, trying to survive torture both mental and physical, I didn't answer him. Not really. He stood patiently by my bedside for a day and a night, me lost and rambling for most of it. Wick appeared next to him from time to time and winked out again as I slipped in and out of sleep.

Since the attack, Borne had changed: He took on a shape more like a vase or a squid balancing on its mantel than a sea anemone. The aperture had curled out and up at the top of that long neck, sprouting feathery filaments (almost as an affectation) that, with a prolonged soft sigh, crowded together and then came apart again like bizarre synchronized dancers. He was tall enough now that the top of him loomed a good foot above the bed. Colors still flitted across his body or sometimes lazily floated in shapes like storm clouds, ragged and diaphanous, layered and dark. Azure. Lavender. Emerald. He frequently smelled like vanilla.

As I lay on my side and stared at him, I could see that Borne had also developed a startling collection of eyes that circled his body. Each eye was small and completely different from its fellows. Some were human—blue, black, brown, green pupils—and some were animal eyes; but he was able to see through all of them. At the time I didn't know what they meant or even that this could mean something terrible. I took it as a kind of exotic adornment, Borne's equivalent of a belt.

When Borne saw me staring at him, he would make a sound like the startled clearing of a throat, and his flesh would absorb all of the eyes except two, which would slowly migrate away from each other, become larger and grow long dark lashes, each of which moved independently from the others and were just pseudopods formed from Borne's flesh. Two impossibly sea-blue eyes in the middle of what would have been the hips of a human being.

The context kept changing. Much later I realized it wasn't just Borne who kept changing with it.

Finally, after three days, I felt more lucid, waking with only slight fuzziness. Wick had gone out, reluctantly, to conduct business. From my bed I said to Borne, "What are you?" It was a dangerous question to match a dangerous mood, and my heart beat faster but I wasn't afraid.

"I don't know," Borne said in a rough yet sweet tone. For a moment I thought he spoke in the voices of both my mother and father. And then, sincerely, almost eagerly, he said, "Do you know what you are?"

I smiled a little bitterly, ignored him, and said, "Maybe I can help you find out what you are." I was still on the worm-drugs and somehow it felt good to be of use, to offer advice, to know myself better than Borne knew himself.

Borne went quiet for a second and his colors dimmed. Then he flared and said, "Is it possible?"

"But you have to be honest with me."

"Honest?" Turning the word over in his head.

"Tell the truth."

A ripple of strong green traveled across his skin. "I can be honest. I am honest." I didn't know if I'd upset him, triggered some other emotion, or if he was simply testing out the word.

"You know a lot about me," I ventured, "but I know nothing about you. Will you answer some questions?"

"I will answer questions," Borne said uncertainly. He might not have understood fully the definition of "question."

"Why didn't you save me from those boys?"

"Save?"

"Rescue. Help."

"I did help." This in an anguished tone and his skin gone entirely black before exploding into reds, then pinks and a roiling green.

I tried to control the trembling of my voice. "Those boys tortured me for hours and you did nothing. They hurt me badly. They even took you, and you're lucky to be here."

Silence. Then, "I couldn't talk until I ... knew them," but I realized *knew* wasn't the word he meant. "I wasn't yet complete? activated? fully aware? until I knew them." Finished the sentence with a kind of frustration for words that caused the feathery pseudopods to straighten like spikes.

"Now you are ... complete? Aware?" I didn't want to use the word *activated* because it scared me.

"More complete. Now that I know them." The eyes on the sides of Borne's head were remarkably human, and I had a sudden sense of them being trapped, passengers. One of the pairs of eyes had been a familiar gray.

Something as sudden as an electric shock or spider bite shot through me, and I knew what *knew* meant. "You killed them," *but not before they hurt me*, the raging, screaming thought behind the words.

"Kill?"

"Cease to be. No longer alive. Dead. Not here."

Confusion shuddered through Borne, a sudden panic. "The ones I know are still here. I know them now."

Those eyes no longer seemed beautiful. They looked ever more trapped and horrible. I turned away from Borne and drifted into unconsciousness for a while. It was easier than facing what he'd said, and yet why would I do that unless I felt safe?

/

6.

My recovery made me stupid, weak. All sorts of ridiculous ideas entered my head. That I lived in an *apartment* and had the flu or a cold and was on *sick leave* from my job until I was better. And when I was better I would go outside with a *briefcase* in hand and walk a few blocks to a *job* in an *office building*, which would entail *shuffling papers*, organizing things on my desk, and *meetings* with other people about *important projects.*

I thought that because Wick had expended ever more energy protecting me, it would be that way forever. My mind laid a trap for me, and I walked into and through it without realizing, carried it around with me.

Wick. Wick and Rachel. Portrait of us, Wick and I, at opposite ends of the frame, half out of the picture. Oddly wary of each other after the attack, for all that he took care of me, perhaps because he expected more blame from me eventually to bolster the guilt he already felt, and perhaps because I did blame him. I blamed him for making me weak, for relying on his surveillance, his beetles and spiders rather than my own traps, many of which I'd dismantled, replaced by Wick's biotech when he moved into the Balcony Cliffs. Was it fair? No. It wasn't fair. But I had my own guilt: I now kept a secret from him, a secret that I was afraid of spilling and one that also might soon change our relationship forever. *Borne can talk. Borne killed my attackers and hid or ate their bodies. Borne is a born mimic. Borne is intelligent.*

Even so, those few weeks contain some of my best memories in the city. Wick would be away, out doing business, gathering intel, providing beetles to his dealers, which left Borne and me ever more time to explore. He'd gotten tired of being in the apartment. On days when I knew Wick would be gone a long time I'd take Borne out into the hallways, prickly with the fear of discovery and stiff from my slow-healing wounds.

It was all a construct by then, this game of not telling Wick that Borne could talk. He had to know; but because I never admitted it and he never brought it up, Borne became an open secret that existed between us like a monster all its own. It made me reckless, as if challenging Wick to confront me. Ignoring the strain on my recovering body, Borne and I would race down dimlit dust-floored corridors, both laughing wildly, Borne afraid of colliding/congealing with the wall and tripping over his own pseudopods and wailing as he laughed, "You're going tooooo fast!" Or, "Why is this fuuuuuun?" When you don't *have* to run and have the chance to run for the hell of it, it becomes a strange luxury.

Then we'd collapse at the end of the hall and Borne, in addition to his usual observation that he was hungry and needed a snack—I now let him hunt lizards and rats so he'd have enough to eat—would ask some of his Questions. He never stopped asking, as if what he was really ravenous for was answers. "This dust is so dry. Why is dust so dry? Doesn't it need some wet for balance?"

"Then it's mud."

"What's mud."

"Wet dirt."

"I haven't seen mud yet."

"No." I would show Borne a photo of a weasel in an old encyclopedia and he'd point with an extended tentacle and say, "Long mouse!" which brought me quickly to the idea of teaching Borne to read, except he seemed to pick that up on his own. When we played hide-and-seek I'd sometimes find him hunched up at the edge of a midden of books, two tentacles extending out from his sides to hold one and a single tentacle tipped with light curling down from the top of his head. He would study any number of topics and seemed to have no real preferences, his many eyes enthusiastically moving back and forth as he read the pages at a steady clip. I didn't believe he needed light, or eyes, to read, but he liked to mimic what he saw me doing.

Eventually I took him to the balcony on the cliffs. I felt he needed a disguise to be safe and found a flower hat with just one bullet hole in it and a brown bloodstain. I found a pair of large designer sunglasses. I had the choice of putting him in either a sheet or a black evening dress that I'd salvaged from one of the other apartments; the evening dress was a little moth-eaten and faded to more of a deep gray, but I chose it because I had nowhere to wear it and it was several sizes too big for me. From the aperture at the top of his head, muffled by the hat, came the words, "We can go now," but if Borne wanted the full ensemble, I wanted the full human. "Not until you grow a mouth," I said, "and a face." It took only a second. All of his eyes went away, then two popped up where appropriate—never gray anymore—and a nose protrusion that looked more like the head of the lizard that he'd eaten a few hours earlier, and a kind of crazy grinning mouth. In the hat. In the black evening dress. He looked so ridiculous and earnest I wanted to hug him. I never for a second understood the trap I'd entered, the gift I'd given. Never realized what other uses disguises might be put to.

We went out onto the balcony. Borne pretended he couldn't see through his sunglasses and took them off. He'd muted his skin to a mottled brown that mimicked my own, and his new mouth formed a genuinely surprised O. "It's beautiful," he exclaimed, "beautiful beautiful beautiful... ." And the killing thing, the thing I couldn't get over, is that it was beautiful. It was so incredibly beautiful, and I'd never seen that before. In the strange sea-blue glow of late afternoon, the river below splashing in lavender, gold and orange up against the numerous rock islands with their outcroppings of trees ... the river looked amazing. The balcony cliffs in that light took on a kind of luminous deep color that was almost black but not, almost blue but not, the jutting shadows solid and cool.

Borne didn't know it was all deadly, poisonous, truly disgusting. Maybe it wasn't to him. Maybe he could have swum in the river and come out unscathed. Maybe, too, I realized right then in that moment that I'd begun to love him. Because he didn't see the world like I saw the world. He didn't see the traps. That was the moment I knew I'd decided to trade my safety for something else. No matter what happened next, I'd crossed over to another place, and the question wasn't who I should trust, but who should trust me. **-bc.**

Stephen O'Connor

THE FINAL FRONTIER

The astronauts turn off their radios during their daily space walk and press their helmets together so that they can talk without being heard. "Leave me alone!" she says to the image of her own helmet, like a golden planet rising amid the warped starscape on his visor. "It's over! Gone! I don't remember any of it!"

"That's not true," he says, compressing the layers of metalized webbing, Zentex and Mylomene between his fingers and hers. "You know it's not."

"Don't!"

The retraction of her hand sends her drifting away from him in a slow-mo pirouette over the top of the module. And beyond her, just over her rotating boots: the blue edge of the whole world.

/

The astronauts are cutting carrots. Her name is Ilka. His name is Bishop. The carrot disks wobble in the air above the cutting board like several dozen tossed coins unable to descend from their zenith. "Of course, you won't have this problem at home," Ilka says, gesturing with her knife at the floating disks and accidentally sending one flipping end over end toward the cabin wall.

Bishop's hand shoots out and catches the carrot before it's gone half a yard.

"Thanks, Bish," says Ilka.

"No problem," says Bishop. "Wouldn't want one of these buggers clogging up the air filtration system."

Ilka clutches her throat and makes a strangle-face. "One of the many perils of space exploration!"

Their mission is called *The Final Frontier* and is the first ever to be paid for entirely by the sale of television rights and advertising. Their cabin overalls and spacesuits are maculate with corporate logos, as are those of the other members of the team, Donald, Franz and Jim, who are jettisoning sewage while Ilka and Bishop entertain the viewers with another installment of *Cosmic Chef.*

The Mission Book recommends that they just be themselves in front of the cameras. But how can a husband's kiss be anything other than ceremony with a billion viewers watching? How can a wife say "Oh, love-of-my-life!" and actually mean it? For a while, Bishop and Ilka sought refuge in irony—

which was easy at first: They had, after all, been married on the gantry just before lift off, she with a veil duct-taped over her visor, he with a bow-tie stuck to the chin of his space helmet, and so it was natural those first days to call each other "shnookums" or "darling spousal unit," their eyes lit by mischief and the belief that their charade was keeping their love sacred, along with everything else that truly mattered to them. But three months of being broadcast to the world twenty-four/seven have made it increasingly difficult to sort the sacred from the charade, and even their officially sanctioned fade-to-blacks have become sources of dismay.

According to their contract, Bishop and Ilka are allowed four two-hour periods off camera each week for "intimate relations." Under the assumption that, as newlyweds, they might be swept away by passion at any moment, they are to signal their desire for a fade-to-black by a French kiss or by a full-frontal embrace with "genital area contact" lasting at least ten seconds. While Ilka and Bishop have never let a week pass without using all four fade-to-blacks, actually managing to be swept away by passion has never been easy, especially given the acoustical transparency of their Seclusion Pod. Of late, their fade-to-blacks have involved little more than dental flossing, whispered bickering and power naps. On the rare occasions that either of them has mentioned their absent passion, they have spoken of it as only a temporary response to nonstop global scrutiny, but privately they have each begun to wonder whether those people they always thought of as themselves are, in fact, only the people they wish they could be.

Now Ilka is peeling an eggplant and Bishop is arranging the shiny, deep-purple strips of its skin in the air to spell out HI MOM! A strand of hair drifts into Ilka's eye and she lets go of the knife so that she can tuck the strand behind her ear. The knife hovers in mid-air, trembling slightly and gleaming in the spotlight like a psychopath's hallucination.

/

Afterward, it would seem to them both as if they had no freedom of will. The first day of Mission Consolidation, Bishop had admired the squared-off tip of Ilka's nose. For most of a week she confused him with Henry, who also had curly red hair. But when Bishop stood on one leg during the neurological exam, she spotted the tear-shaped bulges of muscle on either side of his kneecap and knew instantly he was a bicyclist.

"How'd you guess?" he asked. She tapped her temple with her index finger and said, "I can read your mind."

That night, he was the only one among the dozen or so Mission Candidates who laughed when she told her joke about the penguin and the meat cleaver. And when, after a moment of disconcertion, she smiled and said, "Oh, well, guess you had to be there!" he was, once again, the only one to laugh. She glanced his way, her eyes filled with almost desperate appreciation.

Later, as she was walking out of the Community Enhancement Room with her hands plunged deep in her cargo pockets, her shoulders slumped and her gaze toward the floor, he hurried to her side. "That was great," he said.

"What?" She looked frightened.

He quoted the joke's punch line: "Oops!"

First she smiled, then blushed, then they each looked into the other's eyes and instantly glanced away. That was all it took. After that, they seemed puppeted by forces neither could comprehend nor control.

/

It is possible in space—normal, in fact—to feel the emptiness on every side of you expanding at such a terrific speed that the words "I" and "me" will soon have no meaning, and yet to feel simultaneously the sheer massiveness of the universe bearing down on you with such force that in an instant you will undergo the radical invasion of self normally experienced only by miners in a cave-in, and that half an instant later you will be reduced to such an infinitely slender filament of being it would make little sense to imagine you exist.

Fortunately, the simultaneity of these opposing tendencies of space allows astronauts to achieve a sort of stasis that passes for sanity. But once they are back on earth it is absolutely impossible for them to explain their new reality—their sense that everything is hypothetical, for example, or their altered understandings of the words "hypocrisy" and "hope." This is why, when you run into astronauts at parties, they always have robot eyes, and why so many show up drunk at church, and why at their memorial services their children so commonly say, "I never really knew my father," or, "When Mom said, 'I love you,' it was as if she were speaking a language she didn't understand."

/

The Mission Book lists "fraternization" under "Unacceptable Behaviors" because it "de-facilitates the unity of the Unit," and when Christina asked what "fraternization" meant the first morning of Team Candidacy, Donald, the Team Leader, answered, "It means exactly what you think it means, so don't do it!" At first Christina looked as if she were going to laugh. Then her tongue made a small click against the roof of her mouth and she rolled her eyes. By the time she got back from her weightlessness-simulation flight, her name on the Candidates Roster had been red-stamped NON-SELECTED and everyone drew the obvious conclusion.

It was exactly a week later that Ilka told her penguin joke and, in the hallway outside the Community Enhancement Room, looked into Bishop's eyes and saw the frightened loneliness that matched so exactly the frightened loneliness she herself had been desperately trying to pretend she didn't feel. So, of course, she looked away, and so, of course, at breakfast the following morning, they sat at the same table and talked so casually over their bowls of yogurt and sliced banana, that she was able to tell herself, "There, see—it was all in your mind." And so, that night, when she sat cell-phone in hand on that bench in the cactus garden, wondering why on earth her fiancé Max's amiable babbling about the pet store he managed so irritated her, it was, of course, Bishop who came up from the parking lot, swinging the bag of shampoo and razorblades he had just bought at an all-night pharmacy. With equal inevitability, she was unable to resist making the small noise in her throat that stopped him mid-step. And just when she was assuring him that he hadn't disturbed her—that she only had been listening to the beautiful silence of the desert wind— the coyotes, of course, started their weird yipping and—before she knew what she was doing—her hand sought out his. And when she tried to explain away what she had done by saying, "I always find that sound... I get this feeling... you know... it's like—" she realized that there was no point explaining anything at all, because in an instant her lips would be on his, and his tongue would be in her mouth and they would be breathing each other's breath, making swoony gasps and running their hands up and down each other's backs. And that, of course, was what happened. And, when they found themselves unable to stop what they were doing, they went to his car, and he drove her out to the salt flats where the whiteness running off in every direction so matched the whiteness of the moon directly overhead that it was hard not to feel they were themselves on the moon, even though the moon shining down on them proved that impossible. And when, some hour later, he said, "What just happened?" and she said, "I don't know, but maybe it wasn't such a great idea," he sighed and agreed, and then he said, "But maybe I don't really care." She was silent a long time before saying, "I think I'm falling in love with you." And then she said, "This is crazy!" And then she said, "I don't even know you." "Yes you do," he said, and then it was more than another hour before they drove back to the Mission Compound.

/

The conspiracy theorists are partly right: Our space program may not be taking place entirely on some Hollywood movie set, but we are being lied to about space. The moon, for example, is only half what it used to be. Its far side—the part always facing away from the earth—has vanished. Lopped off like half an apple. Nobody knows exactly when or how, but there are striations crossing the moon's now-flat hidden side that look alarmingly like the markings of a gigantic chain saw.

Things disappear in space. That's become established fact—in certain circles, at least. Many people remember when Pluto was degraded from "planet" to "dwarf planet," but few know that this reclassification was only a cover-up: Pluto had, in fact, vanished. One day, astronomers could find it tumbling along its normal trajectory 3,657 million miles from the sun; the next day they couldn't. It was that simple. The same is true with Uranus and Mercury: Gone. Nobody knows where or how. Likewise, in recent years, the asteroid belt has lost nearly forty percent of its mass.

So far, there has been a consensus among governments and the scientific community: Better not say anything until we know what this means. Probably, it will turn out to be nothing—a data glitch, a misapplied algorithm, a new wrinkle on the theory of dark matter. The last thing we need is people running around screaming, "The end is near!" Think of the rioting that would ensue. The mass suicides! The collapse of moral systems worldwide! No, no, no, say the scientists and heads of state, better that we keep this to ourselves.

Initially, the sole mission of the team Ilka and Bishop were trying out for was to conduct a top-secret investigation of these cosmic disappearances. When Final Frontier, Inc. bought out NASA, it agreed to continue the Mission and keep it top-secret, on the assumption that mass unrest would have a negative effect on television viewing, advertising revenues and the economy in general. It has never been exactly clear, however, how the Mission could be both top-secret and broadcast twenty-four hours a day. The team has received contradictory directives: Never refer to the Mission under any circumstances. If anyone asks, say you are investigating "the space-time continuum." Say you're just doing "pure research." Speak in code. If, for example, you discover another planet has gone missing, say, "I've dropped another pound."

The most recent scuttlebutt is that top FFI execs have begun to toy with the idea of giving up all pretense of secrecy and renaming the show *Who's Steal-*

ing Our Universe? The Truth Nobody Will Tell You! Their rationale: Global strife might take years to reach full throttle; who knows how much money could be made in the meantime?

/

From the earth the moon appears full, and Bishop and Ilka are adrift in the cone of shadow that runs from its flat side off into infinity. They're attending to what is essentially a mile-long windsock, designed to detect the velocity and direction of the gravity-wake left by the moon's departed half. Thus far, however, the windsock has detected no space-time disturbance of any kind, and so Bishop and Ilka have been directed to poke and twist its moving parts and to change its batteries.

The endless cone of the moon's shadow is so utterly dark that, beyond the oblongs illuminated by their helmet lights, it seems to have been flooded with India ink. When Bishop can't see Ilka's light and his own is not shining in her direction, he has no idea where she is. As a result, when he has finally screwed shut the windsock's battery compartment, he accidentally clonks his three-foot-long titanium screwdriver against the back of her helmet.

A metallic voice crackles through his earbuds: "You stupid fuck."

"Shhh," he says.

Ilka reels around, and now the only thing Bishop can see is the blue-white disk of her helmet light shining directly at his visor. Her voice crackles again inside his head: "Don't you shush me! Are you just a total klutz or are you actually trying to puncture my pressure suit?"

"Shhh," he says.

"Uh-oh!" says one of the commentators at Mission Control. "Sounds like a little volcanic activity on the dark side of the moon!"

The disk of Ilka's helmet light drifts at the center of Bishop's vision for a few seconds longer, then shrinks to a skinny lozenge and disappears. He hears the click of her helmet touching his and can feel her fingers pulling at his elbow through many layers of metalized webbing and synthetic fabric. He lets his screwdriver drift on its tether and pulls her waist until their spacesuits are touching front to front. He cannot feel her body so much as the way her movements inside her suit alter her trajectory and momentum, but he finds even such indirect evidence of her physical existence profoundly soothing, in the way that a knocking from the next cell can soothe a man in solitary. She has turned off her radio, he realizes. When he turns off his own, he can hear her stifled sobs coming to him through the dime-size area of contact between the globes of their helmets.

"It's okay," he says. "I understand. You don't have to worry."

Her sobbing continues. He can feel how the heaving of her shoulders is causing the two of them to rotate head-over-heels and to drift ever further from the enormous windsock. "Oh, Bish!" she says at last. "This is destroying everything."

"No it isn't." He gives the side of her suit three comforting pats, which she experiences mainly as a slight shift in the torque of their head-over-heels rotation. "We're more than halfway through," he says. "All we have to do is hang on a little longer and we'll be fine."

"This is making me hate you!"

"No it isn't."

"Yes it is! Every time I say 'I love you' on camera, I feel like a liar and a coward, and I hate you for it."

Bishop doesn't know how to respond to this.

"And why are you always so cheery when the

cameras are on!" she says. "Why don't you just say, 'Fuck you!' and tell them all to go to hell!"

Anger rises in Bishop's throat. His heart kettle-drums in his temples and a featureless fog appears at the center of his visor. He almost shouts, *"Well, why the fuck don't you!"* But when he finally does speak, his voice is calm: "I *am* telling them to go to hell. You know what they want just as well as I do. That's why they chose us. Foster and Lavinia were much better qualified than either of us, but they had nerves of steel. Nothing could stop Foster's avuncular winks or take that gleam off of Lavinia's smile. Who wants to watch that kind of television! FFI is dying for us to curse each other out on prime time. They've been trying to engineer us into a full-scale break-up right from the beginning. Why do you think you're the only woman on the team? Why do you think Donald, Franz and Jim all look like fucking movie stars! Can you imagine the tabloid headlines if either of us showed what we are really feeling? *Star-CROSS Lovers! Hell in the Heavens!* The ratings would go through the roof. And fuck if I'm going to give them that reward."

Bishop feels an alteration in the arc of her spacesuit against his glove. Then the speed of their rotation slackens. After a moment, he realizes that the tension has gone out of her body. Either she has been comforted by his words, or she's surrendered utterly to grief.

There is a long silence. Then she says, so softly he can barely hear her over his flowing oxygen, "Oh, Bish! I keep getting Facebook messages from total strangers who tell me I should dump you for Franz!"

/

Ilka and Bishop had reached the fourth and final tier of Mission Selection when Donald informed all the remaining candidates that NASA had been bought out by Final Frontier, Inc. "This is great news!" he had shouted over the perplexed murmurs and not a few mocking guffaws. "FFI is willing to spend five times NASA's annual budget on space exploration! *Five times!* Think what that will mean!"

Only days after Donald's announcement, Ilka and Bishop were called before Oz Zodmah, FFI's Reciprocal De-lateralization Coordinator: a stout man with a silver speckling of buzz-cut hair across his balding dome and so little distance between his mouth and nose that his upper lip touched the ridge between his nostrils with every plosive he spoke. "I suppose you know that your private affair was never particularly private," he told them.

Bishop turned pale. Tiny, trembling buttons of sweat instantly appeared at Ilka's hairline. "I don't know what you're talking about," she said.

"Our private what?" said Bishop, attempting incredulity but only managing stunned guilt.

"There's no need to pretend," said Zodmah.

"Who's pretending?" Ilka said.

"You know, of course," Zodmah continued, "that under existing regulations you can both be drummed out of the program."

"For what?!" said Bishop, finally managing something close to incredulity.

"You can't prove anything," said Ilka.

"I wouldn't be so sure of that." Zodmah remained silent a good fifteen seconds, shifting his eyes between Ilka and Bishop and smiling at their increasing disconcertion. "But that's neither here nor there," he said at last, "because we want to cut you a deal. We won't court-martial you if you agree to get married."

"Married?!" said Ilka

"Why?" said Bishop.

"You know the reputation astronauts have!

That weird way they talk? How their faces are too clean? You'll humanize the profession and it will be great publicity: *Newlyweds in Space! Stars in Their Eyes! Moon-June-Spoon!* You'll be famous overnight!"

Bishop and Ilka were both silent, goggle-eyed.

"So whaddya think?"

Bishop and Ilka each opened their mouths, but no words came out.

"We'll double your salaries," said Zodmah. "And imagine all the product endorsements!"

/

Things also disappear inside the Mission Module: Jim's tub of hair gum, Donald's left, Velcro-soled WallWalker, Bishop's watchband. One day the team wakes to find no toothpaste anywhere: No crumpled tubes in the Personal Hygiene Bubble; none in the Waste Confinement Canisters; all of the boxes labeled "toothpaste" in the Storage Facility: empty and drifting. Another day it's the same with pretzels. Then Ilka can't find her favorite forest-green washcloth. (She looks everywhere. Three days in a row. Not a trace.) But no one gives any of this much thought. Things get lost. Used up. So what else is new?

/

"Bish?" Ilka says.

"What?" he answers distractedly. They are on another space walk, and he has just assembled the last of the six sections of the new, housefly-green solar panel they're supposed to plug into the side of the Mission Module.

"Uh," says Ilka.

"What?" There is a touch of irritation in his voice.

No response.

The last time Bishop glanced Ilka's way, her face was obscured by the brilliant reflection of the logo-spangled module, but now her visor is crossed only by bright motes and velvet black, and so he can see her eyes clearly: weirdly round and fixed—doll's eyes.

"Ilka?" he says. Then he looks where she is looking.

After a moment, he flings out one arm so that he might turn three hundred sixty degrees to the left; then he flicks back his head so that he might do the same on a perpendicular axis. He repeats these actions four or five times, until, finally, he has no choice but to accept the truth.

No matter what direction he looks or how often: Nothing but those bright motes, that velvet black, a fiercely brilliant sun, and the blue mass of the earth.

No Mission Module.

Gone. Without a trace.

/

"Meteor," says one of the astronomers at Mission Control, when he hears the story. "Beats me," says the other.

Ilka is able to provide no more information about the disappearance than Bishop. She glanced at the module one instant—catching sight of Franz through the porthole, idly twirling a Q-tip in his right ear—then glanced at it again an instant later, only to find that the module had been replaced by stars and a faintly scintillating void. No flash, no shockwave, no sound.

"Sit tight," says Sodastrum, the overnight commentator (it is 3:00 a.m. in Houston). "A shuttle is on its way."

Ilka knows this is a lie, but doesn't contradict

him. What would be the point? "Thanks," she says.

"Back after the commercial break," says Sodastrum, his voice replaced by *The Final Frontier* theme song.

Ilka turns off her radio and touches her helmet to Bishop's. He turns his radio off too. "Do you think they did this on purpose?" she asks.

"Did what?" says Bishop.

"Got rid of the Mission Module."

"Why would they do that?"

"Rescue in Space," she says. "Talk about great television. Once news of this gets out, every TV on earth will be tuned to *The Final Frontier*—no other show will have a chance."

Bishop cogitates a moment. "You're paranoid."

She is silent. She closes her eyes. Then she says, "Hold my hand."

He does. Even when they turn their radios back on, they keep their hands linked. And thus, during the long hours they wait for rescue, they rotate as a single unit, the sun rising over Ilka and setting over Bishop, then rising over Ilka again... Again and again and again. It doesn't stop.

/

Ilka can see the cloud-littered shimmer of the Pacific Ocean hundreds of miles beneath the soles of her boots. For the whole of the three months she has been in orbit, she has never once perceived the distance between herself and the earth as height, but now that distance is a yawning abyss—and she feels as if she is falling into it. Her heart is pounding. She can't breathe. She is gripped by a wild impulse to tear off her space suit.

"You okay?" asks Bishop, pulling on her hand and touching his visor to hers.

"Yes," she says, then: "No."

"Don't worry," he says.

She hears him draw his breath to speak, but no words come. His features are like a series of pale orange half-moons behind his tinted visor.

"How long do you think it will be before they get a shuttle up here?" she asks.

"Sodastrum says it's on its way."

"No," she says. "I mean *really.*"

He shrugs. The half-moons of his face dwindle to quarter-moons, then disappear entirely. "Twenty-four hours." He doesn't sound confident.

"Do you think our oxygen can last that long?"

"Probably."

"Longer?"

"Who knows?"

/

Sodastrum goes off duty and Conrad comes on. Nobody likes Conrad. Before being hired by FFI, he was the MC of a golden oldies show at a radio station in Minneapolis and has the habit of shouting, "Out of this world!" in response to virtually everything Bishop or Ilka say; he is constantly making jokes on the order of, "How's the weather up there?" and "You guys better not be *mooning* us!"

During a commercial break, Bishop hears Ilka say, "Fuck!"

"What?" he asks.

"Jesus!"

"What?"

"Turn off your radio."

He does, and when their helmets are together, she says, "This is so stupid!"

"It's okay." He places his hands firmly on each of her shoulders. "I'm here."

"I just can't stand it!" she says. "That fucking Conrad made me so angry that I started to cry. And now my tears are floating around inside my helmet like a million tiny planets. I keep breathing them in and nearly choking!"

Bishop starts to laugh and can't stop. He laughs so hard his visor fogs up entirely.

"Asshole!" says Ilka, pushing him away.

/

"I'm thinking of something," says Bishop.

"What?"

"I'm thinking of the look on your face that first time in the cactus garden. We'd been kissing and then we stopped to look at each other. You looked at me for a moment, like you didn't know who I was. And then, all at once, I could see it in your eyes. I could see you falling in love."

"Oh, God," she says softly.

"What?"

"Nothing. That was a beautiful moment. That's all."

"I saw you falling in love," he says, "and I fell in love with you too."

They are silent for a long time: Visor to visor. Looking into each other's eyes. Their lips separated by inches of canned air, two layers of gold-tinted plastic, and a vacuum.

"Wouldn't it be nice," he says, "if we could zip these suits together like sleeping bags?"

At this she spreads her legs and pulls on his oxygen pack with both hands, compressing the front of his space suit against the front of hers. Her heels drift in the void, occasionally touching the outside of his knees.

/

They are rotating again. First the sun rises and sets and then the earth. Todd, the CEO of FFI, has come onto their Private Communications Channel to tell them how "personally sorry" he is about their "situation," and that he is "moving heaven and earth" to get them rescued. "We should have a shuttle on its way any minute now," he tells them. And then he says, "There's just one thing... I completely understand, of course, why, from time to time, you guys need your moments of—you know: privacy. That's perfectly natural, especially since you're—well, married and everything. But you have to understand it from our side too. Since we no longer have a video image, your radio transmissions are all we have to build a show around. So we would really appreciate it if you didn't turn off—"

At exactly the instant the earth sets behind Bishop's right arm and the sun rises over Ilka's left leg, Todd stops speaking. He remains silent the entire time it takes the sun to cross in front of Ilka and Bishop and then set again. But this time the departure of the sun is not followed by the return of the earth. Where the earth once occupied more than half their sky, there now are only glimmering stars. The moon has disappeared, too—not just the old, spherical moon, but the new, lopped-in-half moon.

Their radios are more than silent: no static, no hiss of dead air. The silence is deeper than when they used to turn their radios off.

Time passes and eventually the sun also fails to rise, and Ilka and Bishop find themselves entirely alone in the vast emptiness between many billions of stars.

With no stars near enough to noticeably illuminate them, they have become a form of dark matter, but remain linked, rotating, occasionally stirring their limbs.

/

"Look," says Bishop after an indeterminate period of time. He is holding a pie-shaped section of brilliant blue. "It was here all along."

"What?" said Ilka.

"The earth. I don't know why we didn't notice it."

"Are you sure?"

"Of course. Come on. Help me spread it out."

Bishop gives the pie-shape a shake, and Ilka can see that it is actually a disk that has been folded over many times. Taking hold of what appears to be the disk's far edge, Ilka kicks out her feet and is able to drift far enough across space to stretch the disk to its full width. Then, with a second kick, she is able to do the same with another part of the disk, and then another, as does Bishop, until finally they've completely unfurled the disk and the earth once again takes up half their sky.

They pirouette off a short distance so they can survey their handiwork. "Perfect," says Bishop.

"I don't know," says Ilka.

"What do you mean?"

"That's not the way I remember it."

Bishop himself thinks the earth looks a bit blank, but all he says is, "What's wrong with it?"

"I'm not exactly sure."

"Maybe we need to get a little closer."

They summersault back toward the blue disk and find that it is a lot easier to land on the earth than they ever imagined.

"Look!" says Bishop. "We did it! We're home! Why didn't we think of this before?"

"It still doesn't look right," says Ilka. "Where are all the trees? And the color is weird. It's all light blue. And the ground is satiny. I don't remember it being like this at all."

"Maybe that's because it's nighttime."

"How do you know it's nighttime?"

"There's no sun. And look at all the stars."

"Maybe," Ilka says dubiously.

"Of course it's nighttime."

She just shakes her head.

"What other explanation is there?" asks Bishop.

"I don't know. Where's the sun?

Bishop is silent a moment. "Probably on the other side."

Bishop and Ilka walk until they get to the point where the earth ends and a carpet of star-punctuated emptiness begins. They get down on their hands and knees and lower their heads over the microscopically thin edge of the earth until they can see the far side. Sure enough, there's the sun. And now, instead of blue, the earth is completely white, like the salt flats where they drove their first night.

"Oh, my God!" cries Bishop. "Look!"

Way, way out in the middle of the earth is Bishop's battered, copper-colored Toyota Corolla. "I can't believe it's still here," says Ilka.

"How amazing!"

It turns out to be easy to get around to the other side of the earth. They just pull their chins to their chests and roll head-over-heels onto what once had been an upside-down planet. They experience no disorientation as they stand. Walking on this side of the earth feels exactly the same as walking on the other.

/

It takes them a good hour to reach the car, thanks in part to the clumsiness and weight of their spacesuits, which, of course, have not been designed for terrestrial perambulation. "This is it, alright," says Bishop. The car's doors are unlocked and the keys are in the ignition. "Amazing nobody stole it."

"But wasn't your car a Honda?"

Bishop walks around to the back of the car and looks at the stainless-steel lettering above its right taillight. "This *is* a Honda," he says.

"Whew!" says Ilka. "I was getting worried."

He is standing beside her again. "So what do you think?" He takes the index finger of one of her gloves between the thumb and index finger of his own glove.

She doesn't answer, but he can see that half-shy, half-mischievous smile of hers through the reflective visor of her helmet.

"Come on," he says.

"Oh God!" She holds out both hands, palms-up, and shakes her arms emphatically. "How I would love to get out of this fucking thing!"

"Me too." He is smiling. But then his smile fades.

Neither of them moves.

"Do you think it's safe?" she says at last.

"Of course, it's safe! We're home, aren't we?" And with that, he tugs the latches on either side of his helmet and flips open his visor. For a long moment he just stands there with both eyes tightly closed. Then he takes a deep breath. "Jesus Fucking Christ! This is so wonderful! You've got to do this!"

In less than a minute they've stripped off their space suits, their sweat-sodden jumpsuits and even their underwear. Bishop can hardly believe he is seeing Ilka's sleek and shapely body again. He pulls her into his arms, covers her lips with butterfly kisses. After a moment she steps back, laughs and slaps his hip. "Not so fast, loverboy! Wait 'til we're inside, at least."

He opens the driver's door and she runs around to the passenger's side. Once they are both sitting in the car, they start laughing. "Holy shit!" she says.

"Isn't this amazing!"

"This is exactly how it was!"

Their jeans, tee shirts, underwear and shoes are scattered on the seats, floors and dashboard, exactly as they were that first night. Even Bishop's bag of disposable razors and shampoo is lying on the back seat. "Well, almost," he says. "It was night then. And the moon was up."

In fact, the moon is up. But so is the sun. It sits on the horizon, another disk, but dazzlingly bright, with squiggles of blue-red-green flickering intermittently along its rim, and sword-like smears of brilliance running off in four directions like the points of a compass. "It's about to set," says Ilka.

"I think you're right," says Bishop.

They decide to sit and watch it.

But after some fifteen or twenty minutes, it becomes clear that the sun isn't setting at all, but only wobbling unsteadily along the horizon as if it has lost its way. "This is getting frustrating," says Bishop.

"Let's just forget about it," says Ilka.

"No. It *has* to be night!" Worried that Ilka might think he is angry, he looks at her and smiles. "This won't take a minute!"

He twists the key in the ignition, puts the car in gear, and drives across the salt flats to the horizon. The sun is no bigger here than it was when they were waiting for it to set. As he slams the door, Ilka calls out, "Be careful! It's hot! You'll burn yourself!"

He smiles at her over his shoulder. "Don't worry, it only looks hot." As he trots to the very edge of the earth, the sun skittles a bit to the right as if it were running away. Gripping the edge of the earth with one hand, he reaches out with the other, spreads his palm over the top of the sun and pushes it beneath the horizon, as he might push someone's head under water.

When he stands, he's wearing that crooked grin that always gives Ilka a tickly flutter at the base of her throat. He dusts his hands together. "That's that!"

They drive back across the salt-flat and Ilka decides that it looks more arctic than lunar under the moonlight. At one point she even thinks she sees a phalanx of penguins—like bowling pins in tuxedos—in the dimness just beyond the glow of the car's headlights.

/

"So, where were we?" says Bishop once they're parked again at their original spot. Their cast-aside space suits have vanished and, on every side of the white plain, mountains now rise, black against the night sky, except for the orange glow of the Mission Compound several miles to the west.

"I think we were right about here," says Ilka, leaning over and kissing him on the lips.

Some minutes later, Bishop lets his head fall back against his seat. "Oh, wow!" he sighs. "This is such a relief!"

Ilka lowers her head against his shoulder and closes her eyes.

"Remember how frightened you were?" he says.

"I wasn't frightened."

"Yes, you were."

"I wasn't."

"You kept looking out the windows and saying, 'Do you think this is a good idea?'"

"I wasn't frightened. I was guilty. Only a few minutes before I'd been listening to poor Max babbling on happily about his pet shop... and then... Well, it all happened so fast. And I just kept thinking about how happy he had been, and it made me sad. And guilty. I felt really guilty for a while there."

"I guess that makes sense," Bishop says.

They are silent. Holding hands. Smiling into each other's eyes.

/

The windows are fogged in brilliant smears and ragged patches. Here and there the fog has coalesced into tiny, glinting nodes of darkness that gradually merge into droplets. Some of the droplets have run down the glass, leaving behind jagged, night-colored trails.

"I don't remember it being this cold," says Ilka.

Bishop makes an equivocal grunt.

"Do you?" she asks.

"The desert gets cold at night."

"Yeah. I just don't remember the windows fogging like this."

"What about the coyotes?" he says.

"Coyotes?"

He rubs some of the fog away with his hand. "Look."

Through the watery glass, Ilka makes out the moonlit figure of a coyote, not two yards from the car, head lowered, fangs bared. As she watches, one more coyote trots up, then another, then several more, all with their heads lowered, ears back, teeth gleaming in the moonlight. "Whoa," she says. "I don't remember them at all!"

"I do." Bishop smiles. "But they didn't bother us. Right?"

"Guess they didn't."

"Not a bit." He leans over and licks the end of her nose. "The cold neither."

"Guess not." She pulls his lips down onto hers.

/

Sometime later, Ilka sits up. "There's one thing missing." She punches the knob on the radio and Neil Young's "Harvest Moon" begins to play. "Remember?" she says with a big grin.

"Not really," he says.

"Sure you do."

"I don't remember any music at all."

"Yes, you do!" She laughs. "Remember how funny we thought it was that this song should be playing when this huge full moon was shining right down on us?"

"Maybe," he says.

He leans over and kisses her one more time.

Some minutes later, they slump in their seats and look up through the windshield at the full moon. No fog anymore, the glass as clear as winter air. And it's the real moon this time, not the lopped-in-half version.

The original moon. The perfect sphere. **-bc.**

Sarah Gambito

holiday

2

crashing across cousin stars. with deep listening
holes. because we're related. and every wren that
has nested abroad would like to become my
mother. i'd like to lie flayed open upon her twelve
breaking torsos. this blood would weld us to the
chair. and i'd let a crowd in. i'd always thought
that crowds were created in a panic. a great
anti-system of people fleeing fire and nova. rather,
crowd dynamic is more often cultivated because
you run towards. you want concert tickets or
something to do the day after thanksgiving.
they're almost giving it away. this is what she says
as the gold metal hits the outline of her.
she says i want you to find me. i want that you
never give up and you find me.

BRUCE BAUMAN is the Senior Editor of BLACK CLOCK and the author of the award-winning *And The Word Was.* His second novel *Broken Sleep* will be published by Other Press in 2012. His website is brucebauman.net.

SETH BLAKE is an Editorial Assistant of BLACK CLOCK and in the CalArts MFA Writing Program.

SCOTT BRADFIELD is the author of five novels—*The History of Luminous Motion, What's Wrong With America, Animal Planet, Good Girl Wants It Bad* and *The People Who Watched Her Pass By*—and the recent collection *Hot Animal Love: Tales of Modern Romance.*

BYRON ALEXANDER CAMPBELL is an Editorial Assistant of BLACK CLOCK and in the CalArts MFA Writing Program.

TOM CARSON won two National Magazine Awards as *Esquire's* "Screen" columnist. Currently *GQ's* "The Critic," he is author of *Gilligan's Wake* (a *New York Times* Notable Book of the Year) and the newly published *Daisy Buchanan's Daughter*, from which the story in this issue is an excerpt.

KATE GUTHRIE CARUSO is an Associate Editor of BLACK CLOCK and a graduate of the CalArts MFA Writing Program. She has work forthcoming in *Tears in the Fence.* She lives and works in Denver, Colorado.

JUSTUS CAUDELL is an Editorial Assistant of BLACK CLOCK and in the CalArts MFA Writing Program.

SAMANTHA COHEN's fiction has been published in PANK, *Storyglossia* and *Mary Magazine.* She is a graduate of CalArts MFA Writing Program.

PATRICIA CRAM is an Editorial Assistant of BLACK CLOCK and in the CalArts MFA Writing Program. She is a ritual performance artist, designs *Vial* magazine and formerly directed Orbis Nex, an experimental theatre in the Bay Area.

MARISA CRAWFORD is the author of *The Haunted House*, an editor of Small Desk Press and a writing mentor with Girls Write Now. Her website is marisacrawfordforever.com.

GEOFF DYER is the author of the recently published *Otherwise Known as the Human Condition*, which includes the story in this issue. *Zona*, about Andrei Tarkovsky's film *Stalker*, will appear in February 2012.

STEVE ERICKSON is the Editor of BLACK CLOCK. He is the author of nine novels including the upcoming *These Dreams of You*, and the recipient of a Guggenheim Fellowship and the American Academy of Arts and Letters award in literature. His website is SteveErickson.org.

MERRILL FEITELL is the author of *Here Beneath Low-Flying Planes*, which won the Iowa Award, and a novel in progress, *Any Minute Now*, from which the story in this issue is excerpted. She teaches at University of Maryland and is Fiction Editor of *Forklift, Ohio.*

PETER FRANK is art critic for the *Huffington Post*, Associate Editor of *Fabrik*, and Adjunct Senior Curator at the Riverside Art Museum. Widely published as a poet since 1969, he is author of the poem-cycle *The Travelogues.*

SARAH GAMBITO is the author of the collections *Delivered* and *Matadora*, and her poetry has appeared in *The Iowa Review, The Antioch Review, Denver Quarterly, The New Republic, Field, Quarterly West* and *Fence*. She is Director of Creative Writing at Fordham University and co-founder of Kundiman, a non-profit organization serving Asian American poets.

SARA GEROT currently is completing two novels, *Young White Women* and *Doing Crystal*, the latter of which is excerpted in this issue. She is a graduate of the CalArts MFA Writing Program.

ARIELLE GREENBERG is the Poetry Editor of BLACK CLOCK, co-author of *Home/Birth*, and author of *My Kafka Century, Given, Shake Her* and *Farther Down*. She co-edited the anthologies *Gurlesque, Starting Today* and *Women Poets on Mentorship*.

SETH GREENLAND is the author of the novels *The Bones, Shining City* and the upcoming *The Angry Buddhist*, from which the story in this issue is excerpted. He also is a writer for the HBO series *Big Love*.

ANDREW HAUG is the Art Director of BLACK CLOCK. His website is mrhaug.com.

PHOEBE HENRY is the cover artist for this issue of BLACK CLOCK. Her work has been featured in the V&A Designers of the Future Exhibition and she was a regional finalist for Lloyds TSB's Art of Nurture competition in 2010. Her website is phoebeelizahenry.com.

TARA ISON is the author of the novels *The List* and *A Child out of Alcatraz*, which was a finalist for the *Los Angeles Times* Book Prize. Her short fiction and essays have appeared in *Tin House, The Kenyon Review, Nerve* and numerous anthologies. Her website is taraison.com.

JAZMIN AMINIAN JORDÁN teaches children in Northridge, California. Her email address is sheerjaz@aol.com.

DDUM KIM's "History" is excerpted from a novella of the same title.

KYOUNG KIM is the Deputy Managing Editor of BLACK CLOCK and a writer, artist and researcher.

RACHEL KOLB is an Editorial Assistant of BLACK CLOCK and in the CalArts MFA Writing Program.

KATIE MANDERFIELD is an Associate Editor of BLACK CLOCK and in the CalArts MFA Writing Program.

DOUGLAS MATUS is an Associate Editor of BLACK CLOCK and in the CalArts MFA Writing Program.

JOSEPH MCELROY is the author of, most recently, *Night Soul and Other Stories* (from which the story in this issue is taken), nine novels including *Lookout Cartridge, Actress in the House, Plus* and *Cannonball*, the novella *Preparations for Search* and a forthcoming book on water.

JOE MILAZZO is the Assistant Managing Editor of BLACK CLOCK, co-editor of *[out of nothing]*, proprietor of Imipolex Press, and Director of Community Education and Outreach at the The Writer's Garret in Dallas, TX.

ANTHONY MILLER is Editor-at-Large of BLACK CLOCK. His writing has appeared in *Bookforum*, *LA Weekly*, *Los Angeles CityBeat* and *Poets & Writers*, and he is at work on a novel and a book about encyclopedic fictions and secret histories.

KATHERINE MIN is the author of the novel *Secondhand World* and currently is completing *The Fetishist*, from which the story in this issue is excerpted. She has received the Pushcart Prize and grants from the North Carolina and New Hampshire Arts Councils and the National Endowment for the Arts.

RICK MOODY is the author of *The Four Fingers of Death*, newly published in paperback and excerpted in this issue. He also recently released an album of his songs, *The Darkness Is Good*, available on Dainty Rubbish Records.

DWAYNE MOSER is Editor-at-Large of BLACK CLOCK. His art has been exhibited internationally and currently he is co-writing a television project for CBS/Paramount. He has taught at CalArts and Bard College, and works for USC's graduate Fine Arts Program.

JAY NEUGEBOREN is the author of seventeen books including the new collection *You Are My Heart*, as well as prize-winning novels *The Stolen Jew* and *Before My Life Began*, and non-fiction *Imagining Robert* and *Transforming Madness*.

STEPHEN O'CONNOR is the author of the recent collection, *Here Comes Another Lesson*. His website is stephenoconnor.net.

KIKI PETROSINO is the author of *Fort Red Border* and the chapbook *The Dark Is Here*. Her poetry has appeared in *Gulf Coast*, FENCE, the *Iowa Review* and *Best New Poets*, and she teaches creative writing at the University of Louisville.

TIFFANY PROMISE received her MFA from CalArts and hopes to be an art therapist. She writes fiction and poetry and has a penchant for making disgusting things beautiful.

MICHAELE SIMMERING is the Managing Editor of BLACK CLOCK. A writer and designer, she's the recipient of a Fulbright Fellowship for writing and co-founder of Kalon Studios.

MARK SKIPTON is an Associate Editor of BLACK CLOCK and a graduate of the CalArts MFA Writing Program.

CHRYSANTHE TAN is an Associate Editor of BLACK CLOCK and a graduate of the CalArts MFA Writing Program.

LYNNE TILLMAN is the author of the new collection *Someday This Will Be Funny*. The story in this issue is excerpted from a work in progress, *Circumstantial Evidence (Memoir Impossible)*, which will be finished or come to an end, but not to her satisfaction.

ASHLEY TOMECK is an Associate Editor of BLACK CLOCK and a graduate of the CalArts MFA Writing Program. She lives and works in New York City.

DAVID L. ULIN is Editor-at-Large of BLACK CLOCK and book critic of the *Los Angeles Times*. His work includes *The Lost Art of Reading: Why Books Matter in a Distracted Time* and *The Myth of Sold Ground: Earthquakes, Prediction, and the Fault Line Between Reason and Faith.*

JEFF VANDERMEER is the author of numerous novels that have been translated into twenty languages. His fiction has appeared in *Conjunctions* and he regularly reviews for the *New York Times Book Review*. The story in this issue is an excerpt from a novel in progress.

SARAH VAP is the author of three books of poetry including the recent *Faulkner's Rosary*, *Dummy Fire* (which received the 2006 Saturnalia Poetry Prize) and *American Spikenard* (which received the 2006 Iowa Poetry Prize).

LAURA VENA is an Associate Editor of BLACK CLOCK and a writer, artist and translator whose work has appeared in *Tarpaulin Sky*, *In Posse Review*, *The Dirty Fabulous* and the *LA Weekly*. She is poetry coordinator for Avenue 50 Studio and co-founder of Strophe.

SARAH WANG is an Associate Editor at Semiotext(e) and Contributing Editor to *Animal Shelter*. Her novel in progress, *The Black Field*, is excerpted in this issue.

KATE WOLF's work has appeared in *Bookforum*, *Los Angeles*, the *LA Weekly* and *Bidoun*. She co-runs the monthly Five Points Reading Series in Lincoln Heights.

BLACK CLOCK IS PUBLISHED IN LARGE PART THANKS TO THE GENEROUS SUPPORT OF THE

ROSENTHAL FAMILY FOUNDATION

Black Clock is a non-profit venture, published by California Institute of the Arts in association with the MFA Writing Program. All contributions are tax-deductible. It is with the support of donations like yours that our magazine can continue to be one of America's leading literary journals and donations of any amount are greatly appreciated. If you would like to make a donation or have questions about supporting *Black Clock* please consult our website www.blackclock.org or contact advancements@blackclock.org

WE, a few people, have recognized that:

"It is no measure of health to be well adjusted to a profoundly sick society" (Krishnamurti)

AND SO we have have created a magazine, a journal as a place to talk about these sicknesses, these societies, these ensuing madnesses.

VOL. 1 VOL. 2 VOL.3 are available in preview on

FAKEHEAD.com

but we believe in the integrity of the printed objects so we can ship you a copy, anywhere in the world.

"Putting the soul to work: this is the new form of alienation. Our desiring energy is trapped in the trick of self-enterprise, our libidinal investments are regulated according to economic rules, our attention is captured in the precariousness of virtual networks: every fragment of mental activity must be transformed into capital"
-Bifo (The Soul at Work)

More importantly

we're always looking for contributers and collaborators.

VOL. 4 is tentatively titled "The Taxonomy of Desire", so if you have anything to say about mirror neurons and pornography, creative technologies of subjectivity, eating disorders, advertising, virtual reality, and post counter cultural identity, please

send us your work, unfinished, manic or pristine to FAKEHEAD@babymanque.com

OR even just your thoughts on the conservative survivalist doomsday obsession, shock doctrine, post-nationalism, paranoia, cybernetics, terrorism, love, non industrial education models, schizoanalysis, nudity, painting, memory...

Send us your non-confessional poetry, your manifestos, your subversive short stories, your strangest photographs, your love letters to dead gods... It doesn't have to be all smart and shit, honestly. We're just very interested in what's thought provoking and beautiful.

Just check out the website, it will give you a better idea- more visual.
These are very exciting times. Don't let your thoughts be the enemy.

SINCERELY, The FAKEHEAD team. 2011.

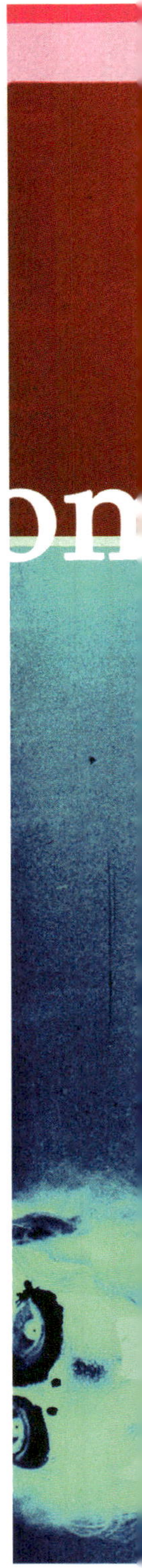

PANK
www.pankmagazine.com

SEE ME. FEEL ME. TOUCH ME.
Handcrafted print from Los Angeles.
Quarterly.
slake
LOS ANGELES
CROSSING OVER
super burger
CROSSING OVER
A CITY AND ITS STORIES
SUBSCRIBE AT SLAKE.LA

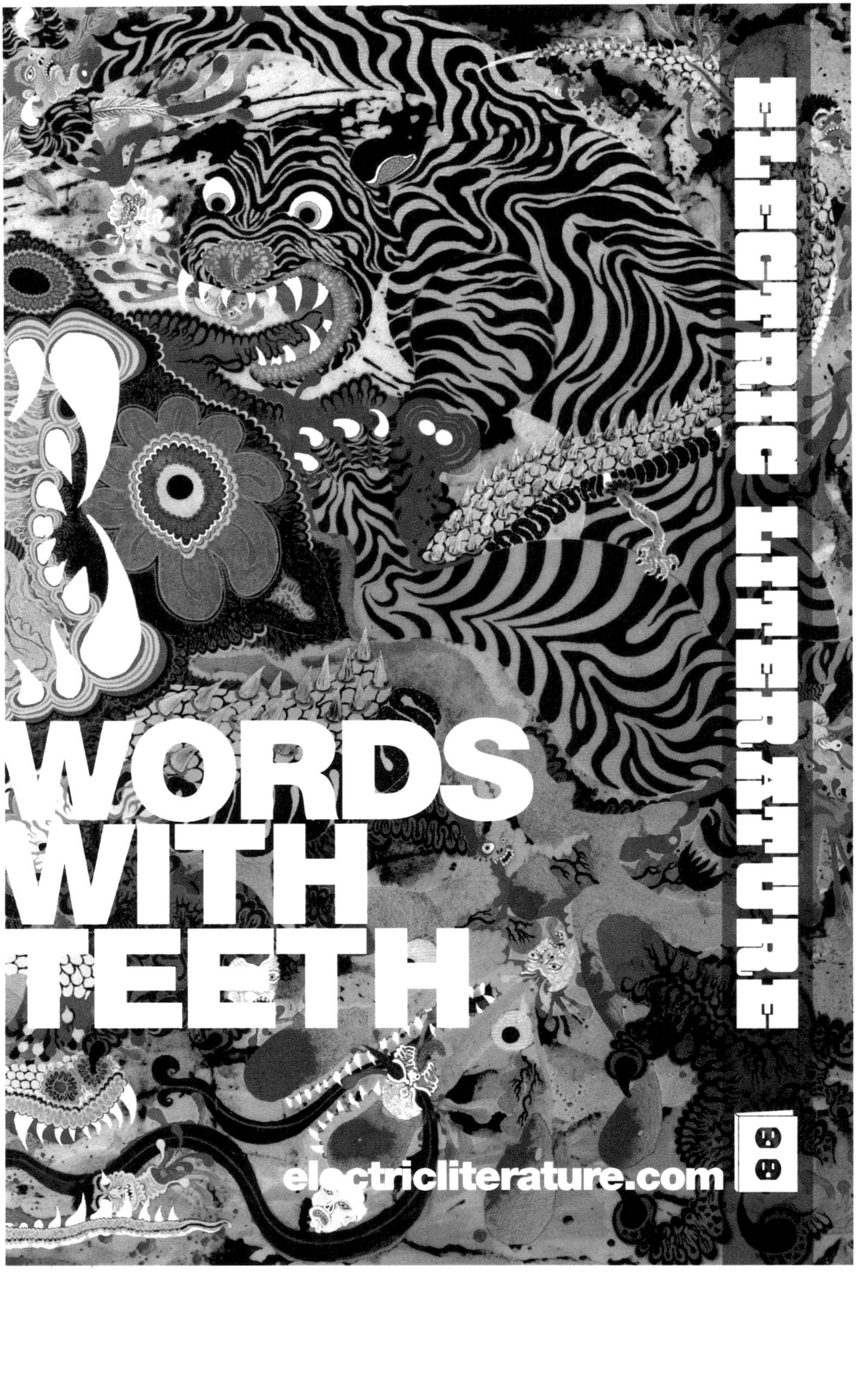
ELECTRIC LITERATURE
WORDS WITH TEETH
electricliterature.com

RECENT BOOKS BY BLACK CLOCK WRITERS

/

JOSEPH McELROY
NIGHT SOUL AND OTHER STORIES
DALKEY ARCHIVE

/

LYNNE TILLMAN
SOMEDAY THIS WILL BE FUNNY
RED LEMONADE

/

JAY NEUGEBOREN
YOU ARE MY HEART AND OTHER STORIES
TWO DOLLAR RADIO

/

TOM CARSON
DAISY BUCHANAN'S DAUGHTER
PAYCOCK PRESS

/

GEOFF DYER
OTHERWISE KNOWN AS THE HUMAN CONDITION
GRAYWOLF

/

RICK MOODY
THE FOUR FINGERS OF DEATH
BACK BAY

/

STEPHEN O'CONNOR
HERE COMES ANOTHER LESSON
FREE PRESS

CPSIA information can be obtained
at www.ICGtesting.com
Printed in the USA
245696LV00007B